THE SCHOOLING OF BOBBY RACK

THE SCHOOLING OF BOBBY RACK

ROBERT CURTIS

ETERNEDITIONS™
New York

"If you're going to try, go all the way. Otherwise, don't even start. If you follow it you will be alive with the gods. It is the only good fight there is."
—Charles Bukowski, *Hot Water Music*

FOREWORD

Bob Curtis was always pushing me to write. He'd want me to write right now. And so I will…

Bob Curtis was a man of rock-solid moral fiber. He saw the good in people, no matter their station in life. He was gentle and kind, and dearly loved his friends. He sang a lullaby for my young daughter which rendered her awestruck, and he rallied like an impassioned political activist to raise money for his best friend, Doc M., when the latter was about to lose his home, and to buy him a new bike when his was stolen.

But Bob wrote, too. That's what he did, and he did it well; it provided him great (and noble) purpose. He was and is a writer. His passion for his art was an inspiration to me; without his presence and influence in my life, I am nothing near the writer I am today—and more, he pushed me to embrace, with unwavering permanence, my own passion for my craft, which in a temporal world of disappointment, rejection, and sometimes frightening solitude, could often be suppressed, but never dismissed. He understood this truth about the creative journey, and this hard-earned knowledge kept him going, as well.

We read each other's work consistently. For years. We encouraged each other, yet offered occasional stinging criticism, even, that lead to temporary hurts and resentments on both sides—but we knew this ego-scarring process was paramount to our growth. We had to tell each other the truth, even if that truth was indisputably and fickly subjective, in order to move forward and upwards to reach the highest levels of our skill and generative potential.

Bob accomplished much with his writing, and he began early. He was already arranging productions of his stage work when we first met in 1987, as undergrads at UMass-Boston; we were both actors in a production of Mac-Beth. He continued with his playwriting (and poetry, too—man, he wrote some potent poetry!) when he he made his first move to L.A., sometime in 1990. I was already living in North Hollywood; he rented a squalid studio in East Hollywood, and he'd take two city buses up to meet me in order that we share pages of his plays and my first short stories. We had thin skins in those days, and there was much shouting and insult, but all of it emanated from that place of insecurity that all young writers live in—and must—until they don't anymore (which is a day that never comes, of course). We drank a good deal together, as well, which had no small part in those fights, and believed we had to as our literary heroes were Kerouac, Jim Thompson, and Bukowksi, and we wanted to be like them in at least the best way we could, given our rawness and naiveté. He finished a good play about the homeless in L.A. that he called Dumpster Frontier, and penniless, hungry, and evicted himself, headed back East.

He wrote, I wrote, we talked by phone, and we hooked up in Boston when I'd return to visit family. On one endless, hazy day we made an epic bar crawl that began at Sullivan's On Tap by the old Boston Garden (the closest we could get to one of Bukowski's old L.A. dive bar haunts), took a vicious turn as we fought and insulted each other's writing all the way from a bench on the Common where we rested between suds to some Rosie's something-or-other Irish pub on Mass. Ave, then ended somewhere in Cambridge, somehow on a conciliatory note—and then not long after my return to California came the the astounding news that he'd been accepted into the Yale School of Drama. Wow!

Our contact was less regular as he negotiated (with bloodied elbows, he intimated) his way through those hallowed halls and black-box theaters, but not long after I received my own admission to U.S.C. Film School—and he was busy writing his plays, and I my screenplays, and then suddenly, it seemed, we had our MFA's, but we had nothing, really, except our work and the knowledge that while we perhaps possessed a certain talent, we had a long way to go before we'd do our best work...but we didn't want to hear that then. Oh, no—not then.

Bob returned to L.A. for round two, driving a van for someone who needed the same moved cross-country, and he lived for the first few weeks with me and my then-girlfriend in Marina del Rey. We enjoyed our new discussions of lit and watched a heap of movies, and he spent some time at a theater company in Venice at which I'd become an active member—but something had changed, in both of us. We craved—no, felt entitled to—writing success. After all, we'd each written a great deal by then, had attended top-notch writing programs at top-tier schools, and it was high time we'd reaped some of those rewards that we felt were ours to be given. I'd had a couple of ultra-low budget films made, and was now seeing some of my stage work produced. I'd asked Bob to direct one of my plays. He had a production at the Lee Strasberg Theater of one of an experimental piece he wrote, and got hired to write a script for an indy producer about the French Foreign Legion. Things were happening for us professionally, but not quite on the level we desired and felt we deserved. And then, there was more drinking. And Bob's Yale girlfriend moved out, and I saw less of him, and he backed out of directing my play at the last minute, and then…something, which I still can't fathom to this day, took place in the way of a significant rift. Bob cut me (and other mutual friends) out of his life, and that was it. No explanation (though I sensed the pressure of competition had a bit to do with it; I certainly struggled greatly with it, and knew it'd had taken its toll on both our psyches and our friendship). I felt terribly wounded; I had no other friend with whom I connected better on an artistic level. No one I could talk books, movies, and craft with like I could Bob. Damn, it hurt. The man made me a better writer, and now he was gone…

Years passed (nine, ten?), and I struggled through some of the darkest days of my life. Addiction, (more) career disappointment, a new career in teaching (the lone bright spot, though that light, too, would fade in time), deeper addiction, the failure of my "final film" to reignite what had never really been a career of any significance, and deepest addiction to the point where I could no longer write. I thought perhaps Bob had left us for good, but I more or less had, as well. I no longer expected his "let's put this behind us" call, and wasn't answering the phone, in any case.

But I got sober, and lucky-beyond-words to meet and marry my wife, Lisa, the greatest champion of my work. I taught writing, literature, and film at several different colleges and one private high school, and struggled to write again. There was little time for the latter, of course, but I had to make the effort. And then, in 2009, another writer friend said he'd run into Bob at a local writer's conference. The news shook me. He was alive and right here in town! I wanted to reconnect with him immediately, but I was fearful that he wouldn't want the same. Still, I took the chance. I had to. Had such a need for those seamless conversations about film, books, and writing. So I reached out…and he responded in kind.

We met (again) at Juniors Deli in Westwood, and it was almost as if no time had passed. We had less hair, of course—but we were both still writing. He'd found a job with the county and had been at it for several years, he told me, and he'd moved to writing scripts. He wrote many, and then had begun to work on a memoir about his days at Yale (poor kid from Hyde Park makes it to the Ivy League, his own take on the "fish outta water" archetype), enrolling in several consecutive writing workshops at L.A. City College to keep him disciplined and motivated. It wasn't long before we were meeting regularly again to write and share pages. He won awards two years in a row at L.A.C.C. for his short fiction and poetry. His literary output was enviable, and he seemed never to tire of the work.

It was immensely satisfying to have my friend back in my life, and we pushed each other to do the best work that we were capable of doing. Bob kept the better part of that wordless bargain. He pecked the keyboard like Elton John his ivories...

Alas, life must and will be lived, and after my daughter was born, there was simply less time to hang out. I know it bothered Bob (never one to "shuck and jive," he told me so!), and I didn't like it, either—but family is family. Bob was still an important part of mine, of course; he joined us for two Thanksgivings in a row at my in-laws in Bakersfield, and we enjoyed a memorable hike to the 9,000-foot peak of Mt. Pinos. He came to speak on poetry to a creative writing class I taught, and I asked him to be a judge for our student literary magazine's annual writing contest. But our relationship became more of the phone call/text/FaceBook message kind. I offered regular feedback as his memoir gained shape, and he gave notes on many drafts of my various scripts. We had a dinner here, attended a movie screening there—but he'd found new interests (singing, improv) and made new friends. He threw a 50th birthday party for himself last June, and I met many of these new pals at the same; it was a magical night where his guests shared writing, singing, and stories. He also reached out to authors whose work he admired—Dan Fante and Mark SaFranko—and got me reading them, too. (Just a couple of months back, he attended Fante's funeral in Santa Monica, and we mourned his passing together.)

Somewhere along the line, he took to hugging me when we'd see each other. You can bet that was an embrace like no other.

His book was finally ready. He'd hired Mark SaFranko as editor, and submitted many a query letter to agents. It was just a matter of time.

He pushed me to take a 15-day writing challenge with his good friend, Nicole, and that's how we kicked off 2016—energized for a productive writing year. He was already at work on part two of his memoir—"the early L.A. years."

We'd talked often of a film viewing/literary discussion mini-fest at my place. But this day didn't work, nor that. Soon, soon—we'll do it for sure.

He attended our housewarming in December (my mom, in for a visit, told me the next day, "that friend of yours from Boston is such a nice guy. We had a wonderful chat"), and then I drove him home from a medical procedure at Kaiser in February. No need to worry, he told me. Just routine. I took him at his word. He directed me to drive by one of Charles Bukowski's old apartments in East Hollywood, one inside of which he wrote so much of his best work; we sat and stared in silence a while. It was a moment that spoke to many years of a shared experience, and what more could be said, really?

Finally, we nailed down a day for our mini-fest: this past Friday, April 22nd. He now told me he'd had some new, and troubling news about his health, but wanted to wait until we got together to offer details. When I asked what he wanted to eat, he said "something plant based," and that was quite revealing.

But that morning, life happened. My wife had to have an emergency root canal, and she was frightened. I assured her I'd be by her side, and called Bob to tell him that, regrettably, we'd have to postpone.

That was Friday morning. He sounded quite relaxed, almost as if he'd not yet gotten out of bed. We talked about books, he bemoaned that he hadn't written in awhile (for him, that meant about two days), but that he was excited about his "L.A. book." He expressed worry for his elderly cat, Dulcinea; he'd rescued her from the streets a few years back. "I'm afraid I might have to put her down," he said, and the pain and acceptance in his voice was palpable. He so loved that cat.

We ended our conversation on a hopeful note. Lunch next Thursday, probably—or maybe we'll try for next Friday to do this mini-fest. I'll let you know. Goodbye. Goodbye...

And so it was...

And now, six years later and change, his book has arrived...*The Schooling of Bobby Rack*.

—Garrett Clancy, April 2022

THE SPARK

I first stated my wish to go to Yale Drama aloud to the president of an insurance company who insisted on meeting all his new employees in person, be they temps or top executives.

"Tell me something about yourself," he said.

"I write plays. I plan to attend the Yale School of Drama," I said without a hint of doubt.

"Hmmm. Good school. What kind of plays do you write?"

"Serious and denunciatory plays." *Serious and denunciatory.* Indeed. I'd read that gem on the back of a Steinbeck novel.

I knew I did not have a special play ready. For Yale Drama, I would need something unique and otherworldly, something that didn't read like the work of all the other pitiful playwrights whining about their terrible childhoods, political angst, or fractured sex lives. But where would that play come from?

One day, while working at New England Telephone, I began eavesdropping on my coworkers as they complained about their jobs, praised their boss's empty jokes, and tele-coached their latchkey children on how to cook a chicken without courting salmonella or burning down the house. I wrote it down. Short exchanges morphed into madcap sketches. Soon these scenes mushroomed into an explosive, existential drama. It said nothing and everything at the same time. The play promptly went off in the U.S. Mail, along with a completed application.

***

In 1992, I lived at home. Me, my sister and father slept in our rooms on separate floors in a Boston triple-decker house bought by my grandmother in 1947. Genevieve Rachaborski died a decade ago. The house hadn't been painted in 25 years. Like Rapunzel, I slept on the third floor trapped in a tower. My sister was sandwiched on the second floor. My dad stood guard on the ground floor with his loud dogs and abundant gun collection. The big bad world of Boston and beyond sprawled outside.

I suppose my sister had become the success of the family. She found employment as a bakery manager at a supermarket chain. My dad had settled on the life of a paranoid eunuch, collecting Social Security Disability and Food Stamps.

Our younger brother dropped out of school at seventeen, ran away, and had travelled most of America by thumb or bus. Last we heard, he'd split Minneapolis for Tucson with plans to get his band back together. TheyHe played punkabilly, or psychobilly, some kind of billy music. I recall them practicing in our damp dirt floor basement. It smelled like spiders and unmarked graves down there. I opened the door and shouted: "You guys sound like a bunch of foul-mouthed elves building a tin shithouse!" That's how *The Foul-Mouthed Elves* got their name. I admired my brother for fleeing our untidy nest and showing some gamble in his soul.

My sister was a big apple-cheeked gal who looked like the star of a la-crosse team. She'd come out to me a few years earlier and I'd said something reassuring. But I changed my tune a few times, especially when she brought girlfriends home to spend the night. But I got over that, and perceived how finding her sexuality increased her confidence and enjoyment of life. I al-most envied her. Why couldn't I be gay and change my life too?

My sister and I had scored the highest on our SATs in high school and won full scholarships to Boston University. This wasn't because we were any Einsteins, but because our classmates were illiterate, and the university had made a sweetheart deal with the city to expand its tax-free property.

After two frantic weeks in which I changed my major five times, I dropped out. All those years as the only white kid in inner-city schools hadn't prepared me for the pretty faces, smiles and wealth I'd encounter at B.U.

Next, I applied for a scholarship to U-Mass/Boston, and got it. U-Mass/Boston was a commuter school with a diverse mix of ages, races and in-comes, far less of a threat to my low self-esteem. I graduated with honors. But that was in 1988. By 1992, I had accomplished very little.

On those evenings when my sister didn't have to work the next day, we would watch television and split a 12-pack. I'd worked enough temp jobs the previous year to get a nice tax refund. So tonight the beer was on me. Never again would life be so untroubled and sweet. Around 9:30pm, as we watched *Star Trek: The Next Generation*, dad called for help. We ran downstairs. Dad told us that he had called an ambulance. We waited until an emergency medical team pulled up to the house. Dad made it down the porch steps and through the front gate without assistance. Then he col-lapsed into the arms of two EMTs who carried him into their flashing truck. We watched them rip open dad's shirt and ready the defibrillator paddles before closing the door.

The idea of my father dying at only 51 filled me with an almost narcotic wonder. The tick of every second became a scalpel slicing into my mind's eye, sharp, probing, demanding instant inventory. Though it felt interminable, it was probably two minutes before one of the EMTs stepped out.

My sister and I looked inside the truck and saw our unconscious father rigged up to an IV drip.

"I'll call from the hospital," I told my sister. From the passenger seat I couldn't see my father. The ambulance sped through traffic with its sirens whooping. But then we stopped halfway to the hospital. The driver ran to the rear of the truck. I sat still until he returned. We rolled on to the hospital. The intercom squawked again. We stopped. I sat bracing for the loss of my sole surviving parent.

My mother had died a year earlier at only 47. She'd been diagnosed with multiple sclerosis a month after I was born. Like the "Stages of Man" evolutionary chart in reverse, she went from walking upright, to leaning on a cane, to hunching over a walker, to sitting in a wheelchair, until she succumbed to a stroke that left her bedridden and without speech for the rest of her life.

Now heart disease might claim my father. Dad had never been much for inspiring me or giving sensible advice, but I didn't want him to go. Part of me sensed the emptiness, the thin membrane between the spark of life and the cold airless nothingness of death. My prayers were rare and my belief in them even rarer. But what else could I do but pray?

The good news was that an IV had fallen out of dad's arm and the ambulance had to be stopped in order for the EMTs to reinsert it correctly. Dad arrived alive at the emergency room.

I sat alone in a waiting room reading a volume of early Eugene O'Neill sea plays. These coarse dramas offered little of interest or consolation. I switched on the TV and watched Charlie Rose on *CBS Overnight*, a few years before his long career on public television began. Charlie was interviewing a young and feral James Ellroy who had just published his fifth or sixth popular crime novel. Ellroy appeared raw and crude. For a national television appearance, he wore a loud red Hawaiian shirt that floated on his skinny arms. I found some comfort watching Ellroy rant on about rogue cops and crooks ruining their lives. Here was a real writer, the kind I wanted to be, prolific, profound and nuttier than a box of crackerjacks.

Later a doctor came in who told me to go home.

"The stove stopped working," said my sister as she opened up. Like an arctic gust the cold air chased me indoors. The oven was opened wide. I smelled the sulfur and smoke of the spent matches piled on the floor.

"The pilot won't light," she said.

This was serious. The ground floor stove had become the house's only source of heat. Our childhood home grew colder and colder. If that pilot didn't get lit soon, the pipes and toilets would freeze solid and burst. I got down on the floor and peeked inside. Damn, but the floor was cold. It felt like a sheet of ice spinning and whistling down a fast river.

"Can you find a toothbrush or something?"

She found one and handed it to me. "It's Dad's."

"He needed a new one." I brushed in and about the pilot stem. I didn't know what I was doing, but made an effort.

"Dad said it needed cleaning. How about a pipe cleaner? Wait." She left and came back. "Here."

I shoved the pipe cleaner into the pilot. It came out filthy with sludge. "Time to try another match." I depressed the gas button. I smelled dog hair, dust, and spent matches. I put three matches together, struck them together and reached inside. The pilot caught. The row of burners blossomed with blue flame.

My sister and I stood in the kitchen waiting for heat.

"How's Dad?" she asked as she held out her hands.

"He's in the ICU. They gave him Lidocaine. It's some stabilizing drug, but it made him freak out. He screamed nasty shit at the nurses and this black doctor." An inapt laugh escaped me.

My sister didn't see the humor. "Jesus," she said.

"I don't think he would have talked all that trash if he wasn't full of drugs and scared."

"He doesn't like hospitals."

"Why should he? They fucking committed him for observation when he just turned fifteen, starved him, drugged him."

"What happens next?"

"They say he needs open heart surgery, a double bypass, maybe triple. But because he's got no money or insurance, they're going to pack him into an ambulance tomorrow and hustle him over to Boston City Hospital."

"I thought they were closing City," said my sister.

"As long as they don't close it tomorrow, we're in luck."

We held our hands out over the warm, working stove. Boston City Hospital had been built seven decades ago by the flamboyant Mayor James Michael Curley whose foxy Irish heart warmed up the old blueblood Yankee town whether anyone liked it or not.

My sister smiled for the first time that morning. "Who do you think Dad hates more, cops or doctors?"

"That's a tough one," I laughed.

"Why did they put Dad in that nuthouse?" my sister asked.

"I think maybe he beat up a midget at 15."

"A *midget*?"

"Yeah. A little person. A dwarf. Whatever. They were friends, but they had a fight."

"When did Dad tell you this?"

"He didn't," I said. "He told me he made friends with an adult midget when he was a teenager, and that they fought."

"Jesus. I thought Dad was tough. I thought he fought only big guys, like bullies, and gang members and spoiled jocks from the north side of the tracks."

"He did. But the midget made him mad."

The oven burned good now. The floor chilled our feet, but the air grew warmer, and we saw no frost when we exhaled. The kitchen felt like a kitchen again. We boiled water and made coffee. Then we considered breakfast.

IVY LEAGUE MATERIAL

It began like an old joke. The improbable met the absurd. Together they begged for a punch-line. A duck walks into a bar, or Robert Rachaborski joins the Ivy League.

The phone woke me at about ten. Too late for a temp job, I mused, only half-awake. Maybe a bill collector? A hard-nosed student loan lady would shout loud threats when she caught me off guard. Most times, I'd just let the machine get it. But today I felt ornery and snatched it up.

"Hello," I said.

"Hello. May I speak with Robert Rachaborski?"

"Uh-h-um. Yeah. That's me."

He didn't sound like a bill collector—too polite. Maybe one of the big grad schools I'd applied to? Perhaps one had bumped me up from the waiting list? So far, Carnegie Mellon had rejected me outright. Brandeis had stuck me at the bottom of their short list, then bumped me in favor of a diversity-friendly female playwright (according to an insider I knew).

"Oh, hello, Robert. My name is Todd Voorhees. I'm the associate head of the playwriting department at..."

I sat up in bed and swung my legs over the side. My feet knocked over three empty beer cans, 16-ounce Black Label tall boys that chimed and clattered across the linoleum floor. I coughed to cover the sound while I slapped my face awake. When I did, I knocked over a fourth can. Flat suds puddled on the floor. I mopped them up with a dirty t-shirt. Whatever Mr. Voorhees was saying, I missed. "Associate...?"

"*Associate head* of the playwriting department at the Yale School of Drama. I'm calling to tell you that you've been accepted. We're very excited about your work."

"You are? Hey, that's great."

"Your acceptance letter is in the mail. You'll be contacted about tuition, financial aid, and all necessary arrangements. In the meantime, I'd like you to come visit us. I'll have our secretary call to arrange an appointment." Mr. Voorhees's voice possessed that composed good cheer you get from a doctor before he gloves up and probes you.

"Sure. Sometime next week, maybe?" I offered.

"That would be fine. So how are you spending your summer?"

"Um...working." I hadn't worked a job in four weeks. It lasted two days. But I did have some house-painting gigs coming up in July and August.

"Well, don't work too hard. Save some energy for a busy fall semester. I look forward to working with you. We'll try to nurture that special talent of yours."

"Yeah. Thanks. I'll try."

We hung up.

Jesus, I thought. *Yale University.* The Yale School of Drama in New Haven, Connecticut, known as the pre-eminent graduate drama program in the United States, the breeding ground for hundreds of Oscar winners, maybe thousands of Emmy, Tony, Obie, NY Critic's Circle and Drama Desk honorees, at least as far as the acting and design departments were concerned. I didn't know how good the playwriting program might be. I'd never heard of any its award winners. But it couldn't be too bad, could it?

I spent the next hour phoning all my friends. The news stunned them more than me. Then I washed and dressed, and went downstairs to tell my dad. He was wearing his usual post-nuclear-holocaust ensemble: a sweater full of runs and holes, drooping grey thermal long johns, and torn polyester slippers held together by duct-tape. He was frying a batch of rock hard pancakes for himself and his two dogs. The canister of baking powder he used was three years old. Canola oil burned fast and hot on the aluminum griddle. Smoke tugged at my nostril hairs. Most of the pancakes came out black on both sides.

"Hey, Dad! They just accepted me into Yale Drama!"

"Is that so? Well, that's got to be something. What happens next?" Dad kept a close eye on his latest batch of flapjacks.

"I'm going down to Connecticut to visit the head of the playwriting program. I'll look at apartments too."

"You? An apartment? With what money?"

"I've got a little bit. I'll start painting houses with that crew in July. My financial aid will kick in the second week of school. I'll survive."

"Want some flapjacks?" Dad offered. He blew on them before he tossed them through the air and into the dogs' mouths. They leaped up to catch them as if they were edible Frisbees. Their claws scraped the torn linoleum floor.

"No, just coffee," I said.

I took my mug upstairs, called a few more friends, then broke out a few of my old play scripts to scan through. I tried to figure out what was so good about them, and why a famous Ivy League drama program appreciated them.

***

The day ended with an impromptu celebration at T.J. Molloy's Tavern, the bar that should have been the model for TV's *Cheers*—though no bar in Boston or anywhere in the real world resembled *Cheers*. For one thing, no one ever got drunk on that show. Maybe I missed it, but I never once saw a guy throw up, or get into a fight, or stumble in with the shakes to order a drink, only to spill it on his shirt. Big Norm sat there all day with a fresh beer, always with the same easy patter and available wit. Just once I'd like to have seen Norm fall completely off his bar stool, scream gibberish, and need to be rolled into a taxicab. It would have been fun to hear Sam the bartender cussing out Cliff Clavin for talking too loud or pissing all over the bathroom floor. Also, the way Norm and Cliff prattled on would have been damned annoying in any real Boston bar. I could just see some Irish construction worker trying to enjoy a quiet pint and telling them both to *"Shut your fookin' daft yaps!"*

Inside Molloy's front door, a large man named Smithy checked IDs. He stood 6'8" or more and had dark lumpy hair and a drooping grey moustache. He was round-shouldered, not muscular, but imposing just the same. His black horn-rimmed glasses often had white medical tape wrapped about the bridge, which made one think Smithy got punched while performing his doorman duties and rarely replaced the broken frames. He waved regulars through, but stopped newcomers. He never spoke, preferring to let the prominent "Photo I.D. Required" sign communicate for him. Smithy sized me up as a semi-regular of appropriate age and level of intoxication and let me in.

I recognized just one of the bartenders, a pink-faced, prematurely balding guy wearing a white long-sleeved shirt, with a black necktie stuffed under the third button. His bushy sand-colored eyebrows were his strongest feature, for they framed his gentle blue eyes with authority. Fergal was his name, though I never used it.

Behind T.J. Molloy's bar loomed a very ordinary collection of bottles. Johnnie Walker Black and Jameson were as topmost as top shelf got. But they stocked more than seven draught beers to choose from, including a German pilsner, a pale India ale, and Guinness stout expertly poured. I asked for a pint of pilsner.

Two middle-aged men watched baseball on a soundless television above the far end of the bar. An attractive woman maybe ten years older than me sat a few stools away. I watched her in the bar mirror. She read a book without much interest, a half-full pint of dark ale in front of her. A mound of curly brown hair tumbled about her head. Her large grey eyes shined wet and vulnerable. She'd enjoyed more than one pint, it appeared, while waiting to meet the male of her nightmares.

She smiled. "Hi. Haven't seen you. What brings you here?"

"The Disney/Bukowski ambiance."

"What?"

I got rescued by the booming voice of my friend Liam Horgan, who was sitting with another friend, Dermot O'Danaher, in one of the booths.

"Robert! Over here!" Liam beckoned with both hands.

Dermot arched his swirling black eyebrows upward.

"Bob!" boomed Liam. "Bobby Rack!"

I turned to the lady. "I'm meeting my friends. Cheers."

She went back to her book. I'd never know her warm mother love, and would suffer immeasurably for the lack of it in the years to come.

I sat and faced my old undergrad pals. The thick, squeaky naughahyde upholstery felt as durable as a crocodile's back.

Dermot was lean and intense. With summer close, he still wore an older man's knee-length raincoat over a black country-western shirt, black jeans, and scuffed black paratrooper boots. He looked like a hipster undertaker and, as usual, as cheerful as death on burnt toast. When he wasn't performing or entertaining audiences, his face appeared frozen. The great French actor and theatrical madman Antonin Artaud once said, "*An actor is an athlete of the heart.*" This made me think of Dermot, who amazed us as a natural actor, mimic, and emotional acrobat. When not onstage, however, he looked like a miserable Irish monk, or maybe what an overworked clown looks like after scrubbing off the day's make-up.

Liam Horgan appeared to be Dermot's opposite in many ways. He sported a purple paisley corduroy shirt that would have gotten him gay-bashed on the Dorchester streets where he grew up. He tried to dress artsy and loud in hopes of meeting more intellectual women who would dig his poetic mind. Liam was half German on his mother's side, a natural with a beer mug in his hand and a ready grin under his thick nose. He looked sturdy but un-athletic, shunning as he did sunshine and all forms of exercise. These days he slicked his hair straight back with pomade. Combined with his sunless pallor, it made him look like a blood-sucking Carpathian Count. He did most of the talking.

"I met her in here at last call, right up there at the bar. She's wearing a little black cocktail dress. Round baby face. Perky nose. Pink cheeks. Looks like the Ivory Snow Girl. I take her back to my place and we do it. Afterwards, I get up to go to the bathroom. I come back to bed and something smells. I mean, *BAD*. 'What's that,' I ask. 'You smell something?' She's lying there with her eyes half-closed, all blissed out. I lift up the covers and *Whewww!* She's crapped the bed! It was awful, like she'd shat out a dead cat. '*What the hell is this?!*' I scream. 'What did you do to my bed?!' Without even opening her eyes she says, 'You made me so relaxed.'"

Dermot snorted and spat his beer. "You animal. You rocked her world. You made the earth move beneath her."

"I made her bowels move!" Liam shook his head. "So I'm past being a gentleman. She's got to go. But she just lies there like a pig in a puddle. I get her on her feet. She's short for cab fare. I give her ten and make her wait outside."

"You saucy cad." Dermot actually smiled. "You really know how to handle them."

"Handle them? I can't housebreak them!"

I slapped the table so hard my hand got numb. Dermot spit a mist of beer on my arm. Poor Liam guffawed and groaned at the same time. Heads turned. We were the loudest people in the bar.

It was a hard story to top, so we shut up for a while and ordered more drinks. A U2 song came on the jukebox. The after-work crowd settled into that mellow, third beer groove.

I added a double-bourbon to my next order. When it arrived, I let it sit there for a minute like brown magic in a sparkling glass. Then I lifted it and let its smoky sweetness curl my nose-hairs before knocking it back.

Liam sipped from his pint of India pale ale. "Don't understand how you can drink that. I drink the hard stuff, I get like Clint Eastwood and want to shoot everybody."

The warm whisky stung my tongue. "Well, it doesn't make me want to shoot anybody. Not even myself."

Tom Frank showed up. He wouldn't sit next to me. He borrowed a chair and placed it so he could sit facing me alongside Dermot. Tom had to be the most normal of us, with his suburban, regular-guy thing going on. He wore golf shirts, gabardine pants, and clean, casual shoes. Liam and Dermot liked Tom, but never saw him much. While we *wannabe artistes* penned poems and tapped kegs, Tom studied to be a teacher while tutoring foreign students for extra cash.

It felt odd to have all three of them facing me like an audience, even as Liam still did all the talking. But I was the man of the hour.

"Our man, Robert," Liam Horgan said. He held out his arms and beamed like a Dutch uncle. He was Bishop Sheen, Zorba the Greek, and Father Christmas all rolled into one.

Back in college, Liam was a regular presence at all of our theatre and literary events on campus. He'd seen all my readings and performances and, even when I turned in a terrible reading, Liam always supported my efforts. He could be a stubborn critic, but you'd never find a more loyal fan.

"Robert," said Liam again. "I've always said it, even after that time you pissed all over my parents' bathroom floor. I pointed at you, and what did I say? What did I say, Dermot?"

Dermot nodded. "I know what you said. I was there."

Liam pointed at me again. "I said, 'I respect that man!'"

"Guess I missed that," said Tom.

Liam aimed his finger at me. "I said, *That man is going to be something special!* He's got heart! Talent! Focus! And he's going to make it, for lots of reasons. For one, I've never seen him ruined by a woman."

I blushed, more embarrassed than flattered. I lowered my eyes, as if reading the table top. "Well, maybe if I got laid once in a while, I could get ruined."

Liam held up a hand. "Plenty of time for that—at the Yale School of Drama. Think of all the fine actresses there. Not like the beer-guzzling Betties in this bar! Just imagine those hot young yoga bunnies staying in shape for Broadway, TV, and film. Can't you see yourself squeezing those high round tits with their sweet strawberry nipples? And fuck the tits—think of those tender young asses!"

"They don't just get in on their looks," said Dermot.

"Shit, he's right," said Liam. "How many audition for that place and how many actually get in? We're talking one out of a thousand gets in. The best of the best. And if they can memorize all those lines and shout 'em to the back of a eight hundred seat house, you can bet they give good head too!"

Tom laughed and snorted. Dermot shook his head like a disapproving Catholic brother.

"Are you kidding me? You're goddamned right they can. They could suck an elephant through a straw!" Liam was pretty drunk and loud, but so were the rest of us. He leaned forward. "And what about those smart designer chicks creating all those sets, costumes, and lighting plots? If they can design a whole stage production, then they know how to fuck too. It's true! Smart chicks are the best in bed. It's a known fact!" Liam pointed at me. "And you're smart too, which means they'll like you!"

23

Liam paused for emphasis, then grew more reflective. "For me, creative writing class was a place to meet girls, deadly insane girls with too many nutty rules about sex. They broke my heart and drop-kicked it into the sewer. But you, YOU were the artist! You're the man, brother!" Liam bellowed.

"You were the real writer," said Tom Frank.

I shook my head. "I'm just a loser who got lucky."

Dermot came to my defense. "No," he said. "No. Don't you ever say that! No one handed anything to you." In his own way, Dermot could be just as sensitive and insecure as me. So when I lashed my own back, he felt it.

Tom agreed. "Dermot's right. It's not freak luck. You deserve it. When you called and told me you got into Yale, man, the phone, in my hand, it felt like a feather. I walked on air."

Liam turned to our friend Dermot. "Dermot is so talented too. Both of you guys! I always said so." Liam squeezed Dermot's shoulder. "I thought Dermot would stay in New York City and we'd never see him again. But you're going back, right?"

Dermot shrugged. "Yeah. I've got to save up money first."

Liam nodded his approval. "Go to more auditions this time. Someone's going to see your talent the way we do."

"How many auditions did you go on?" Tom asked Dermot, unaware that he could pop the lid off a can of angry snakes.

Dermot screwed up his face, scoffed, and snickered. "It's a bunch of bullshit! Doesn't matter if you're union or not," Dermot began. "It's all just a bunch of bogus cattle calls. You wait in line for three hours for a bunch of minty, mealy-mouthed jerks with clipboards. They aren't even real artistic directors or managers—they're fucking unpaid interns! The established companies don't even want to hire anyone anyway. It's just to fulfill some phony agreement with Actors Equity."

Liam smiled. "Well, try to do something with talented folks somewhere. Okay? The important thing is that you get seen."

Tom pressed his original question. "So like, how many auditions would you go on? How many a week?"

Dermot hesitated, then said, "I went on three auditions."

"And how long were you there?" asked Tom. "A year?"

Liam shot Tom a look which said, *Better ease off.*

The whiskey had melted my natural reserve. I launched into a lecture which the sober me would have aborted. "I think all you've got to do this time is get settled in New York. Find a room and a job you can stand. It won't happen overnight. But if you start meeting folks, take classes, and do theatre where you can, you'll stand out. Don't sell yourself short. Find the classy people you deserve to be with. Keep busy. There's nobody like you. You've got all that talent. I mean, really—*they'll come to you.* All you've got to do is show up."

Dermot said nothing for a few hot moments, then smirked bitterly. "It's all a bunch of fucked and burned bullshit! You've just got to do your art and say fuck the system! It's the same people over and over, out in the fancy Velveeta cheese-dick audiences, up on the stage with all the MFA smile-bright actors, in the business offices with all the ART-hole directors and producers, at all the phony auditions exploiting naïve kids with no other choice! It's a total clusterfuck whorehouse trading in broken hearts and human flesh! And none of the bogus gatekeepers and clipboard douche-bags will die soon enough! You can bet it's no damned different in the Ivy League. Maybe worse? Give it six months. Then come back and tell us what it's like at Yale Clown College!"

I knew better than to be offended, but Dermot's words stung. He was a natural actor. Despair and dire prophecy were easy actions for him to play. Even so, I'd rather he hadn't cursed the college where I'd be spending my next three years.

Liam piped up. "Whoa! Tell us how you really feel!"

Travis Edwards walked in, saving us from further argument.

"Hey, Robert. Congratulations. I knew you were getting serious. Did you all read his last play?" Tall, black Travis slid right into the empty seat beside me.

Tom Frank spoke first. "No. Didn't read it. Can I? Can you give me a copy?" Tom asked.

Tom tutored so many foreign students that no cultural and racial road-blocks got in the way of his small talk.

Liam and Dermot waited to be introduced.

"Travis! Thanks for coming!" I pointed everyone out. "That's Liam, Dermot, Tom. Mr. Travis Edwards here will study at the Sorbonne next year!"

Travis was an unusual bird, quite tall, light-skinned, with small wire-rimmed glasses, and a lumpy uncombed afro. He wore a thick wool lumberjack shirt with a dark green tartan plaid. His loose blue jeans had faded naturally. A heavy black garrison belt held them up. Though Travis had strong African features, he spoke with the voice of an articulate Caucasian news anchor reading from a teleprompter.

"Really," Liam said. "Hey. That's the French Ivy League!"

Dermot's mood lifted. "What are you studying?" He liked the French. They were as cold, dark and inscrutable as he was.

"Linguistics, language acquisition, and brain and cognitive sciences," Travis replied.

We sat there absorbing that. Liam waved a grand hand at Travis and me. "All that, and in French too! Look at these smart frickin' people! Me, I'm done with my education, unless the court orders me to another DUI class."

"Travis is from Maine," I explained. "His dad drove a lumber truck. His mom taught college in Canada. Not a lot of black folks in northern Maine, are there?"

Travis was cautious when it came to race matters, but his reply was easy. "Not many, I guess. I remember when I told my dad about getting another scholarship. He said, '*Sorbonne? What is that?*' He just didn't get it. Only thing he thinks black people go to France for is to '*play jazz, smoke reefer and badmouth America!*' Last thing Dad said before he hung up was, '*Well son, if it doesn't work out at that Sorbonne, and you need eating money, you can always get yourself a class two trucking license.*'"

Dermot cracked up. "My Dad tells me there's always a place for me in the police department. But he's going to be the last Irish cop in my family."

I seized this opportunity to razz Dermot. "And aren't we lucky? Can you imagine Dermot here with a badge and a gun? The Aesthetic Detective, Special Poetics Squad, fighting low crimes in high art. Up against the wall, philistine motherfuckers!!"

All of a sudden Liam loved Travis. "Let me buy you a pint!"

Travis shook his head politely. "Oh, no. Thanks. I can't stay. I just stopped by to congratulate Robert."

"Aw come on, just a quick one," begged Liam.

"No. I'd have to drink and run, couldn't get you back."

"Aw hell, that doesn't matter." Liam waved over the waitress. "What do you want, Travis?"

"Um...okay. I'll take a Yukon Jack."

"Yukon what?" Liam raised his eyebrows.

"He's from Maine," I joked. "That's how they warm themselves up there on cold winter nights." An odd drink ordered by an odd guy. Why would a grown man order a sweet 100 proof liqueur with a silly macho name?

Travis offered a unique explanation. "It's the serotonin. I could use a sugar rush. Then I'll have a double cappuccino before I get back to the lab.

I'll be brushing up my thesis until the wee hours. At nine tomorrow morning I have to present the first half to my advisor, a persnickety old theoretician."

We eyed Travis like a candy-striped psychedelic duck.

Liam shrugged. "If that's what he wants, that's what he gets. One Yukon Jack for our France-bound friend! And tell Fergal to blink while he pours it! You hear that, Fergal!!"

Fergal was busy mixing five drinks for a gaggle of college gals, but he found time to nod in Liam's direction.

Our waitress came over. "We don't have Yukon Jack. But we have Irish Mist. Is that okay?"

Liam turned to Travis. "Close enough, my friend?"

Travis nodded. "Sure."

The waitress winked before taking the order to the bar.

"I think she likes me," said Liam.

"She's just constipated," I said.

Dermot and I shared a wild laugh.

* * *

Minutes later I excused myself, telling the table I'd be back after I walked Travis to his train and visited an ATM.

"Your money's no good tonight! Just hurry back!" Liam boomed. "You show those French where it's at, Yukon Jack!"

Out on the street, I lit a Camel Light.

"So what kind of package did they give you?"

"Package?" I asked as we walked.

"Financial aid."

"Oh. Um, it's half-tuition, half loans."

Travis got quiet. "Half loans? Have you thought it over?"

"You mean not go?"

Travis tilted his head. "Well, I make fun of my father, but he did teach me that owing folks money is not a good thing. If it weren't for all the scholarships they want to give me, maybe I *would* drive a truck?"

"No. You don't mean that," I said.

"Three years? Half-tuition? At an *art* school? How are you going to pay back fifty thousand dollars?"

I didn't have an answer. Travis's practicality stung me as much as Dermot's rant in the bar. I said nothing until we stopped at the subway entrance.

"I don't know," I said. "You might be right. But this feels like a big chance for me, even with all the debt."

Travis nodded. "Just think about it. If you go, make the most of it. You've got serious talent."

"Thanks. Good luck at the Sorbonne."

"Back at you with Yale."

"*Back at you?*" I laughed. "Listen to you, Daddy Cool. You getting some smooth in your rap at long last?"

"No. I heard Sean Penn say it in an interview. Later, Ace. Take care of yourself." Travis waved goodbye, and then jogged down the subway stairs.

After another solitary smoke I returned to the bar.

Liam was in even rarer form. He locked eyes with me the second I sat down. "Now before you head off to the Ivy League, where you'll join all the swells, and drink all the fine fruity wines, and spread the tasty crackers with fancy cheeses, there's something I must tell you." He took a breath. "Just be cool. It's not happening to someone else. It's happening to *you*. Watch who you drink with and how much you drink. 'Cause what you say to people when you're drunk, you'll forget the next day. But the people you said it to won't forget it for the rest of their lives. *Watch your ass!*"

"Good advice," said Tom.

Dermot grunted his agreement.

"You're leaving us," Liam continued. "Maybe you'll come back and visit? But I hope not too much. 'Cause there's a bigger world out there for you, and you'll be a big man in it. There's just one thing you need to know before you leave us little people behind, one story that you must take with you as you go forward in life..." He hesitated for effect.

Tom and Dermot raised their eyebrows in anticipation.

"The History of the Boston Red Sox." Liam grew as solemn as stone. The very thought of our old heartbreak team seemed to shave two pints worth of intoxication off his fat fuzzy tongue.

"Oh no, here we go," groaned Dermot, a total non-athlete.

Tom Frank leaned in. "Tell it right," he said to Liam. Tom watched his first Red Sox game as a toddler on his father's knee in 1967, the year of the 'Impossible Dream'. Then, in 1986, he and his dad cried together when the bone-weary Bill Buckner, who would forever be blamed for blowing the series, let the ball slip between his knocking knees.

Liam gave Tom a sage nod. "Robert, you'll be in Connecticut. Lots of New York fans down there. So always remember what my father told me: '*You must hate the Yankees*'..."

* * *

Tom pulled up to my dad's house and parked.

"What's up?" I asked.

"Got any coffee?"

"I could make some. It's late. Aren't you tired?"

"No," said Tom. "I was thinking maybe we could read your play, the one that got you into Yale Drama."

"Really?"

"How long is it?"

"Sixty pages."

"Let's do it." Tom turned off the engine.

At about two a.m., Tom and I stepped onto the front porch. The loose wood swayed and creaked, adjusting to our weight. This noise provoked thunderous barking from inside the house. My dad's two mutts hurled themselves against the door. After thirty seconds of clawing and howling, a light popped on inside.

"Why don't you have keys?" asked Tom.

"Because my dad is a paranoid crackpot."

My dad's hand lifted the dirty lace curtain behind a diamond-shaped window. He squinted out at us with like a mad prospector emerging from a luckless mineshaft. A deadbolt lock rolled and clicked. A metal hook popped free. The door opened.

The dogs rushed us. They reared up on their hind legs, pawed our thighs and sniffed our crotches. Their untrimmed claws scraped the fabric of my blue jeans and Tom's gabardine slacks. Dad neglected to bathe them. Their fur felt as thick and funky as a Kool and The Gang track. The reek of dog dander and grimy, greasy fur punched your nose and scraped at your eye-skin.

"Don't worry." I said. "They haven't bitten anyone's nuts off yet."

Tom rubbed the dogs' matted heads and pushed his way into the cramped kitchen. He sneezed loud, like a chop saw.

"Allergies?"

Tom nodded. He wiped his wet eyes on his sleeve.

As soon as the coffee's ready we'll go up to my room."

My dad shuffled about in his standard sleepwear, sagging, long underwear and an old acrylic sweater peppered with holes. We had no storm windows, so he kept an old bath towel wrapped around his neck to guard him from icy drafts. Dad crowned his head with a fur hat, a Christmas present I'd made for him years before out of rabbit and seal hides, and a raccoon tail. Dad called it his "mountain man hat" or his "Davy Crockett special."

I always had mixed feelings about bringing Tom home. It's embarrassing enough to be twenty-six and living with your father. But the nuttiness, squalor, filth, smells, and self-pity it brought up inside me made it feel even worse. On the other hand, it moved me that Tom could walk in and out of the ugly realities of my world without judging.

"Spread out! Take it easy!" dad yelled. He sounded like Moe Howard of *The Three Stooges* when he shouted at his dogs. But they continued to claw, bark, and bump into each other.

I grabbed both brainless beasts by their collars, dragged them out of the kitchen, and hauled them up onto my dad's disheveled bed. Then I pushed their hindquarters down. "Sit!"

"How are you doing, Mr. Rachaborski?" asked Tom.

"All right," answered my father. "What brings you here tonight? Slumming?"

Tom laughed. "Bob and I are going to read through his play, the one that got him into Yale Drama."

"Oh. His commitment papers. I need to find my earplugs."

"I hear it's pretty good."

"Oh, maybe for a few laughs, I guess. His characters remind me of the fuckin' state cops and Feds who talk too much down at the shooting club. Big-mouthed bastards and they can't shoot worth a shit. They're supposed to protect *us*. Hah!"

I located my dad's dented aluminum coffee dripper, stacked in three sections topped by a pointed lid. When assembled it looked like a surplus missile. I rinsed it out with cold water from the faucet. Somehow, a proper boiler never got installed in our basement. There'd been talk of getting a water heater way back when my dad worked and Grandma was still alive and collecting her pension. But now the money for major repairs was long gone. If I wanted a hot bath or a shave, I filled up a basin with water that I boiled in lobster pots on the stove. I stopped trying to make sense of it as a boy. The problem was that my dad had slipped too easily into the role of momma's boy. After my mother suffered the stroke that made her a permanent hospital guest, my dad and grandma had become joined at the hip. Like an old married couple, they bickered away all their good years while our quality of life never improved a tick.

I lit a greasy gas burner with a match, set a kettle to boil, filled the strainer with coffee, and assembled the dripper. If you measured right, it made tasty coffee.

While we waited, Tom engaged my father with polite small talk between his ragged sneezing. It was absurd, watching spiffy, suburban Tom trade pleasantries with my unshaved dad in his ragman get-up.

"Pretty impressive, huh, Mr. Rachaborski, the way Bob got into Yale University? Hundreds of people apply every year for that program and they accept how many?"

"Five," I said.

My dad shook his head. "Jesus! Imagine all the others who don't get in. Ha-ha. What a bunch of world-class wonders they must be!" Dad shrugged. "Well, who knows. Maybe things can work out for Bob. Or maybe not. From what I see, theatre is no kind of trade. But it beats warehouse work. If you can do what something you love, that's half the battle. But like Jed Clampett said, '*Money sure greases the chute.*'"

Tom chuckled. "Old Jed had a point there. Hey, Bob kind of reminds me of Jethro, don't you think?" He winked at me.

"He eats like him, anyway."

The water started to boil and I poured it into the dripper. I readied two mugs with whole milk and sugar, then reached up on top of the refrigerator for dad's donuts.

Dad's refrigerator was his personal expression board. He collected stick-on magnets from every gun shop he visited, and pinned up whatever newspaper or magazine photos caught his attention. On display was a picture of wolves howling at the night sky. Above it he'd stuck a lovingly detailed magazine photo of an M1 Garand Army rifle cradled in the arms of a World War II Marine. In the center, he'd posted a color newsprint picture of a local Jamaican street entertainer well known in Harvard Square. This happy Reggae character wore black wrap sunglasses above a huge ganja grin. Beneath it were the words "Mellow Out Man" scrawled in black magic marker. Dad said that when his heart acted up, staring at the Mellow Out Man calmed him better than his nitroglycerin pills.

"Want a donut?" I held out the box for Tom.

Tom took a look. "Maybe we can split one."

I filled the mugs to with coffee. It looked like dark gold, the only true luxury available within the shabby digs.

"Let's head upstairs."

Tom nodded. "Goodnight, Mr. Rachaborski," Tom said as we closed the kitchen door behind us.

No reply. Dad's dogs started barking again.

We ascended two sets of stairs in near darkness. I offered Tom the upholstered chair in front of the sewing machine table which served as my writing desk. Then I sat on the edge of my narrow bed. At least there wasn't any dog hair in my spare and tidy sleeping space. The literature in my bookcase ranged from eclectic to intense. Drama classics commanded some space. The rest was a riot of pulp, protest, and angry young men.

I opened the two windows halfway to let the night breezes in. In late spring the air was cool. I knew we'd need airing out since Tom smoked a pack of cigarettes per day despite his allergies. I set out two ashtrays and lit up.

Tom dug out a cigarette. "So where's the masterpiece?"

I slid a cardboard box out from under my bed, pulled out two play scripts, and handed one to Tom. "You asked for it."

Tom read the cover. "*Dirty Dog Loyalty*. What does it mean?"

"Ask a dirty dog."

"I know where I can find some. So who's reading what?"

"There are two parts, Chuck and Gus, plus an occasional walk-on character named Gridley."

"Fire when ready, Gridley," said Tom. "What's it about?"

"It's about sixty pages. You take Gus's opening monologue, then maybe later we'll switch. I'll be Chuck and Gridley in this scene, okay?"

Tom began reading in a mock character voice. He knew me and my humor, and picked up on my rhythms right off. The voice he came up with sounded like a paranoid tragic hero, or a shot-to-shit god groveling in his own ruins:

> "*I remember when it began. We were at war. The Administration was ambitious. A call to action. What can you do for your country? Excellent men responded. Recruited and trained with utmost care. Some were Ivy League, yes. Others were proven managers and motivators. Captains of industry. Men of daring and grand design. But more were just, how can I put it? They were...unconquerably competent. They came from modest means and backgrounds. Not special, and yet brutally unique in their ethics and determination. Men who may not like the dirty job, but who would see it through. Plain, proud characters. Pluggers. Journeymen. Job-holders. Jeri-riggers. The little ants that could! My God, the cheek of it. Cold bold competence. Where did we get such men?*"

I joined Tom and read the role of Chuck.

> CHUCK: *They liked things finished.*
> GUS: *Nothing's ever finished. Never all the way. If the job's finished, we're finished. We're through!*
> CHUCK: *They felt justified, like they'd earned the roofs over their heads and the hot meals waiting at home.*
> GUS: *Sometimes I forget that you were one of them. Once. You were bright and, unlikely as it seems, the best.*
> CHUCK: *I could never run the show like you, Gus.*
> GUS: *Don't you dare pity me!*

Tom puffed his cigarette. He nodded at me. "Wow. This is some mad scientist stuff here. It's like you're reading an insane mind. I'm seeing some bullying bureaucrat locked in a room full of computers plotting the demise of everything good and decent and constitutional. But I don't get it. These Excellent Men, these guys who were The Best—does Gus love them or hate them? Or is his hatred for himself and his own failures? It's confusing. Does Gus admire competence, or fear it? Does he dream of success, or despise the very idea of it?"

"I think all of that. People are complicated."

"So they just cancel each other out. Nothing happens."

"Sounds about right," I said.

"Wow. Bummer." Tom looked disappointed.

For a hot second or two, I was mad at Tom. How could he challenge the entire thesis of my play when we'd barely started to read it? But I calmed myself and kept things polite.

"I don't know, Tom," I said. "I had fun writing it. There are a few good laughs, some vaudeville, a little burlesque. Comedy is king, right? If we can still laugh, who's dead?"

"Okay. It is funny. How do you come up with this stuff?"

"I don't know. I wrote that whole play in a week. It kept pouring out, even if I didn't know what it meant."

"I guess they know at Yale Drama," said Tom.

"That's scary." I nodded at Tom. "It gets better. I think I was just warming up with that speech. Gus and Chuck get into it next. The rest is all dialogue."

Scene by scene, laugh by laugh, Tom and I made it through all sixty pages, stopping only to light smokes. When we reached the end, we sat silent for a minute or so. I can't say it worried me whether Tom would like it or not. But I waited for a good word or two.

Tom started nodding. "This is great. I mean, it doesn't make any sense, but it does. You know? It's like your dad down there with his dogs. It's bizarre and sad, but it's all locked down in street reality too, and funny, real laughs. You could write nothing but comedy if you wanted to. The ending is hard. Does it have to be so sad?"

"Some things you can't slap a happy face on."

"Why not? Don't people deserve to be happy?"

"Maybe they do, and maybe they don't."

"But you deserve to be happy, Bob. Don't you?"

I regarded Tom with respect, but couldn't retreat from my grim world view. "Sure I do. Every loser should get lucky at least once in a lifetime."

"Do losers get into Ivy League drama schools?"

"This one did."

"Well, while you're busy losing at the number one drama school in the country, don't be a stranger, okay?"

"You'll get any news first." I smirked back.

Tom had his points. We could have argued all night, but enjoyed being friends more.

After a thoughtful pause, Tom nodded. "It's a fine play."

I shrugged. "Yeah. It felt like something special. But I don't know how I did it. And I should, I think. Shouldn't I? It sort of wrote itself. I can't explain it. I mean, I keep thinking…Where do I go from here? If this is my voice, well…then I don't even know who's talking." I shook my head and stared at the floor.

Tom shoved my shoulder. "Forget it. It's good meat. Nobody could write that but you. Who else has those characters in their head? That's your magic. Let someone else wonder what it means."

"I guess you're right."

It was four in the morning. I turned off the overhead light and left a lamp on. We smoked cigarettes in the semi-darkness. Our fumes swirled around us and drifted out the windows. The wee hours of the night were a good thing to share with a friend.

"So you're sure you don't mind giving me a ride in August?"

"No problem. We'll get you down to New Haven."

"I'll go down and look for an apartment in July. Want some coffee for the road?"

Tom nodded. We dashed out our smokes. Tom led the way downstairs.

My father was standing in the center of the kitchen. He still wore his Davy Crockett hat, plus a big furry slab of sheepskin draped over both shoulders. A German army rifle rested in the crook of his right arm.

Tom froze in his tracks.

Dad looked at Tom. "We drink. We fuck. We hunt the buffalo." With that, my dad exited the kitchen.

Tom laughed until he started sneezing again. I made coffee.

* * *

The next day I had to get out of the house and explore my old Boston haunts. I felt homesick already, which is odd, because I had mixed feelings about my home city. I'd caught lots of bad luck in Boston, what with sick parents, poor schooling, and little money to bop around with. My good times in Beantown were few. The so-called Hub had handed me a world of hurt.

I rolled out of bed with purpose, made coffee, washed up, and ran out for a bus. I didn't have a hangover, despite all the alcohol, cigarettes, and lack of sleep. When it came to booze, my constitution cursed me. I often found myself the last man standing and somehow kept my body off the floor. Where my mind went was a different story.

I decided to start my nostalgia tour at the Harvey Drew Elementary School where I studied from kindergarten through grade four. The playground looked puny. I walked to the main building. I kept a good distance from the windows, not wanting to disturb anyone, but got close enough to see the blackboards, wall clocks, and hanging fluorescent lights. I saw posted crayon drawings, penmanship guides, and multiplication charts. The loud sounds of children were unmistakable and made me smile.

One of my old teachers came to mind: Miss Patty Petruziello. You couldn't forget her if you tried. She came at you like wild horses over a hill, the most flirtatious, busty first grade English teacher anyone ever experienced. She embarrassed me no end with her stroking, smothering, and wet kisses. I swear that nutty broad licked me up and down like a popsicle. She possessed an unruly pile of frizzy brown hair which tumbled every which way off of her head, olive skin, plump glossy lips, huge dark eyes, and tiny rimless glasses resting on her Roman nose.

Yeah, it was decades ago, and I wasn't even six, but you don't forget a face that smooches you every day for an entire year of your young life. Whenever I tried to wipe her lip gloss and saliva off my cheeks, she cooed sweet words in my ear: "Now you better grow up real fast so you can marry me." I don't remember Miss Petruziello ever giving the other boys the same treatment, so I must have been one hot five-and-a-half-year-old.

But there was one day when I almost fell out of Miss Patty's favor. I don't know what I'd eaten, beans or sausage or undercooked oats prepared by my sick mother, but I had the most evil, uncontainable gas. My little sphincter struggled bravely to protect my anonymity. Through a combination of squeezing, stifling, and slow leaks, I kept my deadliest farts soundless and under the radar. But there was no masking the odor.

Miss Petruziello's nose began to twitch. Her thick hips wobbled and her neck swiveled as she circled the room.

"Okay. Who's making the poopy-doopy smells? The relentless Miss P. stalked the room. "All right. Everyone stand up and get in line. I'm going to smell each one of you. Better 'fess up now. If I find out who's making all the stinky-winky, I'm going to take off all your clothes, then run you up the flag pole in front of the school."

My God—she was going through with it, and the punishment was nakedness no less! Maybe she'd make me marry her too. I feared standing up, and yet I did so without a single hiss or eruption. But I felt as vulnerable as a birthday balloon in a cactus patch.

Miss Petruziello leaned down to sniff the backside of each boy and girl. When she got to me, she lingered. *Oh God*, I thought, *she's going to pull down my pants! No!* But she moved on to the next boy's rear.

I held my gas until the bell rang. When I rushed into the boy's lavatory, I saw the towering assistant principal, Mr. Augustus, with a look of simultaneous relief and embarrassment, making his exit. He nodded at me with a smile, then disappeared up a stairwell. Strange, I thought, to see any adult besides the janitor leaving the boy's room.

Ah, the boy's room. I was safe. Miss Petruziello couldn't chase me in here. I farted with wild abandon. After an extended ass-trumpet solo, I sat in a stall for a while, then flushed. I felt at peace alone in the boy's room. I loitered a while to look out the window and make faces in the mirror. Before leaving, I scanned the open stalls and toilets. One needed flushing. Something abnormally large and dark dominated the child-sized bowl.

I stepped forward with trepidation. My God, how massive. The floater spanned the entire bowl. It could only be the work of the stout Mr. Augustus. I stared down at it in awe. I reached forward, grasped the chrome handle, and twisted. The floater stayed intact through several spins, like a Nazi U-boat caught in a whirlpool. Then it broke apart and was sucked out of sight. I watched the empty bowl fill with clear water. The moment was magical, but also lost forever. Somehow I knew that one day I would be an artist.

I was trying to remember whether Miss Petruziello was cute, hot or sexy when I noticed a black janitor standing beside me.

"Hey. How're you doing?" I said.

"All right. You got a kid goes here?" The man looked ten years old than me. He wore dark blue coveralls and a dirty Red Sox baseball cap. The coveralls smelled of fresh soil, garbage, and pine-scented disinfectant. His plain horn-rimmed glasses hung low on his nose. I could see a pack of Kool 100's stuffed into his chest pocket. His breath reeked like a wet barroom ashtray. His nose-hairs needed trimming.

"No," I said. "I went to school here. Years ago. Guess I'm taking a little stroll down memory lane. I just got accepted into Yale, a graduate drama program, down in Connecticut."

This did not impress him. I don't know what I expected him to say, if anything. But his silent scrutiny grew disturbing.

"Well," he said. "We don't let grown-up folks just hang around. Unless they're parents or teachers or got a job here." The janitor pointed at the two street entrances to the school yard. "You can go out that way or that way."

* * *

Starting in the fifth grade, the City of Boston bused me to the Graterford Elementary School in Roxbury. In 1972, the first year of court-ordered school desegregation began. The intention was to achieve integration between the races. In effect, it meant that black kids got bused into white neighborhoods and, in my case, vice versa. Graterford was seven miles from my home. At the time, I didn't question it, though my neighbors had plenty to say about the situation. Sending someone far out of his way, where he isn't wanted, is a miserable thing to do to a kid and his worried parents. In the past, Southern blacks went through worse for no good reason. But shanghaiing a few white children whose parents lived below the poverty line, while middle and upper class white teenagers went to Catholic, private, and pricey prep schools is abusive and absurd.

Two different bus drivers took us to and from Graterford Annex Elementary School. Our morning driver was Tommy, a big, wild fellow with uncombed brown hair and darting blue eyes. He was probably Irish, though that's a hunch at best and a cultural stereotype at worst. Big Tommy was drunk or hung-over every time we saw him. From the way his blue eyes spun around in his head, he probably enjoyed narcotics as well.

One morning, Tommy stopped at a traffic light. A red-headed young woman in hot pants and halter top crossed the street. Just as the light was about to change, Tommy leaned out of his window and shouted, "HEY, RED! YOU BLOW THE SKIN FLUTE?! WHOO-HOOO!" Tommy popped his tongue in his cheek, slapped the horn twice, and stomped on the accelerator. Before his victim could shout "*PERVERT,*" the bus was blasting through the next traffic light while we kids held onto our seats for sweet survival.

Our afternoon driver, a recent immigrant from West Africa, was a Ghanaian man named Omar. His accented English tumbled into unintelligible grunts unless he shouted and stressed each syllable. We were fascinated by his name. "*Omar! Omar! Omar!*" we'd repeat. Soon it became a chant, and soon it was our song. With our Boston accents, it sounded like: "*Oh-MAH! Oh-MAH! Oh mah mah! Oh mah mah! OH-MAH!*" We slapped the stiff vinyl seats in front of us like African tribal drummers beating out bold jungle rhythms for brave warriors and their fertile young brides. "*Oh mah mah! Oh mah mah!*"

It sure beat "*Row, Row, Row Your Boat*" or "*Frère Jacques*".

One of us started a catchy parody of a song by The Who:

> *"He drives us to school every day. Omar's Magic Bus!*
> *I'm so nervous, I just sit and smile. Omar's Magic Bus!*
> *Roxbury's just another mile. Omar's Magic Bus!*
> *I don't want to cause no fuss. Omar's Magic Bus!*
> *But can I get off your Magic Bus? Omar's Magic Bus!*
> *I want it, I want it, I want it, I want it...*
> *You can't have it!!"*

The ever-patient Omar would look into his rear-view mirror and scold us. "You children behave yourselves or I will stop the bus and put you out in the street!" This was a familiar threat. We believed that Omar would never follow through with it.

"No way, man! You can't kick us out here!" one of us white brats would shout back at him. "This is Congo country!"

"*Oh-mah! Oh-mah! Oh mah mah!*" we chanted.

But one day Omar held true to his word. "That's it! I stop the bus!" He stomped on the brake. We braced ourselves against the seats in front of us. Omar shut off the engine and opened the doors. Silence. Omar didn't blink.

Outside, the big Roxbury ghetto sprawled in all directions. None of us moved or said a word. We stared with wide eyes at the sights of Boston's Blue Hill Avenue and Morton Street. There wasn't a white face to be seen. Grown black men in feathered, wide-brimmed hats and fur-collared coats strutted outside of pool halls, smoke shops, and chicken shacks. I could smell the smoky flavors of barbecue and deep fried food wafting out of local restaurants. Sassy women in hoop earrings and hip-hugging skirts sashayed out of supermarkets, beauty parlors, and rowdy barrooms that spilled the sounds of soul music into the street. During the early 1970s, Muhammad Ali was heavyweight champion, and black folks were beautiful, wild, loud, proud, and did not take shit from nobody!

We looked to Omar for protection. He grinned, letting us sweat a while longer. Then he laughed a raucous laugh that sounded like all of Africa was laughing at a busload of stunted Caucasians. "HA-HA-HA-HA-HA!" He keyed the ignition and steered us back into traffic. We kept quiet until we saw white faces waiting at the crosswalks. *"Oh-mah!"* we sang. *"Oh-mah-mah!"*

Omar shook his head and muttered a mush of curses.

* * *

At the Graterford schoolyard my white pals and I claimed a stairwell for ourselves, just as outnumbered inmates at an adult institution do. We'd sit and watch the black kids practice dribbling and passing basketballs. Only one of us white boys ever joined in the play, Jerome Pasquinel, who could finesse the ball as well as anyone in the yard. As a result, he earned a tenuous place among the black NBA wannabes. The rest of us just sat there looking miserable and bored while we waited for the long bus ride home. There were a few fights, brief scuffles busted up fast by the school administrators who otherwise sat around doing nothing. It seemed like we had five vice-principals and a dozen hall monitors. While underprivileged children of all colors got stuffed into reeking buses, politicians found opportunities to create flunky jobs for their hack friends.

Sometimes one of the black kids would yell, "Hey! Hey, you white boys! Why don't you all go back to Hyde Park?!"

Outnumbered as we were, it took us a second or two to muster the courage to respond:

"We'd love to! Why don't you all go back to Africa?!"

We white kids didn't all find it funny, but we laughed together as a show of solidarity.

The black children waved us off. The administrators looked us over as if we were Klansmen or defendants in the Nuremburg trials. But we were just kids, fresh-faced victims of poverty, circumstance and court-ordered social engineering.

Most of the black kids at Graterford acted cool and easy. I avoided any real trouble with them. My major terror within the walls of Graterford was my homeroom teacher, Ms. Rachel Roth, a stout lesbian with a ducktail haircut similar to Fonzie's on "Happy Days". She wore long pants, baggy peasant blouses, hoop earrings, and the occasional African dashiki, even though she was white and Jewish. In her sandals and slip-ons her big toes and bare ankles were always on display. She had a tough, olive-toned face, a narrow beak of a nose, and furtive dark eyes. Her hard countenance might have been a better fit on the shoulders of a male, Middle Eastern cabdriver. She held that sharp face of hers like an axe above my little elementary school desk.

Ms. Roth's homeroom class was in the basement. Our view consisted of passing strangers' feet and the occasional squatting dog. The lessons bored me. So I daydreamed in class. But my reveries were often shattered by Ms. Roth's sudden shouts. One morning Ms. Roth leaned over me and said, "What are you thinking, Robert? Something's cooking in that head of yours. You want to share it with us?"

Our confrontations often startled the class. Sleeping students woke up and rubbed their eyes.

"What is the name of the first person killed in the Revolutionary War?!" shouted Ms. Roth.

"Thurgood Marshall," said one drowsy student.

"That was yesterday's lesson, Roderick. Pay attention."

"Crispus Attucks," I said with pride.

Ms. Roth did a slow burn. "Yes, Robert." She turned to the class. "He was a black man shot down in the streets of Boston."

"The police shoot him?" Roderick asked.

"No," said Ms. Roth. "Red Coats! British soldiers!"

I stared at Ms. Roth while she lectured us. I studied her post-hippie clothing and large clanking jewelry. Nothing about her escaped my scrutiny. If there was a scratch on her ankle or sunburn on her nose I noted it. But try as I might, I couldn't read her thoughts. She had the same trouble with me.

"What's on your mind, Robert?" Ms. Roth appeared more alien to me than all the black faces around me. She might as well have come in from the third ring of Neptune. But while I couldn't comprehend her origins or intractable opinions, I knew I couldn't mess with such a domineering, far left-leaning New York lady. She would have no patience for the reactionary nonsense my father kept stuffing into my ears.

My dad wasn't radical, but he did visit a few anti-busing protests. He always abandoned them in disgust.

"Too many F.B.I. infiltrators," he'd grumble.

In Ms. Roth's homeroom, I learned to keep my mouth shut and feign great interest in the black history lessons she assigned each morning. I tried not to volunteer correct answers too often. But when she grew frustrated by my classmates' lack of interest, she'd break down and call on me. "Oh all right, Robert. Do you have the answer? Of course!"

"Yes, Ms. Roth." With a tone of gentle solemnity I'd regurgitate all that I'd read about Fanny Lou Hamer, George Washington Carver, Marcus Garvey, Malcolm, Martin, Zora Neale Hurston, Josephine Baker, or whomever. These earnest recitations never elicited a smile or encouraging nod from Ms. Roth.

"That's correct," she would say with the warmth of an iceberg. I had the feeling sometimes that she was thinking, *Wow, I'm really making this little white boy jump through hoops.* It may only be paranoia or delusions of persecution on my part, but in any event, I became quite the black historian and intellectual, if only by default.

"Marcus Garvey wanted all black people to be safely returned to their homeland of Africa," I explained to Ms. Roth.

I told my father all about Marcus G's plan over dinner.

"Ha. We should be so lucky."

I was surprised my dad said this. "Do you hate black people, Dad?"

"No. I don't like the politicians pulling the strings on poor folks. Blacks were the best union men down at the mill. I was shop steward and could always count on their vote. They knew the job was their life. The whites were confused. They thought management would make them bosses if they kissed enough asses."

"But you don't want me to go to school with blacks, right?"

Dad shook his head. "I want you to get a good education."

The ultimate stand-off between big, radical Rachel Roth and little white trash me occurred when she discovered that I failed to cut and sew my own dashiki in home economics class. I stood last in line when the sewing teacher handed out cloth. All she had left was some dull red gingham about as African and soulful as a table cloth. I rejected it for aesthetic reasons, but I couldn't explain this to my big, gay Hebraic homeroom teacher.

"Robert, you finish that Dashiki, and you bring it to class tomorrow after lunch," she ordered.

The next morning, I spread out the plain checkered cloth, cut it to pattern, and tried my best to make a traditional African garb out of a redneck's handkerchief. I fudged the sewing, tore the cloth in places, and then tried to hide my errors by overlapping and re-stitching. When I brought the irregular garment to homeroom that afternoon, Ms. Roth insisted that I try it on. It pinched my belly as I tugged it down towards my hips. This boiled Ms. Roth's considerable behind.

"What did you do here? What have you done to this garment? Take it off! Let me see!" She dug a seam ripper out of her huge leather purse and went to work, but soon grimaced, gave up and resumed our lesson. She paced in front of the class, avoiding all eye-contact. She threw out several questions, but got nothing but wrong answers, dumb looks and extended silences.

"Oh come on, young people. Didn't you do the assigned reading? Am I talking to myself here?"

I knew the answers she wanted, but didn't dare raise my hand. Ms. Roth was still in a rage over the dashiki debacle.

I wanted to smile, but resisted the impulse with everything I had. Inside, I hip-hip-hollered and hurrahed, exulting over my triumph. Because I knew if the damned dashiki had fit, the bitch would have made me wear it all day.

***

During my middle school years, my mother endured a sharp decline. On a monthly basis she was admitted into hospitals. No longer able to function with a cane, she could barely use a walker or adult potty. Then she lost all mobility and became bedridden. By the time I entered eighth grade, she'd suffered a stroke and could no longer be cared for at home. As a ward of the state, she was often shuttled from one chronic hospital to another, usually from a decent place to a not-so-good one, and then on to a succession of underfunded hellholes.

My father's depression deepened. I observed emotional voids widening in my home—like circling bomb craters while scanning for live unexploded shells. After a while, you became numb to the smoke and danger, and sought escape in daydreams of better worlds which were always just out of reach. So you were forced to entertain what fancies you could among the rubble.

My dad smoked his pipe and played with his gun collection. For undiagnosed emotional reasons, he stopped working. He didn't need a doctor to tell him that he didn't give a damn anymore.

We lived with my grandma Genevieve, who paid the property tax and footed the big bills. My dad received enough Food Stamps, AFDC, and S.S.D.I. checks to keep us in welfare cheese, potatoes and Spam. I watched too much TV and consumed junk food like it was heroin. By the eighth grade I ballooned over two hundred pounds. When I reached the ninth grade, I topped three hundred. High school became an emotional blur, a rollercoaster sugar rushes and crashes, a gut-tossing curve on the daily loop-de-loop through the valley of shadows, grief and adolescent gloom. Bullies lurked everywhere. But no one or nobody could make me feel more miserable than I already felt. Who could drop more hate on a self-loathing toad than the toad himself?

Of the dozen or so kids who tried to pick fights with me, most thought better and backed off. The few who persisted I dropped with one punch. I relished that. But I never raised a hand to anyone who didn't push first. My dad and grandma gifted me with good will. I had my moods, but not a mean spirit.

The rain cloud that hovered above was mine alone. No one needed to fear its thunder and torrents. I overfed myself to the point of morbid obesity and, if left alone, could be as gentle as a tree sloth. I brooded blissfully on my own inner misery the way a master guitarist strokes his strings. My instrument was my fouled, unfiltered imagination. It wasn't born fouled. Wonder and joy struggled inside it. My mind churned with complex dilemmas which wanted words and recognition. They begged for a sensible parent's guiding hand. My dreams deserved as much attention as any young person's. They wanted out of the shadows. Not allowed an exit into a better life, they burrowed back into my brain like industrious fire ants.

Though so lonely, I found pleasure in zoning out, and riffing cleverly within the echoing caverns of my mind. Maybe that's why I didn't like to be fucked with? Who were any bullies and assholes to think that they could cross in front of the rolling truck of my wretched reality? If they wanted a piece of my raw raked soul, they'd get it, right between the eyes. Take a bite of my world and choke.

***

By the time I attended Cleary High School, the desegregation crisis had fizzled out. The Boston public school population had been seventy percent white before busing. It became ninety percent non-white after busing. So-called "white flight" to the suburbs, combined with expanded enrollment in Catholic and private academies, siphoned off white participation in the public schools. The integration dream died. But my folks couldn't afford to move or pay tuition, so I remained stuck in Boston public. On the positive side, the bus contracts ran out, never to be renewed. I could now walk less than two miles to Cleary High and would never have to smell a schoolbus's foul fumes or settle my butt on those hard vinyl seats ever again.

At Cleary High my life improved a little. I discovered painting and wrote stories. My black classmates left me alone. We lived on opposite sides of town. It was easy for me to conceal the defeat I left at home each morning. But my white neighbors couldn't help but see the moldy shingles on the face of my grandma's house. They recognized my disheveled father when he stepped out to get mail or hand the milkman a few bucks. They heard him and me exchanging loud profanities, or me and my siblings punching walls and hurling appliances at each other.

I enjoyed the advantages of being an anonymous outsider. I even began to feel fortunate to go to an all-black school, and dreaded a return to white-dominated schoolyards. When I walked by Catholic school playgrounds, I watched the Irish and Italian kids yanking each other's neckties and bloodying each other's noses. I became almost grateful that the federal courts had ordered my poor white ass off to a mellow, all-black public high school. The students I shared space with often treated me kindly. Others tiptoed around me as if I were a sick derelict on the sidewalk. I was a damned sorry sight in those gray hallways with my lumpy clothes and poor hygiene. Even though I looked ripe for ridicule, none of the black kids forced the action with me. The only fights I had were with whites. I don't ever remember blacks jonin' or dissin' me or dropping dozens. I'd never be so lucky in an all-white school. My dad attended those back in the 1950s and got into so many fights that he was expelled and committed to a state hospital for observation.

If anything saved my sanity during my youth, it was art. During high school, I went to Mr. Thomas McCardle's art class every fourth period. I skipped any class I could just to get back to there. Mr. McCardle couldn't care less if I cut a class, defected from the Soviets, or had gone AWOL from the U.S. Marines. He trusted me with the keys to his storeroom, where I could grab canvas and rag papers, paints, brushes, and anything else I wanted to experiment with. I'd set up my station beside a sun-filled window and paint precise, moody images of the river, woods, and wetlands near my house. Sometimes I'd paint people, animals, and automobiles. I must have been pretty good at it, because little crowds would gather and look over my shoulders.

One day, Ogie Coker moved beside me and stood in silence for five full minutes. Ogie was dark and lean and commanded a lot of respect, though he wasn't a tough guy. He had a smooth way with the ladies. He talked easily to every pretty girl in school, and knew all their phone numbers and when their mamas weren't home. But the sly lady-killer stood transfixed over the shoulder of a fat white virgin, nodding his approval.

"You're an artist," Ogie said. "For real."

"Thanks." I felt shy, so it took a lot of strength just to be polite and respond.

Radley Biddle and Nat Bailey joined Ogie behind me. They stared down at my creation and nodded. I don't remember the specific painting. It was probably a dark forest with wetlands, something so delicately rendered you could smell the moss on the trees and see the musky rats skittering over the rocky banks. Back then I composed a lot of swamp pictures.

Even angry little Mustafa Basir stepped up, rubbing his premature beard. "The man's got a talent."

Ogie said it one more time. "You're an artist."

He was the first person to call me that.

THE FABULOUS
CORDELIA GREAVEY

That night I had a theatre date with the fabulous Ms. Cordelia Greavey, critic-at-large for the local Allston-Brighton Tribune. I hadn't told her my big news. "I've got a surprise," I told her when she called to confirm.

"What?"

"I'll tell you tonight."

I exerted some extra effort as I dressed for our evening together. I reached deep into my closet full of hand-me-downs and thrift-shop treasures, selected one of my dad's finest polyester bowling shirts and a pair of slacks instead of my usual jeans or army cargo pants. Because I walked everywhere I wore sneakers all the time. But tonight I decided to wear my suede Billy Jack boots. I'd need to slip them off if some randy mugger frightened my dear Cordelia and needed a quick crescent kick to the face to adjust his attitude.

***

"Why are you putting on the dog?" said Dad when I entered the kitchen. He'd disassembled an M1 Garand Army rifle. The oily metal parts covered the kitchen table. I could smell the harsh odor of Hoppes #9 bore cleaner. Dad owned eight M1 Garand rifles, which he'd purchased cheap through the federal government's ancient Civilian Marksmanship Program, and he delighted in his collection.

"I'm seeing a show with Cordelia tonight."

"Isn't she married?"

"Yes."

"Funny."

Dad's dogs tumbled into the kitchen and barked. I couldn't resist petting the filthy things. Their beautiful eyes looked into your soul, and almost made you forget their fleas, and the grimy, peanut butter texture of their fur.

"When are you going to wash them?"

"I don't know. Maybe next week?" Dad chuckled to himself. "I need to find a tub big enough for all three of us. Then we could all climb into it on Saturday night." He laughed, then started singing his favorite Ernie and Bert *Sesame Street* song. "*Rubber duckie, you're the one! You make bath time lots of fun!*"

I felt something on my hand. "A flea! Jesus!" I nudged the dog away with my foot, then chased both of the dogs out of the kitchen. I rolled up my sleeves and checked for more fleas. I imagined how Cordelia would react if she noticed a flea on her wrist as she reached for a salad fork. This made me even angrier. "What the fuck, Dad! Why do you have to live like a fucking animal all the time?! Shit! Only an asshole lets bugs crawl all over him in his own house."

Our filthy house had been a sore spot my whole life. Oh, I suppose I could have cleaned the place myself, but it was easier to complain. The problem was that my dad just didn't want to earn a buck. His SSDI checks, food stamps, and discount army rifles were enough for him. As a result, the house just kept falling apart all around us.

At 26 years old, and living at home with no job, I had no business complaining. I should have been out in the world building my own nest. But I was a layabout artist who didn't like working a job more than two weeks in a row. Between house-painting gigs in the summer, and the occasional office temp job, I survived—barely.

"This is why I can't bring a girl home!" I shouted.

"You? A girl?" Dad chuckled.

"Or any friends! Or play sports when I was in school! I could have been an athlete, but how could I take a hot shower in this fucking dump! Hygiene is actually important out there in the civilized world, you know, Dad?! Jesus! I never asked for a palace! Just a clean house with basic things that work!"

The dogs tried to sneak back into the kitchen.

"GET THE FUCK OUT OF HERE!" I screamed at the dogs.

"Take it easy," said Dad in an even voice.

"Just once I'd like to see this place clean." I finished washing my hands and grabbed my coat. "If only this house was as clean as your guns."

"If only," said Dad as I went out the front door and slammed it behind me. I immediately came back in and reached behind the door for a big umbrella. "Forgot it's going to rain."

"Don't lose that. It's a good one," said Dad.

It was a good umbrella, made in England, with a thick wooden handle, and cloth as strong as a parachute. I couldn't care less if I got wet tonight, but it would be nice if I could keep my friend Cordelia cozy and out of the rain. Yes. Call me Sir Walter Raleigh.

***

"Bob!" shouted Cordelia with outstretched arms as I stepped off the subway escalator in Harvard Square. She'd just had her hair done, transforming it into a huge shining helmet of tight blonde curls, which looked like spun gold. She wore high red boots with faux fur trim, a plaid wool skirt, a fluffy sweater which made her breasts look enormous, and a cocoa brown belted pea coat. Her hair and neck gave off peachy shampoo and perfume scents. We hugged tight as rush-hour commuters dashed around us. I felt her breasts mash against my ribcage.

She had sure dolled herself up. Her mouth, with its sheen of lip gloss, was small but voluptuous at the same time. Her lips brushed against my freshly shaven jaw.

I had a mad crush on Cordelia, a crush which I barely admitted to myself. Though married and twenty years older, I believed her feelings might be the same. She never dropped any heavy hints, but whenever we got close I felt something electric between us.

I hugged her a little tighter than usual. My life was changing. She'd helped me change it. Of all the recommendations I sent along with my application to the playwriting program of the Yale School of Drama, Cordelia's had to have been glowing and grand. On top of that, I probably would never have applied if she hadn't expressed such confidence in my work.

"So what's your big news?! Tell me, tell me!"

"Well...It's about one of the schools I applied to...?"

"Which one?!"

"Should I tell you now, or should we go sit somewhere?"

"TELL ME!"

"Well, I told you how Carnegie Mellon had me number eight on their waiting list. And how Brandeis put me first. But Yale Drama School...accepted me outright. Yesterday."

Cordelia shrieked. "THAT'S THE BEST ONE! I knew it! I knew it! They made the right choice! But at Brandeis you'd still be in town! Now who's going to keep me company at all these shows?!" She embraced me again. "You're going to Yale!!"

"We'll just have to see as many shows as we can for the next four months." I missed her already.

The sidewalks and streets were shiny and smelled of fresh spring rain as we walked about deciding where to eat. We settled on dinner at a Mexican fusion place: salads, fajitas, and tall iced teas. Cordelia glowed with pride. She beamed across the table at me the entire time.

"I'm coming down to New Haven to see all your shows," she said. "And you'll write me. You better write me."

"I will. When I got stuck in Brooklyn I was grateful for all your letters."

"You were so lonesome there. But now you'll be surrounded by so many young artists and new friends! It's so exciting!"

I wondered about the new friends. Cordelia always picked up the tab when we dined since I was the struggling young writer, but tonight I insisted.

"No," she said. "You need your money for school."

I winked, and for some stupid reason quoted Clint Eastwood from a dumb-ass old cop film: "Are you a lady?"

Cordelia raised her eyebrows.

"Then why don't you just sit there and act like one?"

She frowned. She was a feminist, a liberal's liberal, and no Cro-Magnon act would score points with her.

"I'm sorry," I said. "I heard it in a movie once. Look, you helped me so much. I want to say thanks."

We made our way outside. It began raining. Pop, and whoosh went my big umbrella over both of us. Cordelia slipped her arm through mine. She had big hips, and I couldn't avoid bumping booties with her as we walked. I wasn't looking for a cheap thrill, but got one anyway.

Harvard Square looked good on a rainy spring night. The streets shone bright, blue and silky, with streaks of yellow and red light cutting across the puddles and wet car windows. My big old umbrella felt like a little tent protecting our space as we people-watched and squeezed our way through tight crowds of Harvard students, yuppie shoppers, and foreign tourists. There were also a few desperate homeless people and teenaged runaways, but that night no one seemed too angry.

Cordelia was married to an ex-hippie turned chemical engineer with lower back problems. He showed little interest in theatre, or was too busy to have a night life. I met him once. He was a nice guy with shoulder length hair and a long red beard. On account of his slipped discs and history of back surgeries he walked funny. With a spine made of Swiss cheese I figured that he couldn't be too vigorous.

On the other hand, I brimmed with untapped vigor, but brought next to no experience to the bedroom. The last woman I slept with had proven to be a lesbian entertaining a fleeting fancy that she might be bisexual. She wasn't. That joyless experience nearly ruined me four years earlier. I might as well have been a virgin now. That's why I savored my platonic theatre dates with Cordelia. She was the kind, sweet, wise woman I dreamed of having all to myself someday—if I ever grew up.

Cordelia and I met after I submitted a play to a one-act festival she produced. It was about a hunter who chose a stuffed moose head to adorn the wall of his business office. During a job interview, a prospective candidate brings the moose's final suffering to the attention of the hunter. He performs a passionate monologue detailing a slow death by gunshot, the animal's lungs filling with blood, its organs failing, the fear and panic in its eyes, etc. I wrote a big, heart-tugging aria which made the ladies in the audience gasp and cry. One of them was Cordelia, who aside from being a theatre critic, also happened to be an animal rights activist and anti-vivisectionist. In her Brighton neighborhood she'd become known as *The Squirrel Lady* because of her reputation for rescuing injured animals and nursing them back to health in her home.

After the festival, Cordelia took me under her wing. She read all my plays, helped me get them produced wherever she had influence, and took me to restaurants and theatres all over Boston. What can I say? Sometimes an angel is sent your way.

On the surface our friendship was all innocence. Cordelia would kiss my cheek, and sometimes my lips, but just a quick peck, nothing that entered the danger zone. She'd pat my hand at the dinner table. We sat beside each other in darkened theatres. Sometimes, when bored or drowsy, she'd sigh and lay her head on my shoulder for a second or two. But we never made out or rubbed each other up in a sexual way. Better we hadn't. It would have been beautiful and awful at the same time. Sometimes I wondered if her ex-hippie hubby still believed in free love. Could they have an "open relationship"? Best not to think about that, and just feel blessed for the ways in which Cordelia schooled me, enriched my world, and expanded my consciousness.

Though fairly intelligent, strong, and streetwise, I was an ignorant and unsophisticated young man in many ways. In Cordelia's ever-patient fashion, she taught me how to treat a lady, how to be gracious and grateful, but above all, how to have *hope*. Hope: her grandest gift to me. When I started telling friends that I would apply to Yale Drama, she was the only one absolutely certain that I would get in.

She was also the only grown-up woman left in my life. I'd lost my Polish grandma during my last year of middle school. Just two years ago my mother died. It seemed I always lacked the guiding hand of a kind, sensible, and available female. I didn't think of Cordelia as a mother figure, although I did put her up on a pedestal of sorts. And though I enjoyed the sexual tension between us, she was much more Madonna than whore to me.

As we tried to locate our seats in the crowded theatre, I heard Cordelia gasp, then felt her hand grip my wrist. There was a hurt look on her face as she stared across the room.

"What?" I asked.

"Abby Finkel is here. He wrote something very nasty about me in his column last week."

"About *you?* Why? What did he write?"

"Take a look." She dug a folded up strip of newspaper out of her purse. "Read the third paragraph from the bottom. As if he doesn't trash enough plays, now he's criticizing critics. Read what he said about me. Read."

I read the paragraph in question.

The Sugarplum Fairy Prize goes to the Allston-Brighton Tribune theatre critic, Ms. Cordelia Greavey, whose syrupy prose is so treacly and sweet, one dip of her pen would turn the whole of the Boston Harbor into Karo corn syrup.

"Bastard," I said. "You should throw this out."

"I have to talk to him."

"Why?"

"To show my face. The big mean bully. What a coward. You know he wouldn't say anything in person. I need you to back me up. Stay right by my side. Real close. Okay?"

"Sure," I said.

As the senior critic for Boston's largest and oldest newspaper, Abby Finkel ruled local theater. He looked about ninety years old and couldn't have weighed more than a hundred and twenty pounds wrapped in a wet beach towel. I couldn't believe that this frail man was actually the terror of all Boston stage artists. He wore a striped red cardigan, shiny black slacks, and a bright yellow polka dot bow tie. His round horn-rimmed eyeglasses looked thicker than anything in the Hubble Space Telescope. There were a few wisps of white hair over both ears, but he was otherwise balder than a duck egg.

Cordelia's gait slowed as we approached him. Abby sat just five feet away now. At the last second she grabbed my arm. It surprised me to see her so nervous.

If he wasn't writing about you, Abby did write funny lines. But he relied more on snarky barbs and prickling insults than genuine insight. If Abby ever loved the theatre, those days were gone, and now he only loved to hate it. He relished his reputation for brutal wit and for not liking about ninety percent of what he saw trodding across the Boston boards.

On the flipside, Cordelia liked about four out of five shows we saw, and often tried to be constructive when reviewing shows that turned out to be disappointments, especially if we visited a smaller, struggling theatre company.

"Is this really him?" I said, perhaps a little too loudly.

Abby looked up, at me first, and then at Cordelia, who smiled with all the bravery she could summon.

"Looks like the Crypt Keeper," I whispered, again too loud.

"Hello, Abby," said Cordelia through bared teeth.

"Oh hi, Cordelia. Good to see you," said Abby.

"I see you couldn't resist writing about me in your column."

"Oh I never miss any of your reviews. They're to be cherished. I have so much fun reading them." Abby reclined in his seat, completely relaxed, like a pasha carried above a crowd of peasants. His smug grin was like a permanent gash in his buzzard's face.

"Yes. But is it the wrong kind of fun?"

Abby lifted his palms and shrugged. His bony, spotted hands shook, perhaps from Parkinson's or a stroke. A slight gust of wind could have blown Abby and his bowtie out of his seat. He studied me with a feeble smile. "Fun is fun," he said with a wink. The shriveled old queen was flirting with me!

"Nice tie," I said.

Abby looked down and stroked the yellow polka dots. When he raised his eyes he seemed to be checking my package. "Thank you," he said. "I'll admit that you do have good taste in escorts, Ms. Greavey."

Cordelia bristled, but delivered a cool reply. "He's my friend. He's just been accepted into the Yale School of Drama for playwriting."

"Congratulations," he said. "I'll be looking out for you."

I looked at Cordelia, hoping we could leave now.

"Enjoy the show," she said to Abby.

"I always try. Keep practicing," he said, as a final dig.

"Look," I said. "I don't know who you think you are. Your reviews are petty and mean. They're like mouse droppings on someone's morning pastry. Some people are nice. They're happy about life. It's called kindness.

Anyone against it is just ignorant or hates the human race."

Abby didn't miss a beat. "The Angry Young Man plays were written decades ago, kiddo. You're about a century and a half too late. I hope you've got something new in your trick bag."

He'd nailed me. Bullseye. Every writer's fear is that he's got nothing new.

Cordelia grabbed my arm. "His plays are fresh and brilliant!" She led me back to our seats. Like a perfect lady she sat and smoothed her wool skirt. "Thank you," she said.

Her cheeks were flushed red after her sparring match with Boston's preeminent theatre critic and chief aesthetic assassin. Sparks flickered in her huge hazel-gray eyes. If she were my real date, I would have kissed her hard on the lips right then.

"Thank *you*," I said.

NEW HAVEN

The first train out of Boston's South Station left for Connecticut, New York, and points south at five in the morning. But there was no public transportation at that hour to bring me downtown. I had a lot to do in Connecticut and needed an early start. I would meet the head of the playwriting program, and then search for an apartment with whatever daylight was left.

I decided to walk all the way to the Route 128 Station along the train tracks. It was a six-mile hike through a pitch black, empty stretch of woods, wetlands, and peat bogs. It would be a lonesome trudge, but it matched my mood. Like a hunted character in a film noir, I found more comfort in dark isolation than the crowded light of day.

At 3:45 a.m. I slung my bag over my shoulder to launch my Ivy League reconnaissance. The night air was crisp and rich with the smells of moist earth and budding plants. I heard wildlife in the woods, rustling shrubs, humming bugs, and critters flopping in the dirty river which ran parallel to the tracks. Odd croaks, hisses, and splashes broke the quiet. Twice, roaring trains ripped the silence apart leaving clouds of stinking, sooty dirt in their wake. Distant night birds squawked and rattled their wings. Rabbits leaped in and out of tall grass. Gases bubbled in the bogs. The funk of stagnant water and peat moss filled my nose.

I marched over dark oily soil and crushed rocks. Walking always worked like medicine on me, a way of feeling tranquil but in motion all at the same time. Soon I'd be sharing space with commuters rushing to make a hard buck in New York or Philly.

Amtrak signs warning of arrests and fines for trespassing made me feel like an outlaw, a felon on the run. I followed the rails. I was living "The Defiant Ones," but instead of Sidney Poitier, I was chained to my own rampant imagination. I'd snuck out of Boston with a plan to invade the Ivy League and destroy it. My one-man army would unleash havoc on a pristine city of contented elites, but this time, like Rambo, we'd win. I would strike deep into the heart of the infidel. All my retro, reactionary, under-taught but over-stimulated bombast would mushroom, raining terror down upon a smug, sleeping college town. As my feet crunched the trackside stones, I fancied myself an intellectual terrorist strapped with dramatic dynamite. A satisfied shiver rose up my spine. I laughed out loud.

Almost at once the doubts crept in. Why did I decide to travel by foot alone in the dark? Didn't I deserve to take my place among my peers in broad daylight? The school had admitted me, hadn't they? I carried the acceptance letter with me just in case. In case *what?* Did I expect some intrepid campus cop to sniff me out as an undesirable? *Hey you!* he'd shout but I'd pretend not to hear him. *Hey you! Stop!* He'd grab his walkie-talkie to alert his superiors. *Sir, we have a recalcitrant individual on campus who will not identify himself. Send immediate back-up! Come heavy!* Then as I turned the next corner, the campus Gestapo would greet me with Schmeisser submachine guns. *Und vhere do you tink you're goink?*

★★★

Well before the August sun broke above the horizon I was sitting inside an air-conditioned train. As it rattled down to Rhode Island, the sun was rising. The bar car opened as we reached Connecticut. I stuck to coffee. I felt optimistic and sharp. I wanted to keep a keen edge, to catch all the details of this day. In my lap was my latest play script. I scanned each page backwards, making corrections with a red pen.

As the train slowed to a rumbling creep a few miles from New Haven station, there was an increase in trackside trash, graffiti, vacant lots, torn fences, and abandoned factories with shattered windows. This sort of neglect, vandalism and ruin abounded in former factory towns. But somehow it didn't fit into my image of a city that hosted an Ivy League university.

The train stopped. As I exited the station, I walked by government housing projects. The blocky public dwellings crowded the landscape south of the interstate highway. My prestigious school sprawled over the north side. This grand old college town shouldn't be so much like so many other rundown New England cities. After all, this was where new dramas and musicals succeeded or bombed on their way to Broadway. The swells here once wore tuxedos and top hats, sang Gershwin and Cole Porter tunes, sipped bubbly, and staged musical follies. Big bands honed their fare here before taking Manhattan by storm. Old money students strutted in fur coats and straw boaters to cheer their team on to Ivy League victories.

All that was gone now. From that fallow ghost town assorted strip malls had sprouted. Pizza parlors, chicken shacks, Chinese buffets, and loud college pubs appeared. Once alive with productivity and host to several brand name factories, brewers, and importers, New Haven had boasted a major working seaport. Today it was as bland and dead as any former hub of industry.

***

Since I had an hour before my meeting with the playwriting program head, I took my time walking across the expressway bridge. There were a few more signs of activity on the other side. I started to see students. I turned a corner, and there sprawled my new campus. At the end of a small restaurant row stood sandstone buildings in the Oxford style. With map in hand I walked down this street. Soon I was surrounded by students. I felt intimidated, but kept my Boston strut intact. The pretty female students I saw seemed extra exceptional, because I knew that they had scored 100 points more than me on their SATs.

At last I stood in front of the Drama School, a converted church with brick walls. I reached for the handle of the heavy wooden door. Another student, thin and frantic and with a long mess of blonde hair, shoved his way out. His pink face shone with pock-marked menace. He had the feral quality of a squirrel scanning for acorns and predators.

"Where's the dean's office?" I asked him.

He blinked his watery blue eyes at me. "You're starting school here?" His voice vibrated with high feminine drama.

"Yeah," I said.

"Don't! Which program?"

"Playwriting."

"No!" he exclaimed. "It's a nightmare, abysmal, positively hideous! You want to meet our fearless leader? First door on the left. You know, he isn't even a writer! He never wrote a play in his life. He's a *dramaturg*. Know what that is?"

"I'm afraid not," I replied.

"No one does! The people in the *dramaturgy* program don't know. *He* can't tell you what a dramaturg is."

I didn't know what to say. I smiled. "I'm Robert."

"Llewellyn. Watch yourself." He shook his head and left me.

I entered the dean's office. A man with fat cheeks and a lipless smile greeted me. "Robert?" he asked.

"Yeah. Are you Todd Voorhees, head of — "

"*Associate* head of the Playwriting and Dramaturgy Program," Todd corrected me. "Come. Let's go into my office."

"Hey, uh...I just met this guy named Llewellyn out front. Is he in the...?"

"Oh yes. Llewellyn is one of our finest young writers!"

★ ★ ★

The time came to leave Boston. Tom arrived at my dad's place mid-afternoon. Dad stepped onto the front porch to watch as I packed my stuff into the trunk of Tom's car.

"Any last words of advice?" I asked my father.

"Keep your powder dry."

"But I'm not bringing any gunpowder, Dad."

"Well, then, you'll just have to luck it!" Dad thought better of his comment. "Go easy on the booze down there," he said. "A fool's comfort, that's what your grandma called it."

"Good advice, Mr. Rachaborski," said Tom.

I gave my father a hug. There were no more words or smiles. Dad looked in the opposite direction as Tom and I drove off, as if the distant train tracks and bridges were more interesting than the departure of his eldest son. But at least he stayed outside until we left.

Tom and I both lit cigarettes as we left the dead-end street I grew up on. I pulled an M80 blockbuster out of my pocket, sparked the fuse, and tossed it out the window.

"He's free," I shouted. "The Polish Prince is free!"

I heard Tom laughing just before the big boom. Crows, pigeons, and starlings scattered from telephone wires. One excited bird shat on Tom's windshield.

"Let the pigeons loose," I shouted.

★ ★ ★

We took the I-95 exit into New Haven and found our way to Chapel and York Streets. Tom was more impressed and excited by the neo-gothic, Oxfordian splendor than I expected.

"Now this is the stuff," he said. "The eye-vee League. Look at you, starting things fresh at this big university. It's like you're going to Europe for a grand tour. You're going to meet the best of everybody, from all countries and cultures...."

"Oh sure," I said. "Future presidents, chief surgeons, Supreme Court justices, all the captains and the kings! The wealthiest parents in the world

57

all want their kids to come here. All the dictators, sheiks, tribal chiefs, princes, and robber barons buy their kids a fresh ivory snow start right here. But I snuck in ass-backwards. And my dad has jack-shit."

Tom laughed as his eyes scanned the steeples and spires.

"Maybe a few of these buildings are two centuries old," I remarked. "Most are a lot younger. They're babies compared to the architecture in Europe."

Tom laughed again. "You'd have to say something like that, wouldn't you? Always got to find some way to piss on it and shoot it down, right? I'll bet you think you're better than the Ivy League, don't you? Tell the truth."

I winked at Tom. "I should be seated high in the clouds with all the angelic geniuses gathered about the throne of God."

Tom threw back his head and howled. His laughs at my expense would have been too much if he wasn't my friend.

"Jesus, I hope they're ready for you here," Tom said. "I hope they have a sense of humor, at least."

"They probably don't," I said with a tone of grim prophecy.

Tom pulled over and parked in the center of campus.

"Why are you stopping here?" I asked.

"Don't you want to walk around and look at everything?" I hesitated. "Well, if you want to. We should. I guess. *You* should. I have three whole years to look around."

We walked less than fifty feet and found ourselves inside perhaps the most attractive cloister on the whole campus. The rich grass and tended trees rolled out a quarter-mile in all directions. Museums, libraries, churches, concert halls, and old lecture halls faced the open courtyard. The grass sloped here and there, criss-crossing cobblestone paths and plazas. Palatial columns and arches towered high, while below sat bubbling fountains and sculptures, both classic, and contemporary.

"Wow," Tom said. "If you can't learn something here, I don't know where you're ever going to learn anything, Bob."

"The School of Hard Knocks may take a pleasing shape."

"Aren't you at all happy to be here?"

"I suppose."

"I'm not going to have to come and bring you back home in a couple of months, am I?"

"Not unless they throw me out."

"Good," he said. "I think good things are going to happen here. I think this is where you belong. It's got personality. Atmosphere. The real stuff."

He was awestruck. The Ivy League was a golden grail out of his reach. He was pursuing graduate degrees in ESL and education at his second state college. We'd met in undergrad, where we both fancied ourselves actors for a while. Tom once considered a career in law, but his LSAT scores were so low that only unaccredited law schools would accept him.

Tom's reaction to Yale's stately splendor was normal for an outsider looking in. I would have to attend classes in these venerable buildings whether I admired their design or not. But manmade things never impressed me. If I looked at the Brooklyn Bridge, my first thought would be about the workers who died building it. My second thought would be about jumping off. Bridges conveyed commuting workers to their daily doom. Architecture was a pursuit for men with more money than my dad would ever have. Skyscrapers contained offices full of conniving people hatching sweetheart deals. Such thoughts set the cynical gears spinning in my brain. I was just as paranoid and hysterical as the absurd fictional characters I created on the page. My gloom-and-doom attitude always seemed my greatest impediment to success in life, work, art, relationships, spiritual growth, etc. It probably also fueled my appetite for hard liquor. Such feelings were more nurture than nature, considering my childhood with sick and addled parents. I'd forever expect the Bad Santa to blow up Christmas.

***

It took two trips from Tom's car to move my things into my apartment. Besides my drab clothes and a couple pairs of sneakers, all I had was two folding chairs, an old sewing table to write on, and a few dented pots and utensils to cook with. I would sleep on a three-inch slab of yellow foam until I found a proper mattress. My computer wasn't a computer, just a glorified typewriter with a bird-brained word processing chip. It held the words in one place and was easier to work than a crow quill.

"Nice apartment," said Tom.

It had high ceilings, hardwood floors, a kitchen nook, and a brand new shower and bath.

"You need a good bed though," he added.

"So I can back those sassy actresses onto the springs."

"Good luck." Tom shook my hand with a reassuring grip.

I knew my friend had to leave. I suggested dinner, but Tom had a morning class to teach back in Boston. I felt abandoned, but there was no one to blame. Tom had behaved like a prince. He'd helped me at every step, never showed a hint of jealousy or sent out a single negative vibe. He was happier for me than I was for myself. Damn, I'd miss him. After a tall coffee in a diner across the street, we walked to his car and Tom drove away. As I watched him disappear, I felt as lonesome as a small boy left to contend with his first day of kindergarten.

***

During the week and a half before classes started, I stomped around the whole town. I explored the parks, cloisters, colleges, open buildings, all their connecting tunnels, hallways, and footpaths. I felt like General Patton mapping out potential battlefields in anticipation of war.

But somewhere beneath my sense of dread there was hope. I held it close to my belly like a concealed pistol. I had a chance. Maybe I could make up for all the confused years of isolation? Perhaps I could record over the paranoid conversations with my depressed, chain-smoking Great Auntie? Maybe I could even forget all the anti-abortion tirades and anti-Semitic rants that my grandfather had shouted into my youthful ears? Like Tom said, this might be the place that would liberate the best in me, a special oasis where I could meet and make friends with all the intellectual, attractive, kind, and, above all, SANE people who eluded me throughout my life?

Ha, I scoffed. Hope is the helium that floats everyone's balloon just above the briar patch. Well, I'd floated this high and far. I would hang in to see what happened next.

***

Ten days before the official start of the semester, New Haven was not quite its sassy privileged self. Some students arrived early, but most would pour in a few days before classes began. Except for the city's yearlong residents, the streets were desolate. During the summer, and for a few weeks around the Christmas, New Haven was a black town. The permanent residents eyed me with mistrust, anger, and resentment. Young and old, they roamed the streets like hard-bitten dogs searching for scraps. I saw more homeless people than I expected. Many held their hands, hats, or empty coffee cups out.

"No change," I'd mutter at them.

The homeless men reminded me of my dad. They gathered junk in their carts the same way my dad stockpiled firearms in his closets. The last time my father held a job, I was eleven. Since then he scraped by on food stamps, welfare, and an S.S.D.I. disability check for both his heart disease and depression. I suppose I disliked street people because I had an irrational fear of becoming one. But maybe the fear wasn't so irrational. I didn't have any job skills or savings. Who was I to think I could take a swan dive deep into student debt and somehow find buried treasure? On graduation day, I'd receive a bill for 50 thousand dollars signed Sallie Mae, all for an MFA degree which promised no success and guaranteed hard times.

Most locals I passed in the street were quiet, but on edge, acutely aware of unspoken boundaries. Even though nothing happened, it felt like a war zone, placid on the surface, but straining under the pressures of a tacit truce. A multitude of New Haven Police V-8 interceptors circled the tiny town. But they had nothing to do and no one to protect. Round and round they went like matchbox cars winding around a toy track.

The Yale campus seemed an island of white privilege surrounded by a sea of underclass black ghetto. The disparity of wealth made me think of a banana republic with a puppet dictator and a ruling class living high up in hillside haciendas.

I meandered into a campus courtyard, climbed steps, and sat between Corinthian columns. My sneakers dangled over a twenty foot drop. I looked up the columns on either side of me. Hercules in chains would tear them down with a couple of earnest tugs. I didn't feel up to it. I smoked cigarettes until night came on, then smoked one more before walking home in the dark.

Drama School Dean Zachariah Wodehouse instructed students to call him by his first name. "Call me Zack," he'd say. He welcomed all two hundred or so students each year with a wine and snack party at *Scuzzi's Trattoria*, the first of three official Drama School parties before classes began.

Scuzzi's was packed, even though I arrived only a minute late. Theatre folk are always on cue for free food and drinks. A wall of sound smacked me as I descended into the *al fresco* dining area with its long buffet tables and tarpaulin shading. Servers rushed around replenishing the wine and snacks. A rich smell of spices, sauces and oils wafted from the busy kitchen.

Dean Wodehouse, in a teal shirt and orange necktie covered with images of bananas and kiwis, held court. When he recognized me as a fresh face, he rushed over. "Hi! Call me Zack!" Smiling, he held out his hand. His bald head was scrubbed shinier than anything at the auto show. A ring of unkempt black hair encircled the base of his crown and joined his pointed beard.

"Zack!". I grasped his hairy hand and pumped it with reciprocal enthusiasm. "Great to meet you! I'm Robert!"

Zack saw another new face over my shoulder. "Great! We have wine and snacks. Enjoy!" he said, then escaped to greet another new face. "Hi! Call me Zack," I heard him bellow.

The room vibrated with competing conversations. Eager students chatted each other up with the unchecked enthusiasm of raw youth. The more naïve, the louder they shouted. In my case, the less I knew, the more I drank. My heart beat fast. Sweat soaked my forehead. The students looked good. Some dressed in expensive clothes. Others showed creative spirit with their thrift-shop discoveries.

I decided to crash some conversations. The first student I approached was an affected male. I stood directly in front of him. He had blonde, curly hair and flipped it in a feminine fashion as he jerked his head in every direction but mine.

"Hi," I shouted.

"Oh hi," he said. He snapped to attention, and now regarded me with fierce, unblinking eyes. "I'm Fredric Scott Berg. Call me Scott." He flashed a muscular smile which contained more teeth than feeling. His top shirt buttons were open. A clump of chest hair peeked out. "I'm an actor," F. Scott announced.

I must have worn a skeptical look, because Scott's smile weakened. His vanity-tinged vulnerability made him nearly endearing. Actors seemed sad. They faced long odds. Most lost.

"And you?" Scott asked.

"Playwright," I confessed.

"Well that's what we need. More writers. Actors are nothing without words to speak. We serve the text. Right, ladies?"

A circle of chatterbox females regarded us with coy smiles. "What did you say, Scott?" asked a tall brunette with big green eyes and a smile that made your shoes go loose. Her chin was tucked low. She moved her mouth around each word she, like Ann Margret flirting with Elvis. I looked at her feet. She wore flats and her knees were bent—she was insecure about her height. Though gorgeous, her self-doubt made her approachable.

"This is Robert. He's a new playwright," F. Scott announced. "He's going to give us our words."

"I'm Marjorie." She tip-toed close, then batted her eyelashes comically. "Please write something nice just for me." There was a hint of Southern spice in her seductive lilt.

"I'll start taking notes," I said like Detective Hammer sizing up a dangerous dame. Wow, I thought, Scarlet O'Hara with twice the cup size and legs as long as the Nile.

"He's cute," Marjorie said before returning to her circle. They all resumed shrieking at each other.

A large black man wearing a brown leather blazer, a black turtleneck, and two pounds of gold chains approached. "Scott! What's going on?"

"Julius," replied Scott. "No stress, no mess. Did some Shakespeare in June, then saved my strength for Yale Drama."

"I heard that," said Julius.

Ivory Scott and ebony Julius did the whole ghetto handshake deal in five or six parts. They grabbed each other's fingers, palms, and wrists from multiple angles, then hugged and high-fived, but stopped short of bumping booties or blowing kisses.

I held my hand out old school and said, "I'm Robert."

"Robert!" Julius grabbed my hand and squeezed it with what looked like a fourteen-inch fist. I held his big paw as long as I could, hoping I could avoid the elaborate hand jive.

"Where are you from?" I asked Julius.

"Iowa," he replied with a big smile.

I filed his answer under *"Iowa?"*

"How was your summer?" Julius asked me.

"I worked on a house-painting crew around Boston." Truthfully, I'd worked that job only four weeks, My daydreaming almost got me fired, but my boss had a soft spot for artists.

"Tough gig," said Scott.

"Well he doesn't have those rich parents, Scott," said Julius. "Hell, I'd like to be sitting by a lake sucking up top shelf all summer. But I had to work like my man Robert."

Julius's voice rolled out like a slow boat on warm gravy. A lot of large black men seemed to speak that way in Caucasian company. It was as if they tried hard not to frighten the white people with large sounds or sudden hand gestures.

"Hey," I said. "At least I don't have to remember any lines, just write 'em. I respect actors." Jee-zus. Not only was I drunk, now I sounded as patronizing as everyone else.

"Oh, it's no big thing learning your words. Just like making sure your brush is full of paint."

"Yeah. Uh-huh. I suppose so. I think I need some more wine. Good meeting you guys." I felt nervous and wanted to quit the conversation before I got into trouble.

I did have one compelling conversation with a Puerto Rican playwright from New York City. His name was Fernando—Nando for short. Half elegant Spaniard and half African prince. He was the first person who spoke straight and gave candid advice.

"Write as much as you want, but don't show anything to anyone until you're absolutely ready," he said. "Nobody is going to find your voice for you. Trust yourself. My first year I threw my heart on the table. The faculty ripped my pretty plays to pieces. Oh my God! They screeched and clawed through my heart like turkey buzzards!"

I enjoyed Fernando's colorful word choices. If he wrote as well as he spoke, his plays had to be good.

"What did you do in New York?" I asked.

Nando looked away, then smiled. "Oh, I had a few hustles. Whatever it took to survive." His eyes flashed with sexy pride, but also a discreet sadness. I let this mysterious statement tickle the recesses of my inebriated brain, then decided not to inquire further. Nando kept smiling. I felt awkward, then a bit freaked. Nando wasn't anywhere near as feminine as the actor F. Scott Berg, but I could tell that his sexual boundaries were broader than mine. The way he held eye contact made me think he wouldn't mind expanding my comfort zone. He concluded his pep talk with some succinct advice. "Take your work seriously, but don't take anyone's opinion of it too seriously. If they knew more than you, they wouldn't be here, and I do mean the faculty. If they could really do it, they wouldn't need to teach it."

"Thanks," I said. "Great advice. Pleasure talking to you." The wine had gone to work on me. Next thing, I'd be kissing Nando on the cheek like a continental or, God help me, the lips.

"Anytime," he replied with his holy hustler smile.

I felt a creeping sense of dread that I would soon make an utter and irrevocable ass of myself. The combination of alcohol, pretentious strangers, and my own demons might produce a provocative outburst that could stain my entire future at the Drama School. This thought sobered me for a second or two. Then I grabbed another glass of wine.

Next, I met a beer-guzzling technical designer who could burp through his nose. It had its drawbacks. "Sometimes it makes my nose burn," he said.

I moved away in search of more intelligent prospects.

I noticed an intense young woman with a raucous laugh.

"Hi! I'm Robert. I'm a new playwright."

"I'm Betty," she said in a low voice, almost like a man's. She held her shoulders back while jutting pelvis forward. But her aggressive pose couldn't disguise a paralyzing shyness. Her big eyes got bigger when I moved closer.

"Hard to have a real conversation," I said. "It's like everyone is campaigning for Mayor. So why should I vote for you?"

Betty laughed, a snort followed by tinygiggles.

"You have to be an actress," I said.

She lowered her eyes. "I *have* to be?"

"The way you just laughed. You're free. You let go. Everybody laughs, I know. But with you, it's more."

She looked ready to cry. I imagined that to be the power of her instrument, amplifying her tiniest insecurities.

Hmmm, I thought. This woman might just be a little crazy.

"Do you want some more wine?"

"Sure," she said.

I marched to the buffet and snagged the last bottle of good red. When I returned, Betty was listening to two vigorous first-year actors prattle on. There was no way to pry these eager youngsters off her, so I left.

My head began to spin. I needed to get off my feet, so I sat on a varnished bench, too recently varnished, for the sticky glaze stuck to the fabric of my pants. The sultry August weather had softened it. I rocked from side to side, trying to peel my big butt off the gluey surface.

Ding! Ding! Ding! Dean Zack rapped a spoon on a glass. The crowd grew silent.

I resolved to stand up and separate my ass from its tacky flypaper trap. A hiss slashed the silence as the rear of my pants peeled from the adhesive surface of the bench.

All two hundred members of Yale Drama's student body, plus staff and faculty, heard the big hiss, and turned to look at me.

I blushed. Did they think I farted? I smiled.

None of the bastards smiled back at me.

* * *

The sun set, and night spread over New Haven. When the fresh bottles of wine stopped coming, *Scuzzi's* cleared out fast. I followed a group of students out of the restaurant. They stopped at a streetlight. I hovered behind.

"The technical designers are having a party," said someone.

"Are they cool?"

"No. But they love to drink."

"Where? Is it close? Can I walk?" I asked.

"It's five miles east of town," said F. Scott Berg.

"Who's driving? Can I get a ride?"

Two students looked at each other and shrugged. One of them said, "I've got a pick-up, but you'll have to sit outside."

"Fine. I'll get in the back."

I sprawled out in the truck's open bed, which smelled of gas, rust, and spent beer kegs. I stared up at the stars as the pick-up chugged its way across town. Beside me a young, thin

Asian-American woman lay passed out. She was so still and pale, I feared that she might be dead.

"Hey," I shouted. "Hey!" She didn't move or answer. I put my ear to her face. In my drunkenness, I couldn't tell if I felt the breath of life emitting from her tiny mouth and nostrils.

The truck braked and parked. The driver came back to flip down the truck's rear gate.

"Hey, this girl is out cold! She's not moving at all! Did she OD or is she dead or what?"

"Don't worry about her," said the driver. "She does this all the time. Ninety-pound girls shouldn't mix their medications with tequila shots. Hey, you're a big guy. Do you think you can carry her over to the party?"

"Sure," I said. What red-blooded man would a refuse a chance to carry a lady in distress? It made me happy to have a purpose in the group besides hitch-hiking and hustling drinks. Also, walking into a strange party with an unconscious woman in my arms would certainly make for a colorful entrance.

I picked her up and cradled her in my arms. For the first few minutes she felt light. But after we crossed a third intersection, my arms sagged. "Couldn't you have parked closer?"

"Not in this neighborhood. It's all permit parking. You got her okay? Want someone to take over?"

"No, I got her," I grunted. Ninety pounds felt like plenty more when you were drunk and carrying a person as floppy as a corpse for three blocks.

"There it is!"

I looked across the street to a second floor apartment. There was a crowd inside and plenty of party noise. A passing car blasted its horn and flashed its high beams. The angry man in the passenger seat glared at me.

"Fuck your mother in hell!" I shouted like a South Boston townie after last call. The car sped up and disappeared around the next corner. My fellow Yale Drama students turned around to look at me. You can take the boy out of Boston, but you can't take Boston out of the boy.

By the time we made it up all those stairs, I was panting and huffing like a St. Bernard in a sauna. My companions quickly abandoned me and gathered around a beer keg. I looked around for somewhere, anywhere, to put my burden down. I spied a half empty couch, shuffle-stepped over, and dropped her into the cushions. Her head bounced on the lap of a chubby technical designer, but she still wouldn't wake up. I marched over to the host's fridge and located a rack of longneck beers. The first bottle tasted cool and kind. So did the second. I moved to a table where someone was pouring round after round of whiskey shots. I hung back a bit, so as not to appear a total mooch, but close enough to look interested.

"Want a shot?" a stranger asked.

"Sure," I said.

The hosts lived in a two-bedroom decorated with 1970s motel furniture, enormous table lamps, vinyl-covered kitchen chairs, and loud, plush couches with rough sack-cloth upholstery.

In a kitchenette, a short, bald black man bared his teeth with a hiss after each whiskey sip. His face was plump and oily. He had narrow shoulders and a big square ass. He wasn't the most attractive fellow, but he appeared to enjoy his drink.

I winked at him. "Sweet stuff, huh?"

"Yup," he replied. "You know what else is sweet? Fisting." He bared his teeth and hissed again.

"Okay," I said, backing away. I moved across the kitchen and approached a couple of student playwrights I recognized. They were talking with a technical designer who wore a genuine Stetson hat and a pearl button western shirt. He had the laid-back charm of a singing cowboy.

"Nice looking shirt," I said.

"Thank you," he said. "You write plays just like these folks?" I detected an authentic Texas twang.

"I do. I hope to spin some gold while I'm here."

The cowboy smiled. With his sun-bleached hair, sleepy blue eyes and rusty red face, he looked like a miniature Marlboro Man. "Well, I'll be looking out for some of your spun gold."

"You've been working in the sun," I said.

"Looks like you have yourself. I mended fences on my dad's cattle ranch."

"Really? I painted houses in Boston. So your dad's a cattleman? Never met anyone who raised cattle. Not once in my whole life. How many head does your father own?"

The cowboy's smile vanished. His blue eyes squinted, and his lips tightened. "Asking a man how much cattle he owns is like asking him how much money he's got." His narrowed eyes studied my face for a reaction.

I shrugged. "Hey, it was just a question." I stepped back and let my right arm dangle, as if getting ready to draw a hog-leg pistol. "Wanna draw? Fill your hand."

The cowboy's blue eyes melted. He flashed a big, cow-chip-eating grin.

But I was feeling ornery. "I'm glad your dad's doing well. Mine's got two unwashed mongrel dogs. They aren't worth shit. Happy trails." I turned and moved on.

Man, I was a freak magnet tonight. God knew who or what I'd meet up with next. In the next room, I found a group of five dorky-looking white guys. Four wore baseball caps, plaid flannel shirts, and painter's pants cinched up with wide leather belts. The fifth one wore a Scottish kilt and knee-stockings. He must have been their leader.

I walked in and confronted the kilt-wearer. "Scotland! That's where half my folks are from, down from Nova Scotia. The rest's all Polish, Irish and Belgian? So you're Scots, huh?"

"Yeah," he answered coldly.

"You're supposed say, *Aye!* Hey. Remember that guy? On SNL? *'Ef ets no' Scottish, et's CRAP!'"* I laughed all alone at that one. "Hey, come on. Am I being that much of a dick? It's a party, for fuck-sakes! Have a laugh! You guys aren't drinking enough." I smiled. I knew I was being obnoxious, but these guys were such stone-faced pricks I didn't care.

Kilt Man said nothing. Two of the others forced a smile. The other two quaffed their beers, which they drank from authentic German beer steins with flip-top metal lids.

"Und you have such fine und vancy steins. Hand-forged in Wurms, yah?!" I said this in my best U-Boat commander accent.

The Stein Boys were even less communicative than Kilt Man.

I spotted a gallon jug of Dewars standing open on a table. "Mind if I indulge?" I walked to the bottle and poured. I turned to Kilt Man and toasted him with his own scotch. "I knew some bagpipers in Boston, both Irish and Scottish. You play?"

"No," he said.

"How about a jig? Can you dance a jig? I learned at a couple of Celtic culture festivals. Fun stuff. Know how?"

"No," said Kilt Man. It looked like I wasn't going to get more than a single word out of these guys.

"So this is how you jig. The Irish do a step dance like this. But the Scots cross their legs behind and up and down." I held one arm aloft, and skipped and sawed my legs.

The designers watched me as if they'd just seen a Gay Pride float full of men wearing nothing but blazing orange jockstraps.

"Hey, what do you think? Is this a Scottish jig or what?" I thought I danced pretty damned good. Sure, I was ripped, but then most Scottish folks who'd ever jigged drank a few jiggers of hootch first. I spun around and kicked across the floor once more, then spread my arms. "Now remember how I schooled you, lads and step lively!" I grabbed their bottle and poured myself another big shot. As I left, I flashed them the peace sign.

"Asshole," I heard Kilt Man mutter under his breath.

The bald black fellow who enjoyed fisting still sat alone in the kitchenette. Apparently, no one had warmed to his lewd suggestions. I waved him over. His eyes brightened.

"The guy wearing the kilt in the back room said something about fisting," I whispered in his ear.

I drifted into the living room where the bulk of the guests congregated. The ninety-pound costume designer had regained consciousness. Someone pointed me out to her. She smiled and mouthed the words "Thank you." I bowed.

The blue-eyed cowboy was pouring a fresh round of whiskey. "Want a shot, Boston?"

"Sure."

* * *

The next party was hosted by acting students. The crowd I tagged along with made a liquor store run. I decided not to be such a cheapskate and bought a case of *Dos Equis* Special Lager. The actresses hosting the party hadn't set out even a single six-pack. To them, parties were about dancing. Most of the guests arrived empty-handed and extra thirsty. The *Dos Equis* disappeared in about five minutes.

I proceeded to drink from an open bottle of red wine left on the kitchen counter. Then I persuaded a reluctant third-year actor to let me drink some of the Russian Vodka he'd stashed in the back of the freezer. I got good and oily real fast.

Screaming dance music shook the walls. No one could hear unless they shouted. The living room was packed. Mosten danced with each other. Women danced alone or with each other. There might have been two straight couples on the floor.

I stayed on the lookout for the Betty I met at Dean Zack's *Scuzzi's* party. She arrived late. By then I was far too drunk to make a decent impression. I went over and sat beside her. My words were tender but terribly slurred. I must have smelled like a barroom. Betty looked horrified. But she looked horrified when she saw me sober, too.

Back in the kitchen, an Austrian set designer approached me. She had bright blonde hair and intelligent blue eyes. She tried to talk to me, but all I gave her were grunts. Then I saw Betty dancing with two gay men. This made me mad. Not at them, but at everything and everybody. I studied the party guests and made judgments about all of them. I started approaching them, berating them individually, then as a group.

"ONE OF THESE DAYS YOU'LL ALL HAVE TO SERVE THE TEXT!"

***

I have a vague memory of being driven to my apartment building, then carried up the steps by a pair of gay actors who had danced all night. They coached me through each step.

"Okay. You're doing fabulous. Just lift one foot after another. Left. Now right. Left again. Right. *Fabulous!*"

At over two hundred pounds I must have been heavy for these slender fellows, like carrying three unconscious Asian girls.

"Thanks," I shouted. "You guys are great! Just great! Hey! Did I make any trouble back there?"

"Oh no. You were funny," said one of my handlers.

Even as drunk as I was, I knew that I'd made a complete ass of myself. I didn't feel shame, just worry.

"Did I get into fights or throw actors out of windows?"

"No. There was no thespian tossing, and no fatalities."

"Great! You guys are great!"

They had me inside the front lobby.

"You can find your apartment okay, can't you?"

"Oh, sure! Sure! No sweat!"

They left me there, ran out, and drove away.

After an extensive search, I located my keys in my hand. I aimed my keys in front of me, and took baby steps towards the stairwell which led up to the third floor, my room and my bed.

***

Three days, five kegs, and seven Drama School parties later, I awoke on my bathroom floor, my face flattened against the tiles. Inches away from my lips sat a puddle of congealed purple vomit. I was overcome by dry heaves.

I didn't feel ready to try to stand just yet, so I reached up and yanked my one towel down from the rack. I covered the mess, then crawled out to my mattress. For a number of hours I rolled around and sweated. I cried. I prayed. I begged for grace like a gibbering Jesus freak. I resolved to get a grip and make the most of my luck and life at the Drama School.

I assumed the push-up position. I made it to seventeen, then collapsed. I rested and tried again. This set amounted to twelve. Then I did a few more shivering sets of eight. Trying to do sit-ups was worse. My abs gave out after five. For the rest of the day and night I took only water. My first real meal was a soft-boiled egg on burnt wheat toast.

I thought about Betty, and Marjorie, and a few other pretty ladies in the Drama School. One of them would be mine.

"Make it so," I said aloud. Then I dug into a cardboard box for my copy of *Zen and the Martial Arts*. I re-read a true story about Bruce Lee and one of his students, which I'd read many times before. The student was a know-it-all with several masters degrees who would not stop talking. Bruce offered him tea, then poured the man's cup to the brim, and kept pouring until he'd drenched the table. The student got upset. Bruce remained calm. He told the student, "You have no room for new knowledge. If you are going to learn from me, you must first empty your cup."

I smiled and shut the book. Time to empty my cup.

WAKE UP TO THE TRUTH!

I purchased a clock radio at the Salvation Army, an antique console model made of wood, cloth paneling, and metal knobs. I thought it was a score until I discovered cockroaches living inside it. A little spray of Raid chased them out, then I squashed the life out of them with a Yale Drama Course Catalog.

I focused on my meager breakfast on this Day One Of The Big Diet. Whatever I ate for the next few months would be small, nutritious, and no more than necessary. I turned on the radio and scanned the AM dial. I found five Christian networks and plenty of nattering sports talk. Crap. Where was the weather? Where were the headlines? Then I chanced upon a *basso profundo* voice talking over the tender singing of Teddy Pendergrass: *"Wake up, everybody, no more sleeping in bed. No more backward thinkin'. Time for thinkin' ahead...*

"Good Morning, brothers and sisters! It's time to *Wake Up To The Truth!* I'm your host, Marcus Jefferson, the 'Rebel *With* A Cause.' We speak truth to power and keep it real. This *ain't* Barney time! We've got no purple dinosaurs. Maybe a black brontosaurus if you count our next caller, an original Panther. Good morning, Brother Three-Fifths!"

"Good morning, Marcus. I retrieved the *New Haven Register* from my doorstep this morning, and I must comment on what this paper deems newsworthy. It appears that Howie the police horse is getting a tooth pulled. We've got a big picture of Howie smiling with his big old horse teeth and a fat front page headline. But when I turn twelve pages in to the "News In Brief", there's a little bitty notice which says that infant mortality is on the rise in the urban black community. Now let me ask you, what are this paper's priorities when a horse with a toothache is the top story, and dead black babies get lost in the back pages? Have I gone stone crazy?"

"You are not crazy, brother. You are unconquerably sane."

"Thank you, Marcus. I'm calling up the *New Haven Register* and I'm cancelling my mammy-jamming subscription today!"

I loved these guys. It was the best AM talk I'd ever heard. I planned to investigate Yale's Payne Whitney Gymnasium that morning. But now that I'd woken up to the truth, I would march on down to that mammy-jamming gym, and I sure wasn't going to buy the *New Haven Register* to read on a stationary bike.

Marcus J's show reminded me of all the black history lessons force-fed me in Ms. Roth's fifth grade homeroom class. But perhaps Ms. Roth had succeeded in changing me after all? After listening to Marcus and Three-Fifths, I enjoyed a feeling of elevation, as if a piece of my past had awakened anew. I had little in common with the privileged of Yale, but I knew first-hand about urban life, hard luck and damaged families. The "Rebel With A Cause" had recruited me back into the struggle. I would re-enlist as a soldier in the war on poverty. The class chip would go right back up on my shoulder, and anyone who thought they could knock it off would get their ass handed back to them. I knew this wasn't the best attitude to take into an elite art school, but I would bring it.

My campus map showed me the way to the Payne Whitney Gymnasium, not far from my apartment. Good. It would become my second home when I wasn't sleeping or in class.

The interior was gray and beaten. The fluorescent overhead lamps blinked like strobe lights. Decorating the halls were framed jerseys, trophy cases, and ink drawings of the gentlemen sportsmen from Yale's yesteryears. The sketches portrayed mustachioed boxers in tights, dapper country-clubbers in tennis whites, and shotgun-toting patriarchs with sleek hunting hounds. I enjoyed the old black and white photographs of all-Ivy football games at the Yale Bowl. The men wore fur overcoats and crowned their heads with fedoras, straw boaters, or pork pie hats. They had so much more style than today's crowds with their baseball caps, baggy sweats, and untucked shirts studded with corporate logos. When did men start dressing like boys?

While there were plenty of reminders of Yale's charmed, old-money past, it seemed that none of that old money had found its way back into the gym. I'd seen bad gyms before, but this one made the YMCA look like a resort. The weight room was the shabbiest of all. I couldn't find any machines or free weights that didn't have chipped paint, cracked plates, or torn upholstery. But Yale was better known for its brain trust than its brawn. Members of Yale's football team pumped iron every morning. The majority were Caucasian guys who looked capable, strong, and possessed of a brighter intellectual glint than you'd find in the eyes of most jocks. None of them looked like the steroidal monsters you see in the NFL with their overarching muscles and shiny skin oozing injectable hormones. And no doubt they could negotiate their own contracts and endorsement deals.

I hit the weights so hard that first day that I shivered in pain all night. Lactic acid and bloody inflammation coursed through my raked muscle fibers. I felt like a spit-roasted pig.

Every morning I drank breakfast shakes, and ate salads and half-sandwiches for lunch and dinner. The total was probably two thousand calories or less. On gym days I ate tiny portions of pasta, but only before a workout, not afterwards.

I never believed that I could lose weight and gain muscle at the same time, but that's what happened. Before long I benched over 10 reps of 225 pounds. When I got back up to 315, I'd be happy again. The ultimate triumph came when I started doing one-handed push-ups. I'd first attempted them in a theatre parking lot after seeing *Rocky* in 1976.

I searched all over the Payne Whitney gym for a heavy punching bag. Having something to hit would make my first year at the Drama School go easier. The walls of the weight room were padded with two inches of hard foam. I started going to the gym at five in the morning just so I could punch those padded walls without distracting anyone. Sometimes I was proud of all my early morning thunder and terror. Other times I felt like a mental patient trying to punch his way out of a rubber room.

One morning, while I slammed and battered the foam, huffing like a chubby old bloodhound, I noticed someone standing behind me. He was a tiny Arab fellow as brown as a gopher and almost as hairy. The only place he lacked hair was on the top of his head, which shined as bright as a new apple. He smiled. Then he began shadow boxing and yelling "Boom boom! Boom boom!" He moved beside me, and struck the foam walls with punches that wouldn't snap a cracker. "Boom boom! Boom boom! Boom boom!" He exhausted himself fast, then, after catching his breath, he let loose with a belly laugh. "Ha-ha-ha-ha-ha!"

"I'm Bob," I said as I held out my fist.

"Bob! Bob Boom-Boom! I'm Mahmoud." He bowed and held out his fist. We tapped knuckles, and from then on, no matter where I was on campus, if little Mahmoud should happen to see me, he shouted "Boom boom", and pumped his fists in the air.

After more exploration, I found a heavy bag hanging in the top room of the gym's tower. Yale's Tae Kwon Do Club used that space, but not in the morning.

Dropping from 245 loose and sloppy pounds to 200 lean, hard pounds brought me some welcome surprises. Walking up stairs became pleasant and more fun thanwaiting for elevators. Narrow, form-fitting jeans slipped easily up and down my hips. I didn't have to wedge my bottom into seats anymore. I could shove my butt in any direction and enjoy the space of a chair. My body issues didn't disappear, though. They just became more mental than genuine. When I looked into a mirror, I saw something closer to what you'd find in a magazine, but under the surface, shallow fears still undermined me. I noticed that people treated me differently. Men would get out of my way and look up when I spoke. I got all kinds of attention from gays. Women I thought way out of my league would sneak looks at me. They'd smile, touch their necks and tug at their clothing.

Being a sex object was a thing I'd denied myself during too many years of overeating, bad dressing, hit-and-miss hygiene, painful shyness, or just being angry. I could never figure out what to do with flattery. Now that it came at me full force, I felt defenseless. I'd lived with loneliness for so long that I equated isolation with artistic potency, as if my backed-up libido would someday spawn the mother of all masterpieces. I wanted to break out of this nonsense, but remained repressed. I marched around like an Arthurian knight in armor. I scoffed at love that wasn't chaste, aloof or fraught with obstacles. I looked sideways at adjusted women who just wanted company and fun. Instead, I used up precious time pining for bizarre creatures like Betty Corbucci who were as guarded and sad as me.

But a new body is like any new thing, whether it's a way of dressing, a community, or life at big old drama school, just a matter of getting used to a different view. I'd transformed my shape through discipline. It was time to see if I could impact a whole scary school.

THE AESTHETIC
POLICEWOMEN

I arrived on time for the playwrights-only Drama 2 Workshop, moderated by our plodding program head, Todd Voorhees. The rehearsal room had a dry, old attic smell from two hundred years worth of students. There were fifteen movable chairs along with the fixed theater seating. Per Voorhees request, we sat facing each other in a circle.

Today we'd hear the first act of *Rock of Aegean's, A Wildly Irreverent Take On The Greeks,* a three-hour rock opera with more lyrics than a Bob Dylan boxed set. It contained revenge plots, murder, masks, cursed families, and a chorus much like in ancient Greek plays. The playwright had brought along a cassette player to share his original music.

For more than two hours without a bathroom break we read the play aloud and listened like good scouts. I was cast as the Chorus. Though I had plenty of lines, it disappointed me that the playwright hadn't asked me to read the lead. His main character Agamnumbnutts had an abundance of grandiloquent dialogue and got to spout gem after gem:

> AGAMNUMBNUTTS: *A splendiferous psychedelic halo surrounds his head like a glam rocker's rainbow shag show wig!*

The writer's powerhouse poeticisms were impressive. But with ninety-seven pages to go, we were in for a long afternoon.

> AGAMNUMBNUTTS: *An Hephaestean buzzard-beaked stab of mortification rips through my nether tract inciting a riotous blast which ricochets off the porcelain, and generously fills the airspace with a ginger mist!*

That was his best yet. What a payoff! And to think he probably just meant diarrhea. Imagine two hours worth of such textual contortions. It would require endurance. But Yale Drama playwrights are made of steel. Our class had started at noon and was scheduled to end at two. But with one minute to go, Agamnumbnutts was still in rare form.

AGAMNUMBNUTTS: *Our mounting woe alone is misfortune's mad dog daddy in these forlorn Irish wolf-hound hours.*

Two wolfhound hours and counting. I needed to urinate. I wasn't the only one. As I squeezed my thighs together and crossed my legs, I spied others doing the same thing. One man kept yawning into his armpit. Another woman searched her skirt for pills of lint, plucked them, and made a tidy pile.

AGAMNUMBNUTTS: *This coalescence of quietude is but an ephemeral calm before the cyclonic megaphones of Promethean vehemence which await us all.*

That would be me in the men's room in about twenty minutes. Jesus, what a Snagglepuss scribbler this guy was! How did he come up with this stuff? You had to admire the unrelenting quality and quantity of it. He could manufacture his own Disneyland out of anything in the dictionary. I didn't understand how Irish dogs, glam rock, or ginger mists coalesced into anything resembling ancient Greece, but the playwright appeared quite convinced of the merits of his work. He sat there smiling, his eyes wide, with his chin resting on his fists.

Finally it was over. We applauded. The class lasted an extra twenty-five minutes so that we could give the writer some feedback. Most of us tried to earn merit badges for constructive criticism. A slight argument erupted when I suggested that the playwright could cut many of his compounding metaphors.

"You know," I said. "Sometimes he uses five different metaphors to describe the exact same thing. They're fresh images. But why not just choose the best one and cut the rest?"

Voorhees frowned and stared at me. His close-set brown eyes flickered. There was something reptilian about his face. It made me think of a lizard waiting to shoot out its tongue at a passing horsefly.

A clique formed to defend the writer's choices, including Professor Voorhees, who launched into an impromptu lecture.

"Language in itself has energy and drama," he said. "It has its own cumulative power." The Professor then used his favorite expression: "*There's a fundamental notion at work here.* And that is whether or not words alone create great theatre. I argue that they can. Words themselves are the life-blood of a true theatre, a theatre without plots, without three well-made acts, without characters defined by their poor choices, fatal flaws or formulaic back-stories. I argue that the basic unit of drama is the word. Stage poetry lives or dies on a syllabic level. I have sat with audiences and witnessed as sprawling wordscapes gathered momentum and swept over the crowd like storms. A text that seemed inert on the page blossomed and became a horizontal avalanche. Everyone in the house felt it, a chance awakening, a tectonic shift in the unconscious, a manifestation of the unseen. We experienced a verbal sea change, just by the way the playwright ordered and trussed together his words."

This ornate concept was too much for a Boston lad educated in public schools.

"Yeah. I feel the same way," added one of my classmates. "I like plays that aren't afraid to explore language and find the energy. Energized wordplay, that's what it's all about. I like anything with energy, lots of energy."

Try a few D sized batteries up your ass, I thought.

The playwright stared at me as if I'd just felt up his mother. His dark eyebrows bristled with anger and confusion. *Fuck him.* I'd be a lot gentler with his mother than any producer would ever be with his overstuffed, fruitcake plays.

In moments like these, my mind retreated from rationality and sought comfort in violent chaos theories. My eyes drifted above the heads of my classmates and explored patterns on the dirty windows. I wondered how Professor Voorhees got tenured, and why he leased a luxury apartment decorated with antique furniture, rare fossils and framed prints, while other men lived out of cardboard boxes and gibbered over fortified wine.

Fundamental notions? Shit. I must have been thinking this too loud, because I felt Professor Voorhees's eyes on me.

"The language in today's play has transformative potential, and should not be discouraged," Voorhees declared for my benefit. "As I said to everyone in our very first class, *descriptive* criticism is welcome in this workshop. But be careful with *PRE-scriptive* commentary. We observe and describe here. We don't dictate. We don't dismiss." After a deliberate pause, Mr. Voorhees withdrew his judgmental gaze, and then regarded the rest of the class.

I was angry. I made a fair comment, it seemed. People with fundamental notions should be able to have fundamental disagreements. But I knew I couldn't win. Voorhees was much more educated than me, and had a war chest full of quotes, footnotes, and ready references. *Go fuck yourself*, was about all I could tell him with any authority. As horizontal avalanches of words go, that would have been snappy and succinct, but far too prescriptive for his tastes.

Professor Voorhees raised a hand and announced, "We still have an open slot next week. Would anyone like to go?"

I raised my hand. Voorhees ignored me, but when no other hands went up, he gave in.

"Okay," said Voorhees. "Robert will go next week right after Wendy's first piece. Does anyone want to take Robert's originally scheduled slot later in the semester?"

"I'll take his slot!" shouted Wendy Grushkin.

Wendy was a petite Upper East Side gal with an elfin face and big, matronly breasts that would have been ungainly on a woman twice her size. Her large chest and permanent smile made me think of Nurse Ratched in Ken Kesey's *One Flew Over the Cuckoo's Nest*.

Professor Voorhees checked his schedule. "Wendy, you're scheduled for the first hour next week and also on November sixteenth. Robert had November second. Do you want to switch your sixteenth for his second?"

"Oh, forget it then. I don't want that slot," said Wendy.

"It's only two weeks earlier," said Voorhees.

"I need all the extra time I can get," said Wendy.

"Okay. Hmmm." Voorhees frowned and fussed with his list some more. "Robert will go three times this semester, I guess."

I didn't understand why anyone would not want to have his or her plays read aloud in class as early and often as possible. Considering that we had three years to try and fail, and maybe improve our craft before graduation, the Yale Drama playwrights were the laziest bunch of anal-retentive nurslings that I'd ever met. All they needed to do was present a single act of one new play each semester. That's twenty to thirty pages, double-spaced. Half of each page is taken up with character names and stage directions, so it's more like ten pages of fiction or less. But every student playwright wanted to go as late in the semester as possible. The way my classmates sat on their precious plays, you'd think they were all constipated geese withholding a treasure of golden eggs. By the time their work was read, the dialogue was so delicate and airy I had to wonder what had inspired the plays to begin with. It seemed as if they had beaten all of the original impulse out of the work with ten thousand hammer strokes. The words that remained were flatter than the paper that held them, as bland as triple-distilled baby urine, too weak to stink.

My classmates ruthlessly targeted the clichés in each other's work. Originality and innovation were the most prized of Professor Voorhees's fundamental notions. But the kinds of risks which created revolutions just didn't happen in our frigid, passive-aggressive workshops. Class after class, plays without plots or recognizable human characters were praised and patronized. Most became minimalist exercises so empty of emotion and devoid of detail that they were critic-proof. *How can you criticize what isn't there?*

Other plays loitered over unexplored intellectual ideas. Pretty words, aphoristic flourishes, and fancy language abounded. Everyone was a master metaphor-mixer, a genius of the aphorism, and an expert with the precarious, yet delicately extended simile. They scraped the skin of their individual angst, but once flesh parted, and blood appeared, they smothered it to death with abstraction. Each play was stifled with a frilly lace pillow before it could scream.

I felt useless in these classes.

As an undergraduate theatre student, I embraced writers like Eugene O'Neill, and Arthur Miller, and especially Clifford Odets more than I ever should have. Cliffy was the rat prick bastard who crushed Frances Farmer's artistic dreams and sent her back to her mom and the madhouse. Nevertheless, I thought of theatre as a tool of conscience, a club to combat injustice, a set of chains to drag the richest man down before the judge's bench. And the audience must be implicated.

I read more contemporary dramatists, like Samuel Beckett, and Harold Pinter, and their American imitators like Albee, Sam Shepard, and David Mamet. I arrogantly dismissed them all, except for Beckett. Beckett fought with the French Resistance in WWII and wrote plays like a man who knew he had one foot in the grave from the day he left the womb.

The theatre I dreamed of creating lived somewhere between the rough speechmaking of Eugene O'Neill and the forlorn pauses of Beckett. After watching productions of *Death of a Salesman,* or *Long Day's Journey into Night,* or *Waiting for Godot,* you wanted to change the world, embrace a lover, fight, cry, kill someone, maybe yourself, or save someone. After listening to the timid, inscrutable plays at Yale Drama School, all I wanted to do was hide my contempt while my plummy peers oohed and ahed and gave each other's esoteric creations big sloppy tongue baths. These unrelenting love sessions left me feeling low. I walked out of these workshops in a cloud of confusion and vague sadness. I wondered if I'd ever crawl out of my funk and make great art. I still believed good stuff could be written for the stage. I just didn't think it would happen at Yale Drama School.

The only fair response to this merciless mediocrity would be to write the dangerous dramas I thought belonged on the stage. Unfortunately, I didn't have one ready for next week.

***

There were two short pieces presented in that day's Drama Two workshop. Number one was the first act of Wendy Grushkin's play *Downtown Deena, A Girly Fantasia in NYC.* It told a little story about a chubby New York girl who eats 12 hot dogs from 12 different street vendors as she walks all the way from 42nd Street down to Greenwich Village. En route she has conversations with stereotypical Manhattan-ites: hawking vendors, homeless people, slumming uptown matrons, frantic actors rushing to auditions, but mostly with herself. The character delivered her lines directly to the audience. Wendy's play was fun, but it left one longing for the classic structure and gravitas of *Laverne and Shirley.*

The second piece was my play *Townies,* about a couple of childhood friends from a Boston neighborhood who meet at the state unemployment offices and start arguing. I believed in what it said about poverty, class conflicts, and the challenges of the underprivileged. Its thesis was that the folks who most need to get along and protect each other are often the least equipped to do so. But I worried that the play was all thesis and no drama. I figured that eighteen pages wouldn't cause anyone too much grief, but when the first few lines were read, I could tell my script was a dead cat stuck just above a sewer grate.

The class grew restless fast. There were no laughs where I expected them. I scanned my classmates' faces for reactions. They looked like patients in a chronic hospital. Some of my dialogue provoked sniggers and headshakes, especially when my characters made aggressive comments about race and gender. The only student with half a grin on her face was Wendy Grushkin. But she always smiled –– Prozac, most likely.

The play was loosely based on my experience working in a mail room with over a dozen black guys. They didn't understand why a white boy with a college degree sorted mail. I didn't understand why a man making seven dollars an hour would father five kids. Tensions grew. Threats were made. I got fired.

Whatever conflict there was in my play unfolded in a clumsy back and forth argument. One character had a college degree and no job. The other had a felony record and no job. They judged each other for twenty minutes —that's all. I didn't know how to end the play, so I threw in a security guard to order them out of the unemployment office. It was a stupid finish which introduced an unnecessary third character. I could see now that my play was too simplistic and old school for its own good. Its style of social realism was brave when Zola did it, fervent when Odets and Arthur Miller used it, and on its way to becoming very dull when Paddy Chayefsky and Rod Serling pumped out their work in the early days of black and white television. Toss in a few flying saucers and alien life forms, and my play might have made a fair *Twilight Zone* episode. Otherwise it was total shit.

Sometimes you just don't know how much a thing stinks until you rip off the lid and sniff. When the last syllable of the closing stage direction was read, I slumped in my chair like a death row inmate who had just received the best of Old Sparky. I wished the smell away, but it hovered like a fart trapped in a space suit. I wanted to ask Professor Voorhees to skip the discussion, but I knew he wouldn't have it. Then I thought, *Why the hell not?* Maybe I could learn something from having my nose rubbed in my work. But what could I learn? Awful was awful. Perhaps I needed to be punished? Yes, that had to be it. I was a bad boy begging for abuse. Who would crack the whip first?

Wendy Grushkin and Marla Starrett trampled each other's first sentences. "I think," they both began.

"Oh, I'm sorry," said Wendy. "You go."

"Oh no," said Marla. "No. You go first. Please."

"Okay," agreed Wendy. "I think the language lacks energy. He uses strong words, but there's no impetus or originality. The voices are undistinguished. He doesn't take risks with his language choices. The talk is ordinary. I don't know if I care about these people or want to spend time listening to them."

Wendy was right, but her comment still made me want to rape her with *Roget's Thesaurus*. But Wendy proved to be the good cop.

Bad cop Marla stepped in next. "Well," she began, "it's like that old grandmotherly expression: 'If it's not nice, necessary, or useful, tick a lock.'" She pursed her lips shut and mimed turning a key, which made the class laugh "So I don't really know what I should say, if anything."

Voorhees smiled. "Go on, Marla. Say what's on your mind."

Marla smiled. I suppose she was a handsome enough woman, with her good skin and curly blonde hair. Her eyes shined silver blue. Her lips were thin, but still sensual. Her square flat forehead, sharp nose, and high cheekbones gave her the stubborn look of Clint Eastwood's sister.

"Well, I don't know what Robert was trying to do here," she said, "but it doesn't seem like much or that he tried too hard." She paused and shook her head in a show of frustration. "If plays don't use heightened creative language, then what's the point? People used to care about what they brought into this class. I wish they still did!" Marla looked down and froze like Rodin's *Thinker*.

Tyson was champ again in those days, and I wasn't sure who hit harder. I tried my best to relax and roll with the blow. A thousand words in my defense would not bring Marla back to my side, and calling her a bitch would be one word too many.

Wendy Grushkin raised her hand and spoke the second Voorhees acknowledged her. "I agree. That's what I meant about the lack of energy, I think."

Marla smiled at Wendy. They beamed at each other. From that moment on, I nicknamed them Cagney and Lacey, the Aesthetic Policewomen. Wendy was the chunky brunette. Marla was the butch blonde. As the stern captain of their squad, Voorhees kept them in check. They worked me over pretty good in the interrogation box. I expected we would all have more run-ins over the next three years, and unless I became a better writer, or jailhouse lawyer, I'd get the worst of it every time.

***

The next day I sat in Voorhees's cramped little bomb shelter of an office. The morning sun blasted the window shades, and made everything hot and close. It seemed airless and weightless in there, like a NASA demo capsule.

"You know, from the way you mix up the names, and forget half the plot, I'm guessing you didn't read my play even once."

Voorhees gripped the edges of my playscript and leaned forward over his desk blotter. His chair creaked. His dark eyes squinted under bunched up brows. I saw my play twisting in his hands like a powdered cruller spilling red jelly. I also saw all my other plays piled neatly on the metal bookshelf beside his desk. *God*, I thought. *My worst first drafts, and he has them all stacked there like evidence of my insanity.* "Don't you ever doubt me," hissed Voorhees with a tight, deliberate mouth, chewing the words like oily fish bones, and then spitting them at me. "If I read that play, I read it at least *ten times!*"

This flash of raw anger from the normally calm Voorhees surprised me. I looked back at him like Bogart stone-walling an aggressive district attorney. I played it tough, but then wondered if he might be right. If my play sucked, it sucked. If no one laughs when you're done telling the joke, it wasn't funny. I considered backing down. Yeah. Let him win this one. He needed the little victories more than I did. Or did he? No sense burning all my bridges my first year here. Just play along. But I wasn't going to apologize. Hell, no. Apologize for what? For being disliked and dismissed? He obviously hated my play, barely read it, and openly sneered at whatever I tried to say. I could butt heads or back down. Hold my ground or hold it between my knees. And why start a war with the man responsible for my education? But the guy was a dramaturg who hadn't written a line of dialogue in his life and had no business teaching playwriting to anybody, especially in an Ivy League MFA program.

But still, maybe there was some karmic reversal at work? Maybe I came here to be *his* mentor? Perhaps the universe shoved us together so we could learn important life lessons from each other, and create wisdom and karmic rectitude? Maybe the high road had been paved for us long ago? As the Muslims say, our stories were written by God long before we were born. But it was up to me to take that first wise, brave, and generous step.

I considered saying something less antagonistic and more agreeable. I was just about to and almost did. But I stopped. I jumped off the Peace Train. I chose war. Let the bridges explode, the cities burn, and all the dead float down flaming rivers. Perhaps I was an insecure loser making a dangerous enemy and kicking his own bright future into the ash heap?

I looked straight into his eyes and said, "Ten whole times, huh? So like, the tenth time you read it, you still didn't notice that the lead character's name was Mike and not Mark?"

"I know what I read! This piece was messy and difficult. This is not your best artistic effort. It failed to engage me in any significant way. Somewhere around page 25 or so, I just had to *put it down*. This is not the kind of writing that got you accepted. When I compare your submission material to this, it's as if they were written by a different person."

"So, I can't even *try* a linear style? Everything has got to be just like the submission play? If it's not your kind of nutty catnip, can't you play along?"

He fumed. "Your submission play worked on several levels."

"It was two guys talking about their crotches and terrorizing each other for sixty pages!"

"That held my interest! This doesn't!"

After a pause, I said, "Okay, okay. Bad is bad. But I've got something new, something nice and screwy and cryptic just for you. It'll be on your desk Monday morning."

Voorhees was still angry. That I would presume to know his tastes provoked him. "Monday," he hissed. "I'll be expecting it. You know," he said, "the first year in this program is probationary, and I have asked some students to leave."

"Sure." I grinned, knowing my next play would tickle the misfiring neurons in his old-school, hippie skull. I'd written this new piece as a lark, a parody of a parody of the kind of theater I hated. But as long as I didn't tell Voorhees or any of my classmates that, we'd all have fun.

BETTY AND BERGMAN

Her name was Betty Corbucci. She was rare and radiant, a misplaced gem in a sea of trinkets. Sure there were plenty of sexy, intense women at Yale Drama. But with Betty, it was more than just hormones. When I looked into her eyes, I saw something crazy that made me feel less crazy.

Every chance I could I talked to her. We worked on the same production, me with the run crew backstage, she acting under the bright lights out front. The play was a graduating student's thesis on *commedia del arte*. Betty had a puny but busy part. She had more costume changes than words. Each night she became an angel, a bunny, an orange, a berry bush, and a sheep. The sheep got the best laughs of the night for saying "Ba-a-a."

I slogged scenery for seven work study dollars an hour. I cared so little that I allowed the fly scenery to thud down onto the stage. The stage manager would shake his head. Once he came over to criticize me, but my guard dog growls scared him off. I snarled a lot during my first months at the Drama School.

For her first entrance, Betty wore an angel costume fashioned with white satin, wired chiffon wings, chenille trim, glow tape stars, and discreet splashes of glitter.

Unaffected and earthbound, she didn't seem aware of her looks. I imagined her as a feisty resistance fighter outwitting rat bastard Nazis in an Italian neo-realist movie. I became convinced that Betty was an actress of rare, raw power. She was Anna Magnani, Vanessa Redgrave, and Vivien Leigh all rolled into one. And she would soon be Bob Rachaborski's girlfriend. Aside from her unique eyes, nothing else about Betty seemed quite perfect. Her face was oval, with a nose perhaps too big, and a chin too small. Her waist, hips and thighs all seemed a bit thick. But when you put everything together, you had a gal who was warm and desirable.

From behind the curtains, I watched her float across the stage on her diaphanous wings. When she performed I never missed a cue. I handled those fly ropes like the lilting strings of a harp. The scenery settled without a whisper or a shimmy. I would have lowered and raised the pearly gates on God's command just to let my angel Betty out to play. It wasn't enough to adore Betty from afar. I needed her. I hadn't tried sex in years. After a stretch of chronic unemployment and failed attempts to live on my own, I'd moved back home with my paranoid father and all his gibberish, despair, and squalor. This backslide had squashed the last drop of confidence out of me.

Sure, I lived in my own apartment now and attended the famous Drama School. But the old insecurities still clung to my scarred hide like a blast of skunk juice. For so long I'd believed I possessed nothing material or spiritual to offer a young woman. I knew nothing about how to win the right mate. My concept of courtship was as savage as a wild boar hunt. I rushed blind into unmapped jungles, dodged tusks, and made Hail Mary lunges. But no matter how horrible or awkward my attempts to woo Betty might be, I would not quit until she was mine.

The monster play production consumed our waking hours. There'd be no first date until we got our lives back. In the meantime, I wouldn't let Betty forget me. I hovered close. Sometimes she'd stiffen when I cornered her while her classmates were watching.

"Do you want to see a movie with me?" I asked her two days before closing night.

"Yes," Betty said. "I'd like that." She smiled, then escaped to get an early start on a costume change.

Well, it worked. Now I needed to play it cool until we got past the first kiss and clothes came off. For the first time in a while, that didn't scare me. I felt trim ready to snatch the tiger by the tail, swing it over my head, and toss its striped ass back into the jungle. I'd been throwing the iron around all semester. The Rock was ready to party naked. Although other actresses cast their sweet moonbeam sex vibes my way, my choice was Betty. Only she possessed that freaky magic that made me feel like I was howling with my own family of junkyard dogs.

The big, boring *Commedia del Arte* play closed with a thud. The half-empty house cleared out. The bars outside filled fast. There'd be no drinks for us. We'd strike the set no matter how long it took. Betty and I would meet the next evening.

I grew concerned about the date. Theatre folk say that the purpose of the first rehearsal is to get to the second. I hoped that my first outing with Betty wouldn't be my last.

***

The sun set and the streets darkened early in November. Yellowed leaves scudded along the streets with the rise of each chill wind. I rang Betty's apartment at five-thirty. She buzzed me up. Her place was clean, colorful and full of soft, fluffy furniture. It looked like the set for a children's TV program.

Betty wore a black sweater with flared sleeves, faded blue jeans, and suede boots with short heels. I admired her shiny thick midnight hair. Her face was pale from lack of sleep.

"I'm burned out from last night," she said. "How are you?"

"I got in a little nap and ate a late lunch."

"Good for you. I wasn't so lucky."

We took turns staring at each other, and then at the walls.

The ball was in my court, I thought, so I started talking. But I must have confused that court with a baseball diamond, because I launched into an endless inning of foul tips, forced errors, and embarrassing swings at nothing. As usual before some of my most disastrous dates, I launched into a monologue about my childhood, and all the misery and sickness it contained. I don't know why I did this. Perhaps I needed to confess before I could accept grace into my life? Self-pity is not sexy. Betty's sleep-deprived eyes were closing. She'd almost drift off, then blink herself awake. But did I stop talking? No. I covered every grade in the Boston Public schools and all of my mother's hospitalizations before Betty raised a hand and grunted.

I shut up.

She stared at me for a hot moment. "You don't date much."

"No."

After a pause she asked, "Do you want some coffee?"

She prepared two very strong and large mugs. "So what's this movie we're going to see?"

"An Ingmar Bergman film about young lovers who run away from their parents and live free until their money runs out."

"Just like us, huh? Okay. Let me finish my coffee."

Betty put on a bright red pea coat with a matching beret. If she could survive my monologue and still go on with our date, good things were still within reach.

Walking across town shoulder to shoulder, I felt comfortable with her. She started smiling. There was a childish skip in her step. She darted across intersections and tried to beat every traffic light. Twice she was nearly run down by a car. I felt like a dad out with his wacky precocious daughter.

I bought the tickets and we took seats in the middle of the theatre. Betty arranged her coat on an empty seat, then crowned it with her beret.

Other women I took to movies like this one would groan when they saw the old black and white footage streaked with scratches. But Betty laughed at the image of a young girl trying on hats and grinning at her own cleverness. For a 1948 film there was a good amount of nudity. I snuck a glance at Betty. She turned and winked. Would I get lucky tonight?

After 90 minutes or so, the credits rolled.

Betty smiled. "That was good."

On the way home we walked slower, stopped at each intersection and waited for green lights like good citizens. When we got to her door, I moved closer. My plan was to lean in for a kiss. But Betty turned her face at the last second and rested her chin on my shoulder. We hugged each other tightly.

"I had a good time," she said.

"Me too. I'm going to call you. Okay?"

"Yes. Call me," she smiled, then ran upstairs to her place.

Date one, I said to myself. Looking good, Chico.

THE SPOOKING OF
LEOTIS JENKS

Professor Voorhees grinned as if I'd just fed him a spoonful of caramel custard. Autumn had arrived in full swing, and his small office felt more temperate and calm. He leaned forward and held my play script with both his steady hands just above his desk blotter. "I was very pleased to read this new piece of theatre. The language has momentum and constant surprises. This is the kind of creativity I expected from you."

"I knew you would appreciate it," I said.

"Will you offer this as your first Playwrights Collaborative Project?"

"Do you think I should?"

"It would be a good fit, wouldn't it?" he said. "All you would need is a good director and a strong lead actor. I could approach the heads of our Directing and Acting Departments, tell them about your piece, and ask them to read it right away. Perhaps with my influence, we can provide the best available talent. Would you like me to do that?"

"By all means," I said. "Would you?"

Voorhees squinted at me.

"I want the best show possible." My daft Miss America smile didn't melt, but it was all I could do to keep from cracking up. I'd written the play strictly for laughs. I felt it had little artistic or humanistic value.

The professor studied me with a cool expression. "But we'll need to read this in Drama 12 first, with a director and a cast that I approve of. Who do you see in the role of Leotis?"

"How about Artie Giacometti?"

Artie was the best character actor in the school.

"Yes. He'd be good, wouldn't he? Hmmm. Yes. We'll try to do your play right, Robert. My first criterion in mentoring any collaborative endeavor is that I must work with artists of consequence."

I nodded like a good boy. "What more could I ask?"

BLUNDER WITH BETTY

It didn't take me long to screw myself out of a good thing with Betty. I was a self-saluting toad too busy smooching his own insecure ass to be anyone's prince. If I had asked Betty about her shows, I would have understood the artistic and emotional risks she undertook. I would have been there, rooting for her the whole time. Instead, I left town.

Somebody offered me a ride to Boston. Why not, I thought. After two months with the Ivy League elites, I deserved a getaway. I said yes, even though Betty performed that weekend. I didn't know it was her first lead role in her most challenging acting assignment yet. So while she'd be wrestling epiphanies, I'd be in Boston getting loud with booze-hound buddies. I left a bone-headed phone message on her machine.

"Hi, Betty. I got a free ride to Boston. I'm going to see friends and family. Bye." As soon as I hung up, I sensed that I'd done something irreversibly foolish. Is it wise to skip town when the actress you adore is opening in a show? When I returned to New Haven on Sunday, the light on my phone machine was blinking. I pressed play and heard Betty's voice.

"Hello, Robert. Got your message. I hope you had yourself a good old time in Boston. You know, I don't think you need to call me anymore. Goodbye." Her voice rasped resolutely. It sounded as if she'd left it all on the stage that weekend, like a true heroine of the theatre.

My body felt light, like an empty garbage bag caught in a gust of icy air. The only part of me that didn't feel weightless was my heart, which sank down deep inside me. I brooded for an hour, then picked up the phone and left a lame, rambling apology. The truth was that I felt no guilt, just frustration with myself. I didn't care much about anyone's shows. I'd been at Yale almost three months, saw five new productions every week, and hadn't liked one yet. Well, what the hell. I'd get past it. Guys do worse things to women and still get the best action. I'd make it up to her. I didn't have class till noon the next day and felt like getting very drunk. The liquor stores closed at eight. It was 7:45. I moved fast.

DRAMA 12

Drama 12 began in the fall of 1929, the year of the crash. It had been founded by Gerald Pearce Burkewood, who had defected from that crimson place with his famous playwriting workshop. It was said that G.P. Burkewood enjoyed a close friendship with Eugene O'Neill, but I don't know if O'Neill was aware of it.

Drama 12 was unofficially known as "Drama Dozens," a phrase which must have been coined by a playwright who had experienced the class at point blank range. The class became a principal chopping block, where tenderfoot playwrights were handed their asses by grandstanding faculty and useless student dramaturges on a regular basis. It was just that sort of sanctimonious den of precision clusterfuck which can only occur in the hermetic classrooms of academia.

In Drama 12, old has-been writers, competitive students, and budding hack critics could point out the shortcomings of anyone brave enough to create fresh material. They did so without restraint, repercussions, or any real world consequences. The literary life has one thing in common with the sport of boxing: there are always more experts than practitioners. I suppose there are writers' rooms in Hollywood studios where scripts are quibbled over and disemboweled by committee in the same way. But at least there's something on the line there: blockbuster money to be made, a TV season to fill with fresh episodes, corporate sponsors to court. In grad school there's nothing at stake but over-boiled egos. As the old college joke goes:

> Q: Why is there so *much infighting among university faculty?*
> A: Because the stakes are so low.

Today my play *The Spooking of Leotis Jenks* would be read in Drama 12. Professor Voorhees sat in the front row and beamed as though he'd just shat a platinum rabbit. I sat in the middle of the room. The front row seemed too eager-beaver, and the back would be like hiding. From where I sat I could experience the reactions around me.

Up on stage, my director, Jane Dunwich, conferred with the cast Voorhees had chosen. Jane was one of the most creative people I ever saw in action. She asked lots of questions. If she didn't like what she saw and heard, she'd say something so wise and tender you couldn't help but want to please her.

Voorhees had done well by me, no doubt. Jane would direct, and the very best character actor in the school, Arthur Giacometti, would read my lead character. Artie could make any dialogue sing like a forest full of songbirds. Each tired word, each overused phrase was sweetened and made fresh by his agile tongue. All the student playwrights wanted Artie G. to polish their turds and put an appealing spin on them.

Artie sat center stage on a wooden chair. The other actors were seated beside him on folding metal chairs. Jane took a seat in front of the audience, and then nodded to Artie, who stared straight out at us and assayed the role of the be-spooked peckerwood Leotis Jenks.

> LEOTIS: *Y'all ain't getting shit outta me!*

This got a laugh. God knows why.

> LEOTIS: *Y'all are just goin' to have to learn it the hard way like I did, back-asswards, bent-over, and fucked and burned within an inch of your lives. Get yourself worked over by experts like I got done, and then you'll know this whole goldang world ain't much.*

Artie snorted and spat. Then, after a mournful pause, he threw back his head and let out a painful scream which subsided into rocking moans and sobs. Wow. What an actor. What an immaculate ham. That wasn't in the script. But it sure tenderized the transition into Leotis's confessional monologue.

> LEOTIS: *I'm sorry. Oh division and desperation. We are so alone on this earth when all's said and done.*

My dialogue trotted out a whole lot of cornpone twaddle which combined the worst of Sam Shepard with the best of the Deputy Dawg and Foghorn Leghorn cartoons I'd enjoyed as a child. I slapped in plenty of borrowed Poe and stolen H.P. Lovecraft as well. Artie made the most of it and scored regular laughs from a class packed with his peers. He was as Southern fried as a rich kid from Connecticut could be.

> LEOTIS: *Forgive me, folks. It's just—all upon me again. It is here, dear people, that my memory grows frail. For as my tale nears that fatal phone call, I cannot retain*

all what was spoke. It seems a kindness that I cannot. No mind could know the whole of them. No mind could contain them and survive the night.

The play went on like this. In pungent terms Leotis told tales about gruesome deaths, messy sex and bodily functions. But I tossed in some silliness for relief.

> LEOTIS: *I was halfway through a rack of Bud pounders, and quite calm, considering the heat and the hard day's work behind me. The Mexican wrestling program was on TV, and a rare bout was in progress. Midget triple tag teams were fighting for three tiny championship belts. The vicious Los Diabolitos challenged. While the kindly Poco brothers fought for retention. I was rooting for the latter myself. I remember it clearly. There was Tito Poco, Paco Poco, and the sibling considered the most loco Poco, the legendary Tampico Hammer, Otto René Poco. All wore their trademark tiger tights. I confess that I was amused watching these six sad little men bouncing each other's heads on the canvas, if only to fulfill my normal human need of entertainment? But now, how indecent a spectacle it seems.*

The last third of my play grew quite grim. A terrified Leotis talked about evils only he could perceive. His paranoia consumed him. First it rose like a creeping tide, and then it bashed him against the jagged edges of his unconscious like raw stormy surf. In the end, it drowned and devoured him.

> LEOTIS: *And then came the end of everything, all my little boy wonder, my retreat into present insanity. Might I say that the sounds I heard were deep and hollow, distant, yet so terrible close? It was as if the voice of all evil hollered warning through a wall of shaky red jello. And this is what it said...*

After discussing the role with me, the actor playing The Vision of All Evil based his character on Playwriting Chair Todd Voorhees. The actor gave an exaggerated impersonation of Voorhees's frigid monotone. It sounded like William S. Burroughs after huffing a balloon's worth of helium.

VISION OF ALL EVIL: *Reeky feet a ticklish treat. Toe jam! Shucky-shucky wow. Count ten whole toes, just one nose, bowl of brains, length of throat, heart and veins, all she wrote. Empty head stuff with bread. Drained brains. Early to bed. Chugga chugga, chit'lins. Chugga chugga, okra. Suc-co-tash! Ma? Ma? I want my Maypo!*

The crowd laughed, but by the end, they laughed only for relief. Artie found a human character rooted in the mulch of my indulgent ramblings. His Leotis became a man facing death with genuine fear, pain, and rage.

LEOTIS: *I will not trumpet further warnings on cold deaf ears that offer no sympathy. I know I'm just a poor ignorant boy from far away hills, and that my small notions don't travel far in a big town like yours. I say what's next for myself, in the unlikely hope that I can regain my former good health:*
The lazy body is the devil's workshop.
One man's socks are another man's mittens.
A lesbian is a lesbian is a lesbian.
And if you stick your finger in the kitty,
you're gonna get scratched.

The look on Artie's face as he brought the play home put all the spook into *The Spooking of Leotis Jenks*. He looked like a man destined for Hell and ready to drag the whole audience down with him. After the last stage direction was read, the class applauded. Artie nodded his head for more applause.

The actors left the stage. Professor Voorhees arranged two chairs center-stage and beckoned me to join him. We sat beside each other facing the crowd.

Marla Starrett raised her hand first. "I loved it. I really did. I'm, I'm just so impressed by this piece. Such a strange and creative piece of writing, Robert. The use of language is so clever and odd, but it succeeds so well!"

I said nothing and nodded with mild gratitude.

Wendy Grushkin raised her hand next. "I agree. It's great. Just great. I don't get all of Robert's humor, but..."

The class laughed.

"But others seem to," Wendy continued. "Robert has really broken barriers with this piece. He is declaring his originality as an artist."

Broken barriers? I felt like I'd just broken wind through a megaphone. The next student who raised his hand was Artie Giacometti. I feared what he might say because I respected his gifts. It was okay if he liked my work, but I hoped not too much. The play was half a gag and I wanted him to be in on it.

"This is the kind of material an actor loves to work on," said Artie G. "I know the play is kind of out there."

The class laughed again.

Voorhees turned and grinned at me like a proud dad watching his son win a baseball trophy.

Artie waited until the laughter died. "But for real, this character is huge, and he has all this wild language to live through. The words do so much of the work. They take the actor on a journey. Maybe not always where the actor *wants to go...*"

The class laughed again. There was a rumble from the back of the auditorium.

"The title says it all!" peeped the raspy voice of resident acting guru and Dean of Academic Affairs Bill Michter. "*The Spooking of Leotis Jenks*. We watch Leotis getting spooked, until he becomes a spook and can only haunt an empty shell of himself." Bill Michter was a god to his acting students, so they all dutifully nodded and applauded their mentor. Dean Michter almost never attended Drama 12 classes. But apparently, he had taken an interest in my play or, more probably, Arthur Giacometti's reading of it.

Then Voorhees offered his own inimitable commentary. "There's a fundamental notion at work in Robert's piece."

Oh my God. Was there? I turned to look at Voorhees.

"Because Robert took his time, and invested his own unique imagination at every step, he has created a work of consequence. Each moment of interaction between the artist and the text demands probity and personal inventory, first from the writer, then from the performer. The best, most evocative stage moments occur when the membrane between actor and text becomes permeable. The abominable transmogrifies and merges with the beatific, ketchup and bourbon stains become bedfellows with epiphanies, bodily functions live beside grace notes, nudging each other for prominence. Conflict evolves from just the way one odd word rubs against another, creating subtle frictions, or perhaps even invading and vivisecting neighboring phrases. Language itself is laid bare and opened wide for discovery. What we have just seen here is how a theatre of language can work. When it is working, and this play is *working*, an instant of life itself as it is fiercely probed becomes an aperture to infinity. Whether it is grappling dwarves, steaming cow pies, or empty cans of beer rattling down a windswept alley, the minutiae of life appear bright and crisp and even more clearly to be the guides to eternity."

A long silence ensued. At last, not knowing what else to do, the students applauded.

I couldn't look at Voorhees. If I allowed myself to grin, I might have spontaneously combusted into laughter. If I'd frowned or smirked, it would have been far too public a challenge to Voorhees and his notions. I stifled my confusion and held my contempt in check. Okay. The play was better than I thought. It engaged Artie G.'s imagination enough for him to create a human character with a large dramatic arc. But come on. Grappling dwarves as guides to eternity? Cow pie epiphanies?

I felt used. Voorhees's elaborate assessment had more to do with his Ivy League ego than my intent. How could he use my silly play as an opportunity to float out one of his sacrosanct *fundamental notions?* It was bullshit. The only thing keeping it airborne was the hot air Voorhees expelled. Was this what my play had been about all along? A self portrait of abasement and immolation on the altar of academic elitism?

Oh God. Yeah. Fuck me. Maybe? Perhaps the play was my own premature epitaph for a fast, flaming death at Yale Drama School. *I* was Leotis. I was the skull-fried hick strapped down in a chair and interrogated by rowdy demons and phantom inquisitors. It was me, Bob Rachaborski from Boston, going mad, and Voorhees himself was the Vision of All Evil, and now he'd claim my bloody name and write it down in Yale Drama School's *Book of the Dead.*

Man, this public attention freaked me out. I wasn't paranoid. No. Not clinically. That would be an insult to the folks wearing rags, pushing shopping carts, and screaming curses into random mailboxes. But a panic overtook me. Okay, I thought. Cool it. Voorhees is just nuts. So was my dad and my grandpa, and so are lots of other folks who pay taxes, walk their dogs, and subscribe to *The New Yorker*. I'm not crazy, just disgusted and cranky. Get a grip, Bobby. I willed myself into a passive trance and waited until the class ended so I could exit safely with a crowd of students.

I stumbled home in a daze. The chill autumn winds tugged at my loose clothing. I buzzed and fidgeted all over. Some folks get stage fright before a play. In my case, it became post-stage fright, or perhaps post-traumatic stage fright. Yes, PTSF. Bobby Rack discovers a new disease. Alert the media.

What had just happened to me? Words were spoken and opinions offered, but now it was one big, spinning, inscrutable blur to me. The class members had spoken with comfortable authority about something only I knew the origins of. How could they be so sure of themselves? Could my play really be more than the cartoon flatulence I'd intended? I don't know, maybe. But it wasn't a window to infinity. It couldn't be. I'd written that play for an audience of one. And between my dear old friend and me, we knew the play started as nothing but a creative caper.

But how could a class of a hundred people with degrees and good dental work all be wrong?

I kept walking home, where I planned to turn off my phone and burrow into bed. I even passed a liquor store without stopping. Man, Drama Dozens had sure dropped a ten megaton mind-fuck on me.

* * *

Two weeks passed before I saw Betty in person again on a bitter November morning. Since it was Sunday, the streets were empty. She was standing outside the Drama School in her red pea coat and beret. The wind tossed dead leaves around the street.

"Hi," she said, in a voice as crisp as the dry leaves.

"Hi," I said. That single word took more out of me than a Hamlet soliloquy. I walked on. The cold wind scraped my face. I felt hollow. My skeleton rattled inside me like a rusty length of chain. Every footstep thudded hard on the sidewalk, jolting me from my toes to my teeth. I was heartbroken to the bone. But something about the way Betty said "Hi" gave me hope. She was angry. When she hissed that greeting I felt heat. Hissing and heat is sexier than sterile indifference.

In the following days, I learned something about the performance I'd missed. It was an old European play translated into English. Betty played a mentally challenged farm girl who was repeatedly raped by an itinerant ranch hand. For much of the show she performed in the nude. Horrible things happened to her again and again, and she didn't know why. It sounded like early Fellini, or the best of German Expressionism.

Regardless of her role, it was a play I would have wanted to have seen. Damn, what a good show it must have been! Not only did I miss Betty's brilliant acting, but also a chance to see her naked beauty. I'd let my contempt for all things Yale Drama undercut me. As with all my lessons throughout life, I'd learned this one good and hard. In the future, I'd ask around and get the scoop on the cast, crew, and "suck quotient" on all productions before making any more hasty escapes to Boston.

PCP

The acronym PCP might make for a punchline if the underfunded Playwrights Collaborative Projects weren't so sad, small, and under-rehearsed. Each playwright's script got a reluctant director and a cast of third string actors not otherwise engaged in more important Yale Drama School and Yale Repertory Theatre projects.

The hierarchy at Yale Drama was topped with the mainstage Yale Rep season shows, which were professionally staffed and cast with union artists. The faculty often supplemented casts and crews with unpaid students. The budgets of Yale Rep shows ranged from twenty to forty thousand dollars and more. Ninety thousand was the largest budget I'd heard of. The subscriber base funded only a fraction of the costs. The rest siphoned off funds from public and private grants, alumni endowments, and residuals from famous plays making the rounds of the regional theatre circuit. I suspected that endowment money set aside for students might also be pilfered, but what did I know?

I received a Eugene O'Neill Scholarship one year, but it was only a letter, with no mention of money. Voorhees explained vaguely that the funds must flow back into the institution to "help lower every student's tuition".

Each Yale Rep show ran about seven weeks. The run of a show had not been extended since Dean Wodehouse took over the Rep, but in theory extended runs were still possible.

Just below these flagship productions were the directing students' third-year thesis projects. They received budgets of three thousand dollars and runs of three weekends. The student directors often supplemented their budgets with money from home, depending on the wealth and enthusiasm of their families and friends. The acting faculty also staged a song recital each year for the acting students. This musical production required professional accompanists at union rates. Most musicians travelled up from New York City and received a *per diem* for meals and travel.

At the very bottom of Yale Drama's dog-eat-dog pile lay the playwrights' PCPs, with maximum budgets of no more than two hundred dollars and a run of three performances in a single week. Playwrights Collaborative Projects never had assigned designers. The faculty allowed PCPs a mere eighteen days of rehearsal, including tech. Whether you got a competent cast or director was a roll of the dice. It was best to expect snake eyes. No playwright I knew ever beat the house. Writers got the worst choice of available talent. Worse still, our resident acting guru, Bill Michter, often used PCPs as opportunities to stretch the range of his more limited students. If a role demanded subtlety, he would cast his most abrasive actor. If the character demanded a seasoned leader of men, he would give a young, effeminate actor a crack at it. If it were up to Dean Bill Michter, Woody Allen would have played Rocky Balboa and Conan the Barbarian just so that Woody could expand his range.

Because Playwriting Chair Todd Voorhees and Acting Chair Bill Michter grew fond of my play, I received better treatment. Leave it to me to complain about being a faculty favorite, even if it was ever so brief.

Arthur Giacometti was not available to star in my PCP production. He was starring as *Peer Gynt* in Ibsen's fantastical masterwork of the same name. Artie G. does *Gynt*. Great for him. But maybe not so great for my spooky play?

My director, Mikolaj, was a closeted gay Ukrainian man who always wore a dirty gray overcoat and a permanent frown. He looked like your classic rain-coater sneaking in and out of a triple-XXX Pussycat movie theater. On those rare occasions when Mikolaj did smile, he looked like the village idiot holding steaming meat pie in his hands. He was perfect for my play.

The role of Leotis was given to a scrawny, intense actor named Donatello Poncia, an Italian-American. Who better to play a panhandle peckerwood with a Welsh surname? Donatello, or Telly, as he liked to be called, wasn't the same kind of fast-talking natural actor as Artie G. Telly liked to brood and make very deliberate preparations. He avoided uncalculated risks. He liked to sniff around his characters and ask his directors a thousand questions before he committed to any action or gesture. However, if you held his hand long enough, he delivered. To his credit, he was sensitive and scrappy. He enjoyed passionate arguments with his collaborators. I'd lucked into a feisty, committed actor.

There was no design team or run crew whatsoever: no prop-master, no costumer, no make-up artist, no one to design the set, the lighting plot, or the sound cues, no one to even Xerox two-sided paper programs. Playwright's Collaborative Projects were not very collaborative after all. A director, a stage manager, and a dramaturg staffed my PCP—that's it. "What's a dramaturg?" folks like to ask. Think of pasties on a drag queen. Imagine a eunuch on his wedding night. Consider that Diet Coke you ordered with an 8,000 calorie, triple meat pizza. Then ask yourself: what could be more useless?

But our dramaturg proved to be kind and perceptive. He researched every last pop culture reference in my dialogue, and deduced pretty much all of my inspirations, from Dylan Thomas to Bob Dylan to the Heckle and Jeckle cartoons. However, when it came time to offer advice on my production, Voorhees elbowed my bright young dramaturg aside and assumed command.

"Robert, I've observed several fundamental complexities in your piece that I feel your actors are emotionally surfing over," said the professor. He hovered and wouldn't leave until I spoke to Mikolaj in his presence.

This forced me into an awkward position. I wasn't the play's director. Which was good, because I didn't possess the tact, subtlety, or experience a director needs to communicate with sensitive actors. I never bothered to translate Voorhees's cryptic criticisms. I merely relayed his comments to Mikolaj, who conveyed them to the actors, who were saddened and confused by them. Fortunately, Voorhees went off to find other playwrights to warp and frustrate. In his absence, Mikolaj calmed our actors, and coaxed them into taking greater risks.

"We have a rich text," Mikolaj announced. "I don't know what it means, but I feel its tensions. This play excites me! I know what to do with it!" Mikolaj turned to me. "It may not be what you expected, but it will be bold. It will have truth!"

I shrugged. "If you're excited, I'm excited."

"Good." Mikolaj turned back to Telly. "You will be the focus, Donatello. You will be the exact center of this play. We will not be using tired stage conventions of text and space. Your performance must be pre-expressive, elementary, and rooted in the power of your personality. I have made extensive study of the empirical and anthropomorphic techniques of Eugenio Barba!" (Mikolaj pronounced this: *Eww-hen-ee-oh Barr-Bah!*) He kneeled before Telly. "We will learn how *your* body generates energy, and maximize it! The performance you create will be dynamic, decisive, and alive!"

Shit, this guy was good. Telly ate it up. Before long, Mikolaj persuaded Telly to perform the strangest exercises. I walked into rehearsal one time and Telly seemed to be standing upside down on his neck. On another occasion, he walked backwards on all fours and skittered about like a beetle. I half-expected Telly to grow invisible wings and levitate next.

Our stage manager was the only genuine Southerner involved in my cornpone creeper. He was a sober, church-going Christian out of South

Carolina, and seemed more open-minded, polite, and liberal than all of us Yankee agnostics put together. No one asked his opinion of the show, so he never offered it.

One day, as we took a break outside the theatre, I offered him a cigarette, which he refused. "So what do you think of the play?" I asked.

"Well," said the stage manager. "It's got atmosphere for sure. The words crawl under your skin the more you listen to them. I don't know what the purpose of the strange sexual content is."

"You don't think a guy like that would say those things?"

"Never met a person like that. Don't know as I would ever want to. But just because someone might say something in real life doesn't mean it's stage-worthy."

"You mean like an imitative fallacy?"

"It's just my opinion. Your actors all seem excited about it. I'm responsible for the cues, not the content."

I could only admire his responsible nature. He did his job as stage manager, plus all the work of our nonexistent designers. He located a big blocky torture chair for Leotis, riser platforms, and dusty cowboy getups from the student costume shop. His lighting plot was modest but moody, casting long bands of cold gray and blue light across the stage. The set looked like a Vincent Price dungeon in an old Roger Corman horror classic.

Sometimes Mikolaj ran about the stage waving his arms, painting images in the air with his delicate hands. Just as often, he would kneel down beside Telly, to gently caress and cajole him.

"Now we must focus on the moment. Feel every vertebra in your body. Every spectator is tied to each single segment of your backbone as if by fishing lines. When you move, you pull them with you. Your eyes tell them where to look and what to see. They cannot look away. Your pre-expressive tensions grip them before any idea is transmitted. If the audience were filled with jungle natives who did not know a word of English, they would know all of your feelings."

After one week, Mikolaj and I started to get excited. Telly was dynamite in the most recent rehearsal. He worked slowly, but oh so thoroughly, from the outside in, then back out again with surprising force. He displayed the poise of a Shakespearean player along with the honest gravity of a New York method actor. Telly walked into the rehearsal room every day with a magnanimous smile and offered a big bright hello to all. But when he sat down to play Leotis Jenks, his face slackened, his eyelids drooped, and he became a man denied sleep, food, and all human contact for a week. Like any great Italian racing machine, Donatello Poncia could climb from zero to sixty in seconds.

Two actors played supporting roles in my play. One was a real Texan, or half-Texan anyway. His mom lived in Amarillo. She'd married a man from Chicago. Hearing this Chi-Tex actor speak his lines with his mother's accent was a pleasant surprise. Somehow my invented dialogue fit that twang. I must have had some inbred peckerwood in me somewhere, even though I'd never lived further south than South Boston.

The actor cast as The Vision of All Evil was our other great stroke of luck. At six-feet-three and hairy as a bear, this fella was a strapping Sephardic creature. He bore a resemblance to Popeye's nemesis, Bluto. Mikolaj and I agreed to dress him up in a little boy's sailor suit, complete with short pants and knee socks. Whenever he took to the stage, The Vision of All Evil sucked his thumb or an oversized lollipop. At his final cue, he mounted a boy's metal tricycle and all 225 pounds of him pedaled onto the stage. After circling a terrified Leotis three times and startling him with shrieks, hiccups, and shrill giggles, the Vision of All Evil fell off his tiny trike. He crawled over to Leotis for a tickle session, and fondled Leotis's face, hair, and clothing. Donatello Poncia was not a large man. So when the Sephardic Colossus starting ripping off Telly's shirt, it looked like a big daddy ape peeling a banana.

The Vision of All Evil didn't have much dialogue, but he made the most of it by giggling, groaning, burping, hiccupping, whistling, sighing, screaming, snorting, farting, hissing, harrumphing, and whatever else he goddamned felt like. None of this was in the script, but it worked. Insecure actors need their little victories and a playwright must be open-minded.

***

The Spooking of Leotis Jenks had its workshop premiere on the day Charles Bukowski died in March of 1994. It was scheduled for just three performances: Wednesday, Thursday and Friday at 4 PM in a fifty-seat black box theatre. Attendance was light since there were four other productions rehearsing on Yale Drama's and Yale Repertory Theatre's main stages. Only fifteen students came to the first show. The space looked vacant, and, despite the actors' efforts, it felt like nothing more than another dress rehearsal. But the small crowd was alert and laughed.

Forty people turned out for the Thursday show. The actors were comfortable, and they let loose. The audience laughed at almost everything.

They laughed at the show and laughed at each other laughing. A couple of guys in the back row looked ready to wet their pants. The female patrons laughed, too, but not as much as the guys.

I spotted Betty Corbucci in a center aisle seat. Her eyes never strayed from the business on stage. When the show ended, she didn't stop to offer congratulations. She didn't say hi or even look my way. But she was smiling as she exited the theatre.

The final performance was packed with exhausted actors on break between back-to-back rehearsals and productions. I watched them slurp coffees and chomp down snacks in the stairwell. It looked like chow time at the dog kennel. Then they all shuffled inside and sank into creaking wooden seats. I could tell they resented being there. They'd much rather have been eating hot meals, napping, or sexing up their neglected sweeties.

The lights dimmed, then rose on the pale, sunken face of Leotis Jenks. As Telly began to peel the onion and unmask the character, no one seemed tired anymore. In fact, folks leaned forward and focused on his every gesture. But no laughs yet. I worried that this crowd might be too critical. Sharp fingers of ice stroked my spine up and down. Today my play would speak for me. Whether an audience would listen was the question.

I was an unknown in the Drama School. Telly, too. He had never been regarded as a standout among his peers, not like Artie Giacometti. Telly's classwork was respected, but before my play he'd never been cast in a lead role at Yale Drama. Now, for the first time, his classmates saw what he was capable of. When he started talking about sex, they finally laughed.

> LEOTIS: *I've read a little of what you call erotica, and it has informed my intercourse. It surely has. But you know, the best loving I ever experience still seems to happen by accident. I remember one time a friendly neighbor lady stopped by the barn for a bucket of milk. She came into the stall to watch as I obliged her. I had both my hands under the heifer a'tugging away, when she just leaned over to watch, and one of her breasts fell right out the top of her house-dress. She didn't bother to put it away. It was a large and lovely thing with personality like a friendly face. If it had teeth, it surely would have smiled. She blushed. I blushed. Things heated up fast and we had a real humdinger of a yummy time.*

Once everyone else began laughing, I chuckled too, out of relief more than anything. I used to think it masturbatory to laugh out loud at your own material. But if you can't hoot and holler at your own nonsense, why should anyone else? After all my battles with Voorhees, the snarky critiques from my classmates, and my romantic blunders with Betty, I needed a blowout in a safe place. I still had half a semester to go before I was no longer "on probation."

I laughed at everything my fantastic cast did. I laughed at Mikolaj's painful frowns, his dirty-old-man raincoat, and his endless Eugenio Barba-isms. I laughed at the great Donatello Poncia, who should have been playing Hamlet instead of telling Southern-fried dookey jokes. When I spotted the frigid Voorhees giggling into his fingers, I laughed loudest.

When my play got serious again, and Leotis began to get spooked out of his miserable busted gourd, I kept laughing. Heads turned. Voorhees looked ready to shush me.

A true artist, Telly never lost his concentration. He rode that nuthouse play of mine round and round the track, won every race, and brought all the horses home. Despite the lack of money, designers, crew, a stunted rehearsal and all of Voorhees's dramaturgical meddling, the show had blossomed into something far beyond my expectations. They were my words, but they belonged to the characters now. I was watching fine, skilled actors invent in the moment and delight an audience.

I was humbled.

MY BRIEF BUT TORRID AFFAIR WITH BETTY CORBUCCI

Betty had plunged a thorn into my heart and kept twisting it all year long. We'd started to date early that semester, but I blew it by skipping town when she performed a leading role. I'd known it was a stupid thing to do, but sometimes stupidity has a life of its own, and you get dragged into a dumb-ass move by inertia. Betty accepted no apologies, and didn't speak to me for months. Then, all of a sudden, she liked me again.

One day I heard her shouting "Hi!" at me from across a crowded street. I crossed over.

"Hi, Betty. How are you these days?"

"Good!" She smiled brightly. "How about you? I don't see you so much anymore."

"Oh, I've been burrowed in. I'm trying to write something good that will get the faculty off my back. The only time I go out is to the gym or for classes."

"You look good. Things must be working out. I think you're going to create unique things. I don't know if they'll make you famous or rich, but they'll be special."

"My play went up last month. I saw you in the audience, but you didn't say hi afterwards."

"Sorry. Your play was so...imaginative, so imagistic...and tender. See? You can be sensitive. You're not that hard." She punched my shoulder with her fist.

"Thanks. So, do you want to go out again?"

"Sure," she said. She squeezed my arm, then rushed off. "Got a class. Call me!"

I did. We went to a movie the next night and ate sushi instead of pop-corn. The sushi stunk up the back rows. I worried that the smell would annoy the other patrons. Later on, we found an empty church on campus and went inside.

"I like churches," said Betty. "This is a quiet church."

"Aren't all churches quiet?"

"Some have too many statues and saints, and stories in the stained-glass, too much screaming iconography or idolatry. This one's not so busy or loud." Betty walked to the front and found a table of unlit candles. "Can you light this?" She lifted one taper which I lit for her with my lighter, then she used it to light up all the rest.

"You sure it's okay for us to use these candles?" I asked.

"Yes. As long as we tell the truth."

"You mean I can't lie at all?"

"Nope. Not in church." She smiled.

We sat in a pew near the front. A gentle draft tickled the candlelight, which danced on the walls around us. Betty's eyes took on a spooky gleam. Her pale skin glowed. She wore pendulous earrings made of gemstones and sharp slivers of metal. They looked like a pair of dream-catchers. She wore a black sweater with a high turtleneck collar. Her dark hair splayed out over her shoulders, like a high priestess in an occult horror film. I hoped that this time around she'd prove a good witch and not a wild wicked one.

"You look so serious," I said.

Betty grew self-conscious. Her eyes looked sad.

"What's the trouble?" I asked.

"I'm usually by myself when I visit churches. Sometimes I feel like I'm all alone in a dark place. Then I come here and I'm better. But still alone." There was a hint of old heartbreak in her voice.

"You don't feel alone right now, do you?"

"No. I feel good."

"I'm glad we got together again. Too bad the year's almost over. Sorry I upset you. Sometimes I don't know how to treat people right. I just hadn't been on any dates or been with a woman in a real long time."

She smiled. "See? It's easy to tell the truth in here."

"How about you? What's your secret?"

"I've never found any men in the Drama School who wanted to be with me. They might take me out once, but the next time I see them they're dating one of my classmates."

It seemed that neither one of us had experienced love in a long time. I probably had more cobwebs in my crotch than she did. We weren't innocents, but we weren't as slutty as your average theatre student. But Betty and I longed for something more. For the first time all year, I felt connected to someone. When we stood up to leave, I took her hand. A donations box sat on a table beside the exit. I dropped in what I thought the candles might cost. Betty approved.

After our movie/sushi/church date I walked her home. We hugged for a half hour in front of her place. She let me kiss her once or twice. As I held her in my arms, she'd lean back like she was about to fall to the ground. It was a trust exercise—she wanted to see whether I'd let her drop. I must have passed the test, because she invited me upstairs for some petting. I got her panties halfway off. She let me paw her big round bottom and all around her magic sauce-box, but every time I reached for the prize she'd grab my wrist—more trust games.

* * *

It took a puppet show to finally get me into Betty Corbucci's bedroom. The puppets started as a classroom exercise given by my favorite writing teacher at the school, Ms. Margot Cody, a beautiful Navajo woman with almond colored eyes and long black hair. She instructed us to write a play with two roles, then to perform it ourselves using puppets. Maybe I took the project too seriously, because I created the maddest, most colorful puppets in the class. I made them out of socks, pipe cleaners, and carefully cut pieces of brightly colored sponges. They looked as ferocious as Balinese three-headed demons. I practiced with them in my apartment for hours and had too much fun. I even brought the act down to the local pub to show my playwriting classmate Reymundo Diasanta—Rey for short.

Rey was a soft-spoken gay Filipino who enjoyed scotch as much as I did. He came out to his elderly parents years ago, but still acted closeted to the rest of the world. He wasn't a delicate character though. He'd been one of the first members of Act Up during the AIDs crisis. He'd stood his ground against angry clergy, rowdy Reaganites, panicked homophobes, sadistic gay-bashers, and the NYPD. Whenever Rey spoke about the 1980s in New York, sparks crackled in his eyes. I don't know what he missed most: the young sex, the tumultuous times, or just feeling alive. I think we both felt prematurely dead.

"Such bright happy puppets," said Rey. "And such flaming colors. Are you sure you're not gay?" Rey liked to flirt with me. It was safe and silly.

"I'll lend them to you for the next Pride Parade."

"Oh no. You must design a whole new float just for me."

"How about a disco Lady Liberty with a glitter tulle?"

"See! You have to be gay!" Rey was buzzed. He talked and laughed too loud. My banter and puppeteering skills amused him, but not the local

109

barflies. When one of the crispy-looking bartenders began staring, I stuffed the puppets into my bag.

I leaned over to Rey. "Hey, listen. Just go up to that big bartender and say: *'Hey you! Yeah you, Fozzie Bear! I want a blue martini with two lichi nuts, and a champagne back.'* Then untie your ponytail, shake it all out, and say, *'Because baby, this hair is coming down tonight!'* I'll back you up."

Rey turned to look at the fat, hairy, six-foot-three bartender, who looked like a football linebacker gone to seed.

"C'mon, Rey! Let's do it! I've never wrecked a bar!"

Rey turned back to me and smiled. "You're sick."

* * *

I performed a G-rated version of my puppet show in class. Everyone seemed to enjoy it. However, it was the X-rated version I performed in the Yale Cabaret which thrilled the Drama School and secured Betty's affections. I'd concocted an evil bit of guerrilla theatre when I was in a nasty anti-Drama-School mood, and I performed it with a scorching lack of restraint.

Betty was sitting on the aisle as I strutted down to the Cabaret stage. I squeezed her shoulder and wiggled a puppet under my arm so only she could see. She laughed and covered her face. Betty's shining smile was a comfort, especially given all the other skeptical mugs I saw as I climbed up under the bright lights and faced the crowd. Everyone in the school had branded me a character. Some knew about my absurd, aggressive plays. But otherwise, I was a recluse who kept his contempt hidden.

The cabaret's emcee didn't even know my name.

"I think...this guy has some puppets for us, folks."

So without a proper introduction, I dragged a chair center-stage, hung a black coat over it and crouched down behind it. I slipped on my puppets and raised them into the lights. One puppet was a suffering playwright. He sported a yellow sponge nose, big purple ears, and crossed eyes. He spoke in a gentle Southern accent like a fugitive from a Georgia chain gang addressing his Redeemer:

> *"I was just a plain country boy from far away hills, new to the big town, and unschooled in the evil ways of men mad with power, and their untidy machinations."*

The other sock puppet had a red nose, orange ears, and long yellow fangs. He stood for Professor Todd Voorhees, the head of our playwriting pro-

110

gram, and my nemesis at the Drama School. Voorhees spoke in a low but prissy register, kind of like Mr. Rogers, but without the kindness, patience, or personality:

> *"The first year at Yale Drama is probationary, and I have asked some students to leave."*

The plot of my puppet show was simply a recreation of my many clashes with Professor Voorhees in his cramped office. Voorhees thought the plays I wrote were full of dull 1950's kitchen-sink realism. I pigeonholed Voorhees as an emotional cripple who wouldn't know a well-made play if it bent him over in Times Square and buggered him in broad daylight.

We both had our points.

My yellow-nosed puppet gave the evil Voorhees puppet a good dressing down, cussing out him, the other faculty, and the whole school with language that would make a felon blush.

I raised my head above the chair and peeked between my puppets to see Betty's reaction. She was beaming like a young mom watching her boy sing the National Anthem.

> *"Now I'm just going to close my eyes and pretend you've got a pair of pretty lips."*

My hillbilly puppet then subjected Professor Voorhees to a series of degrading sex acts. This drew loud applause and laughter from fellow students. My puppets and I took a bow.

Betty met me outside. We started walking to her place. She smiled but didn't say a word. I understood that I needed to follow her, and that something fun was going to happen. We climbed the stairs to her apartment in silence. She closed the door behind us. She didn't switch on any lights. She took off her coat, her sweater, her zippered boots, and went straight into her bedroom. I stood out in the dark of her living room like a clueless jackass. Then I heard Betty moan from her bedroom: *"Where are you?!"*

I didn't miss that cue or my next entrance. I joined her in bed. We groped and rolled around in our clothes for a good long while. Soon the moon and the streetlights outside revealed us to each other in all our naked glory. Even though I was a gym rat back then and in the best shape of my life, I remained self-conscious, especially about the stretch marks left over from my obese teenaged years.

"You have a beautiful body," said Betty.

For once in my miserable life, I accepted the compliment in the spirit it was delivered. "*You're* beautiful," I replied as I slid back into bed beside her. She had lovely olive skin and I slowly and firmly rubbed my palms into every part of her. She made the sweetest, most feminine sounds. Betty's breasts were a perfect size, with plump, yummy strawberry nipples. Her behind was abundant, bouncy, and round as anything in a melon patch.

Holding and touching Betty felt like the most important thing in the world. The fact that I'd not had sex in years didn't matter. Even if I didn't know how to make her happy yesterday, I was learning every way possible to do it now. The sounds she made guided me. She smelled great. Like a good actor, everything I tried was bold and freshly invented.

"That was the best," she said when we were nose to nose.

I didn't know what to say, but figured I couldn't go wrong telling her "You're beautiful" a few more times.

Later on, she slid under her covers and curled up. She wanted to sleep. But like a kid with a new toy, I wanted to keep playing. My penis refused to go down, not with Betty's gorgeous lovely everything lying right next to me. She tucked her butt into my lap. I wrapped an arm around her. There was no way I was going to get any sleep. But I controlled myself, and let my new love slip into sweet deep slumber.

As I looked past her sleeping form and at the streetlights beyond her window, I felt mighty lucky. I could have been alone in my own place that night or out there walking the empty city streets smoking a dirty cigarette, but instead I was inside a cozy bedroom with a warm woman. After most of a semester and one game after another, Betty and I had finally arrived at the best night of our lives. Maybe I was making too much of it. Sometimes when you finally get what you've been begging for so long, it's a letdown. That wasn't the case with Betty. Love was good.

Later, I slid out of bed and into her bathroom. I was too stiff to pee, so I masturbated first. While she dreamed honeyed dreams in the other room, I dreamed of her big olive-toned bottom and beat out a good one.

I was a hell of a man.

***

Though I got only two hours or less of sleep, I woke up smiling. I felt like I'd discovered something unique. *Wow, what is this great stuff?* I was a dreamy-eyed rube plopped off a turnip truck.

That morning, Betty and I ate some of the leftover sushi from our movie and church date. The other night I wasn't so sure about raw fish. Today I savored each ripe, nasty bite. Betty picked up my long-sleeved dress shirt and slipped it on. We sat on opposite couches, smiling at each other.

"Last night was fun," I said. I stood up, crossed the room, and bent to kiss her.

"Yes. It was." She wrapped her fingers around my neck and held my lips to hers for a good long time.

***

Two days later, our happy April ended. We had only a few weeks left to enjoy the nutty buds of May. The warm weather brought us outside for long walks on tree-lined streets, into old Yankee graveyards, and through fragrant flower gardens in bloom. We drank the darkest Turkish coffee, and kissed hard and slow in shaded doorways. One day it rained and we escaped into a natural history museum. Betty looked ravishing with wet hair. We smooched savagely in front of stuffed saber-toothed tigers and wild wooly mammoths.

She wore a fun new outfit for each time of day: flowered print dresses in the morning, short skirts in the afternoon, and slinky cocktail dresses at night. Our evenings never got old. We enjoyed more sex than sleep and slept awfully late.

"I think I love you," she said one afternoon.

"You *think?* Well maybe I love you too?"

We weren't ready for more than thinks and maybes and settled for another kiss.

***

One good morning led into a few more great weeks, and then to an awful afternoon when I brooded about Betty's upcoming flight back to her family on the West Coast. We held each other in bed. Her eyes were heavy and dreamy with love. But I just kept growing angrier. Why was she so sweet on me now, with only a few days left? If she'd let me get next to her earlier in the school year, we'd have something more grounded and durable to last us through our separate summers. All we had left were these precious few hours of fear, lust, and frantic coupling. Then she'd take that plane back to Petaluma, California, and I'd be on a train to Boston.

We smooched hard and pulled at each other's clothes. We both felt it. This was going to be the last time for a long while. I was moody, like a bear awakened too fast from hibernation. How could she put me on ice like this?

"What's wrong?" she asked.

"Nothing I say can change anything."

"What did I do?"

"I suppose I can write to you. Will you answer my letters?"

"Yes." She paused. "Talk to me."

I pushed her away. She cried a little, then turned around and yelled at me. "Why are you being so mean? Do you like being mean to women?"

I couldn't explain myself, or why I'd want to hurt her feelings. My brooding transformed into sadness and regret. Betty left the room. I followed her. She brushed her long dark hair in front of her bathroom mirror.

"I'm sorry," I said, and then I couldn't help but cry. It had taken me all year to find a woman I could experience all these feelings for. Now she'd be gone in five days.

Betty let me hug her. She hugged me back.

"Never trust a crying man," I said with a wink.

She said nothing. We held each other.

* * *

Summer overtook our few brief weeks of fun and discovery. Betty retreated to her hometown on the opposite coast. She took a job pouring California's finest in Sonoma County. I painted houses for rich gay people in Boston and drank tap beer with native Irish painters and wallpaper-hangers. When she stopped responding to my love letters in mid-July, I knew something was wrong. I dialed her phone number in Petaluma and left messages with her mother, who had never heard my name.

I kept busy with physical work in Boston. I stood on ladders, a rag wrapped around my face, scraping shingles and sanding endless walls. Some of the paint was old, hard, and full of lead. We did the job and washed the poison out of our pores as best as we could. I worked from first light to first dark. When I hustled, I could forget Betty. On Friday nights, the painting crew drank heavily, as a warm-up for Saturday, when we drank more heavily. It felt good to fix things with my hands. I could control a scraper or a sanding block. But Betty remained far out of reach. It hurt just to imagine what she could be doing, and with whom.

***

When I returned that September to our mystical Ivy League scene, all the romance was gone from the stark Connecticut town. My naïve first-year dreams were gone, replaced with blunt realities. I would not visit Todd Voorhees's office once that first semester of my second year, even when he asked me to. I wasn't on probation anymore.

Another gal with more game and sizzle than Betty soon sank her painted claws into me.

Her name was Sally.

WELCOME WEEK II: LIVE HARD AND DRINK FREE

Q: Why won't a shark bite a Jewish-American Princess?
A: Professional courtesy.

"If I could only turn back the clock to when God and her were born!"
—Bob Dylan, *Shelter From the Storm*

I watched the young couples in the bar laughing and nodding and sipping their beer every ten minutes. I didn't usually drink in loud pick-up bars with horny twenty-somethings. It just happened to be nearby and open. The open air space, ample seating, and the ten beers on tap sucked me in.

I was drinking with Ted Hinton, a guy I'd met for the first time only twenty minutes before. A 6'4", thirty-six year-old Okie, he'd recently been accepted into the Yale School of Drama to study playwriting, just like me. He'd tracked me down to get my thoughts on the program. I gave him an earful.

"Forget this preeminent-drama-school-in-the-country happy horseshit. They don't teach craft, character, psychology, or anything about being human or telling a sane story about it. It's just snarky critiques and mediocre mind-fuck. An aesthetic inquisition, that's all, a crock of high art crap. There's no humility and nobody even has a sense of humor."

Ted didn't quite believe me, but he was too polite to argue. He presented himself as a gentle, tender hulk of a guy. He didn't seem to want to move too fast or talk too loud for fear of startling people.

The first significant question Ted asked was, "Are you gay? I mean, it's fine, but...I just wanted to be clear."

"No." I winked. "Disappointed?" I laughed. "Yeah. I haven't proven it lately, but I'm straight. How about you?"

"Oh. Yeah. Me too. Straight." Ted was embarrassed. We ordered two pints of some microbrew release that had won awards at various local beer-fests. It had less personality than Budweiser mixed with barley tea, and smelled like someone had drowned a petunia patch with pumpkin juice and panther piss. For the next round I'd switch to Coors. Bad as the homemade suds were, the high alcohol content chilled my rant. I actually began to say positive things about the Drama School.

"The actors here are like racehorses. They shimmer and glide and snort, you know? Fine looking beasts. Thoroughbreds. The women aren't all gorgeous, but they can act. Great voices, presence, power in front of an audience. You just want to jump up on stage, bite their asses, get lockjaw, and be dragged to your death."

Ted laughed.

"The guys couldn't fight their way out of a paper bag, but they've got acting chops. They won't all get famous after graduation, but one out of ten will work for the rest of his life. Lots of them will win Emmys and Oscars and you'll see why—I mean, aside from being totally connected up-per-middle class pricks with money from home. Some of them do have real talent." I took a big gulp of the muddy summer brew, winced, and stuck out my tongue. "The designers are pretty amazing. Most of them will drop the theatre like a hot rock when they graduate. They'll run to Disney or Dream-works and start building soundstages for blockbuster movies." I shook my head. "I don't know why they want writers here. No writer out of this place has won a Tony or a Pulitzer in over thirty years. And never an Oscar. Embarrassing."

Ted looked skeptical. I decided to shut up about the Drama School and listen for a change. He told me how he drove a feed truck up and down the Midwest for years, from Iowa to Texas, then about how he ended up married and in a Bible college because a girl he liked wouldn't go to bed with him otherwise. The marriage ended as soon as he joined a community theatre and met a plump stage manager who actually knew something about good sex. Ted's most decadent days of tomcatting began when he became a staffer in the Texas legislature. Apparently, Republicans do "Do it". Then he reeled off his acting achievements on various Southwest stages, mostly starring roles in old warhorse plays like *Inherit the Wind, The Crucible, Cuckoo's Nest*, etc.—small pond stuff that got him lots of babes but no money and no Equity card.

Between the old stories of amateur theatricals, one of us would step up to the bar for another round. It was my turn now. I stood at the bar beside a long dark lady who sat alone. She seemed to purr when I slid in beside her to address the bartender. We made eye contact, then looked away quickly—scared of what, I don't know. I felt some heat there, but I made no effort. Schmuck. As usual, too shy for my own good. I walked away with two pints.

Ted and I sat for a few minutes regarding the room, until two young females slid into our booth and sat right beside us.

The one next to me was the prettiest. She had feisty brown eyes, full lips, and a strong but perky nose. Her face was so sexy and serious that I didn't even notice her body. But when I glanced down I saw that she was a drop dead delight. She leaned towards me. The whole world shrunk to the space between her face and mine.

"Hi," I finally blurted out.

"Hi. I'm Sally. Trudi and I just got in. We're New York girls. We decided to get a drink."

"I'm Robert. Maybe I could get your next one?"

She smiled. Her eyes were smoky and mischievous. She picked up her pint and drained a full two inches off the top. "Maybe? If I'm still around?"

Well, she could drink. I wondered what else Sally could do, and if she'd do it with me? I had a scary, crazy feeling that she would. For a layabout playwright, I looked okay these days. I'd spent the summer prepping and painting houses. I looked tough and sporty in a white t-shirt, and what little hair I had was sunny blonde. Forget that I used to weigh three hundred pounds. Block out those traumatic snapshots of my bloated, paralyzed mother helpless in her own waste. With a body image and mother issues like I had, it was a wonder I could even talk to a girl, much less be picked up by one.

"I bet you play sports," said Sally. "Let me guess. Hockey? You look like a hockey-playing stud."

Sally laid it on thick. But I was afraid I'd soon find a way to screw myself out of a good thing. I tried to hide my terror, but my heart jerked and jumped inside me like a squirrel scrambling within my ribcage. If Sally was scared, she didn't show it. Instead, she held eye contact, jutted out her chest and licked her lower lip. There was something feral about her. Not dangerous, but unwavering and on the prowl. It was like a female panther had invaded the room, and now it wanted to lick me.

"No. Never played hockey." I smiled wide. "See? Still have my teeth. I took Tae Kwon Do for four years. Trained as a boxer for a while, but never competed. Not a team player, I guess. Lone wolf."

"Lone wolf"—why did I say that? Lonely jerk was more like it. I lowered my eyes, grabbed my pint, and drained a third of it. The glass felt real in my hand, and I needed reassurance. Sally's easy expression didn't change. After I set my beer back on the table, I thought, *"Okay, relax. Maybe this really is happening to me."*

"You should never box. You have a nice nose." Sally studied me a second or two, and asked, "Do you like my nose?"

"Yeah. It's fine."

She needed more.

I caught Tim giving me a discreet nod.

"Am I beautiful?" Sally asked.

"Sure," I said, with no sugar added. I sensed she wanted more, but I got cocky and wouldn't give it to her. If she was disappointed, she didn't show it. She sat back and sized me up like a gypsy fortune teller who'd already collected her fee.

I bought rounds of Coors until I ran out of money. Then Sally started buying them. I spared her my anti-Drama School rant, and we exchanged sexy small talk and hungry stares.

"I'll bet your father has dogs and a lot of shotguns," she said. She smiled when she saw me hesitate.

"How did you know?" I pictured my dad cleaning one of his surplus army rifles and rubbing out fleas on his arms.

"Oh, I know," Sally nodded. "I know." She sat there like a cat with a canary, and the canary was my pecker.

For an extended moment, which might have been five seconds or five minutes, Sally and I stared at one another. I didn't have a clue about her dad's unique proclivities, but suspected that I would soon learn an awful lot about hers.

We leaned forward at the same time and kissed. We kept kissing. It was rude and raw, and it must have looked like we didn't care who watched or what they might think. And we didn't.

***

Despite her impersonation of a randy, man-eating *femme fatale*, Sally declined my offer to walk her home. She gave me a long kiss goodbye before confessing that she was a performer joining the Drama School's elite acting program. "We'll be seeing a lot of each other, big guy," she said winking her eyes.

We were outpatients in the same institution. No wonder we connected. Before we parted, Sally invited me to a poolside brunch with her and Trudi the next morning. The restless Trudi held the bar's front door open and shook her head.

***

At ten the next morning my phone rang.

"Hello."

"Hi, Robert!" chirped Sally like a songbird.

"You didn't have to call. I was going to come over."

"Oh, don't flatter yourself. I'm just making sure you didn't oversleep. Better come now or we'll start without you."

My apartment at 100 Hyde Street stood three blocks north of the campus in what was unofficially known as the DMZ, that indistinct borderline between Ivy League privilege and the large surrounding ghetto. It took twenty minutes to walk from there to Sally's high-rise just south of campus, but I made it in ten.

"Sally Garfinkle, apartment 1509," I said to the doorman at the 100 Joy Street Apartment Towers.

He grabbed the phone and called Sally. "Go on up."

The elevators had yellow pillowed walls and long mirrors with roses etched into the glass. I pressed number 15. I could see my reflection in the closing doors. Man, that summer house-painting gig had kept me tan and trim. I glowed with health and looked good in my clothes. With my powder blue swim trunks and bright white sleeveless shirt, I was a real summertime sport. Apartment 1509 was protected by a metal security door. You'd need a small tank to get through that monster without the tenant's consent. I knocked.

"Robert?!"

"Hi. How are you?" I stepped inside.

"We girls be chillin'," she said in a dead-on impersonation of Rosie Perez. I'd soon learn Sally was a gifted mimic. She performed a whole repertoire of New York personalities, from weary Yiddish grandmas and waspy society matrons to meter maids, spicy Latinas, and various ghetto cutie-booties. Who Sally really was would prove to be the hard thing to pin down.

"Like the breezes in the treeses," I replied.

Sally popped her cheek with her tongue. "Nothing popping but the peas in the pot. And they wouldn't be hopping if the water wasn't hot."

I followed her into her apartment. She wore a flimsy tie-on skirt wrapped around the bottom half of her cocoa brown bikini. Trudi watched us with raised eyebrows. I got the feeling she knew men well enough to discern that I wasn't a major threat. She seemed more concerned about Sally making a fool of herself.

"Would you like a Mimosa? Are you hungry? We have fresh strawberries, grapefruit, and bagels from my mother's favorite bakery. Come out and sit on the deck." Sally led me outside.

From fifteen stories up, you could see New Haven's downtown and seaport, the Connecticut hills and wilderness to the east, and the very tip of Long Island out beyond the harbor.

Sally handed me a huge glass. Her version of a Mimosa consisted of champagne with a splash of juice. Three of these and we'd never make it to the pool. She appeared to have had two already, so I drank fast to catch up.

She sat opposite me with her legs crossed high and let her hair fall over one eye. So far it had all been one long cruise down easy street and every light beamed green.

"Trudi and I went to high school together in Scarsdale. We're best friends. We've laughed and cried and made all kinds of *mishigas* together." She said this without looking at Trudi.

"You're lucky. I don't have any friends from high school. I was the only white kid in most of my classes. They were good enough kids, I guess. All God's chillun' got wings. I don't give a shit. If my folks were rich, I could have gone to a real school and come here to the Ivy League ten years earlier. But I had no money behind me. I didn't learn very much about black culture. I was too much of snob, or my head was too far up my ass. My mom lived in hospitals all that time. She died two years ago. I suppose I wouldn't have been happy anywhere."

Sally's eyes seemed to cross and cloud over, but it may have just been the champagne catching up with her.

"Sorry. We just met. It's a nice day. Seems like I always have to confess my sins when I meet someone."

Sally patted my arm. "Sorry about your mother. What do you mean, sins?"

"Nothing. I don't know...sins against me, I guess."

"*Against* you?"

"Not sins, really. It's nobody's fault. But you still feel bad, even if it's all a big accident. Let's forget it. You look great. Did I tell you you were beautiful last night?

"I don't know. Did you?" Sally squinted suspiciously.

"If I didn't, I was a goddamned jackass fool. Because you are the most drop-dead gorgeous woman I ever set these sweet green eyes on. How about we make another round of drinks and truck all this glamour downstairs?" Errol Flynn couldn't have rolled it out any smoother, and maybe I even meant it.

Sally ate it up like a chocolate covered sundae with nuts and sprinkles. Trudi pursed her lips and snorted. We all stood up and Sally led the party downstairs.

The pool water gleamed bright and clear as glass. I dove right in. Sally and Trudi stayed dry and sunned themselves on beach chairs. They whispered to each other while I plopped and flopped about in the water like a happy walrus. I thought I heard Trudi say "He's gorgeous," and then Sally make a yummy "Hmm-mmm" sound in reply.

Sally stood up and strutted slowly around the pool. Her wrap disappeared. She shouted "Catch!" and landed butt-first in my open arms. After two quick kisses and she went back to sunning herself with Trudi.

After two more of Sally's booty-flops, it was time for her to walk Trudi to the train station. I climbed out of the pool slowly, trying to hide the incorrigible erection I'd sported all morning. Sally and I made a date for that afternoon. She sent me home and took Trudi upstairs to pack. When I saw Sally next, she'd be without a chaperone, and her own woman entirely.

***

That afternoon Sally rang my apartment and I buzzed her up. She wore a denim skirt and sleeveless white top. She'd washed her hair. It was full of bounce and smelled like warm honey.

My place was beyond Spartan, but at least I cleaned it regularly. A king mattress with soft cotton blankets took up half the floor space. I had one smooth round table with matching chairs. My worldly goods and garments were tucked away in closets and tight drawers. I'd forgotten flowers for the table. I bought a single bottle of a wine. Beyond that, all I could offer Sally was cold beer, cigarettes, and home-made spaghetti.

After eating and smoking, we dropped down to my mattress and horsed around. I rubbed up her legs and buttocks and lower back. She let me squeeze and tweak her plump pointy breasts through her blouse, but shoved my hands away when I tried to push up her tight skirt. She snapped her legs shut and offered me her behind to rub again. I gave her little spanks

122

and squeezes, while I kissed around her neck and under her ears. The little sounds she made were feminine and fun, but I'd always ruin it by reaching between her legs.

"No," she said. "It's too soon." And then when I reached for my fly, she shouted, "No!"

I gave up. I laid my head beside hers on my pillow. We both smelled like garlic and beer, but in a raw, contented way.

"We're going to have such good times," Sally said.

"Are we?"

"Maybe you should take a walk down to the Student Health Center and get a blood test?"

"A blood test? Did you get one?"

"I had one months ago. After my last relationship."

"Who with?"

"An attorney. He worked for my father. We lived together. But I wasn't happy."

"Think I can make you happy?"

"I want you to. I want you to so-o bad." Sally's eyes half-shut. She slid across the pillow to kiss me. "Just get a little slip of paper that says negative and all doors will open."

For the rest of the day I acted the good boy. We went outside and sat on the swings in a rusty old kiddie playground behind my building. Sally told me that the Garfinkles left Germany before the war and that her mother's people were Seidelbaums by way of a Polish shtetl.

"Hyman Garfinkle was a mechanical engineer. He made his money making mainsprings for machine guns during World War II."

"That's the most important part."

Sally checked to see if I was patronizing her. "Oh yeah. Your dad's a gun nut, isn't he?"

"He's not a nut. He's just crazy about guns."

"My dad has his own law firm on Madison Avenue. His nickname is the Velvet Panther, because of his smooth, deceptively gentle style in the courtroom."

"The Mel Torme of torts."

"Ha. My daddy would like that." She said. "Garfinkle is not so bad, as Jew-bag names go. But I'm going to change it."

"To what?"

"Well, what I really want to be is a performance artist. Or a really classy comedian, you know? My absolute favorite performer is Eric Bogosian. I saw all his early downtown work. I just love him. But I sure as hell don't want to be Sally Bogosian. I could go Sally Allen like Woody, but that's too fake Jewbag. Carlin is too Irish. I've been thinking Bruce."

"Like Lenny Bruce?"

"Yeah. Sally Bruce. That's Lenny's mother's name. Sally Bruce. Bruce Willis. Three syllables. Sally Bruce."

"Garfinkle is kind of cute."

"Cute don't win at cards, big guy." Sally smiled. Our lips were bruised and swollen by now, but we kissed yet again.

I leaned back and watched some homeless guys sorting through a dumpster. "Guess I'm sort of a Steinbeck character, a mongrel white American. My dad did some amateur genealogy. He said our first folks landed in Nova Scotia in the sixteenth century. Some Scotsman started a brewery up there which failed. Then some other Scot sailed to Boston in 1711 on a ship called the Lion. Later, a Belgian boated from Brussels, and then a Butler arrived from County Clare. The most recent was Bronislaw Rachaborski. The first job Broni got was inside a foundry, inhaling molten metal fumes. He quit and found work in a steel mill. He unionized that mill and became its first shop steward. He was a good union man, but a mean father. He wasn't healthy enough to fight Hitler, so he took it out on his only son. But the worst thing he ever did was die young.

"My Dad was nine when he lost his father. Hard little kid. Kept getting in nasty fights with every bully in town. Had a long juvenile record by the time he calmed down. He married my mother at eighteen. Then mom got sick with multiple sclerosis. It wrecked my dad. He wasn't a bad fella. He would have been better if he could hold a job. Me, I stayed away from trouble as a kid. But I seemed to stay away from fun too."

Sally reached up and brushed my hair. She was watching me and listening. Some women would pull away when I launched into war stories. Others would patronize. The nicer gals zoned out until I was ready to have fun again.

But Sally stayed with me. I felt her warmth and. the kindness in her eyes. It was something new. She seemed so brave.

"Well, there you have it. Everything you need to know about my fucked-up family and the history of American labor."

Somehow I couldn't just shut up and kiss her. No, I tried to squeeze out one last, self-inflicted parting shot.

But Sally laid a cool finger across my lips and followed it with a kiss. She got off her perch, nuzzled my neck, and whispered in my ear. "It's okay.

You can take it all out on me. I'll take everything you've got."

"First I got to get my results from the Health Center."

We went out for pizza, and drinks. We strolled and people-watched, hugged, and held hands like a newlywed couple. At long last I walked her home and kissed her goodbye in front of that same frustrated doorman. Sally disappeared into the golden elevator and I returned to the sidewalks of New Haven.

***

There would be ample occasion for Sally and I to make public asses of ourselves during Yale Drama's Welcome Week. I feared for her. She had a rich girl's status to lose. The fact that she whored for no one meant nothing. In the theatre, whores were human resources. It wasn't uncommon for theatre students to seduce a dozen of their classmates within a single semester. But as one bisexual vixen told me while in the process of breaking my heart: "Promiscuity should not be a judgmental word."

Sally and I were guarded with our feelings and genitalia. We'd both begun as ugly ducklings in middle and high school, Sally as a dorky gal with emotional problems in wealthy Westchester County, and me an obese white boy surrounded by underprivileged blacks in Boston's public schools.

Sally's dad was generous and loving when he came home from his law firm, but her clean freak mother washed her hands a hundred times a day. When mom wasn't clutching bars of soap, or drenching countertops with disinfectant, she riddled her nervous daughter with criticisms.

From first glance Sally and I homed in on each other as freaks of the same misfit stripe. We wore our freak badges on our sleeves and were still raw and nuts enough to dream of bringing real drama into a drama school. We might not have been all that glamorous, but I like to think that we were standouts in the whole unholy dog show.

***

The first party Sally and I attended together was Dean Wodehouse's annual meet-and-greet at *Scuzzi's Trattoria*. Sally wore a tight, tangerine-colored top and a short white skirt. Her brown hair was bouncy and bright and smelled like fresh fuzzy peaches in picnic basket. She was nervous about meeting her new peers and professors. I'd met most of them before, but Sally had big Ivy bright stars in her eyes. She squeezed my hand as we descended the steps into *Scuzzi's al fresco* dining area. Her body vibrated with neurotic tension. She smiled, but her eyes were wide and fretful.

"It'll be okay," I whispered in her ear.

She squeezed my hand harder. "Thanks."

"Want some wine?"

"Please."

"Red or white?"

"Yes," said Sally.

I decided to start us off with white because it was most plentiful. We tossed down two glasses. As we started on number three, Sally was calm enough to engage with her fellow actors.

Lots of men hovered close to Sally. Wearing fat, hammy smiles five actors in succession introduced themselves. They pretended to be nice guys at the same time as they were sneaking looks at her behind. Bastards. They tried to score with any first-year meat. But I trusted Sally. Even though we'd known each other less than a week, we were already joined at the hip. But still no sex, not until I got my test results. It appeared that Sally had inherited her mother's virus phobia. But I wasn't going to argue against safe sex. Besides, she promised that I could do anything to her once a doctor certified me STD-free.

"Like what?" I'd asked.

"Anything," she said. "It's all going to be yummy with you." Then we'd roll around in bed, kissing and petting for hours. Between my aching wood and her soaked panties, I believed we were building towards the sweetest consummation.

It got to be fun watching the predatory actors plying their greasy charms. They sported an unshaven, magazine model look that included lots of hair gel and bleached teeth. They winked, capered and grinned as if they were the most charming fellows God ever breathed life into. *Bunch of big silly rent boys.*

One earnest thespian dominated Sally's time too long for my taste. I moved in to rescue her—or maybe rescue myself. When I got close, I heard his pitch.

"Today's theatre has lost the efficacy of its myth. Don't you agree?"

"Oh sure," said Sally.

As Mister Efficacy turned to me, Sally stuck her finger inside her mouth and mimed gagging.

When I wasn't looking, yet another grinning fool moved in on Sally. "So you're new! That's so great! They audition so many, but always find the most interesting people. It's an art, the way the faculty assembles such a rich company. I don't know how they do it. It's great. Great. Just great!" He hadn't let Sally get in a word yet.

"Oh yeah. Great." Sally winked at me.

She knew how to handle herself better than I could, so I backed off and let her finesse her train of admirers. Still, it scraped my nerves. She and I had spent every waking hour together for the last week. It felt like new love. But maybe one of these glorified chorus boys could turn Sally's head?

Truth be told, I envied the Drama School actors. The acting program was far tougher to get into than the playwriting program — it was next to impossible. Only a few hundred playwrights applied for five open slots, but thousands of actors auditioned every year. In the end, the school accepted a scant sixteen. To bring your best and keep your cool through those auditions took poise and grit. It also took a lot of hope. Maybe that's what made me jealous. The odds were that one Yale Drama actor in twenty would act professionally after graduation. What did they have to smile about?

I walked over to my buddy Rey Diasanta and wrapped an arm around his shoulder. "Rey! How the hell are you?!"

Rey opened his arms and gave me a gentle, good-gay-guy hug.

"Hey, I heard a great actor joke over the summer," I said. "A famous film producer is addressing an audience of young filmmakers. He says, '*The first thing a producer must learn is this: All actors are schmucks.*' A man in the crowd stands up and says, '*Sir, I am offended by that remark.*' The producer shrugs and asks, *Are you an actor? No,* the man says, *I'm a schmuck!*'"

Rey laughed. "I see you found a girlfriend."

"Can you believe it? I should call my dad. He'd be proud."

We both looked at Sally, who'd pulled herself away from all her male admirers and inserted herself into a crowd of actresses. Sally winked at me.

"She likes you," said Rey.

"Uh-huh. Don't tell her who I really am, okay?"

"If she can't figure it out, I won't do her any favors."

I noticed that Sally was now drinking red from a glass so full it sloshed over her hand. It didn't stay full long.

Betty Corbucci glided by with a big, batty smile on her face. "Hi hi hi hi!" she trilled, and kept gliding.

"What's with Betty?" Rey asked.

"I don't know. Three months ago we were in love. She stopped writing to me in the middle of the summer. I wanted to ask her why. Then Sally fell into my lap."

Sally slipped between us. "*Moi?* In your lap? Sounds yummy." She copped a quick hug and bit my neck. "So I've been telling everyone about the new big guy in my life."

"How about all the hairy-legged gigolos checking you out?"

"Please," she scoffed. "I don't date actors."

"Sally Garfinkle, this is Rey Diasanta. He's a playwright."

"Are you?! You look like such a sweetheart."

Rey smiled. "Hi. Why won't you date actors?"

"They're self-obsessed, neurotic wrecks, and they spend all their time looking into a mirror. I don't compete with a mirror. Gaw-w-d, it seems like I've lived and breathed, shared food and clothing, scripts, shoes, make-up, mirrors, and dressing rooms with actors 24/7 since the day I left junior high. Trust me. That's why I'll always be a writer's wench. I like to be around you brainy boys who won't steal the fucking underwear off my sleeping body."

A few heads turned in our direction. Sally hadn't bothered to check over her shoulder. A few folks wore pissy reactions on their faces. One plump stage manager had heard her every word.

I tried to control the damage. "Whoa! Tell us how you really feel! What about the female of the species? Aren't they just as needy and dangerous?"

"Oh, I know I'm a high maintenance bitch." Sally slurped more wine. "But I'm worth it." She nuzzled noses with me.

Rey interrupted our kanoodling. "I would take one of those big superficial guys and do him right in front of his own full-length mirror."

"Take your pick, sweetie. I'm sure enough of these boys are AC/DC." Sally snatched a fresh glass of wine off of a waiter's tray and drank it. Then she grabbed my neck and pulled my ear to her lips. "Wanna know a secret?"

"Tell me."

"I'm a big hairy cunt," she hissed into my ear.

Rey took that as his cue to replenish his wine glass.

"Nice meeting you, Rey!" Sally shouted. "You look so wise and sweet! I'm sure all of your plays are brilliant!"

"You scared him away," I said.

"All those gay boys think a girl's pussy is full of teeth." Sally ground her body against mine as if we were alone and everyone else was motel furniture.

"Want to go home?"

"Too many parties today. I have to meet everyone." She nosed her way into my shirt and kissed my chest.

"Maybe just for a nap?" I suggested.

"Nope." Her pelvis pushed flush against mine and moved all around. A few party guests took notice.

"It's...kinda public here."

Sally mashed her lips against my ear. "Would you do me in a public place?"

"Um...maybe. Not now." I maneuvered Sally into a less conspicuous corner and put my body between her and the rest of the room. The party was winding down, and we were quite drunk.

"But would you? Would you drag me into the bushes and attack me? Would you yank down my skirt and do me hard?"

"That could happen."

"Mmmmm." She nuzzled my ear. "Would you pee on me?"

"What?"

Someone tapped me on the shoulder. When I spun around, I was met with a woman's smile.

"Can we borrow her for a while? We're going out for pizza. It will be just us first-year actors. Can you come, Sally?"

"Can I?!" Sally shrieked with joy and embraced her new classmate. "Oh, we're all going to be such great friends!"

* * *

I promised to pick up Sally after her first-year-actor pizza party. They celebrated at a popular pizza parlor in the center of campus that had red everything: walls, ceilings, picnic tables, jukebox, and big brick pizza oven. All that red made it look like a fire station. Despite the old school brick oven, the pizzas tasted like oily cardboard. On the plus side, the pitchers of beer were nice and large. When I arrived, the first-years were swapping stories about the day they learned of their acceptance to Yale Drama. It was Sally's turn.

"My parents took me out to the Four Seasons," said Sally.

"How did you get reservations?" someone asked.

"My father made them," said Sally, as if getting a table in that place was as easy as ordering a taco off a truck. "We drank so much champagne! I was screaming and sobbing all night. The whole restaurant watched us. My father announced to everyone: '*Our daughter just got into Yale Drama! She tried three times and now she's in!*' Dad bought champagne for the house. '*My beautiful* Shanie *is going to be a great actress!*'"

Sally was a fun storyteller. She drank enough that day to kill a small horse, but remained upright and lively. Her eyes crossed and uncrossed, but she never slurred her words. It reminded me of the interviews with Judy Garland when she would tell crazy show biz stories with a quadruple gin in one hand and a bent cigarette in the other.

"Then our waiter came over," said Sally. "He asks me, *'Did you really get into Yale Drama?'* *'Yes!'* I screamed. *'That's fantastic! You're so lucky. I auditioned five times. You must be good.'* Now every waiter in the restaurant and half the kitchen staff was gathered around our table. *'We're all actors,'* they said. *'Wonderful!'* Daddy shouted, *'You're all very brave!'* The waiters brought us free dessert. Then Dad left a tip that was twice the size of the bill. *'George!'* Mom screamed. But Daddy said, *'Honey, they're all actors just like our darling Sally!'*"

Sally wasn't ready to leave. I ordered a pint and pulled up a chair at the far end of the table. I felt out of place among actors. The beer helped. The actors started pumping quarters into the jukebox, which led to group singalongs: *Sweet Caroline, Margaritaville,* and *New York, New York.* Why I didn't leave or go and throw myself under a truck, I can't explain.

As a grand finale, Sally climbed on top of the table to sing along to Jimi Hendrix's cover of the Trogg's *Wild Thing.* She threw her hair all around, stomped across the table, and rattled her rear like Tina Turner. Even though she was wearing panties, you could see every crease and toe of the camel. Pitchers of beer teetered as she strutted. *"You make everything...groovy! Yeah, wild thing! Yeah, wild thing! Yeah yeah yeah, wild thing!! Oh s-s-s-sock it to me!"* She jumped into the air and her heel landed on the edge of a pizza tin. A greasy slice flipped up and slapped her bare calf. Then she started backpedaling and lost her balance. She screamed *"WILD THING!!"* once more before falling off the table, and into the laps of several unhappy actors. No one got hurt, but a few thespians got a shower of draught beer and tomato sauce.

I guided Sally out the door, then escorted her home. She held my arm and nuzzled my shoulder all the way. We had another party to go to later that night. Good angels, protect us.

***

The next party was a barbecue and keg affair in a playwright's backyard. He and his wife owned two giant shaggy dogs. White fur covered the lawn furniture and dog droppings hid deep in the overgrown, sun-burnt grass. The dog deposits were hard to avoid, as one of the first-year actors discovered.

"What the fuck?!" he exclaimed.

This was just the kind of public transgression that a *yenta* like Sally could stick her surgically-altered nose into. "Who throws a lawn party and doesn't clean their lawn?"

This event defined Sally's mood for the next few hours. When someone took the last hamburger off the grill, she shrugged. "When a Jew throws a party, there is enough food."

One thing there wasn't a shortage of was beer. The hosts supplied a large keg and lots of cheap stuff in the fridge and coolers. I'd brought along two six-packs of a German pilsner.

I didn't enjoy cadging other folk's specialty brews, but when I opened our host's fridge and found that all of my fine pilsner had disappeared without myself or Sally getting a taste, the rules changed. I saw some fancy European bottles with an elephant on the label. I grabbed two. After we I finished them, I grabbed a couple more. As I was about to enjoy my second, a bald, red-bearded dude with scabs on his head and a can of Schlitz in his hand accosted me.

"You know," he hissed. "I brought that Elephant beer. Do you think maybe I could enjoy some of it? You can drink this instead?" He shoved the can of domestic swill into my face. "No," I said before returning my attention to Sally.

The guy walked off and brooded in a corner for the rest of the night. I felt guilt over his precious suds, but not much.

"It's a party. What a creep," said Sally.

I winked. "He ain't no Jew."

Sally smiled for the first time since we'd arrived.

The sun set, and our host switched on some bug lamps and floodlights. Sally and I kept drinking on our empty stomachs.

A white guy with blonde dreadlocks and flowery tattoos from his eyebrows to his ankles passed Sally a lit joint.

"Don't smoke that," I warned her.

She took a long toke, kept puffing and raised an eyebrow at me. She took another greedy tug then passed it my way.

"No thanks," I said.

She shrugged, and then handed what was left back to White Dread. Dread didn't look like he'd spent any recent quality time with a bar of soap. I wasn't against drug use per se, but you never know what some strange cat likes to roll up in his papers. I smoked something once that was dusted by some punk rockers. I ended up sprawled on a park bench for two hours while I waited for my body to cooperate with my desire to stand and walk.

"Why did you have to do that?" I asked Sally.

Her eyes were shining red and bright. A madcap grin spread across her lips. "The devil made me do it!" She took two more tokes. Then she beamed a bemused smile at me.

At that moment a chubby female playwright stepped in front of us and snapped a photo.

Sally waved at the air with her hands. Her pupils spun in her skull like marbles. "Jesus! Now I'm blind! Who let her in?"

"She's paparazzi. She thought you were Glenn Close."

"I don't look like that ugly bitch, do I? Jesus, I'm clinically blind here! I'm going to need a cock-sucking seeing-eye dog now!"

I had not heard Sally curse quite like that before.

My chubby classmate was crushed. She'd meant no harm, but Sally wasn't through with her.

"Why the hell don't you tell someone when you're going to use that thing?!"

"I'm sorry," the playwright said with trembling lips.

I waved her away, then squeezed Sally's shoulders. "Take it easy. She's my classmate. She likes me."

"Good. Now she can go back to chewing her cud."

"That's mean. Is that really you?"

Sally looked up. Her disdainful frown morphed into a mask of sadness. A flood of Jewish guilt overtook her. She started crying, not quiet sobbing, but loud bawling and blubbering. "God, you're right! I'm such a cunt! I have to tell her I'm sorry. Let me go tell her."

"You've scared her enough tonight. Listen—I spotted some whiskey. If I go get us some, can you keep out of trouble?"

I went into our host's kitchen. As I poured some whiskey into a pair of glasses, I noticed a stranger grinning at me like I was his new best friend. He was big and fat and wore a dark bird's nest beard and a black beret on his bloated head. Laughing, he waddled in my direction.

Uh-oh, I thought. *Where's my schmuck repellent?*

"Hey, you've got a wild one out there, huh?"

"Call me Mr. Lucky."

"Ha! How long have you two known each other? You married?"

"We just met."

"No?! Seriously?! Wow! You guys are the freaks!"

I let the offense slide. "Who's your girl?"

The Bearded Froggy pointed out his lady: she had a nice plump shape, ice gray eyes, and a face that belonged on a journeyman boxer.

"Oh. Didn't notice her," I said.

I went out looking for Sally.

"Where'd she go?" I asked aloud.

"I don't know," someone answered.

I found Sally hiding in a dark corner of the yard. She was sitting on top of a barrel behind a storage shed, her face buried in her hands as she sobbed.

"What's the matter?"

At the sound of my voice she looked up. Her face streamed with tears. "I checked my make-up and saw my skin! I'm all blotchy. My lips are peeling. My nose looks like a big red golf ball. Oh God, my face is falling apart! Could I have leprosy? There's dry leprosy and wet leprosy. Is dry worse? My face won't fall off, will it?"

For one second, I feared she was serious. I had that fight-or-flight feeling one has when encountering the truly psychotic. Then it dawned on me that hyperbole was one of Sally's hobbies. "Don't talk crazy."

"Just tell me my face isn't going to fall off! Can you do that?! Is it too fucking much for you? Are you any kind of man? Or are you some macho bastard who likes to terrorize women and kick their little hearts off a cliff? I bet you are. A real bully. Pimp mentality. You'd pimp me, wouldn't you? Right out on the street!"

In awe I watched Sally's outlandish aria. "You're funny."

"What's funny?! Why are you laughing?! I bet you put something in my drink. I'll wake up with my ass turned inside out and locked up in the trunk of car." She glanced at her compact. "Oh God, my face! I've never looked this awful. Maybe I drank away my looks? Have I drunk away my looks? Is it too late? Tell me it's not too late." Her monologue could have rambled on for hours. I grabbed her shoulders and kissed her.

"You're the most attractive woman anywhere."

"Just *attractive?* What about my skin? Will it be okay tomorrow?" She touched her face and mine.

"Sure. All you need to do is hydrate."

"Okay." She grabbed one of the whiskies and drank it down.

"Not that! Water! Let me get you some. Stay put."

When I got back, Sally was still perched on top of the barrel. I'd put together a care package from our host's kitchen: water bottles, whiskey, canned nuts, cheese crackers. I twisted open a bottle of water and handed it to Sally. She upturned it into her mouth and drank half.

"Can I take you home now?"

She shrugged.

"Let's go," I said. She offered the slightest resistance as I took her by the arm.

As we emerged into the yard, which was full of students, Sally whispered into my ear. "Act like we just had sex."

"What?"

"Pull at your clothes. Strut a little. Grin like you just enjoyed the best blowjob of your whole life."

Sally put on a dreamy smile, pulled at her bra straps and re-arranged her skirt. Her legs swung loose and wide, as if she'd been riding a horse for ten hours. She clung to my arm, rubbed her face on my shoulder. "Oh, I'm ruined," she said in a well-trained stage whisper. "You've wrecked me for any other man."

The crowd regarded us with a mix of disdain, envy, and amusement. Sally owned her audience. She was Joan of Arc, Lady Godiva, and Marilyn Monroe singing Happy Birthday to JFK. I smiled. The semester hadn't even started and somehow I'd found the best playmate in town. When I led her out to the street, Sally stopped. I tried pulling her, but she rooted herself like a stubborn horse.

"We're going to take a cab, right?" she asked. "I'm not going to walk five frickin' miles!"

"It's a half-mile at best. Let's go."

"No!"

"I'll carry you." I scooped her up and wrestled her onto my shoulders. It was an awkward maneuver. I almost dropped her. I didn't care. She scissored my neck and screamed like a lady wrestler. I squeezed her ankles.

"Ouch! You're hurting me!"

"Behave, or I'll chuck you into a hedge."

She pinched my ears.

"Or maybe into a dumpster and close the lid?"

"Put me down!"

I pushed her over my head and set her down like a ballerina. She wobbled a bit, sneered, and turned her back.

"I'm going back to the party to get a ride."

"Fine. I've had enough."

"Get back here!"

"Sorry, but if this is how you're going to act, I've got to go. You need a nap, or a night in detox, or maybe an extended holiday in a rubber room."

"I've already been."

"I bet you have."

"You do not know how to care for a woman."

"What does M'Lady require at this time?"

"Rent a clue! And rent an R while you're at it, Mistah Boston Cream Donut. *Let's go to the Welcome Week PAHTIES, Sally. You need time inna rubBAH room. You needa night in de-TAWX. PAHK YAWUH CAHH at the bottom of a frickin' lake!*"

"I'm not your shrink or your nurse. Good night."

"Don't you dare abandon me!"

Just then a taxi appeared.

"TAXI!" Sally shouted. The cab braked. Sally ran over and jumped in. I crossed over to look inside.

"Get in," she ordered.

"Maybe I feel like walking."

"GET. IN."

The cabbie leaned over and looked at me with imploring eyes. I think he was afraid to be alone with her.

The cab took us to Sally's apartment building and stopped. Sally looked at me.

"I spent all my money on the beer I never got to drink."

A stony silence settled between us. Sally opened her purse and paid. We got out. She turned her back to me and cried.

"Can I go home now?" I asked.

She cried louder.

"I guess I'll come in."

Sally walked and cried at the same time. I followed her into an elevator and up to her apartment. We reclined on her bed in the dark bedroom. The moonlight shone in. There was noise from the street below.

"So, did you really spend time in a rubber room?"

"I was 5150'd once."

"5150'd?"

"Involuntary commitment. I had a little *freakout* in the city. Tee hee. I'd been walking around all night, miles from my apartment."

"I see. So you do walk sometimes."

"That night I walked everywhere. I stopped in places for drinks. But I wouldn't let anyone talk to me. At some point, I wandered into a reggae club, hoping to toke some stray ganja."

"What did you do in there?"

"Just dancing. No one tried to back me into the boy's room. They knew

I was a sad girl and let me dance. If I'd walked into another bar room that far out of my mind, I'd have been gang-raped on a pool table.

"Later, I did a line of coke in the ladies room. Men offered it to me all night. I didn't want it that bad. When one of the girls got generous, I jumped. She and I went outside to smoke ciggies. We laughed and laughed. Then my laughs turned into screams. I kept screaming. I couldn't control it.

"It must have gone on a while 'cause the cops arrived. Then an ambulance. I noticed a long line of black folks in clubbing clothes. I wondered what cool club this could be that had such a long line out front? Then I realized that nobody would wait in line to get into that filthy cave of a fucking club. They were out there to watch me get strapped onto a stretcher and rushed to Bellevue. I put up a little fight with the officers. I yelled like some film noir *femme fatale* getting dragged to the gas chamber. The cops laughed. They knew I didn't mean it."

For a while Sally and I said nothing. I wasn't frightened by her revelations. I only felt closer to her. My family had a mental health history. But the main thing Sally and I had in common was a deep streak of self-loathing.

I reached into the sack of contraband I'd assembled at the garden party. "I found a jelly jar in the recycling bin and made us a stash." Whiskey sloshed around in the jar.

"Got in himl," said Sally.

"Excuse me?"

"It's Yiddish. God in heaven help us."

"You know I don't understand any of that yiddley diddley stuff. Bo Diddley, I know."

"We'll just have to give it up to God. That's what we'll have to do. Go with the love."

"Oh it ain't all that big a thing, is it? Have a snort."

She gulped some down. "Hmmm. Tastes good."

"Must be the grape jelly." I put my arm around Sally and pulled her close. "It'll be okay with us."

"Will it?" she said with dramatic desperation.

"Sure." I hugged her closer and started humming. My humming grew into singing. The song was an old country ditty my dad had on vinyl. *"A preachment, dear friends, you're about to receive, on John Barleycorn, tobaccky, and the temptations of Eve."*

"You've got to be kidding." Sally rolled her eyes.

"Oh-h-h...ONCE I was young and I had a good life! I had enough money to last me for life! Then I met a gal and we went on a spree! She

taught me to smoke and to drink whiskey!"

"Oh, I don't think I could teach you a thing."

"Cigareets, and whiskey and wild, wild women! They'll drive you crazy! They'll drive you insane!"

"Great. I'm dating a hillbilly playwright. My mother would be so proud."

"Cigarettes are a blight on the whole human race! A man is a monkey with one in his face! Cigareets, and whiskey and wild, wild women! They'll drive you crazy! They'll drive you insane! Write on the cross at the head of my grave: For women and whiskey here lays a poor slave."

Sally couldn't resist, and joined me on the chorus.

"Cigareets, and whiskey and wild, wild women! They'll drive you crazy! They'll drive you insane! They'll drive you crazy! They'll drive you IN-SA-A-A-NE!"

We kept kissing while swapping the jelly jar.

***

I got Sally out of her panties for the first time in the wee hours. She let me lick and tickle, but wouldn't let me in.

"Okay. That's enough. I've let you go too far."

I reached for my pants. "Just let me beat one out!"

"No!" She grabbed my hands before I could unzip.

If I were any kind of man, I would have taken her by force. But I figured I could wait a couple more days. My STD test results would be ready on Monday. I didn't tell Sally this. I intended to ambush her and demand immediate service.

***

A week later, I strutted into Sally's apartment wearing a greedy grin. I produced a white slip of paper and held it out. "Look, mom! No VD! Time to get naked."

"No!" Sally held up her hands to defend herself.

"Oh, it's all on now! The dick is coming out!"

"No. Don't you think I'm worth waiting for?"

I placed my hand over my zipper. "Sure you are. I'll wait five more seconds. Four, three, two..." She tried to run, but I caught her. "Aren't we ready?"

"I just don't want us to rush. Can we go get a drink?"

"But all the fun's here."

"Just one?"

* * *

At the nearest bar one drink became many drinks. Sally rubbed up against me in the booth. I continued to brood.

She began talking dirty. "I want to open your pants and see what all that strut is about. Mmmmm. I want to taste you. You can do me whenever. You can wake me up in the middle of the night. I don't care if you pre-jac all over my ass. You're the king. I just want to make you happy. You can yank down my skirt in an alley or drag me into an empty classroom." She mashed her breasts against my arm. "I think I love you."

It was too soon for love. I whispered, "You're beautiful."

The waitress came by. I signaled for the check.

It was late when we got back to Sally's place. She left the lights off and bared her full breasts, which swung out like those of an early 60s pin-up girl. Then she knelt, undid my jeans, and gave me half a treat. A condom soon appeared.

"I'm dripping," she said. "I'm so wet. See what you do to me. Now you know. Now you know."

Yes, I knew. But the problem was that we were too goddamned schnock- ered. We made a good start, but our numbed bodies collided and crashed without any tenderness. Inertia kept us going for a while. At some point we gave up.

"Next time, we fuck first and drink afterwards," I said.

"Okay. Fuck first."

Sally kissed me, then turned around to be spooned. We stayed like that till she fell asleep. It felt exciting just being beside her. I buzzed all over. So what if she was crazy and a bad drinker? I couldn't wait to have her wide awake again.

BLUE BETTY

The first time I saw Betty alone that autumn was in my favorite liquor store. She had a bottle of wine in each hand. I said hello, then followed her home.

Betty's place looked messier than I'd ever seen it. Clothes both clean and dirty sat in piles on the floor. She hadn't straightened her bed covers. The air smelled stale, as if she hadn't opened a window in weeks.

"Why did you stop writing to me?" I asked.

"I slept with someone else. I didn't think you wanted to hear about it."

"I waited for you. You know that? I did."

"It was nothing really. It just happened. I thought it didn't mean anything. Most people in the theatre are pretty loose. I didn't want to hurt you. I couldn't lie to you. I just hoped you wouldn't worry about it or feel bad."

"I did."

"I'm sorry."

"Was I not enough for you? Was I too much? I mean, *why?*"

"It wasn't you."

I walked over and grabbed her.

She fell softly into my arms, but turned her face away. "Don't sex me up. I've been in dance class. I need a shower."

I put my hands on her shoulders and looked into her eyes. "You and I could have still been together."

Betty smiled. "That's okay. I'm sure your new girlfriend is great. Everybody is great. Everyone is beautiful when you get to know them. To know someone is to love someone." She rattled off the words with a fake grin. She might have been the greatest of actresses up on stage, but her forced cheer did not convince.

I stared at her and wondered if she and I should get back together somehow. I loved her. It just seemed like too much had slipped and drifted away. Our happy spring was gone forever. Maybe we could have stirred things up again, but Betty had a remote side. I wasn't sure if I wanted to navigate my way back into her forbidding little world.

She uncorked some red wine and poured herself a large glass. She poured me one too. I drank it, then left.

I'd just finished with one crazy actress and was now getting started with one who was even crazier. Would I ever love Sally Garfinkle in the same way I'd briefly loved Betty Corbucci? Well, Sally had a bombshell body and supplied plenty of sex, which sure beat staying at home and playing with sock puppets. She didn't leave me much time to pine or mourn.

* * *

Later that semester, a cloud of despair settled over Betty. She began to drink hard, often, and alone. The way she moped about the campus reminded me of a lost madwoman in a gothic novel. One day I saw her in a black hooded coat with a long scarf that whipped about her neck in the chill autumn winds. She hovered at a crosswalk. The light changed to green and the walk sign flashed, but she didn't move.

"Hi," I said, drawing up beside her.

She turned and forced a broad smile. "Hi. How are you?" Her cheeks flushed red, which brought out her bloodshot eyes.

"Oh, good, I suppose. Writing a little. Arguing too much with my professors. How about you?"

"Okay. Okay. Okay." She said the word differently all three times. None were believable.

"Can I walk you home?"

"Sure," she said as she stepped off the curb. A car horn blasted. I grabbed her arm.

"Good boy scout, walking little old ladies across the street." Betty chuckled to herself.

I stepped into the crosswalk and reached for Betty's hand. She clutched at my fingers and hurried beside me.

"Are you going home for Thanksgiving?"

"Yup. Back to good old Sonoma County."

Once we got to her lobby door, I hesitated. I had no intention of going inside with her. Betty unlocked the door.

"Okay. See ya in the funny papers!" she said.

"Take good care of yourself." I meant it. The sadness in Betty's gaze was raw and awful. Looking into her eyes felt like teetering on the edge of an abyss.

"Goodbye," she said, and disappeared up the stairwell.

Near the end of the semester, Betty got cast as Lady Macbeth. That spooky play fit her perfectly. Each syllable, each gesture, cracked the air with bold precision. Her alto voice trumped and trounced all the squeaky guys onstage with her. I watched her performance in awe. I doubt Dame Judi Dench ever did it better. Even Sally agreed that Betty was a terrific actress.

Sally and I waited outside the dressing room and congratulated the actors until Betty came out in her street clothes. She looked exhausted. Great actress that she was, she'd left it all on the stage.

"Brilliant!" I said. "You were so good up there!"

"Thanks," she said with a wistful smile.

Sally stepped up. "Amazing. *Mazel tov!*"

"Thanks. Excuse me," Betty said. A long line waited to congratulate her. They gushed and stroked her. Some even genuflected.

Later, I thought about telephoning Betty just to reiterate how good she'd been and share my impressions of what made her work exceptional. But my feelings for her were still too strong. And it wouldn't be fair to Sally.

After *Macbeth* closed, Betty left school for several months. She began to see a clinical psychologist back in California. When she returned, she looked heavily medicated and sat around scowling in her classes. She'd put on twenty pounds. She found a psychologist at the Yale Medical Center who must have done her some good, because by next spring she was back to smiling.

I needed to see a shrink myself, but I was too busy getting loaded and laid, besides writing my angry little plays—among other vices.

BIG BAD BOSTON
BASTID PLAY

The last student play I'd seen was some kind of juvenile schlock-fest packed with gastrointestinal humor and clunky puns. A 112-year-old blind, black street musician(actually a 25-year-old doing a bad Morgan Freeman impression) narrated the play. It seemed to be about a paranoid Chinese-American boy tilting nightly with cartoonish demons that leaped in and out of his clothes closet. The action was laced with random Asian-assimilation themes, latent bi-curiosity, and a mute dwarf who kept darting out of the wings.

With plays like this dominating Yale Drama's student stages, I didn't know what I should write, or how it could ever be favorably received. I felt naked and naive before the esteemed Yale professors and students with their clear bright eyes and well-fed grins. I tried hard not to let anyone make me feel small, so I struck the pose of a streetwise Boston kid, complete with a strut. The pose masked both tenderness and raw ignorance, giving me the shrewd look of a man working his own angle and winning on his own terms. It was both bullshit and one hell of a bluff.

But the armor worked both ways. While I enjoyed its protection, it also made me doubt or distort any incoming information. I looked every gift horse straight in the teeth and saw pitchforks sprouting from the gentlest tongues. I could not distinguish help from harm, crooked from straight, or the best advice from the very worst. I snapped at the hands that tried to feed me. If there was any way to butt heads with opportunity or screw myself out of a good thing, I found it. Instead of creating fresh theater, I argued with the immovable faculty. *If only I hadn't taken the bastards so seriously!*

I could stay at Yale or go home. A real man would have left, but I stuck around to see what would happen next. As Richard Gere shouted at his relentless Sergeant in *An Officer and a Gentleman*: "I GOT NO PLACE ELSE TO GO-O-O!!"

The pen is mightier than the sword, which was just as well, because with a sword I might have hurt someone. I found no civilized place to dump my anger but on the page. So I sat at my desk, faced my cheap, boxy word processor and leaned into the task.

My new play, *Bye bye, Mr. Boston Cream Pie,* was inspired by stories I'd heard about Boston's Mayor Kevin White who was first elected in 1968 and served till 1984. Mayor White would negotiate his most delicate transactions in the privacy of a hotel room in Boston's Parker House Hotel two blocks from City Hall. His Honor would hold forth on a queen-sized bed while a parade of campaign contributors, city contractors, cronies, lawyers, legislators, and union bosses dropped in one by one to propose sweetheart deals.

I tried to imagine my way into that private hotel room. The mayor by himself wouldn't do, so I created a police commissioner, who also happened to be the mayor's lifelong friend and confidant. Together they would look like Commissioner Gordon and Police Chief O'Hara on the old *Batman* TV series. You'd half-expect someone to shout out, *"Begorrah! Devilish clown prince of crime! Oh, if I only had a nickel for every time that Joker has baffled us!"*

The plot was simple. The mayor is at his career's and wit's end. He's facing corruption probes by city, state and federal auditors, as well as ongoing criminal investigations. Local radio talk shows and tabloids gave him only negative press. The single lifeline that might save him from public disgrace is a favor from the president he helped elect. The play's central moral dilemma is sparked by an offstage event: a hate crime against a Jamaican immigrant on the streets of South Boston. Offstage is not the best place to put your inciting incident, but I made the best of it.

Why a vital young man like me wrote about comically decrepit characters nearly three times his age is hard to explain. These senior citizen roles would be challenging to cast under the best professional circumstances. Considering that the average age of Yale Drama's acting class was twenty-four, my desire to explore the moral and mental decay of sexagenarians was ridiculous.

The reason I decided to throw these aging white powerbrokers up on the stage was likely my indirect hostility towards my father and grandfather, and direct hostility towards Yale Drama's self-important faculty. The art most of Yale's professors tried to sell us students fell frequently into abstraction, often utterly plot-less and incoherent to any wider audience. The professors were PhDs who fancied themselves social democrats and informed liberals. They voted Democratic and yet I saw them as the worst kind of closet conservatives.

New Haven had a huge homeless population and the PhDs stepped over these men and women each morning just like everyone else did. New Haven's unemployment, school dropout, and crime rates soared disproportionately high for such a tiny town. The infrastructure of the greater city had sunk beyond decay. Yale was the largest single tax payer in the city, but paid taxes only on its so-called *non-educational* property.

Meanwhile, the university's tax-free campus shined pristine, and New Haven's police force was the highest paid and best equipped in Connecticut. You could even say that besides Yale University, crime and law enforcement were New Haven's only growth industries. Tolstoy once famously asked, "What then must we do?" And Samuel Beckett answered, "Nothing to be done." Nothing to be done?! Surely the great minds gathered at one of America's towering Ivy League colleges could see this urban blight sprawling around their snow white paradise. Shouldn't all the resident PhDs apply their high ideals and abundant intellects to this shameful, barefaced neglect? What would Jesus do? Where was the radical empathy of the true seeker? Was being an artist really a matter of hiding behind the walls of forbidding gothic architecture and artfully framing agony and fear in the abstract for privileged audiences?

What pissed me off most of all was that the Ivy League elites wore the badge of culture on their chests. They represented a greater aesthetic. They were the embodiment of high art. Me, I was low comedy. And I resented those contended bastards running the show.

But rather than seek my own peace and progress, I flooded with anger at what was incomprehensible to me. On the other hand, the faculty was wise. They spent very little emotional energy on me. They understood that there wasn't any way that I, with my half-assed public school education, could argue them off their fortified high ground. Nonetheless, I tried.

I took the worst stereotypes of Boston neighborhoods and characters and invested them with as much humor, humanity, and wit as possible. It played like Archie Bunker on steroids, *Dirty Harry* with a rhyming dictionary, or Tricky Dick Nixon communing with his Silent Majority, but this time, we'd get to win. I shot-gunned all sacred cows and firebombed all things politically correct. If the characters used racial, ethnic, or sexist humor, I tried to make each punchline irresistibly hilarious. When my characters talked about broads or babes, I made them as smooth as Sinatra. My cops would all have crew cuts, close shaves, sunburned necks, and waste no time reading Miranda rights to rotten apple punks. Bob Hope would golf with presidents in Palm Springs. And Robert Rachaborski would bring it all back to life on a proscenium stage.

It was an absurd and doomed task, no less than an aesthetic suicide mission. But I had to do it. I had to.

CAROL CUTRERE

The faculty cast Sally as the rebellious but sensitive small town Carol Cutrere in the Tennessee Williams play *Orpheus Descending*. This first year director's project had a shoestring budget. The director, Billie Sadler, was a large, affable gay woman who looked like the Michelin Man with granny glasses and a crew cut. Billie's bright, tender voice did not jibe with her butch exterior. When she spoke, she sounded like a sensitive schoolgirl narrating her own gothic novel.

Sally and I ran into Billie in the street when we were on our way out of a beer and pizza joint and she was on her way in.

"I'm so excited to work with you!" Sally lied. "How should I prepare for the role?"

"Just read the play. We'll start fresh in rehearsal," said Billie.

"I'm going to watch all the Tennessee Williams films I can. I've already seen the PBS version of the play with Vanessa Redgrave, and the Marlon Brando film *The Fugitive Kind* with Anna Magnani. Oh, isn't that Anna Magnani magnificent? I've watched both films twice already!"

"You shouldn't have done that," said Billie.

Sally's smile collapsed.

"I want to see your fresh interpretation," Billie explained.

"I was just trying to understand the play." Sally's tone rang with hurt and insecurity.

"That's okay. Just go back to the script. We'll make our own discoveries in rehearsal," said Billie.

Watching trim, sassy Sally seeking the approval of this dowdy giantess was odd. Her insecurities about her talent were obvious. She needed a positive word from Billie, otherwise, her afternoon would be ruined.

Billie touched her shoulder. "You'll be fine. Study the script." She sensed that Sally needed more. "You have a wonderful vulnerability for this role. See you at the read-through." Billie walked on by us and ordered her pizza.

On the street, Sally turned to me. "What's wrong with watching the filmed versions of *Orpheus Descending*?"

"Nothing. You wanted to learn about the play. I understand. If I was going to play King Lear I'd be watching Laurence Olivier's *Lear*, Paul Scofield's *Lear*, all the BBC *Lears*. I'd watch Kurosawa's *Ran*. I'd listen to *King Lear* recordings by John Gielgud, James Earl Jones...I'd look for the Robin Williams version, the Fred Flintstone *Lear*."

"Robin Williams never played frickin' *King Lear*!"

"I know. And we're poorer for it."

"What does she mean *a wonderful vulnerability*?"

"It means you're vulnerable and wonderful at the same time."

Sally squinted at me.

"And when you're wonderful, you're just a little bit vulnerable. And when you're vulnerable, you're terribly...."

"Oh shut up!" Sally snapped and punched my arm. She shook her head. "Everybody in this school hates me."

I leaned in for a kiss. She turned away. Then she changed her mind and kissed me hard. It was a sweet greasy kiss that tasted of olive oil, oregano, basil, hot red pepper and love.

Sally did acquire a vulnerability that was breathtaking. Gone was her girly New York strut. Instead of flaunting tight jeans and short skirts, she began to look awkward and shamed. She pushed her knees together and her trim brown thighs somehow became pasty under the bright rehearsal lights. Even her abrupt New York accent seemed to warm up and melt into a rural Southern lilt. She grew to trust her peers. She played her part in a collaborative experience.

They called it *work study*. Sorting programs and ushering were the least of it. Imagine striking electrical equipment from ceiling grids or filling dumpsters with slabs of dry wall at three in the morning. One unfortunate first-year actress found herself compelled to clean animal cages for a visiting circus act. The poor gal gagged and sniffled and cried the whole time. Yale Drama was a feudal combine that chewed up more talent than it spat out. We underfunded students were its peasant fodder. These low crimes of high art continue to go unpunished.

My worst work-study experience at Yale Drama left a rope burn about my brain that may never heal. It branded me a cynic for good and a curmudgeon before my time. The faculty stuck me on the run crew for a big-budget, so-called comedy. I forget what the title was, and wish I could forget the rest. It hoped to be a pretentious parody of a high art play in which a doctor of psychiatry and a language acquisition scholar coach creative mental patients competing for MacArthur genius grants. Think "One Flew Over the Cuckoo's Nest" meets "Rocky" as written by a dude dressed as Gertrude Stein. Various pseudo-outrageous artsy stereotypes trotted in and out, including a man who did the same unnatural things with zucchinis that performance artist Karen Finley did with yams back in the 1980s. One character wore a silver lamé space suit and blasted things with a Silly String gun. Another nerdy creature wore flippers and an inflatable duck around his waist at all times. The psychiatrist had a neglected wife played by balding middle-aged man in a pink bouffant wig and glittering cocktail dresses. The language acquisition scholar carried a clipboard. The actor playing this scholar pretended to scribble significant scientific data, but anyone in the first ten rows could see that his pen was still capped and his pages were blank sheets.

The most offensive aspect of this production was its cost, which ran up to one hundred and thirty thousand dollars. Some of this went to the large union cast and crew, but most funded the prime building materials used to construct the elaborate set.

The director explained that she wanted the thrust stage to be "springy and bouncy" because the play was a comedy. In accordance with her wishes, the stage would be raised, tilted, and extended into the audience. Carpenters built an entire floor upon a floor. This required a huge supply of wood for the ribbing and strut-work underneath. Then they mounted layer upon layer of plywood, foam and particle board. This single part of the set cost the most. The carpenters could have built three one-bedroom bungalows with the same amount of lumber and labor.

The director got her springy set, but the play averaged one laugh every twenty minutes—perhaps $20,000 dollars per laugh—before half-empty houses comprised mostly of non-paying students, bored reviewers, and a dwindling assortment of long-suffering Yale Rep subscribers.

The actors knew the production was a lame duck that missed the winter migration. They kept their spirits afloat by performing practical jokes on each other backstage. I found some amusement in observing an escalating feud between Silver Space Man and Inflatable Duck Boy. Duck Boy emptied all of the Silver Space Man's Silly String guns, thus rendering him impotent before the live preview audience. In retaliation, Space Man deflated Duck Boy's inflatable bird five minutes before his entrance. This led to a confrontation in the green room.

"Don't touch my duck! It's my duck! So hands off!"

"Hey. We're talking about a duck."

"I'm a professional!"

"Oh. And I'm NOT a professional? They teach you how to keep a kiddie pool duck inflated at Julliard, did they?"

"STOP TOUCHING MY FUCKING DUCK!"

I couldn't help laughing at this clash of the titmice.

"See," said Silver Space Man. "He knows it's a joke!"

Duck Boy whipped around and flipped me the bird. When he saw that my shoulders spread twice as wide as his, he covered his middle finger. "Sorry. I meant him!" Then he ran off with the deflated duck flapping about his waist.

The crime of the century—or at least the semester—occurred after the show closed, when the set got struck. All that expensive, premium pressure-treated lumber took over 24 hours to break down, tear up and transfer to a pair of dumpsters, all to be towed to a landfill somewhere.

A security guard in the parking lot outside the theater shook his head. "All that good wood going into the trash," he kept repeating.

I took a break from my strike duties and lit a cigarette. "You could build your own Xanadu out of all that, huh?"

The guard didn't get the reference, but got the idea. "Shit, I'm in a furnished room. My ex-wife has the house. The judge doesn't care. But a single room with a hot plate and a shared bath is better than a jail cell."

I offered the old guy a cigarette.

"No thanks," he said. "I want to enjoy life someday."

I decided to call it quits. I was getting paid work-study wages, seven bucks an hour. The crew boss got pissed when I left. But what could she do, fire me from Yale Grad school?

BOSTON CREAM PIE
IN THE FACE

Bye-Bye, Mr. Boston Cream Pie would have worked best as a farce, like Genet's *The Balcony* or an absurd chamber piece in the style of Harold Pinter's *The Birthday Party*. A little abstract grease on the window would have given it a shimmering opacity which might have fooled folks into thinking it was challenging contemporary art. Instead, I took the most difficult road possible: I wrote it as a straight drama about a friendship about to go through a life-changing conflict. I suppose I was shooting for some *shifting-spirit-of-the-times* epiphany in which two old white powerbrokers realize that their old parochial ways do not speak to their changing city anymore. But it wouldn't work. I'd created some fun, edgy moments, but as a whole it played like a kitchen sink bitch-fest, and not a stylish one like *Who's Afraid of Virginia Woolf?* It was more like *Boys in the Band* with only two boys, or *That Championship Season* with only two corrupt public officials.

They say the best love stories are written about two men. Good examples would be *Midnight Cowboy*, *Of Mice and Men*, and *The Shawshank Redemption*. I had created a love story of sorts. I believed it wasn't sexual, but with two male characters in a hotel room and a queen-sized bed center-stage, my play must have looked pretty goddamned gay to anyone walking in off the street. To compensate, I'd thrown in small female roles, one loyal old Mayor's Secretary, and a young manicurist/prostitute named Aileen who would lounge about in her underwear. Both female parts were thankless. The Secretary scolded her reckless boss with snappy one-liners. Aileen cracked a few risqué jokes, but mostly looked sexy doing nothing at all. I suppose I'd put her on stage out of mild homophobic panic.

Byron Foster, my director, was without doubt gay. I liked the little round wooly bear, with his curly brown locks, his plump crumb-catcher moustache and frizzy soul patch. I met Byron at a party where I overheard him describing his favorite episodes of *Bewitched*. I waited for him to pause, then chimed in. "I never liked *Bewitched*. The guys all acted silly and fussy. Elizabeth Montgomery was cute as Samantha, but cool and stiff. I liked

I Dream of Jeannie, with Barbara Eden in her genie costume. She was sexy and girly, you know. Yeah. I just couldn't get into *Bewitched*."

Byron raised an eyebrow and shot me a look that said, *Well, duh, ya big straight bastard!*

Byron was a huge fan of Ingmar Bergman's slow-moving, psychological dramas and liked to work side-by-side with actors to develop deep characters and relationships. I can only guess what attracted Byron to my big bad Boston play full of corruption, sleaze, and racially-charged content. Maybe because he was a white Southerner from North Carolina. One thing Boston and some Southern cities shared was racial tension. As Byron was a member of a persecuted minority, I expected him to be more sensitive and less willing to offend than me. But he wasn't. The provocative, politically incorrect aspects of my play excited him. He seemed to get a perverse thrill at the idea of creeping under his audience's skin.

"I can't wait to put this up in front of an audience." he said. "It's going to be intense. It'll be like Clarence Thomas's Senate confirmation hearings!" Byron could be freaky, sweet, and sincere all at once. As much as I disliked Yale, it gave me a chance to work with madcap misfits like him.

He and I sat down, talked casting, and made a short list of our top picks. The lead role demanded a flamboyant and fearless actor. Not only was our Mayor a charismatic public figure, he was also an alcoholic, a whore-chaser, a corrupt grafter, a cross-dresser, and a candidate for early senility. But Byron didn't have any luck casting the production. Only six character actors among Yale Drama's twenty-five available male performers could even hope to play seasoned old men. Dean Michter told Byron that the school's best character actors, Thomas Boyd and Artie Giacometti, were otherwise cast, along with the other four actors on our short list. It was hard to believe that all six of our top choices were unavailable during my short production slot. More than likely, Dean Bill Michter planned to indulge in some of his creative casting. He found perverse pleasure in shoehorning his actors into roles no one would ever expect to see them play.

"I have just the right actors!" he told Byron. "They may not seem like they can play older, but trust me, they're sleeping giants!"

Our two giants appeared human-sized at best. It wasn't as bad as watching a fifteen-year-old play Willy Loman in a high school production of *Death of a Salesman*, but what I got were two 23-year-old leading men. Put them in business suits and they looked like junior execs and law clerks, not a Boston Mayor and Police Commissioner.

The two actresses cast were wonderful. Too bad they had tiny supporting roles and that I understood women about as much as a mosquito understands a bug lamp. They spoke two percent of the play's dialogue at best. The actress playing the Mayor's secretary was too smart and gifted to play a dowdy old lady with a mere thirty lines. She spent more time fitting a gray wig than she spent onstage. The other actress had sassy, doll-face charm and plenty of talent. But she did not like what my play asked her to do. I wanted her to be naked onstage, or at least bare-breasted, like the women in those R-rated 1970s exploitation movies I grew up watching at the New Pixie Theatre in Massachusetts. *Why? Because I was an artist!* Hey, you can't blame a guy for trying. But our dear Aileen insisted on being dressed in at least her panties and bra. We compromised on a brief topless scene in the second act. Otherwise, she and the other actress performed like real troupers who scored big laughs with the few lines I'd written for them.

My Mayor revealed his cross-dressing habit in the third act. The joke, as I intended it, was the sight of this burly curmudgeon stuffed into a red evening dress. However, the actor cast was a trim gay man with delicate features. He had sky blue eyes and high cheekbones that shined like fresh gala apples. When he put the dress on, he looked better than half the actresses in the Drama School.

My play received its first public workshop in November of 1995. Had the audience been mostly old white guys over 55, it might have gotten some laughs. But a twenty-something Ivy League audience found no amusement in it. I heard a few reluctant chuckles during the play's two-hour-and-ten-minute presentation, but most of the laughs came from me and Byron, and an odd, middle-aged Australian special research scholar who sat there red-faced and searing drunk. I couldn't tell if the play worked. Unless there are audible sighs or sobbing, you never know for sure. However, I did see folks leaning forward during a few tense exchanges of dialogue.

Watching my wildest inner thoughts spoken aloud by actors in front of a crowd gave me a prickly-all-over feeling. My play regurgitated a lot of my father's and grandfather's peculiar poisons. The worldview was white and hostile. The climax of the play, when the Mayor gives a racially-charged lecture to his friend, came across like Robin Williams channeling Enoch Powell. Enoch, for whoever needs to know, was the British Tory MP who gave the infamous "Rivers of Blood" speech before Parliament in April of 1968, three weeks after Martin Luther King's assassination. Enoch's thesis was that noble white England and its genteel way of life would be consumed and destroyed by waves of black and brown immigrants from the collapsing colonies. It ended Enoch's career in politics.

My experience as the lone white boy in public school classes had embittered me, and I just couldn't stifle the urge to piss off my politically correct faculty and peers. Growing up in the era of Boston's court-ordered school desegregation, I blamed the judges and corrupt politicians of Massachusetts for my early poverty and poor schooling. I also blamed the so-called grownups who'd raised me.

My maternal grandfather was the one true bigot I had known. Race didn't trouble him. But anti-Semitism gave him immense purpose and pleasure. His two favorite subjects were the Jews and abortion, or as he called it, *MURDER!* I still couldn't forget him sitting in his mustard brown kitchen pounding his scarred breakfast table so hard that his coffee cup rattled in its saucer. Grampa's apartment always smelled vaguely of urine and unwashed clothes, like a hospital, minus the disinfectant. Visits to him always made me think of death.

"The world rose up against the Jews before and it will happen again! Everyone thinks they're so smart, but the ones I knew weren't so smart! They were more clever than smart. They snuck around with their ears and eyes open, and stole all their ideas from the smarter people around them."

Hmmm, I thought to my young self. *Isn't that how people get smarter? By listening to smart people and watching how they do things?* But that would be far too logical for grampa, who by now was shivering in his chair, spittle hanging off his bluish lower lip. What fine fiery rages old granddad had! It would have been fun to see him square off in the boxing ring with a 70-year-old Jew in his own weight class, preferably one with Golden Gloves experience. But grampa never punched anything but kitchen tables, or his wife or daughters when he was younger. By the time she turned sixteen my mother's younger sister Carol had had enough. Grampa slapped her with an open hand and Auntie Carol punched him right in the mouth. That ended that.

During grampa's vicious arias my eyes would drift. Sometimes he slapped my forearm to get my attention back, a gesture which both surprised and angered me.

"Hey, let me tell you another funny thing about a Jew who got too smart for himself! Ha ha ha!" The unfrosted light bulb above wasn't flattering to his mottled, bald head and old gray tee shirt peppered with small holes. The laugh lines around his mouth weren't delicate or sweet. But despite his bunched brows and fiercely knotted forehead, there was something soft in his eyes. He was a lonely person who needed an audience just as much as any tortured comedian or out-of-work actor. Some part of grampa realized he was a failed old man fighting epic battles with the ghosts of Jews in a tight, grimy kitchen with just enough space for a table and three rickety chairs. The only weapon within reach was a butter knife filthy with cream cheese, herring, and pumpernickel crumbs, and the only funny part of it all was that his food was probably kosher.

"Some Russian Jew tried to cut in front of Ginty at the Senior Center's Christmas buffet. So Ginty tells him, 'Wait your turn.' 'I was just looking,' says the Jew. 'Get to the back of the line!' Ginty raises a hand to smack him. That shut him up and sent him skipping. *Pushy!* They want everything that everyone else has got. They want it first. And they want it for free. Imagine a Jew cutting in line on Christmas! Ginty schooled him. He ran like a rabbit! HA HA HA!"

Grampa's father put him to work as soon as he could stand and hold a wallpaper brush, but he did save the money to send him to college: Boston University, Class of 1934, Bachelors in Business Administration. Grampa tried to get jobs in high finance during the Depression and afterward, talking his way into a few, but he could never hold them for long. He just couldn't get along with his co-workers, especially the Jews. On top of that, grampa was a rabid anti-FDR Republican in the highly Democratic state of Massachusetts. He was so public in his hatred of President Roosevelt—or "Rosenfeld"—that two FBI agents once paid him a visit in order to interrogate him as a possible traitor during World War II.

Eventually, grampa forgot high finance, and made all his money as an independent wallpaper hanger. He resented this, drank heavily, crashed a few cars, and terrorized his wife and two daughters. My mother, shy, plump, and religious, was his oldest child, so she got the worst of it.

As he grew older, grampa mellowed on every subject except for his two favorites. When his wife got sick with Multiple Sclerosis, he did all he could to comfort her. She became bedridden and trapped in their apartment for the last ten years of her life. Grampa had no life besides her. Local widows pursued him because he remained tall, slender, and very handsome in his dark mohair suits. But he would have none of it. Either he'd lost all interest in sex, or he preferred the stoicism of his role as God's Lonely Husband caring for an invalid wife.

Even though I did not share my grampa's worst opinions, they did shame me and wormed their way into my system. I felt stained and damaged. The hate scorched like acid or corrosive poison and burnt a few holes in my skull when I was a child, and I had a paranoid fear that I'd always be a little wet-brained whenever a hard rain fell. A ten or twelve year-old shouldn't have to school his septuagenarian grandfather, but I tried:

"But isn't Israel this little country surrounded by big Arab countries full of oil? Dad said it was like a postage stamp in a football field, and all they grow are tiny oranges."

"Your dad knows nothing! They're murderers! They bomb their neighbors with missiles we build and pay for! They murder Christian civilians in Lebanon with our bombs! Can you believe it? A Christian country pays Jews to kill Christians! But why should anybody be surprised in a country where it's legal to murder innocent children!"

"Legal?" I said.

"I'm talking ABORTION! MURDER! And you can bet a lot of Jew doctors give abortions in those clinics! Murderers!"

Even though I stopped speaking to my grandfather as an adult, I could still see the shine on his uneven teeth and hear his percussive shouts popping in my ears. I try to convince myself now that I wrote bigoted characters into my early plays because I wanted to understand them. But it was my past that gunked-up my system. I had to write it out. So much unchecked shit—unprocessed material as the psychologists say—blocked up my inner world. Without a Freudian doctor in my life, where else could I ever put my mess but up on stage? It reeked and roared, it was unconquerably strong and undeniably dynamic, but also degrading. It just couldn't be processed or polished. It was like serving an undercooked slab of fantastically marbled steak drowned in cold barbeque sauce, moldy mushrooms, and rancid onions. The audience could stab and slice at it, but they'd have a hell of a time getting past the rot and rawness to parcel it into digestible chunks.

I didn't regret that my early plays were undercooked, stinking, and leaking blood. I only hoped that the so-called preeminent drama school in the country could have helped me with them. *If not here, then where?* I felt like I was trapped in a bad marriage or a dysfunctional family. At times it seemed as if I was acting as my own lawyer in a protracted case in front of an indifferent judge. I knew that the drama school teachers weren't my parents and that I hauled more of my own rotten family baggage with me than they could ever dish out. Still, art seemed such an intimate thing. Artistic collaboration brought folks closer than most families. The goal was to touch the heart and move people into higher states of feeling and consciousness. Was I asking too much to want someone to touch my heart and make me feel encouraged? I suppose I was. When folks aren't giving, you have to start taking. That's street reality.

After the first performance of my play, I watched the audience file out in silence. I decided that stopping to say hello to anyone wouldn't do me, them, or anyone any good. So I left. I marched straight out of the theater on a windy autumn afternoon without making eye contact with anyone or once looking back. I saw Byron, my director, out of the corner of my eye chain-smoking Camel Lights and shuffling in the cold, but didn't acknowledge him. I should have. Sally was in rehearsal all afternoon and couldn't comfort me.

I was alone.

I bought a bottle of some second rate scotch and a rack of generic beer on the way to my apartment. No sense getting fancy when all you want is to get numb.

Once home, I packed a glass with ice and filled it to the rim. The ice crackled. I drank a beer while waiting for the cubes to melt. I put on a Rolling Stones cassette because I needed to hear noise outside of my own head. I reclined on the frameless mattress, propped up my head with three pillows, and sipped the scotch. Not bad. I got up for refills, to light a candle, and to flip a few cassettes. Bob Dylan was next. He made me feel more hip and gritty in my woe. I didn't slug the scotch, but let it leak into me like watered-down laudanum. It wasn't a pretty scene: a man in his prime hitting the bottle and hiding in his apartment. But sometimes a firm bed and an empty room is the best medicine.

Forty-five minutes after fleeing my play like an abject coward, my buzzer rang.

"Hello?" I said into the speaker.

"Bob?! Are you okay?!" It was Sally.

"I'm fine. I'm not in a great mood, but come up." I buzzed her in, then greeted her at the elevator.

Her cheeks throbbed red and sparkled with tears. "Bob, I heard you walked out on your own play." She sobbed as if her own show had bombed. I put my arm around her as we walked inside.

"That's not true. I waited until it was over and then I left. I just didn't want to talk to anyone. I should have talked to the director, the actors, and said something. I feel bad."

"No. It's okay. I was so worried."

"The show was a big sick elephant that died too slowly."

"It was just the first performance."

"There are only two more. Maybe it'll get better, I don't know. You always hope against hope that your show is good, even when it sucks."

"It doesn't suck," said Sally.

"Well then, it blows. Or maybe it sucks and blows at the same time, and just hovers there, and won't go away. What are you doing here? Don't you have rehearsal?"

"I left," said Sally.

"What? What do you mean you left?"

"Oh, who cares? Our bitch stage manager whispered something about you while I was backstage waiting for a cue. Once I'd heard you left your own show, I was useless. I wish I could have been there for you! I'm sorry!" Sally touched my face.

"No. No. What did you do? It's my play," I said.

"After dropping a bunch of lines, I begged Cassie to let me come to you. She said no. So I just left."

"Sally! You can't do that!"

"What else could I do?! Oh, I know—the fucking show must go on! People think they're so goddamned important around here. My boyfriend's a wreck about his play, and I'm supposed to stand backstage with my legs crossed, and my thumb up my ass waiting to say two frickin' lines for some big butch director with a mouth full of marble cake?"

"You should have stayed."

"I'll live. How are you? How was the show? It must have gotten some laughs."

"Not many."

"Come on. I know they laughed. What did they laugh at?"

Sally sipped from my glass and puffed from my cigarette.

"Well, it was hard to resist the gorilla suit bit."

"See! I told you! I bet it was hilarious!" Sally squeezed me, kissed my ear and forced a smile out of me.

"I'll sit in the front row tomorrow," I said.

"I'll sit next to you."

"Don't laugh too hard."

"What do you mean?"

"Just don't fake it."

"What do I ever fake? So did Sarah take her top off?"

"Yeah. But she covered up with her arms."

"I've got better boobs than her." Sally paused and then asked, *"Don't I?"*

"Of course."

"*Of course?* It's very simple. You say yes or no. Which is it?! WHICH IS IT?!"

I answered by pulling her top off. She wanted to say more, but I attacked her with everything I had. You can't end every argument that way, but if you can get away with it, it's grand.

A couple of times I wondered what my grandfather would think of my crazy Jewish girlfriend. And then I just didn't.

CHRISTMAS AT DAD'S

Sally would enjoy her holidays with her family in Scarsdale. She had a long list of family gatherings to attend.

"Why can't I come? Don't they want me around?" I asked.

"You know that my parents adore you."

"I *know* that? How about I take the train into the city and join you for a couple days?"

"There's no place for you to stay. This is family stuff. I won't be having any fun."

"Who are you going to kiss on New Year's?"

"Nobody," she moaned. "I'll miss you so much!"

I said "Bye" and hung up without arguing. I didn't know what Sally's folks really thought of me, but doubted that she fought very hard to get me invited to their festivities.

One of my male classmate once told me: "That little princess is going to eat you up like her last wild oats."

I didn't like to think of myself as the last raw oats in my spoiled sweetheart's feedbag, but perhaps it was true. Maybe I'd spend my Christmas all alone in the empty college town, just me, my radio, and the liquor store. Boston was only a three-hour train ride from New Haven, but I didn't fancy squatting in my dad's squalor for the holidays. My gay sister and I got along, but she didn't have much time for me since she discovered girls.

When you're alone it's hard to keep a grip on your sanity. They say no man is an island, but I survived despite myself. I was enjoying my new Yale grad student lifestyle. I wrote. I exercised. For the first time in years, I had an unsoiled, uncluttered apartment with abundant heat and hot water. I wasn't a triple-decker kid from Boston anymore—I was an Ivy League drama student. At Yale, I was rooting and rebuilding myself, investigating my new identity as a man and an artist, scrapping with scholars and flirting with feisty actresses.

Back in Boston, there'd be nothing to do but work dull, dead-end jobs and fend off my dad's filth, nonsense, and slobbering dogs until I could afford an apartment.

Aw, hell. I phoned my dad.

"Bob—I was just thinking of you. I tried to write you a letter tonight, but your sister brought her girlfriend home. It's hard to concentrate. It sounds like they're going at each other with baseball bats up there."

"Jesus, Dad. I need to hear *that?*"

"Oh, they must be terribly in love," he said.

"Dad, I was thinking I'd come visit you. We could cook a turkey. And I could see some of my Boston friends."

"Sure thing. I'll fix you up with some blankets. I just washed the dog off some of them."

* * *

It was after nine in the evening when I arrived. The house was dark, the street quiet, and the icy boards beneath my feet groaned and crackled. Dad's dogs began barking. I didn't bother to knock. Dad pushed a curtain aside and peered out. I imagined a pistol in his hand, safety off. He opened the door.

Inside, the house smelled like a cave full of wolves. Smoky and Shady were good-hearted, but barked like unholy attack dogs. Clumps of dog hair sat in dusty piles in the corners and all along the baseboards. Dad wore a dirty bathrobe, sagging long johns, and some wool boot-liners that he'd salvaged for use as slippers. The booties were wrapped with fresh silver duct tape.

"Nice moonboots, pop. Do they help you defy gravity?"

"No, but they keep my feet warm."

"You ought to gather up this hair and build another dog."

"That's an idea."

I opened the refrigerator and looked inside. Dad still drank whole milk and ate jumbo eggs, even after surviving triple-bypass surgery. He stocked ground beef and bacon, too. On top of the fridge, he'd stashed a box of individually-wrapped, cinnamon powdered donuts. I took one.

I phoned all my friends to let them know I was in town. Those that answered were busy with close family, in-laws, possessive wives or girlfriends. Others had gone out or split town to holiday elsewhere. I left lots of messages.

When my sister heard I was coming, she decided she'd take off with her girlfriend, a bulky Puerto Rican bombshell who used to trick for crack. I met them as they were making their exit.

"Oh hi, Sis. You almost missed me."

"Almost doesn't count," she said with a grin.

We weren't huggy by nature, but shared a brief embrace.

"You look goo-ood," said my sister's girlfriend, Melba. "What happened? You lose weight?"

"About thirty-five pounds."

"Wish I could lose some," she said as she swept her hands over her stout body. It seemed comfort food had replaced that old nasty crack cocaine. Melba adored my apple-cheeked sister and would no doubt defend her with her life as they holidayed in the *barrio*.

"Merry Christmas," said the girls as they went out.

I chatted with my dad for a few hours, then went upstairs where I slept until the next afternoon. After washing up in the sink and cooking a late lunch, I sat around catching up on my dad's health issues and financial woes. None of it was pleasant news, but I acted the good son, nodding with sympathy.

There wasn't much to do in my old neighborhood on an icy winter's night. I could take a train into downtown Boston to watch the Christmas crowds. But wandering the city streets with my collar up wouldn't make for much Christmas cheer. So I kept my dad company. We shared less common ground than ever. His conspiracy theories, paranoia, and reactionary assessments were good fodder for absurdist theater, but not much else.

"The whole country was lost in 1959," said Dad. "We gave up the ghost. The sixties were no fun. The scariest time. Peace and love was a bunch of crap, a total myth. The country was terrified. Everyone feared the worst. They got it. Black folks got smart in the fifties. White folks threw away their minds in the sixties and never got them back."

I didn't even bother trying to decipher his cryptic pronouncements anymore. They were plump, inscrutable onions best left unpeeled. I listened, winked, and kidded him. His gun talk was fun and masculine for a while. Thanks to Dad, I knew more about which bayonet is best on a British Lee Enfield Jungle Carbine than 99.9% of the population.

Holding dad's guns felt good in a boyish, cops-and-robbers sort of way. It also made me feel a little stupid. I never wanted to shoot anyone, not even myself. Russian roulette with one of dad's revolvers nearly tempted me, but deep down I wasn't suicidal, but just lonely and bored. I'd rather have had a clever friend to laugh with.

Later that evening, while searching through an upstairs room for some of my old theatre texts to read, I opened a drawer that used to contain my socks and underwear and found my sister's dildo collection. I closed the drawer. Dildos and guns seemed to be the Christmas toys of choice in my childhood home. Perhaps I could hang an assortment of both on a Christmas tree. I could use bandoliers of ammunition for tinsel, and maybe a triple-ripple pussy plug for the star. But alas, no tree adorned our old house this year.

I decided to go out to a local Cleary Square barroom. That felt stupid, too. But what else is there to do on a friendless night two days before Christmas?

***

The Cavan House sounded like a traditional Irish pub, but it was just a grimy dive for locals. It amused me to see all the bent and collapsed fencing that surrounded the makeshift parking lot. So many drunk customers plowed it down on a nightly basis that management stopped repairing it. Wire grates protected the front windows from disgruntled customers. But the inside looked clean enough, even if it smelled of half a century's worth of spilled beer. The barmen poured fair Guinness, but most regulars drank Bud out of the bottle, along with shots of cheap whisky like Ten High, Jim Beam, and Old Thompson. My nose-hairs still spark and smoke just thinking about Old Thompson.

That's what I ordered. I was sniffing at my second shot when I got slapped on the shoulder.

"Bob Rachaborski's back in town! Hey hey!"

Jerome Pasquinel held out his hand. I took it. He gripped hard, mashing my knuckles together. Jerome wasn't a big guy, but his hands had grown hard and thick from pushing down on a jackhammer all day.

"Big Bobby Rack! You home for Christmas? Still at school? Didn't drop out, did you?"

I shook my head.

"Good. Yale, huh? That's got to be special. Hey, this here is Tommy McGrath. Look at that face. He's just a kid, twenty-one, bright, happy as a puppy, and full of cum."

"How are you doing? You knew Jerome from high school? Was Jerome a big bad pirate back then too?"

"Sure," I said. "King of the seven seas."

Jerome introduced his other buddy who wore thick glasses and had short black hair that looked like a Brillo pad. "This is 'Poindexter' Ricky Pancino."

Nobody pushed the charm louder than Jerome. He made me think of what might have happened to Mark Wahlberg if he hadn't scored as an underwear model, rapper, and movie star. Jerome was better looking than Mark, but not the same kind of winner. In high school, Jerome was the lone white player on the basketball team. During their best season, he broke his ankle jumping and landing foot first on a loose ball. But he couldn't accept walking on crutches. After two weeks, he sawed off his cast with a steak knife. He never returned to active play.

"So, Bob, we were going to drive to the Braintree Mall. Nothing going on here. No girls. Come out with us."

"Okay," I said.

Outside, we circled Poindexter Pancino's car, a 1977 Ford Landau LTD. It was a huge, black V-8 boat smattered with dents and splotches of brown primer paint. The interior smelled of gas fumes, cannabis ash, and spilled beer. The engine thundered, quaking like a washing machine full of cherry bombs. A trail of black smoke tumbled out the back end like a pall of doom. Some found its way into the car. I coughed and gagged as the fumes scraped my throat and lungs.

"Open the fucking windows," barked Jerome.

Jerome did all the talking. "Yeah, she was fat. But big tits make up for everything. This girl could *fuck*. You know what they say: Fat chicks are like mopeds, fun to ride, you just don't want to be seen riding one."

Poindexter parked near the mall entrance. Jerome slapped Tommy on both shoulders. "Be cool, Tommy. Take your time."

Tommy looked grim and edgy, but he winked and gave us all a Bruce Willis smirk. We watched him walk into the mall.

Jerome turned to me. "Tommy is ice. I saw him walk into a store and come out with five pairs of Levis under each arm. The look on his face, you'd think he was the manager."

Ten minutes later, Tommy walked out with seven leather jackets still on their hangers.

"Pop the trunk," said Tommy. He dumped the coats inside. He held up his bloody hand. "I stabbed my thumb breaking off one of the security locks."

"The ice man strikes again!" Jerome squeezed Tommy's arm.

"You guys do this much?" I asked.

"Yeah. We only get caught maybe once a month. Jail's not so bad for just a night." Jerome winked at Poindexter.

"Oh shit!" shouted Poindexter.

"It's the cops! They're following us!" shouted Tommy.

"Oh shit! SHIT! SHIT!" shouted everybody.

For a second they had me. I panicked, thinking there might be drugs in the car. Since Reagan's *War on Drugs*, you could get a 10-year minimum conspiracy sentence just for *knowing* someone who possessed felony quantities of narcotics.

Somebody slapped my shoulder. "HA-HA! We wuz just kiddin' ya! Did you see his face? Bob was scared." They all howled.

We parked outside the Cavan House again. Jerome went into the bar, then came back out with six guys. He sold each of the leather jackets for twenty bucks a piece. One guy bought two. The last guy bartered some cocaine and pot for his garment. Everybody was happy. Someone rolled a pair of joints. They went round and round our little circle. Then we went inside.

At a narrow side bar near a window that faced the street, Jerome spread out lines of blow with a cardboard coaster. He rolled up a new dollar bill and snorted up the first two lines. "Come on, Bob. Come on. Have some. Go for it, Bob."

I backed away. "No. You guys enjoy."

I hadn't been offered free coke too many times in my life, but as usual I declined. Cocaine scared me. I never forgot how the Boston Celtic's 1986 top draft pick Len Bias died of *cardiac arrhythmia* during a cocaine binge on my birthday. Len was a 22-year-old, 6'8" competitive athlete. Cocaine snuffed him out like a mouse in a medical experiment.

The Cavan's owner, Declan Donovan, picked up the phone and made a show of dialing 911. It seemed like the old man stared directly at me. When all the coke disappeared, Declan dropped the phone back into its cradle. The police never arrived.

Jerome was hyped. He strutted about the floor. He snuck up and hooked his arm around my neck. "Bob, you big boy! Remember how I called you that in school? You Big Boy!!"

"Oh, yeah."

"Hahaha! We fucked around a lot in those days. Remember that time in biology class, when you cut up a frog and found a beetle in its stomach? I told you to '*Eat it!!*' You stood up and grabbed me by the collar. Man, we almost got into a *big* fight!"

"It wasn't all that much."

"Dude, you got so mad! Haha. You Big Boy!"

"Good times."

A pair of big-haired ladies walked by. They had pretty, painted faces, full single-mom breasts and behinds wider than the barstools. Jerome whispered. "See Connie Roy with the black hair and tits? I fucked her. Not good. I had to do *everything*."

"She's standing right there," I said.

"Aw, she knows. You want to try it on with Connie, go ahead. Just talk to her. She'll go home with you, even to your dad's place. McGrath goes with her now."

Tommy heard his name dropped by his hero and walked over. "Jerome is the pirate, a total pirate. He's the swordsman who swings through here on a rope. He fucks any girl he wants."

Jerome went on spilling dirt about his female conquests, most of whom were in the bar that night. "See her? A sweet ride. I busted three nuts in a row inside o' her, till she pushed me off. *'I gotta sleep,'* she said. But I'm getting old. I can't fuck all night anymore. Shit, I'm thirty."

"Too bad," I said. "Listen, I'm going home. I need to go say good-bye to Declan. I'm a friend of the family."

"No! Where're you going?! Come on. Just hang out."

"Good seeing you. Maybe I'll stop around before I go.".

I crossed to old man Declan, who was counting piles of fives, tens, twenties, and more than a few fifties. "Hello, Mr. Donovan. How are you? How are your sons doing?"

"Hello, Bob. Leo has his plumbing business. Gerry's a hotel manager in County Cork. They're making good money, both of them. Timothy's in school for a masters in social work."

"Sorry about that mess earlier. I barely know those guys. I was sitting at home with my dad and got bored."

"That's all right. Be a good fella now. Say hello to your father." Declan winked and continued counting his wads of cash.

✱ ✱ ✱

When I got home, Dad told me that I'd received two calls, one from Sally, and the other from my old Dorchester friend Liam Horgan. Liam had long since moved to Arlington, Massachusetts, a haven of liberal elites and PhDs five miles north of Harvard. It was a far cry from Dorchester Avenue's gangland Irish barrooms.

"Liam!" I hollered into the phone. "What's up?"

"Bob! Well, here's the story. Samantha decided to get back on the pipe for the holidays. She stayed clean six months, kept taking her anti-depressants, and then said, '*What the fuck*' last night, went out to score, and crashed with her ex, a three-hundred-and-twenty-pound opera singer named Maurice."

"That's awful. So sorry to hear that."

"Yeah. What are you going to do? If she wants to crawl back down a crack pipe and shack up with Jabba the Hut, fuck her! And you know what? After her spree, she'll want to move right back in with me till she finds a new place. All her crap is here. Nothing is over till it's over. But screw it. Bob Rachaborski is back in town! Bobby Rack! Let's have a Summit of Giants!"

"All right, fellow giant. What's the plan?"

"A film called *Leaving Las Vegas* opened last month. It's still playing in a tiny theater downtown. Listen to this: "*Nicolas Cage plays an alcoholic Hollywood executive who loses his job and family, moves to Las Vegas with a plan to drink himself to death, and meets a prostitute who loves him without trying to upset his nihilistic agenda,*" explained Liam.

"Sounds like a new Christmas classic!"

"I knew you'd dig it. We can go bar-hopping after, then go to my place. I've got movies and enough beer to float a battleship, plus a couple of Swanson TV Turkey Dinners."

"Just like momma used to make. See you Christmas, Liam."

I hung up, then dialed Sally at her parent's home.

Her mother answered. "Oh, hi, Bob. I'll get her." That's all Mrs. Garfinkle had to say before putting down the phone.

"So what are you doing with all that family?" I asked.

"I'm miserable. I miss you," said Sally.

"Come on. Did you light the Menorah and spin the dreidel?"

"Nothing so exciting. I miss you so much. I told my parents I'm going back to campus a week early. It'll be our playtime
-- just us."

Sally's voice warmed me. On a cold, lonesome Boston night, it felt like the blanket every baby cries for.

"Are you okay?" she asked.

"It's rough. But I'm not a stranger to it."

"You can take it all out on me. Give it all to me."

"I'd never hurt you."

"I know. But I want it all. It's all love with us."

After more sordid promises and endearments, we hung up. I found my dad on his bed disassembling a German Mauser *Karabiner*-98 bolt-action rifle. "Hey, dad," I said, "do you want to go down to your shooting range tomorrow?"

"Sure. Yeah. Why not? Probably won't be a soul there."

On Christmas Eve, Dad and I emptied an assortment of pistol and rifle ammunition into paper targets. Dad shot better. I was way behind on practice, but I remembered the basics: aim—-breath control--squeeze up the slack--BOOM.

Towards the end, Dad and I took turns with his 1911 .45 Colt automatic pistol, the classic sidearm of both World Wars I and II. We must have put a hundred rounds each of dad's hot re-loads through that automatic. BLAM BLAM BLAM!

"Good. Good," Dad told me. "You're keeping them on the paper. But you're pulling low and right. Don't grip too hard. Don't push the gun at the target. Let the weight settle. Rest it in your hand. Squeeze the trigger easy with only your finger, just one easy stroke."

Dad's encouragement felt good. It was the mentoring I needed, especially after a semester's worth of discussions with the Drama School's icy, smug, unfunny faculty.

After two hours, all my gun-rust was gone. I became almost as good a shot as my dear old dad. BLAM BLAM BLAM BLAM! I confess I enjoyed it immensely.

Guns weren't my first choice for Christmas cheer, but when life hands you lemons, make lemonade. Next thing, I'd have at those dildos.

Just kidding.

JAGGED CHUNKS OF
MAD CRAZY LOVE

The wild night started innocently enough. We met up for fun, like any young couple. Sally's rehearsal for what I called *The Brooklyn Pigeon Play* got cancelled. I found her in the lobby of her building. She jumped up into my arms and wrapped her legs around my waist.

"I missed you!"

As the elevator took us up to 14, we climbed all over each other like a pair of monkeys racing up a coconut tree. The moment her apartment door slammed behind us, we fell to the floor. Sally's skin still glistened with warm sweat from her dance class. She hissed into my ear, then bit down hard and almost took off a piece of the lobe. When we made it to the edge of the couch, I yanked down her spandex tights. Her buttocks spilled out, and said, *Hi!* I grabbed her bouncy hips with both hands. How did I ever get so lucky?

Later, we raided Sally's fridge, but there wasn't much in it except for a few diet cookies which we gulped down with cream soda. Actresses starve themselves. Sally and I were still too lazy to venture out, so we forgot about food and fell onto her bed. We kissed, tongued, and sucked each other's mouths like bottomless bowls of candy. Her full lips were natural, unlike her sharp nose, which had been deftly shaped by a Scarsdale plastic surgeon. A Mediterranean bump had been removed, but it still had a long, Bob Hope slope.

We decided to save some for later, after we'd gone out for some food and drink.

"I'm taking a shower," said Sally.

I joined her under the water for a while, then stepped out. I looked inside her medicine cabinet for some mouthwash. There I saw her collection of anti-depressant and anti-anxiety pills. "Which of these are you still taking?"

"Just the Zoloft and the Effexor. The others are old."

At last she stepped out. We toweled off and dressed.

I put on a fitted long-sleeved shirt, button fly jeans, and black navy oxfords. Sally wore a knit blouse, a wavy print skirt, and sassy espadrilles.

Her legs stretched out long, lovely, and brown. Half of that warm coloring came from her Mediterranean roots, the rest she'd soaked up poolside last summer in Westchester County. I'd spent my time off painting houses with Irish working class heroes in Boston. I wasn't very heroic by comparison, but they liked having an artist in their midst. I'd been accepted into a fine arts program and these hardscrabble lads regarded it as a much bigger deal than I did.

"So what're we doing, gorgeous?" I leaned in for a kiss, but Sally pushed my face away as she brushed on her make-up.

"Let's go out for a drink."

"Solid," I said.

Within four walls our behavior was raw and childlike. But when we hit the street, we affected regal poses like a couple of famous race-horses trotting before the bettors in Kentucky. What an arrogant and pretentious pair!

We walked past a stoop where a group of twenty-something black males sat and talked. I braced myself, but there were no catcalls. The guys on the steps just nodded and wagged their heads at each other. Whatever words they exchanged weren't loud enough to be heard, much less offend. Sally probably appeared more intimidating than me. She had her own strut. Her parents might have wealth, but it was earned the hard way in a single generation. They were determined people who had lost most of their elders in the Holocaust and struggled for the privilege of spoiling a daughter. Sally had not paid the same dues, but she was a tough Jewish girl with attitude just the same.

Hell, here she was dating a poor fella like me. Sex and romance were the glue that held us together. But maybe I was just her chosen pet.

We made it to the Sea Dog, which had become our pub of choice. The drinks weren't the strongest, but they poured them fair and the price was right. The décor was nautically-themed of course, with anchors and buoys, skiff paddles, life-preservers, and crossed harpoons adorning the walls. That pair of whale-stabbers always worried me. Sally and I got pretty ripped whenever we hit the Sea Dog. I feared that one night we would liberate them from the wall and commence jousting.

Florence, our favorite waitress, walked over. "How are you both doing tonight?" she asked in the rock-crusher voice that matched her craggy face.

"We're great. Can we have a plate of bacon potato skins, some stuffed mushrooms and some hot wings, please?" asked Sally.

"What would you like to drink?" Florence rasped.

"Two rocks margaritas," said Sally without looking at me.

Hm. This was going to be a tequila night. I never knew which would end worse, our Cuervo escapades or our wild whiskey nocturnes. And when would the argument start? We'd already reached our sex quota, but hadn't fought once all day. It would happen soon enough. A few drinks would get things rolling.

"Should I get my nose fixed again?" asked Sally. "Shortened? Made more perky?"

"Absolutely not," I replied.

"You don't know what it's like for a woman in the entertainment industry," she whined.

"It can't all be a beauty contest," I said. "Look at Rosanna Arquette, or Angelica Huston, or Sigourney Weaver. They're cute, but they were never pretty."

"Those rich bitches had connections up the ass!"

"Then get more connections, not more surgery."

"You really have no cocksucking clue how to make me feel better, do you?"

"I'm such a useless boyfriend. You should trade me in for someone connected who can pimp you out properly."

"I'm not a whore."

Sally and I could be tactless in that rude, uncensored way that children can when saying just what's on their minds. When we took off the gloves, things got ugly fast. Sally obsessed over her looks. Most often, she'd be searching for a compliment but I'd whack her with an insult instead. I knew exactly what she wanted, but preferred to withhold it. She wanted me to tell her she was the most beautiful woman anywhere, and that her plump, pendulous breasts were actually high and perky, and that her plastic surgeon had not cut too little from her nose, but just enough, and that my sweet Sally was a goddess who had drop-dead gorgeous everything from head to toe, and that I worshipped every last precious insane inch of her beyond any sense and all the not-so-unbreakable laws of nature.

That's what Sally wanted me to say. But the opposite tack made things livelier fast. It also made for the most amorous apologies the morning after. It reminded me of that old joke about the sadist and the masochist who meet in a bar and go home together. The sadist ties up the masochist and the masochist asks, "Well, aren't you going to whip me?" And the sadist grins and says, "No." This joke was my love life. I hate to admit it, but mistreating each other opened the door to our best sex. The door swung both ways. Sally loved to call me a creep and fool who didn't know how to treat a woman.

I'd take it on the chin and dish it right back. Instead of ladling on the honey, I'd withhold my praise and watch her fume.

It wasn't as if I didn't praise Sally's beauty all the time. God, I must have told her she was beautiful and that I absolutely loved her twenty times a day. How many times did she have to hear it? Should I have to perform Romeo every night, plus twice on Wednesdays and Saturdays just because she was insecure? I enabled her, or maybe we were two of a kind caught up in our own reciprocal addiction.

Sally began talking about how her rehearsals were going.

"I think Bill really wanted to challenge me with this part," she said. "It's a big role and maybe I could do without the monster makeup, but I think I'm going to really break out with this character. I'm going to blow everyone away."

The role in question was Plopface, the disfigured sidekick to a ghetto philosopher in the Brooklyn pigeon play. Bill Michter, the preeminent acting teacher of our famous drama school, challenged Sally's treasured glamour by casting her as teenaged boy street hustler with a giant inoperable pink mole bulging from his left cheek. I'd seen the make-up studies in rehearsal, and the glued-on blob of pink play-dough made my sexy Sally look like a refugee from the old Star Trek set.

"The play is overwritten," I said. "Your character has got some good poetry to spout, but the face thing, the big growth, mole, tumor, whatever it is, that's just a gimmick. I mean, come on, Plopface? That's not a character. That's just a bad amalgam of impersonal nouns. Sure, you can find some strengths in the character and make some truth in moments. You're a good actress. But you've got to play through all that make-up. Bill is a prick. He just likes to warp and frustrate young actors' minds. You should be playing Maggie the Cat or Antigone or Ophelia. Instead you're a rubber-faced cartoon in an overwritten comic book. How does that make you a better actress?"

Sally didn't say anything. Her eyes zeroed in on me like an infra-red hunting scope. With three margaritas in me, it was easy to ignore my tactless mistake.

"You bastard," she hissed. "I've worked hard on this part. This character is a rapper and a poet. The words are not the best, but I've made them my own. I'm saving this playwright's ass. You of all people should appreciate how hard I've worked."

She started to cry in that bold, sudden way that only well trained actresses can. Fake or not, I'm a sucker for a woman's tears, so I backpedaled. A little.

"I'm sorry. The guy is a good writer. But he could use an editor. He tries to say the same thing with five different metaphors. Why doesn't he choose the best one and cut the rest? But it's all good for you. You're right. You're saving his lazy ass. You're going to make his words soar."

Soar? Jesus. Even *I* didn't believe me.

Sally eyed me like the bacteria on the bottom end of a microscope. Would I ever get off the petri dish tonight?

"Two more margaritas, please," Sally called out.

Florence wobbled in her tracks. "Rocks. Right."

"C'mon. You know I didn't mean anything," I said. "It's just another student play. They all suck. Mine too. But you'll make the best of it. You like rap. You're not a singer, but you've got the moves. You did all those Hip Hop dance classes."

"They all suck," she repeated. "Every play has to suck, don't they? Especially my roles. Anything I do has to suck!"

"Why are you busting me? You hate everybody. Tell me one classmate you like or even respect. Nobody. You hate everyone. You think all the other actresses in the program are either fat horses or stupid sluts, and that all the guys are women-hating homos or arrogant pricks."

"They *are!*" She started crying again. She could melt faster than an ice cube in a blast furnace. "They're all a bunch of fucking animals in this school! But I thought I could at least count on you. I thought I could trust my boyfriend, who's supposed to love me and make me happy. This is the first part Bill cast me in which isn't just a walk-on or a two-word sneeze, and you have to destroy it for me! Well I hope you're proud of yourself, Mister Destroyer! I hope you're real fucking happy!"

I stopped talking. I regretted upsetting Sally so much. But she didn't own all the high ground, like she thought she did. She ridiculed and despised the whole school. She laughed when her classmates failed. But she had no sense of humor whatsoever about herself. If she could pretend that the Brooklyn pigeon playwright had written something of value instead of a protracted mess, what did she really think of my plays?

"Well I'm sorry I cast any doubts upon your stunning debut as Plop-face."

"It is a stunning debut! You bastard! You don't deserve a girlfriend like me!"

"Funny. Sometimes I think the exact same thing."

We drank the next two rounds in silence. Occasionally we barked a few harsh insults at each other, but mostly we just stared at one another with unwavering menace. By the time big Flo hollered for last call, we were ready to crawl across the table and claw each other's eyes out.

Out on the street, we shouted a lot of nonsense at each other. Sally slapped me hard across the face like a wronged wife unleashing her wrath upon a deceitful husband. I took the blow and didn't flinch. But it hurt. The hateful look in her glazed eyes hurt more, even if it was all booze and bark.

Then she jumped up on top of a parked car and stood there with clenched fists, like Sally Field standing up in a union hall. She shouted down at me: "TELL ME I'M BEAUTIFUL, YOU FUCKING BASTARD! SAY IT! SAY I'M BEAUTIFUL!"

At this point, I abandoned Sally and walked home. She'd become impossible and shrill, a total harridan, and things would not get any better this side of detoxification. But a real man would have walked his woman home.

The next morning I called Sally and profusely apologized.

"Come on over," she cooed, smooching into the telephone.

In ten seconds I had my pants on. I got to Sally's place in ten minutes, and they were off again.

***

"I don't care if John Grimes survived cancer. It should kill him next time. John Grimes is a fucking animal as well as an abysmal actor!" These were some of Sally's more big-hearted assessments after a long day of back-to-back acting classes.

"What happened?" I asked.

"Nothing. He just started doing unrehearsed bullshit in a scene we'd been preparing for weeks. I stopped the scene and pulled John aside. *'What the fuck are you doing?'* I asked nicely. *'I'm having an experience,'* he says. Great. My mom's chihuahua likes to have his experiences on a newspaper. Then he tells me I'm sabotaging his scene. *'Sabotaging your scene, John? I don't think so.'* Then do you know what John Grimes said? *'Don't you play an action at me!'* Dr. Wallick didn't care. All actresses are pieces of ass to him. He fucked a future Oscar winner in 1976 and now thinks he's the King Shit God of Acting Mentors. Oh, and then that stupid Juanita Jackson took sides with John. That brown bitch is dumber than a box of rubber doorstops. Seriously. How did she get into this school, an Ivy League school, for cocksucking-sake? Want to hear her latest? She actually said this, I swear to frickin' God, she says, *'You mean to tell me that Israeli people are Jewish?'* *'Um...Yeah,'* I said. *'Oh,'* she says, like it's the news of the century. *'Well,*

Sally, I learn something new every day!' Oh my God. I can't bear it. I can't bear it anymore. Oh suicide, where is thy sting?"

"Do you want some lunch?" I asked.

"Is it laced with cyanide?"

"No."

"I could eat," she said.

We sat on the big orange couch in the center of her apartment. Yellow afternoon light filled her sundeck and spilled into the room. My arms were around Sally, but you couldn't call it cuddling because she was fidgeting and fuming. You can't cuddle the Tasmanian Devil. I'd learned to listen peacefully to Sally's brutal arias until she was finished. Once she'd talked herself out, a pleasant afternoon remained possible. If I just steered her gently towards catharsis and comfort, clothes would be shed and everything would be worthwhile again. However, if I interrupted her or took sides, no one got any good loving that night. But when she wished cancer relapses upon classmates, I wondered what kind of woman I was dating. Sally acted tender towards me, but I was her boyfriend. If I were a competitive peer, how high might I place on her shit-list?

I didn't know John Grimes or Juanita Jackson. When I saw them, they seemed attractive and pleasant. But because Sally blasted both with such disdain, I never befriended them. I didn't pursue friendships with any of Sally's classmates. They were off limits, *verboten*. It was always Us against Them, and if I wanted *Us* to be naked tonight, I could never side with *Them*.

I'd wanted to break up with Sally before, but this time it felt serious. All of my previous attempts fell apart, and proved to be lame, half-hearted and half-assed. I'd march over to her place determined to tell her we were through. But as soon as I entered her apartment, she'd distract me with a sudden crisis. Sometimes she'd already be crying and inconsolable about a wrong allegedly done to her by a competitive peer or faculty tyrant.

Other times, Sally would greet me at the door wearing just panties and a smile. If Sally in black lace panties cried over a crisis, I was a goner. She'd walk into my arms, lay her face against my chest, and all my break-up bravado would melt, imploding like two scoops vanilla ice cream in the noonday sun. We'd move to her bed, and soon I'd be wiping her tears with one hand, and tugging at her undies with the other.

***

I sat with Ted Hinton in a barroom, the last place anyone finds honest courage. Later in the evening, this place would be packed with beer-chugging college kids. At two in the afternoon, it was a dark dive with a sad smattering of retirees, functional drunks, and scratch ticket players. They nursed domestic tap beers as they watched *The Price is Right* on snowy old TVs.

"She's too much," I said.

Ted grunted. He'd heard it all before.

"We're always fighting. Then she's depressed. She stays in bed all day like someone died. All I can do is hold onto her and wait for her mood to change."

"Hmmm," replied Ted.

"It's not like anything is my fault, but I have to pick up the broken pieces and sort them out."

We drank, put down our beers, then lifted them up and drank again.

"She's an attractive woman," remarked Ted.

"We're too close. It's like we're a couple of kids in the sandbox with no one else left in the world to play with, like the world has been through a total thermonuclear holocaust, and we're the only humans left, just her and me, trapped inside a bomb shelter or in one of those geodesic bio-domes or something. It's hermetic, desolate, oppressive."

I mixed too many metaphors or used too many ten-dollar words for Ted's tastes. He blinked and belched quietly.

"I've got to break up with her. But I say that all the time. How? She's got me. I mean, maybe I'm whipped? But whipping is relative, don't you think? If the woman is hot, the sex hotter. Well...I mean...I think it all depends upon the quality of pussy a guy is getting whipped with, am I right? If it's lovely and sweet, then whipping is a small price to pay, cheaper than a night out, and you still get the sex."

Ted lifted his head, almost as if to affirm that I had said something profound or soulful, but then changed his mind and looked away. After a pause, he asked, "Do you like that beer?"

"It's all right. You know I like dry German beers."

"Mmmmm," said Ted. "Crisp pils."

"Okay. Whipped is whipped. But I drive her crazy too. She's begging for compliments. I don't give them to her. And unless she's really depressed, I mean flat, dead-dog-on-the-road depressed, she never withholds sex. Sometimes I'm so annoyed, *I* don't even want to do it. Then we'll fight until I give in and give it to her." I grabbed my face with both hands. "Oh my God, I am whipped. I'm ruined if I don't crawl out. I've got to get away from her."

I sat up straight. "Okay. I'm breaking up with her. I guess we can't be friends anymore either."

Ted cleared his throat. "I've found," he began with a creaky voice, "that the only thing that works...is a clean break." He grabbed his pilsner, drained the last of it. That one full sentence seemed to have taken a lot out of him.

"No contact?"

Ted did not reply.

"Okay," I said. I took out my wallet. "Another?"

Ted shrugged, then grunted.

I held up one finger to the bartender, pointed at Ted, and then left enough money on the bar.

"Wish me luck."

Ted said nothing. The bartender slid him a fresh draught.

Halfway to Sally's place, I had what reformed drunks call *A Moment of Clarity*. I resolved to part ways with Sally, yet here I was, heading straight back to the same old hypnotic honey pot, that which had held me enthralled for over a year now. Once I stepped inside the circus ring of her apartment, I'd be undone. The real world would disappear and I'd be in Sallyland. *Abandon all reason, ye who enter here.* I'd never been able to resist all her happy charms before.

I reversed direction and walked back towards my place. I knew Ted would still be at the bar. But drinking with him all night would not solve anything. I needed to retreat to my own cave. I needed to think this Sally craziness through.

At one of New Haven's crappy, under-stocked little supermarkets, I bought some meat, vegetables, and potatoes. I would make a rich, nurturing stew. I'd cook it slow. I'd let it simmer all day.

The moment I stepped into my place, I picked up the phone.

Sally's machine picked up. "Hey-y-y! This is Sally. Please leave me a brief message. This means you, mom. Peace, ya'll!"

"Hey, it's me. I need to talk to you about...."

Sally snatched up her phone. "Bob." I heard her phone fall off the desk and bang on the floor. I imagined the plastic, pigtail cord knotted up like a clump of dreadlocks, all twelve feet reduced to three feet of tangle.

"Yeah. Hi. Listen," I said. "I'm thinking we need time apart. Things are getting crazy between us. Too many fights. Too much bad feeling. I feel like I'm becoming this awful person. I'm sick of feeling angry and being mean to you."

Sally paused. "I thought you were coming over."

"Do you think that's a good idea?"

"Yes," she said.

"Do you really?"

She didn't answer.

"Look, I'll...I'll call you in couple days. I need to be alone right now. I need to think about stuff."

She sighed. "We don't have to say yucky things to each other. We can be sweet. Can't we?"

"Maybe. Not today. I'm going to hang up."

Sally said nothing. I could hear her breathing.

I hung up.

Her voice was tender, vulnerable, and sweet. I knew that if I listened to it much longer, I'd be jogging over to her place and buying flowers along the way. She'd order up some Chinese food with her dad's credit card. We'd be super kind to each other, for a while, and then there'd be some brooding, slow kisses. We'd live in the glow and frolic of joy all afternoon. But sometime not so late in the evening, Sally would remember my plan to part with her. She'd begin to resent it immensely. Her eyes would smolder, cloud over with rage, and while she would have enjoyed our sexy afternoon, spite would override all of our bliss. She'd start in on me. *You didn't want to come over. As good as I am to you. As much as you know I love you. I'm all yours. But what are you to me? Creep. Big creepola.*

"Creepola" was a term of endearment she'd borrowed from her mother. She would then pour herself a large glass of hard liquor. Instead of sweeping in to reassure her with apologies, I'd pour my own. Once we were sufficiently oiled and unhinged, the shouting would start. If she started crying after one of our exchanges, I might make a stab at being kind to her. *Oh come on. You're beautiful. You know how I feel. I adore you.* But it would be too late. She wouldn't buy it. She'd know I was after more sex or just some quiet so we could sleep. *Bastard. You know you despise me. You hate me just like every other cocksucker in this filthy slaughterhouse of a fucking school!*

I disconnected my phone and started my stew. Even though it was storming outside, I opened all of my windows. I lit a few fat candles and watched the flames jump and jerk. The wind tossed hot wax over the sides. The dampness brought a chill into the room, an atmospheric nippiness, a safe taste of Mother Nature. I put on a sweater as I worked in my kitchenette.

Though New Haven was a college town, there wasn't much good radio. I scanned through the AM dial and settled on my default station, a black public affairs channel. In the morning, I listened to their loud radical talk about urban neglect. But in the afternoon they switched to the smoothest, old school R&B standards and solid gold soul. As I chopped vegetables, I listed to songs about heartbroken folks going outside in the rain to cry, losing love on lonesome highways, and torn lovers not wanting to be the first to say goodbye. When Rose Royce sang, "Love Don't Live Here Anymore", I thought of Sally alone in her apartment and what an idiot bastard I must be. Then the Isley Brothers rescued me with "Work to Do".

"Woman, I've got work to do!" I shouted.

As my stew simmered, I reclined on the bed, reading through a book I'd already read ten times. I can't say I did much focused thinking about my struggles with Sally. It was more a vacation from the relationship grind. The stew smelled grand. I filled a big bowl and ate it slowly, sopping up the last of it with broken chunks of stale sourdough bread. I closed the windows and turned up the heat. I returned to my book and read until I grew drowsy, then slept for twelve hours. World War Three might have begun, but I wouldn't know until I woke up.

About noon the next day I reconnected my phone. It rang immediately. I picked it up and said, "Hello."

No reply. Just breathing.

I hung up. I answered three more of those voiceless calls over the next two hours, then left for the gym. I enjoyed an amazing workout. On the way home, I stopped at an Indian buffet. I pigged out all by myself. Back at my place, my answering machine blinked bright red. I pressed play. Thirty seconds of slow breathing, and then CLICK.

I decided to get some writing done. I turned on my ancient word processor, which looked like a toaster oven with a keyboard. I edited the dialogue in my family drama *Mother Rose On Ice*, shaving off syllables, hoping to turn heavy, maudlin lines into elegantly rendered dialogue. The phone rang. I let my machine monitor Sally's breathing.

At about eleven that night I fell asleep. Thirty minutes into my slumber, my door buzzer went berserk. It rang five times before I rolled off my mattress. I doubted it was a drunk trying the wrong apartment. It could only be the police or my romantic destiny coming to claim me.

I pressed the receiver. "Hello."

"Bob! I'm coming up!" Sally announced.

"No, you're not. Go home. I'll call you tomorrow."

"Buzz me up! Now! I'm coming...!"

I took my finger off the button. The intercom buzzed and buzz-zuzzed.

There was no way to disconnect it or turn it off. I considered duct-taping a cushion over it. I smothered the buzzer with a pillow. The muted buzzing continued. I pressed the intercom again. "Get out of here!"

"Robert! Buzz me up right now!" The pillow muffled her voice, but now she sounded scarier, like a kidnapping victim trapped in a premature grave.

Three security doors stood between Sally and me. Once she got past the lobby, she'd need a key for my floor, and then the door to my studio apartment, my last line of resistance. The buzzing ceased. Someone had let her in.

I could cower in my darkened apartment, but instead I ran out to catch her on the stairs before she got close. I folded my arms and waited at the top of third floor stairwell.

Sally smirked when she saw me. "What are you doing? Posing for a comic book?"

"Why are you here? I told you I needed a break."

"Let's go inside your apartment. I want to sit down."

"You couldn't keep it together for just one day? I told you I would call you."

"I am not going to stand out here in the stairwell like a crack dealer. Now be a *mensch*. Take me inside."

"I'll walk you home."

"You'll walk me home? Oh. Aren't you the sweet goodnight prince? I could've been mugged or raped or murdered walking all the way over to this hellhole."

"No one asked you to come."

"So what have you been doing with yourself? Have you been keeping busy? Have you been productive while I've been stuck in my bed crying and contemplating suicide? I hope you didn't worry too much about me."

"I've been relaxing."

"Good for you. I've been plotting to hang myself with my pantyhose. Yes. It's become that sordid. Have you got any rope? How about some twine? Twine might be nice."

"Let me walk you home."

"TAKE ME INSIDE NOW!" Sally's face was red and quivering.

James McAdams, the ever likeable "Jimmy Mac", star of Yale Drama's acting department, with his tousled brown hair, blue eyes, and Crest commercial teeth, appeared on the stairwell. He carried a bag of Thai takeout, plus a 2-liter bottle of Fresca. His affable smile disappeared when he saw us.

Sally forced a smile. "Oh hi, Mac."

"Hi," said Jimmy.

After he left, Sally sat on a step, folded her arms, and buried her face in them. I sat three steps above her. She was mortified. I didn't care. By now, our reputation for being the craziest couple in Yale Drama had grown to legend. I'd once overheard a tipsy theater management student say: *"Bob and Sally? They're cra-a-zy. Completely certifiable. But they'll probably end up married."* It bugged me. I thought of Frank Sinatra driven mad by the aloof Ava Gardner, or Richard Burton trading snarky barbs with wild, violet-eyed Elizabeth Taylor. They had big sexy fame. Sally and I were just nutty unknowns.

"I'm going to walk you home." I walked to the bottom of the stairwell. "Let's go." I held out my hand. She slapped it away.

Outside, New Haven's streets were empty. Apart from homeless people pushing carriages and diving in dumpsters, the campus was deserted. Sally and I walked side by side without speaking. We reached the awning that led to her lobby door.

I stopped. "Okay. You're home."

Sally turned to me. "I want you to escort me upstairs and put me in my bed."

"I don't think that's wise."

"Don't think. Just take me upstairs. Make sure I'm safe in bed and ready for sleep." She walked into the lobby.

"I can make you safe. I don't know about me."

"What you don't know about yourself is plenty."

Sally's doorman sat at his station looking miserable. His pompadour stood taller and greasier than usual. His handlebar moustache drooped on both sides of his slack mouth.

"How about I just put you on the elevator?" I asked.

"How about you yank your head out of your ass?"

"Will none of my good deeds go unpunished?"

"Oh. You did a good deed? Alert the media."

Our arguments always ended in a standoff. After a while, right or wrong didn't matter. I gave in. "Okay. I'll take you upstairs and tuck you in."

I turned to look at the doorman, who didn't appear to be entertained. He shook his head. He took out his police baton and whacked the top of his doorman's desk. "This is what I do!" he shouted. "This is all I ever do! My life! Can you fucking believe it?!" He re-holstered his club and shook his head.

I escorted Sally up to her apartment with the intent of sitting with her until she fell asleep. She undressed and slid under her covers. I sat fully clothed on the edge of the bed.

"I'm going," I said.

"Go ahead," Sally muttered, her face pushed into her pillow. Then she started crying.

I let myself out and walked home.

The next day, I received a couple more voiceless calls. The machine took both.

I telephoned my favorite professor from my first year at Yale, Ms. Margot Cody, a tough cookie television writer who had won a few awards for Off-Broadway plays. We weren't close. I don't know why I presumed I could ask her for advice about my love life. But she seemed the type who would give no-nonsense answers. That's what I needed.

"She won't give up," I told Margot after a ten-minute explanation of recent events.

"Do you really want her to?"

"Yeah. I think so."

"Because I'll tell you the truth, Robert. Nine times out of ten I give folks good advice, and they do the exact opposite. I've had this conversation too many times. People think I'm sympathetic. I'm not. No one's paying me to be a shrink."

"Okay. Forget it. I'm sorry to bug you."

"Well you have bugged me, so let's get it over with. If you know this girl is bad news, then ride out the breakup. Don't whine about it or expect it to be easy. From what you've described, I don't think this can ever become a mature, long-term relationship. You two are designed to destroy each other. What will happen is that she'll destroy you if you let her, then she'll marry a lawyer just like her dear old dad."

My phone beeped, and the voice of an operator cut in. "Is this Robert Rachaborski?"

"Yes."

"You have an emergency phone call from Sally Garfinkle."

"You're kidding. Can I say goodbye to someone first?"

"Yes," said the operator.

"Margot, it's her. She said it was an emergency and the operator cut into my line."

"Wow. She *is* hard core."

"Could I maybe call you back later?"

"I hope not. But if you must."

Robert Curtis

"Thanks. Okay, operator. Put her through."

"Bob! Why don't you have call waiting?"

"I was on the phone with my professor."

"Why don't you ever talk to me when I call?"

"Because all I hear is breathing. Look. I have nothing to say to you. If you've got to talk, say your piece. Tell me when I can hang up. Okay? Go."

After a prolonged silence, Sally hung up.

I decided to spare Margot Cody another call. Instead, I phoned an old friend from Boston named Peggy Carnahan, a pug of a gal who looked like Jimmy Cagney with Farrah Fawcett's feathered hairstyle.

Peggy had her own prescription for my troubles: "The only thing that works with women is to shove another girl right in their faces. Tell you what, I'll pack a bag of my sexiest outfits and come down this weekend. I'll hang all over you, kiss and squeeze you in public until she gets the idea."

"That sounds kinda extreme."

"This situation calls for extreme measures."

I told Peggy I'd consider it. I hung up. The problem with Peggy's idea was Peggy. Back in Boston, she'd tried to get me drunk and out of my pants more than once. If I allowed Peggy to visit, she'd jump me for sure. Then I'd have two nutty babes breathing into my machine.

Who could I call? My Dad knew as much about adult consensual sex as a Catholic priest. My friend Rey, an unlucky gay bachelor, could only shake his head in sympathy. Why grown men tied their nerves into knots over vaginas was a mystery to him. I wasn't wise enough to find a clinical psychologist, even though they were free at the Yale Student Health Center for anyone currently matriculated.

I called up Ted Hinton and asked if he wanted to meet for a drink. We met at the same dark dive, only now it was crowded with shouting undergrads. Ted elbowed us little drinking room at the bar. We stood there sucking up pilsner beers and iced whiskies. There were a lot of young women around. None of those privileged Ivy League lasses had Sally's mad gleam in her eye. Calm and sweet women could only belong to more adjusted men. Or so I thought. As usual, my low self-esteem was doing all the talking. These gals were definitely within reach. They checked me out. A sane man would have selected the finest young lovely in the room and went on the hunt, but not me, no. I needed to see insanity in a woman's eyes to help me feel less insane.

"Where have you been?" Ted asked.

"Home, taking care of myself."

182

"I should do more of that. Your girl has been asking about you. She bugs me every time I see her."

"I'm sorry about that. How is she?"

Ted paused. It wasn't a conversation he wanted, even though he'd brought it up. "She was sitting in here with a table full of actors last night and laughed louder than anyone. Two hours later, I saw her walking home by herself crying." Ted winked at me. "Try a shot of Dickel."

Ted signaled the bartender. The bartender poured us two Dickel bourbons. We drank.

"Nice, huh?" Ted grinned. "Cheap, but full bodied and smooth, with a little nibble on the end. Tickles the tongue."

Ted kept talking, but all I could think about was nibbling Sally's body and tickling her with my tongue.

"Jack Daniels went downhill," Ted continued. "It used to be 86 proof. It was popular and sold a lot in clubs. But people got buzzed too fast. They bought fewer rounds. The distillers reduced it to 80 proof to increase sales. But Jack is not real bourbon anyway. It's corn liquor, a sour mash."

Ted should've been a distillery tour guide. "So how's your play going?" I asked him in order to change the subject.

"Well, my play is about God, I guess, but I don't want to name Him as such. So I made it into science fiction. You see, these space aliens visit this small Texas town, and one is the transmogrified essence of Buddy Holly. A few of the elderly folks actually saw Buddy in the flesh before his plane crash in 1959 with Richie Valens and the Big Bopper. The old timers really do recognize the rockabilly legend."

"Uh-huh." I nodded, paying little attention. I was hung up on *transmogrified*, a large word for Ted.

"Then this young waitress in the town diner falls in love with Buddy, not knowing he's a space alien. But he's just sort of an alien, really, more of a restless spirit on a quest, an angel fallen from the stars, if you will, but not holy holy, *Hey, look at me, I'm an angel*. He's just a regular guy from another world trying to make things right for himself and his past, for this wide-eyed waitress gal, for the town, for all humanity, I guess."

Ted's play idea wasn't grabbing me. While he rambled on, I tried to imagine Sally in a waitress uniform with a white apron. Nah. She was too uptown for that. How about a maid's costume with black stockings, a feather duster, and a foreign accent?

"Huh?" I grunted. Ted had apparently asked me a question.

"I said, that's where the God angle comes in. Now should I call him the Grand Old Dad, the Galaxy's Original Dude, or maybe The Big Guy?"

Sally called me Big Guy sometimes. "Um, I...don't know about that. Just call him Jeff or Topper or Waldo or something."

"Waldo?" Ted's eyes crossed and uncrossed, as if he suspected that I was patronizing him.

"You know—just call him by a name. If He's God, we'll know He is by what He does, right?"

Ted got serious. "It's a spiritual play, but I don't want it to be a sermon. I don't want the audience confused either."

"Oh, I wouldn't worry about that, Ted."

"Now with the waitress, I'm wondering if she should have a sexual relationship with the visiting Buddy. Or is that un-angelic activity, not in keeping with his noble galaxy quest?"

Five days ago I'd enjoyed my last un-angelic activities with Sally. My body missed her.

"Well, if it's consensual and he doesn't have VD or anything. Is the alien Buddy going to get her pregnant?"

"Oh no," said Ted. "That would be another play entirely."

"Yeah. It would have to be." I slid off my bar stool. "Hey. I need to go."

"You don't want one more for the road?"

"Nah. Talking to you about your play just makes me want to go home and get to work on mine," I lied.

"Well, okay then. Happy writing."

I exited the bar and didn't look back.

As I jogged home, I thought about Sally. That girl was mad for me. I was twice as mad for wanting to leave her. Sure, we fought and shouted, mostly in public. But we also comforted each other at a creepy, elitist university. We drank too much. But as long as we didn't drive, rob convenience stores, or mainline heroin, who cared? The first, best high we had was each other, and no one could bottle that in Kentucky or suck it up in a syringe. Right about now I needed a hit of my dream stuff.

I ran into my building and leaped up flights of stairs. I left the front door of my unit wide open as I moved to my phone and dialed Sally's number.

"Hello," she answered.

I panted to catch my breath, "I miss you."

We listened to each other's breathing.

"I miss you too."

I felt tender all over. It would be unmanly to admit how much I needed her right then. "Can I come over?"

"Come on over."

"I'm coming."

*   *   *

Later that semester, Sally and I went to see Ted Hinton's play about the Southern barflies who gather at a local tavern in a small town where a UFO who is actually Buddy Holly had landed. I expected more about the relationships between the lonely characters and that the UFO hysteria would just be what brought them all together, a shared dream that united them, something that gave them a family away from their empty homes and broken families. But Ted went in the wrong direction. For him, the aliens became real. They arrived as emissaries from more intelligent life forms that were trying to save us from ourselves. He didn't drop the God angle either. The characters talked about the Big Guy and the Galaxy's Grand Old Dude. So instead of actual human conflict, the play became a protracted science fiction sermon, the very thing that Ted had hoped to avoid. He called his play "Bright Light In The Sky" but a more apt title would have been "I Have Seen The Light In The Sky" or "How Saint Anselm And The Space Aliens Saved Our Town's Soul".

During a blackout, Sally leaned close and whispered into my ear. "He gets accepted into the best drama school in the country and he writes an episode of *Hee Haw?*"

DRAMA DOZENS

LITTLE CHARLIE: *Ooo ooo ooo ruh. BZZPHST!*

DAD: *I swear I'll shove a meat thermometer through his brain.*

MOM: *Shush!*

LITTLE CHARLIE: *Ooo ruh ooo oo. BZZ-PHRUPHZZT!*

DAD: *Corn. All the time corn. Waxy green beans that taste like crayons. No one can cook a chicken around here. Can't cook a chicken or a steak. Who can't cook a steak? Just stick it in the broiler, a couple minutes on each side.*

LITTLE CHARLIE: *Emm em emm.*

MOM: *I've had enough.*

DAD: *What exactly does it mean when someone has "Had enough"?*

LITTLE CHARLIE: *Emm em emm.*

DAD: *The little bastard wants his M & M's again.*

MOM: *Don't say that! He hears what you say.*

DAD: *He'll just spit them out all over the place like watermelon seeds.*

MOM: *If that was all that kept you happy.*

One of the most interesting student plays that I heard during my three years at the Drama School was written by my friend and classmate Rey Diasanta. Rey's play offered us a disabled child named Charlie, with next-to-no motor skills, and a tongue that moved to just one side of his twisted mouth. Charlie couldn't form words or make his parents or siblings understand him, so he created meaning through repetition of the few sounds available to him.

The Drama 12 class gathered to listen to Rey's new play. The house consisted of third-year actors and directors, dramaturgs, and all the play-wrights—perhaps 50 students altogether. Five actors read Rey's play aloud.

Charlie's mother, father, and siblings bickered about the same unchange-able things. Little Charlie tried to divert and undermine these destructive re-curring tensions with his passionate but seemingly nonsensical interjections. In time, he achieves an impact. His family grows happier, more unified, and productive without knowing why, even as Charlie's health declines to the point of near death.

You would think such a story might appeal to young fine arts students. But because Rey chose to dig deep with Charlie, to find a challenging voice for a challenged character, the audience reacted coldly. Charlie didn't charm and amuse audiences like *Forrest Gump,* Owen Meaney, *Simon Birch, Rain Man,* or any number of cute and cheeky disabled, mentally ill or challenged characters.

Rey didn't just *pretend* to create a language with less than ten one-sylla-ble sounds. He invented one. His play had the painstaking commitment of a world class linguist or a metaphysics scholar detailing a doctoral thesis. The play forced you to feel, to suffer, and struggle in the way little Charlie had to fight to communicate with his disintegrating family. A brilliant child-mind sat trapped inside an immobilized body.

We as an audience were faced with a dilemma. Like everyone around Charlie, we were annoyed by his incessant hoots, hisses and repetitions of unformed words, and how he'd beg for M&M's and then spit them out. But what would you—or anyone—do with only ten elusive sounds and a family tearing itself apart?

A paralyzed boy tries to save his emotionally crippled family. I believed it was brilliant. But because my classmates could not sit contentedly in their seats and cheer "Run, Forrest! Run!" they grew resentful. When Rey's read-ing ended, the applause was weak and brief. The audience looked uncomfortable. So began perhaps the ugliest session of Drama 12 (or "Drama Dozens") that I ever participated in.

"I don't know why people bring in plays like this!" said six-foot-four Julius Burrell, a black former college football player who dressed in leather jackets and turtleneck sweaters like Shaft. "*Who* is talking to *who*? Are there actual *characters* here? What are we supposed to play as actors? The family doesn't talk to each other. The crippled boy just moans, makes crazy noises, and spits candy all over the place. There's no communication." Julius's brows knotted tightly. He pronounced his words with such force, you'd think he was addressing a prison riot instead of a playwriting workshop. His voice echoed off the paneled walls of the old rehearsal hall.

"We're trained in realism—Chekhov, Ibsen. We don't even attempt Strindberg our first year," said Jimmy Mac, a handsome, blue-eyed wonder boy who still banked healthy residuals from a successful commercial and soap opera career years before attending grad school. "But with this play, I don't know what questions to ask, let alone the answers. If we knew what to play, we'd play it. We'd apply the techniques we've learned."

Dark blonde, curly-topped, azure-eyed Jimmy Mac grew up the next door neighbor of an Oscar winning film director, with names like Al Pacino, Jerry Orbach, and Faye Dunaway dropping by and patting his head at garden parties. He was dating the gorgeous biracial daughter of another famous film and TV director. He already had an agent and manager waiting for him to graduate and get busy making money again. He was an actor who wanted to direct. Fuck Jimmy Mac.

Julius and Jimmy were best friends, and quite popular in the Drama School. I used to think they were okay guys and even wondered if we could be friends. But no more. Today they both wore angry looks on their faces, as if someone had thrown a rock at their grandmas.

My classmate Rey threw no rocks. His plays were raw, odd, and a bit inscrutable. But they also had heart and soul and risked disaster with each fresh and unique line of dialogue. He wrote bold lines like a young sexy poet, even though he was closer to forty than thirty.

I sat mutely while my buddy got dismissed by these Ivy League hams. I knew Rey's plays were good. There was unexpected poetry and elegant lines in Rey's work that only he could think of. But I couldn't pinpoint what held his plays together or made them dynamic theatrical experiences. Watching his plays felt like watching obsessed lovers communicate in a strange foreign dialect. The language tumbled out in choppy, unexpected chunks. It erupted with oddities and surprises. It conjured existential moods, like the work of

Fellini or Antonioni, or maybe Samuel Beckett by way of the Pacific Islands. But how could I communicate my perceptions to stubborn actors trained to sing along to their same old naturalistic player piano?

I felt for Rey. I wanted to stand up and say: *Fuck you! Leave him alone! You know nothing about how great his stuff is!* Not a well-reasoned argument, but the subtext would be clear.

My body shivered with queasy electricity. I felt scraped and jittery all over. The Irish whiskey I'd shared with my neighbor Ted Hinton last night didn't help. I became worried that I might say something very foolish.

My own looming public disgrace was a few spoken words away. My hand shot up. *No, Bob, don't,* I begged myself. *You want to set the bastards straight, but you can't. They wouldn't understand anyway, no matter what you said.* My inner voice was right. But it had become more than a debate now. Two big, pretty-boy actors had abused my friend. I didn't think I could argue these know-it-all gigolos off their high ground, but maybe I could spoil their day with a few choice words.

My body felt weightless as I straightened up and held my hand even higher.

"Robert," said Professor Voorhees.

"Yeah," I said. "I-uh, I don't know where to start. But um…Yeah. What to play? Actors always say the play isn't ready, or that it's not playable. But maybe it's not always the play that isn't ready. Maybe it's you guys who aren't ready some times?" *Careful, Bobby,* I told myself. *Take it easy. Keep it polite.* "Maybe what's on the page is something that you've never seen before, and *you* are not ready to play *it*? Or maybe you can't? Of course, it's only the new plays that are always '*unplayable*'. With a dead playwright, you have to step up and deal, serve the text, dig for subtext, you know, like you're supposed to." I shut up. My hands were shaking. I closed them into fists and forced them behind my back. I'd addressed Professor Voorhees, but now I looked at Julius, Jimmy, and the rest of the class.

There was a dry silence. Big Julius glared at me like an opposing tackle. Jimmy Mac looked at me as if I'd just called Julius a porch monkey. All the other actors turned to regard me. Yes, I'd made myself the hot turd on the wedding cake.

A few playwrights, dramaturgs, and directors might have seen my point. But directors are diplomats, playwrights protest only on the page, and dramaturgs, well, they're the court eunuchs in the Kingdom of Drama.

Julius spoke first. His voice rose in volume with each word. "I've played all kinds of scripts in this school, and I haven't missed a single student production in three years, as a performer, producer, writer, director, or audience member. I've done new plays, old plays, classical, Restoration, Greek, Shakespeare, comedy, tragedy, absurdist...!" He was shouting now. "But this play," he said with a sneer, "it just doesn't give me nothing to work with." He used a double negative, just to remind us that he was black, I guess. "Maybe it helps the writer to hear his words spoken out loud? But I don't get a...a thing out of it!" He'd almost said *damned*.

For a second, I was back in a Boston public school hallway facing another black tough who wanted me to pay for his lunch, or give him my carton of chocolate milk or my textbook because he'd lost his on the bus. But sweet baby Rey came to my rescue.

"Why are you shouting so much?" said Rey.

"I'm not shouting!" Julius shouted.

Rey shook his head. "I'm sorry if my play upset you so much. This is not what I wanted. We don't have to discuss it anymore. It's okay."

An awkward silence followed.

"This is your discussion, Rey," said Professor Voorhees in a Mister Rogers *'It's a beautiful day in the neighborhood'* voice. "Please, let's continue. Who else has something to say? Someone new, please. How can we nurture Rey?"

Julius looked guilty. Even though he dressed like a 1970s pimp, he thought of himself as one-hundred-percent civilized, a loyal good-guy friend to his swinging, pseudo-Rat-Pack buddies like Jimmy Mac, and a butter-sweet gentleman with the ladies. "I was only expressing my opinion. If I raised my voice, I'm sorry," he said in the most tender tone he could muster.

I almost felt sorry for Julius now. There was an adolescent "Wally Cleaver" whine in his normal voice. He often tried too hard to sound cool, confident and strong, smothering that graceful feminine side which all great male actors have.

Julius grew up a Midwestern kid in Iowa public schools as lily white as my Boston schools were black. He'd won football scholarships and played well until drug abuse and a knee injury took him off the field. It hadn't been all babes, applause, and spotlights for Julius during his first year at the Drama School. The faculty gave him the tiniest roles in mainstage productions. He played voices in Greek choruses, Shakespearian soldier walk-ons, and murderers with two to three lines of dialogue, tops. When they finally gave him meaty roles, each one seemed chosen to feminize and emasculate him. In a single semester, Julius played a Harlem drag queen, a big mama blues diva, and even Oprah Winfrey in a comedy revue.

Jimmy Mac stepped close to Julius and pointed at Rey with two fingers in the tradition of President John Kennedy. "I think you're the one who may be taking yourself too seriously here. Julius may have become a little excited, but he's one of the most generous actors in the whole department. Ask anyone."

Rows of heads nodded.

Rey shook his head. "I didn't write this play to make him mad at me or disappoint anyone. It's okay if Julius doesn't like it. But why is he so upset?"

"I'm not upset. I..." Julius stammered.

Professor Voorhees intervened again. "This argument is not useful. Does anyone have any new thoughts on Rey's play? Perhaps someone else we haven't heard from yet?"

Jimmy Mac ignored Professor Voorhees and spoke to me as if it were my play. My statement about actors not up to the challenge of a new text still stung.

"The language isn't focused," he said. "The characters don't interact. Performers need to know what to source and who to play to. There are solo shows and soliloquies where an actor works from inside, but there have to be clues, text that points to subtext, moment-to-moment realities that rise into supra-realities. Words must mean something."

"Yeah!" Julius nodded.

Jimmy Mac and Julius were one tough salt-and-pepper duo. Perhaps I had bitten off more than I could chew by challenging this Mutt and Jeff act.

"All words have meaning. You don't see words on Rey's pages?" I asked.

"Yes," said Julius. "But too much of it is this little boy talking nonsense and making noises. The characters aren't listening to each other."

"They aren't?" I asked.

Rey spoke up. "Don't actors do a gibberish exercise?"

There was a pause while Julius considered this and Jimmy Mac tried to think up a clever response.

"Yes. We do a gibberish exercise. It's an improvisation," he said. "One actor leads the group with gibberish commands and the group responds realistically. The goal is to achieve a unified, shared experience between the actors." A light went on behind Jimmy Mac's eyes. He grinned. "So are you saying that we should play this text as gibberish? That we should just spit out Rey's words like gibbering idiots?"

"No. You should be yourselves," said Rey in all innocence.

The class laughed. Even Voorhees chuckled.

To everyone's surprise, one of the more gifted directing students stood up. James Beckwith was the son of an army general who had held a high appointment in Nixon's administration. All of his ancestors served as career soldiers ever since George Washington crossed the Delaware. James, however, broke with family tradition and pursued a career in the dramatic arts. He was prematurely balding, with a doughy, boyish face, and the thinnest lips. His pinhole of a smile seemed quite sincere.

"Rey, I thought your play offered us a rich, rewarding, brilliant, and unique point of view," said James. "You are a true artist. But you have to understand that these young actors are about to graduate. They will be pursuing work in commercial film and television, and trying very hard to build careers playing TV detectives, doctors, young parents, crime victims, and distressed lovers on soap operas. Your heightened language and fine poetry may not help them hold up a bottle of shampoo or astringent and sell it to a national audience."

Great, I thought. *The bastard will be the dean someday.*

"Excellent point!" said Voorhees. "Let's end here!"

I heard many affirmative grunts. Some even applauded.

I looked at Rey. Rey looked at his feet.

Jimmy Mac, Big Julius, and I stared at each other like gunslingers in a spaghetti western. Class had run five minutes over time. Students rushed out. I wondered if Rey would be in shape for a beer. I doubted it. I could have taken the back door to avoid Julius and Jimmy Mac. But I walked right between them.

Outside I lit a cigarette and waited. I wanted to see how Rey was doing. When he came out, he chased after big Julius. "Why won't you talk to me about my play? You had so much to say in class. What are you worried about? You're so big. I'm just a little brown gay boy!"

Julius started to run away from Rey.

I smiled. My friend was doing just fine.

CABARET BOYS

Necessity was the mother of this drag queen bastard. For two weeks, I became the big diva on campus. It was the only time I ever wore women's clothes, and it forced a make-or-break moment between me and Sally. For a little while I crashed her turf and brought the drama.

The faculty had not cast Sally in one leading role. But I snagged the female lead in the funniest play on campus and fell into it ass-backwards. Big Bob would burst his cocoon and blossom. Two divas would cling to their fragile, frantic love. Above all, the show would go on.

I owed my new star status to Ms. Dusty McCorkle. Besides writing brilliant plays, she'd traveled the world and once worked as a Vegas showgirl. One of the photos from her dancing years was on display in her apartment. Her boyfriend Max would point to it and shout in his Bronx accent, "Isn't she a beauty?"

Dusty's plays were all set in her native Tasmania and based on her eccentric family. Everyone loved her work. But there was a problem. Her characters were Tasmanian matrons, and apparently no actress in the nation's preeminent drama school was equipped to play them. While some faked a fair Down Under accent, few found the delicate trail of Dusty's wit.

It got worse in the workshops where writers cast each other. When we read Dusty's plays aloud in class, they sounded flat. We knew her work was good, but the comedy didn't show up. Then, one day, Dusty asked me to read a female lead. The first line I read got laughs, then the second and all that followed. They say a good comic knows what he's doing to earn each laugh. I took my best guess and played what was on the page. I suppose I'd dreamed of playing a middle-aged lady ever since I was a child staying up late to watch *The Benny Hill Show*. In my early teenage years, Benny Hill was God. Who else could play both Liz Taylor and Richard Burton in the same sketch?

> LIZ:*The doctor examined me all over today and said I had the body of a seventeen year old girl.*
> DICK: *Did he say anything about that big fat bum of yours?!*
> LIZ: *No! He didn't even mention your name!*

I doubt that Benny Hill's brand of drag offered comfort to young queens trapped in repressed communities. But Benny's big-breasted laughs and boyish approach to all things sexual freed the libidos of little straight boys everywhere.

I became Dusty's go-to-guy for female roles. This extended into the advanced workshops where student actors read our plays aloud. No one complained when I, a mere playwright, got plum roles in Dusty's readings. A large audience increased my confidence. Though I never studied voice, my enthusiasm sent the text to all corners of the room.

The apex of my collaboration with Dusty was reached when she claimed a thirty-minute slot in Yale's cabaret venue. The show was "Pageant Ladies", a farce about backstage machinations at a church pageant presented in honor of the Queen's first visit to Tasmania. Dusty gave me the leading role in her down-under *All About Eve* story.

In fact, all of the female roles were cast with men. We had Jomo Kifimbo, a six-foot-five, ex-college hoops star with proud North African features. He looked handsome enough, but no excess of cosmetics could make his face any more feminine than Ernest Borgnine's ass. We had Bart Barboza, a hairy Brooklyn guy with a toucan nose. Bart feigned an okay Tasmanian accent, but still sounded more New York than Pacific Islander. Then we had Blaine Arden, the only honest-to-God gay boy in the cast. Blaine was fond of sweets. It showed. He wasn't tall or pretty or athletic, but he had abundant humor and charm. He told mad stories about growing up gay in Savannah, Georgia. Blaine's parents sent him to military school hoping it would redirect his orientation. The chief form of punishment there was corporal. Rebellious students were ordered to lower their skivvies and then spanked with canoe paddles. Blaine would roll his eyes and say, "How anyone thought that would make this gaybird fly straight is beee-yond me!"

Sarah Jean Bailey, the single genuine female in the show, rounded out the cast. Sarah played Archie Biddle, the shy church handyman. Sarah was attractive, but it didn't take much make-up and loose clothing to draw out her masculine side.

It was great. I had the starring role, a colorful supporting cast, and between butch Sarah, burly Jomo, Bart's *shnozzola,* and Blaine's outsized ass, I was the prettiest fella in the show. This delighted me perhaps more than I should say.

The luckiest stroke occurred when Sally got cast in Ted Hinton's "Bemoan, Beweep, and Bewail". The Cabaret producers decided to pair a dark one-act with Dusty's comedy. Ted's piece was a muddled dirge about a housebound paraplegic who has strange dealings with sexy neighbors. I suppose there were psycho-sexual undertones at work, but a capable psychiatrist would be more interested than a cabaret audience. In any event, Sally had lots of lines, and we could kiss and squeeze each other backstage. There were hazards. She and I were prone to public fights and the not infrequent alcoholic binge. Hopefully we'd keep our cool, and not terrorize the cast and crew.

The time came for costume fittings. Not only would I wear a dress, but also a Malayan sarong. Our pageant celebrated all corners of the British Empire and the glory of God that graced it. An unfortunate moment occurred when Blaine emerged from the dressing room in his costume. He'd insisted on a pair of simulated breasts. The designer gave him a size 42 triple-EEE brassiere packed with puffed polyester. Blaine shook his fake knockers in our faces.

"Great tits," I joked. "She gave you a great ass too."

Blaine's smile disappeared and he rushed outside.

I felt awful. I'd forgotten how big Blaine's butt already was. Any padding there was God-given. Through a frosted window, I watched him puffing a Camel Light in the chill air. What could I do? Go after him in my dress and apologize? I could just see the pair of us on the steps, two fellas in women's clothes, one in tears, and the other saying, "I'm sorry, Blaine. I didn't mean it. Your ass isn't too big—it's beautiful!"

Later Blaine snuck back in. We made it through a dress rehearsal. I stepped on Jomo's lines and he corrected me. I respected his expertise. Still, when a towering athlete clutching a powder blue purse whispers advice in your ear, it's hard to stay composed. I promised it wouldn't happen again.

Sally's rehearsals weren't going so well. Ted didn't want to direct, so he'd asked an inexperienced young woman to take charge. She talked clever, but had never directed a play this side of high school. Ted's work boasted two *femme fatales*—my Sally, and Ms. Tatiana Egorova, a woman who'd played Chekhov to great acclaim on Moscow's grandest stages. Her facial expressions leapt from placidity to overarching passion in a flash. Russian accents are coarse on some tongues, but Tatiana's gentle lilt trilled as sweet as an Irish grandma's. She also had the calmest ice-blue eyes I'd ever seen. One long look from Tatiana and everyone started sobbing over lost cherry orchards. Sally feared getting upstaged, but there were no worries of that. The young director pushed and begged, but Ted's play sat like a flat rock in a puddle. The two divas stood by and watched while the playwright switched from beer to whiskey.

Speaking of whiskey, Sally and I indulged one night after rehearsal. Long days of rehearsing and classes wore us out. Sally suffered most. The acting program was a dawn-to-dusk boot camp that included daily instruction in dance, voice, speech, and scene study. Actors rehearsed for readings, workshops, and mainstage plays, where they understudied the union rep actors. Playwrights attended just three drama workshops that met once per week. The rest of the time we were supposed to write brilliant plays or lounge around dreaming them up. We had elective classes too. But professors outside the drama school treated us like visiting royalty, giving us easy grades.

Sally had also been cast in two concurrent productions with small spear carrier roles. Between both she had eight lines of dialogue. Ted's cabaret piece gave her more words, but not good ones. Meanwhile, I starred in a crowd-pleasing farce. And so, after our third, fourth, or perhaps seventh cocktail, Sally's eyes hardened. "Mister Big Shot," she grumbled. "You had to be a big shot. Remember that Billy Joel song?"

"Sure," I replied.

"Everybody hates me in this school," she said. "Hummmph. Well the feeling is mutual."

"Tit for tat," I said.

Sally snickered. "You don't even like my tits."

"I love them."

"Sure," she shouted. "Now that I'm all fat you love them! Now that they're all bloated and busting out everywhere! I can't be this fat! I can't!"

"You gained five pounds," I reminded her.

"You're the big star now and you don't even have tits!"

"I look good." I smiled.

"Oh, do you? So that's what all this is about? You think you're more gorgeous than I am, don't you?"

I hesitated while considering this, knowing it would irritate her immensely.

"Yeah! That's it! Mr. Pretty Boy! You with your sexy green eyes and cute blondie *face-illa*. You bastard. Say it. Tell me you think you're prettier than I am!"

I looked Sally in the eye. All this talk of tits made me horny. I started sweet-talking. "You're the most beautiful woman in the whole school. You have the sexiest lips and eyes, the most gorgeous body. You know it."

Sally moaned. "Then why won't anyone cast me in anything?!"

"You're too much woman for them. I don't know. It's only your first year here. They have to give you a lead sometime." I touched her as I said this and pulled her close. She wept on my shoulder. I set our drinks aside and didn't mention refills.

★★★

Opening night.

"Hello, dear," Bart trilled as I entered the dressing room.

The boys were primping. Bart hadn't shaved his wooly legs, but opaque hosiery hid his fur well enough.

"Hello, darlings," I said.

In a long lavender dress and a wild beaded bonnet, big Jomo looked like some rough downtown trade. It would take one brave freak to pull over and pick him up.

My dress glowed with blue and violet hues. My beige hat sported a pink band ringed with golden flowers. The cobalt shawl draped about my shoulders couldn't disguise my meaty deltoids.

Once fitted, I searched for Sally. I found her languishing on the stairwell above the theater. She was wearing a long green evening dress. The color shouted louder than an Irish-American inebriate at South Boston's Saint Patrick's Day Parade.

"How are you, beautiful?" I asked.

"Miserable. The play's a nightmare. Look at this dress."

I opened my arms. "Come here. Let's have some loving." She walked into my embrace. "That's it. Sock it to me, biscuit."

Sally's gloom lifted a little. She giggled.

"You look gorgeous," I said.

"I look green."

"On you, it's the dearest color in the world. You're springtime, a whole bright season in one sexy dress."

"Sweet talker," she said.

"Most women would look like a pool table in that thing. But you look like you stepped out of a technicolor musical. Like Maureen O'Hara. You're the most Irish Jewish girl I've ever seen. Besides, green is Kermie's color. Kermit the frog."

I felt an erection coming on. To proceed was unwise. It would be difficult to hide major wood under a polyester dress.

"You're such a guy," she said. "No dress can hide my man. You're my big guy. You know what that's like for a girl? To have my own big guy? I feel safe with you."

"Don't worry, babe. I can outfight and out-fuck every drag queen bitch in the building." I kissed and caressed her.

"No," she said. "Later."

"Why not?"

"Everybody's downstairs."

I tiptoed to the balustrade and looked down with trepidation. On the landing below stood the entire cast of Dusty's show. They'd heard our every word. What the hell. At least we were being nice to each other.

Bart winked when I came down. "Hey, Kermie."

My cast-mates snorted. Jomo popped his cheek with his tongue and said, "Every drag queen bitch in the building?"

Everybody laughed. I blushed. More laughs.

Jomo preened in my direction and held up his palm. We high-fived and snapped our fingers over our heads.

***

"Five minutes," shouted the stage manager.

I slipped backstage. A recorded church hymn faded. The lights fell to black. A capacity audience adjusted themselves in creaking chairs. I followed a trail of glow-tape to my mark. A spotlight rose on the back of my bonnet. I turned to face the light. Loud laughter. I still hadn't uttered a word.

Our twenty-five minute show seemed to fly by in ten. I could be shy to the point of paralysis offstage, but under the lights in a tight blue dress, I was fearless. The irony did not escape me. I'd come to Yale to write serious plays. Instead, I was prancing across the boards in pantyhose.

The play concluded with a monologue both smug and vulnerable. My diva character triumphed, but at what cost? She'd trampled her lifelong friends to reach the top. Fade to black. APPLAUSE. Lights up. I waited in the wings while my fellow players ran out to take their bows. I went last. More applause.

In the hot cramped dressing room, job one was to get out of sticky female clothes. But the doors flapped like hummingbird wings as well-wishers rushed in to shower us with praise.

An intense, intellectual actress named Samantha Pryor walked up and placed her face just inches from mine. She had furtive dark eyes and a body with tight, round, hot everything.

"You found her humanity," Samantha said. "The Widow Gibbons was vulnerable, sweet, but also lonely. You didn't condescend to the character.

We loved you out there."

"Thanks," I said.

Sally watched from across the room. So did Samantha's boyfriend, Bart Barboza.

Samantha touched my chest where I'd shaved my cleavage. She caressed razor stubble, small cuts, and tiny pink welts.

"Ooo," she said. "A little irritation here, I see."

If I were any kind of a man, I would have scheduled a ruthless tryst with Samantha. All the actors did it like rabbits. Life's short and only so many bunnies would hop my way. Samantha lingered a while longer, but I played the good boy. I'd have Sally to myself after I shed my dress. Sammy Pryor was trouble. She was dating Bart. I didn't need any more backstage drama or I'd have a real *All About Eve* story on my hands.

When the crowd left, Sally and I embraced.

"I'm so proud of you," she said. "You did such a good job. Everybody's talking about it."

"You were lovely tonight. Your timing was perfect."

Sally scoffed. "Please. I survived. You were the star."

She studied my face. "You know you're good, big guy."

We hugged. "I love you," she said.

"I love you," I said.

On our way home we detoured through the old campus. It was a cold, damp night in late autumn. Wet evenings with creeping mists brought out the enduring qualities of our centuries-old university. Sally and I looked for signs which might prove that our love would last longer than a few short semesters. The outward gloom rendered everything obscure and out of reach. Fog dulled the sharp towers and softened the glow of the fake gas lamps.

Sally and I held each other close while we walked. Nights like these made you believe in brilliant futures.

The first time I saw playwright Theodore "Teddy" K. Lee was at a party during the Drama School's "Welcome Week". He smiled a lot and would only drink a beer if others insisted. The beer became a prop in his hand which rarely met his lips. There was something raw about Teddy. His features were broad and flat, and he had the oddest pointed ears, more outer-Mongolian than Beijing businessman. He came from upstate New York, the son of immigrant but professional parents. He'd gone through prep school and Princeton before making his way into Yale. He liked hard rock music, graphic comic books, and dated a plump redhead from Wisconsin named Joanna Hansen. Joanna was a scholar who studied theatre history and dramaturgy, which meant she hovered around artists but wasn't accepted as one. She and Teddy never talked or touched while at parties, but always arrived and left together.

Most writers are shy and live larger lives on the page than in social exchanges. Teddy came across as too gentle to scare anyone. Even though he stood five eleven and square-shouldered and seemed very serious, his voice and gestures were small. He parted his hair on the side like a schoolboy. He wore small wire-rimmed spectacles. His cheeks always seemed to be unwashed, pink, and puffy. Seated in our writing workshops, Teddy would pull his NY Yankees baseball cap down low over his eyes and sink as deep into his chair as possible, as if drooping low enough might allow him to disappear through a secret trap door in the wooden floor.

On a cold winter day the playwrights-only Drama 2 class gathered to hear and critique Teddy Lee's newest play. We assembled our usual circle of fifteen writers and faced each other. Ted shyly passed out copies of his script, stopping to assign roles for individuals to read.

"Would you read Billy Clubb?" he asked me.

"Sure," I said.

"Thank you so much," said Teddy.

Billy Clubb?? *Who's playing Nancy Nightstick*, I asked myself. I'd soon find out. Oh, would I.

I don't know what I or anyone else expected from Teddy the day we read his play aloud. Perhaps his work would be polite, parceled into three well-made acts, and then embroidered with all the twenty-dollar words he amassed at Andover and Princeton? We were in for a surprise.

The themes were rape and domination. The first act contained a series of brutal attacks, in which a woman dressed as a man proceeds to rape men with a strap-on phallus. A few of the victims are dressed as women. After the attacks, two of the men cry. One becomes catatonic. Another, a sexist thug named Billy Clubb, seemed to enjoy being raped. Teddy assigned me that role and I played it to the strap-on's hilt.

"Oh! Oh yes! Fuck me, cruel mistress! Mommy!"

In a later scene, the tables are turned. The woman dressed as a man is ambushed by the men formerly dressed as women. One of the rapists shouts: *"Freak out with your prick out!"* After the brutes have run a rape train on her, the woman retreats into victimhood. She turns her violence inward, curses herself, and subjects her body to disturbing mutilations. Then her violence bursts outward again. She attacks her own female community. She rapes a meter maid who looks like her mother, as well as a virginal schoolgirl.

Some of the writers remarked that Teddy had courage.

"You're very brave," said Wendy Grushkin.

Others thought he might offend people.

Some, like me, withheld comment, thinking: *What the FUCK?*

***

Teddy K. Lee's provocative rape play *Rage Train* was slated for the first PCP (Playwright's Collaborative Project) slot that semester. For his politically incorrect, combustible play to succeed, it would need the most tough-minded talent available. Gutsy, original artists who could look past the play's sensational aspects and locate a core of humanity just *might* be able to save it. They could possibly even turn Teddy's freaky vision into something dynamic and undeniable.

Yes, this is always the hope of the playwright in a system that favors writers least. But too often the sodden donut crumbles and sinks to the bottom of the coffee. Then it's just empty seats, broken hearts and a lump of soggy crumbs in a mug.

One night, after indulging in a loud argument with Sally, a bad one that would require a night apart before makeup sex, I decided to go out for a drink by myself. I chose a tavern which was popular with actors because of its proximity to Yale Drama's theaters and rehearsal spaces. It offered lots of wooden booths and large tables. On weekends, Yale Drama students dominated the space. Since it was Monday, I figured it would be empty.

Who should I see at the bar but Teddy Lee. He was drinking draft beer out of a pint glass. I ordered bourbon on the rocks.

"Hi, Teddy. How's your show going?"

"Oh, it's...going...someplace, I guess."

"Drinking already?" I winked.

Teddy chuckled. "Just getting started."

"It's a great life if you don't weaken."

"Sure." Teddy smiled, but it was forced.

"You've got balls to put that out there," I said. "That play is a bombshell. I mean, I like that it's controversial, and I don't give a damn about it being politically incorrect. But your play, man, wow, that is wild stuff! You really go for it. All the way. If I wrote it, I'd go ahead and stage it. You write it, you step up and represent it, right? But I'd be nervous too. You know that some people are just going to hate it? I mean really hate it? You know that, right?"

"Umm. Yeah. I suppose," said Teddy.

"Can I get you a drink? What do you want?"

"What are you drinking?"

"Bourbon on the rocks. But this is a hundred proof. They pour hard here. You okay with that?"

"That's fine." Teddy smiled a sleepy smile. When his bourbon arrived, he took one small sip to assess the potency, then drained the whole glass.

"Whoa," I said.

"Sorry."

"Hey, it's your drink. Knock yourself out. Another?"

***

A week into *Rage Train*'s rehearsals, the Yale Women's Center learned of the play's rape theme. They quickly assembled a protest rally before even reading a word of the play. They issued a press release which the *Yale Campus News* published. A representative of the Women's Center read it aloud at the rally:

"We've been informed that this play *Rage Train* contains at least five violent acts committed against women. One out of six American women has been a victim of a rape, or an attempted rape. Globally, one in three women experience physical or sexual violence. These are your sisters, your mothers, your daughters. We find this unacceptable. Violence against women is at a crisis level. Those of us who have volunteered in rape crisis centers and battered women's shelters know this too well. We hope that the Yale School of Drama will reconsider this production. If they proceed with it, we will protest. We will stand up for women. We will stand up for victims. If the Drama School insists that this is a freedom of expression or censorship issue, and that they will stand behind this playwright's misogynist vision and fetish for violence, we hope that Yale Drama will provide time for a proper post-performance discussion. We hope that those responsible for this play will have the courage to confront an audience of women and listen to their concerns. Because these are life and death issues. Thank you all for your support."

The afternoon of the rally, I received a phone call from the *Yale Campus News*. A year earlier I'd offered them my services as a movie and theater critic. It landed me free tickets and extra writing practice. I'd met the caller, a kid named Willie "Skip" Whittaker, or something thereabouts, who happened to be the feature editor. He must have watched too many movies about reporters, because he ran around wearing a cheap straw hat, a seersucker blazer, and a red bow tie. The crazy kid also talked too fast, like Cary Grant in a Howard Hawks film.

"We want the skinny on the *Rage Train* play," said Skip. "You're a playwright, huh? So you must know the author? What's he like? Will he talk to you? Will he let you in to watch rehearsals? Do you think he'd give you an exclusive?"

I stopped Skip before he asked any more questions. "I know him. I had drinks with him just last week."

"Could you ask him if you can write a story?"

"You know that this is just a student play with a hundred-and-fifty dollar budget?"

"The way the Women's Center is barking at the moon, I think this play might be big news. If you write it, I'll run it. What do you say? Can I count on you? Can I?"

It felt like a mistake, but I said "Sure."

"Awesome sauce!" said Skip before hanging up.

I picked up my Yale Drama call sheet and phoned Teddy Lee. He found it flattering that someone would actually write a story about him. It seemed innocent enough, writing about a play in rehearsal. But it turned out that I needed the approval of the director, Todd Voorhees, and Dean Bill Michter, before I could enter the rehearsal space as an observer. Dean Bill even wanted a first read on the copy too, but I told him no. Benito Mussolini had nothing on Yale Drama's faculty. After a day of deliberation, Dean Bill gave me the thumbs up.

The director assigned to work with Teddy Lee was an officious West African man. His name was Oletun Osazuwa, Ollie to his peers. If he understood a play enough to be moved by it, he was competent. If he didn't, he took the path of least resistance: patronizing the writer, pampering the actors, and nodding robotically at whatever drawings, models, or costuming the volunteer designers unfolded in front of his face. Ollie only wanted to write, develop, and direct political plays about the tragic lives of everyday Africans. He wanted to bring plays about his homeland to all corners of the world. Yale was just a career move for him.

However, something about Teddy's gender-bent sexual violence energized the usually passive director. He sat Teddy down after the first reading and shared his feelings.

"This is an important play," began Oletun. "In my homeland, rape has become a tool of political terror and oppression. Why do men do such terrible things? I believe your play gives us a chance to explore this question."

Ollie had no clear stage concept, but searched for one. He consulted with Teddy. But Teddy couldn't say where his play sprang from, as if it were some afterbirth of his unconscious slapped to life and bawling for its misplaced mother. Without a solid concept, Ollie could only throw Teddy's bold images up on stage and hope they found form and stayed erect.

Speaking of erect things, the casting of the play's strap-on star became their only bit of luck. Rosalie Bryant was a wild, emotional actress who could steal any scene that wasn't bolted down and chained. Unfortunately, she was also super-sensitive and too easily wounded by criticism and gossip.

Teddy could comfort Rosalie when she was in a mood to be comforted, but couldn't come up with the first clue for how to deal with her when she got irrational, angry or loud. Ollie got results from Rosalie with basic politeness, firmness and compassion. He possessed a radical and unshakable empathy which he'd brought with him from his war-torn African homeland. He tried to get answers and inspiration from Teddy, but the playwright grew more shy and withdrawn as rehearsals progressed.

Sometimes Rosalie arrived in a contemplative mood. She cornered the director and writer with questions about the play's overall arc, her character's objectives and super-objective. Ollie confronted Teddy. "What makes a woman want this kind of revenge? Why doesn't she run away or hide or try to forget?"

"I don't know," said Teddy, waving his arms.

"There must be a core...some spark in her character...some event that made her a wild warrior instead of a weak victim?"

"I don't know," said Teddy, turning away.

"Ms. Bryant needs to know," said Ollie. "She will have to find these answers with or without you."

Teddy attended all the rehearsals, but offered little help. He kept his distance from the stage. The back row wasn't far back enough for him. If he could have crawled into the back of the theatre and peered out through two holes in the wooden paneling, he still wouldn't have felt safe.

As a playwright, I recognized Teddy's terror. I often felt fearful, defensive, and gripped by a fight-or-flight urgency when confronted by relentless questions from faculty and peers. Skilled theatre artists ask practical questions about what a scene offers and how to play it. But insecure detractors wanted to psychoanalyze or pigeonhole a writer and his/her creations. They got personal. *Where did this come from*, they'd ask. *How could you write this? How do you know people like this?* The impulse was salacious and disparaging, not creative.

But I can't speak for the inscrutable Teddy K. Lee. He must have just had thinner skin than most.

By contrast, Rosalie could be as sporty as a Roman gladiator in rehearsals. She gamely wore the strap-on vibrator, and giggled with both her male and female co-stars during the succession of simulated rapes.

"OKAY, BOYS. READY TO GET RODE HARD AND PUT AWAY WET?" shouted Rosalie like a drag queen Henry the Fifth as she strutted in after a break. She was a very pretty woman, but the sight of her with that strap-on was devastating. Whatever crush I once had on her dissipated.

After the first rehearsal I approached Teddy. "You know, Teddy. I think this could work. As crazy as this play is, it's got mystery, real darkness, and a strange momentum that's hard to dismiss. It's like somebody's nightmare sprung to life. Just when you think the violence is exploitation, you're surprised, almost touched. It's hard to describe, but it's got its own dream logic and inevitability, even its own truth."

My praise seemed to make Teddy nervous. He chewed his lower lip. "Thanks," he blurted out, before backing away and leaving the rehearsal hall.

Ollie gave precise directions to Rosalie: "The phallus must be up and out. Hips forward. Buttocks tucked and tense. Lower your diaphragm. Breathe deep. Shout! Shout loud like a man! Walk like you have a real penis. You must create the anger and violence of a man. This is not just penis envy. This is penis revenge! Treat your phallus as if it were a deadly weapon ripped from the hands of your worst enemy!"

Ollie's tone was as direct as a policeman's. Rosalie might be totally untethered and bouncing off the ceiling, but Ollie kept both feet on the ground. He seemed to wear Rosalie down with his persistent instructions.

Teddy experienced a brainstorm halfway through rehearsals: he came up with a completely new ending. He rushed into rehearsal the next day with brand new pages. His hands trembled as he gave them to Ollie. He was giddy.

Ollie read the new scene with care, and then began to nod his head. "Very good. Yes. This is the ending we needed."

Basically, the new ending went like this: after an epiphany of sorts, the protagonist locks her sights on her male attackers and, one by one, takes her revenge. She corners the last male rapist in his family home and binds him to a chair with duct tape. But she has somehow misplaced her strap-on. What to do without her plastic sword? After some foreplay, she is still able to rape the man because he is helplessly priapic with a perpetual erection.

"Say "Fuck me!" Say "FUCK ME!" she commands.
"Fuck me. Fuck ME!" the man hollers between moans.
She rides and rides him as the lights fade to black.

Not surprisingly, the male actor whom Rosalie would sit and bounce on liked the new ending.

The only person not thrilled with the scene was Rosalie.

Ollie called the cast together to read through the scene immediately. There was some haggling over the nudity required.

"Excuse me. But I need to be wearing something," Rosalie demanded.

She scoffed at the idea of a body suit. "I don't want people to even *think* that I'm naked!" When Teddy suggested a dominatrix costume, Rosalie almost blew her top. "What are you guys going to write next, a scene with a donkey in Tijuana?"

The actor whom Rosalie's character would mount and ride suggested a Catholic schoolgirl skirt.

All the males in the room nodded.

Rosalie waved her hand. "Whatever."

They began rehearsing the scene. Only halfway through it, Rosalie stopped and sat down in the center of the stage.

"What's the matter?" asked Ollie.

Rosalie just shook her head back and forth.

"Please talk to me, Rosalie. I can't help you if I don't know what's going on. Please," begged Ollie.

"I feel ridiculous up there," Rosalie confessed.

"You must take yourself seriously. Art is a serious job."

Rosalie sobbed. Teddy left the rehearsal hall again.

"He is a weak man who wrote a strong play. This is how it is with writers. A sensitive man feels a powerful truth that no one else can see, say, or write down."

"I don't think I can do this," said Rosalie.

"If you quit now, you will feel even less strong later. Sometime in the future when you need strength, you will remember how you gave up today, and you will give up again. I was scared to leave Africa. I was afraid to follow my dreams. I almost left the airport before my flight boarded. But I went to London. I went to America. I will see the whole world! Be strong! You are an artist! Artists make apologies to no one!"

"Okay. Okay." Rosalie wiped her eyes, and then jumped when she heard the hall door open.

Oletun looked up as two chatting actors strolled in.

"THIS IS A CLOSED REHEARSAL! YOU MUST LEAVE! NOW!" shouted Oletun in a bad-ass Shaka Zulu voice. I'd seen a lot of brothers pull the scary-black-man act back in the Boston public schools, but never a native African. Ollie was the best.

"Oh, sorry," said the intruders as they disappeared.

Ollie pointed at me. "And you too! You must go! Rehearsals will be closed from now on. My actors need my care and protection. They need a safe place to explore."

"Thanks, Ollie," said Rosalie wiping her tears.

Teddy crept back into the room when it seemed that Rosalie's crisis had subsided.

I fought an urge to stay and listen through the door, but feared that Ollie might catch me.

ANOTHER NIGHT
IN PARADISE

Because Melvin was Sally's pot connection and classmate, I tolerated him. He and I sat waiting in the lobby of the Yale Repertory Theatre wearing black and white usher's outfits.

The lobby was bright and tidy, and decked out with red carpeting, a chandelier and two trophy cases full of theatrical awards. It offered comfortable seating for guests, but often grew cold because of doors that swung open. Most patrons retrieved their tickets from the box office before the show. Each entrance and exit sucked just a little more heat outdoors.

Sally arrived late. She joined us wearing a white angora sweater which made her look like a fluffy indoor cat. She sat in my lap. The house manager scowled when she saw the unsorted programs lying on the carpet near our feet. I snatched up some programs and stuffers and got us started. Melvin reached down for a few, too. Sally stayed put.

Melvin's mother was a blonde Atlanta belle who married a light-skinned black academic back in the Sixties. The marriage didn't last. Melvin endured. Like most of the bright yellow characters in academia, he was acutely aware of his blackness.

Ever since forced busing in the 1970s, my hometown of Boston developed a reputation. The news media portrayed the city's white underclass as rabid bigots. Because of this, Melvin felt compelled to subject me to endless litmus tests every time we met. *Hey, Rob, what do you think of Affirmative Action? Do you agree that today's prison industrial complex is an extension of the old plantation system? You ever date a sistah? Would you marry one?* My answers were neither provocative nor patronizing, but always left him wanting more.

"I'm going to supper with the folks down at The House tonight," Melvin would announce to any white classmates within earshot. *The House* was shorthand for Yale's Afro-American Center. If it wasn't supper with the folks, Melvin would be off to a black solidarity conference, a West Indies steel drum celebration, or some Christian Soul Fellowship Fish Fry.

When I smirked at Melvin's public proclamations, he'd squint at me. I thought about grabbing him by the arm: *Please, Melvin, stay and eat with us tonight. You know you're more European than African! Come celebrate your whiteness!*

Sally leaped out of my lap and onto her feet. "I have to rehearse a Strindberg scene with Prentice. You fellas can sort these programs, can't you?" She left. We didn't protest. Melvin grew up a mama's boy and did what women told him to do.

Sally didn't have any straight male friends, but she rehearsed with her male co-stars all the time. When you dated an actress, it came with the territory. She was always playing some man's wife in a Strindberg, Chekhov, or Ibsen scene. Sally also met with Melvin to smoke joints and discuss old school rap music. I had no doubt that Melvin wanted to get into her pants, but that wasn't what bugged me: it was his supply of dime bags. Sally and marijuana did not mix. She already took fistfuls of prescription pills and drank like a crew of Polish sailors. Add cannabis to the mix and she became difficult, bouncing between extremes of paranoia, persecution, and unbridled bitchiness.

To avoid Melvin, I vigorously stuffed programs.

"Hey, Rob," Melvin said.

Uh-oh, I thought. *He's talking.* Melvin had a cuddly quality when quiet. The problem was that he never shut up.

"So check it out. I've got an idea. I think a cat like you would dig it. You're a big strong man. I know you would enjoy a chance to explore this kind of hyper-masculine territory."

Jesus, I thought. *Is this muppet making a pass at me?*

"What it is, Rob, is I got this idea for a play."

After a long pause, I broke down and asked, "What is it?"

"Do you know about Joe Louis?"

"Yeah. Heavyweight Champ 12 years. Longest reign ever."

"Was it 12?" Melvin asked.

"He beat Jimmy Braddock to win the belt and finally lost to a young Marciano, when Joe was old and burnt out from cocaine. He fought exhibitions for the Army during World War II. But the IRS harassed him the rest of his life for back taxes. He lived in a mental institution for a while. Paranoid delusions."

Melvin raised his eyebrows. "So you know about him?"

I glanced down the stairwell, hoping Sally would rescue me. Guests arrived. Melvin and I stood up and passed out programs like a pair of Jesus pamphleteers. He pitched me his idea for a play about the famous black boxer about whom he knew nothing.

"First, you write it," said Melvin. "Then I'll read your drafts and give notes. I'll play Joe, 'cause I look like him. A trainer will teach me how to box like DeNiro in *Raging Bull*."

"So I do all the writing and you do all the acting?"

"Yeah. That's it. Perfect. And maybe we can throw in a romance? Like with Joe Louis's wife? Or a mistress?"

"Marva Trotter? Or Sonja Henie?" I asked.

"Who?" Melvin asked with a squint.

"Trotter was his wife. Sonja Henie was a Norwegian figure skater he had an affair with. Henie dated Tyrone Power too."

"Wow. White girl, huh? Tyrone was black too?"

I said nothing. If he didn't know Tyrone Power was a white movie idol, it would be too much to explain. In Melvin's defense, he was only twenty-three. At twenty-eight, I knew little about a lot of subjects myself. But I wasn't asking anyone to write a full-length play for me to star in.

I knew about boxing because of my dad and grandfather, both boxing fans, plus my childhood barber Sal D'Mazzio who, to paraphrase a famous movie, *"coulda been a contender"*. Sal was a scary barber, but his boxing talk was smart. Many times Sal nicked my tender young ears with his scissors. If a styptic pencil couldn't stanch the flowing blood, Sal would break out a vial of epinephrine and demonstrate his skills as a cut man. Then he'd slap me on both shoulders and shout, "There you go, champ! Ready to go three more rounds! For the title!"

As Melvin went on talking, I thought about him in the role of the mighty Joe Louis. The Brown Bomber possessed a perfect physique and power with either hand, jolting power he could deliver from any angle. The only thing that Joe could not do, which Sugar Ray Robinson could, was fight while moving backwards. But that didn't matter. Moving forward, Joe steamrolled his challengers. Joe's trainers had to retain twenty sparring partners because he kept knocking them all out. Joe survived the racism of his time by making a show of politeness and piety. White male boxing fans put aside their prejudice and became addicted to his immaculate violence. To the public, Joe Louis appeared to be a humble, married Christian man who supported our soldiers. But in the privacy of gangster hotels, he used cocaine, shot craps, and backed many a starlet onto the bed springs. When he went to work in the ring, he had an icy shine in his eyes, like a tomcat toying with a crippled bird.

The only thing Melvin and Joe had in common was light skin.

"Did Joe Louis fight any black fighters?" Melvin asked.

"Jersey Joe Walcott, Ezzard Charles, Jimmy Bivins...." Before Melvin could say another word, I raised my hand. "Look," I said. "This sounds good. I'm flattered. But I've got my own projects. Writing a Joe Louis piece on spec, with me doing all the work, that's too much." I took a breath. "It's a great idea. For *somebody*. If you're that passionate about it, maybe this is something you need to work on yourself. I'll give you feedback. If you decide to put some effort into it, I'm happy to help."

Melvin looked hurt, then angry. He didn't say another word.

After the final curtain fell, we threw open the doors. After the audience left, we entered the messy theatre and stooped to pick up abandoned programs, ticket stubs, empty water bottles, used Kleenex and other assorted trash. When Melvin and I were finished, Sally appeared. Her eyes gleamed red and smoky.

"Enter Ophelia," I said.

She raised an eyebrow. "More like Juliet."

Melvin stood up. *"Arise, fair sun and kill the envious moon, for thou art far more fair than she!"*

She smiled. "See. He knows."

Melvin grinned and bowed, happy to have upstaged me, the little gold-toned ponce.

As we walked Melvin to his place, he and Sally started rapping together, something about Biz Markie and *The Vapors*. I felt like a dad out with his two noisy kids. When we reached his stoop, Melvin nodded and said, "Peace."

I had Sally to myself again. As we approached her apartment, she asked, "So what did you guys talk about?"

"You," I said. "What else?"

She giggled.

When we got upstairs, we drank some tequila, lit up some of her new stash, and got naked. The envious moon watched us through the window. There was a furtive look in Sally's eye. I took another toke and hoped for the best.

***

I forget how it started, but sometime in the wee hours I found my hand wrapped around Sally's throat. We had stayed up half the night drinking, toking, laughing, loving, and fighting. She may or may not have taken her before-bedtime pills.

If Sally's father knew that I'd had my hand around his little girl's throat at three in the morning, I would have been in big trouble. Sally adored her father. His wealth and protection had been the only rock in her insecure young life. I'd read somewhere that women who loved their fathers always made the best girlfriends, and that, conversely, a woman who hated her father should be avoided.

I didn't hate Sally, though it seemed I might strangle her.

She'd become hysterical and began shouting. She couldn't stop shouting. She kept mad-dogging me, lunging, shoving, grabbing and shaking me. It grew loud enough to wake our neighbor, a working nurse, who pounded the wall with her fists.

No two year-old could bring a better tantrum than Sally. There was no rhyme, reason, or single target for her rants. She barked stuff like: "*Fucking one-way cocksuckers! This cocksucking school for motherfuckers! It's a cocksucker clusterfuck! Full of pigs, fat horse cunts, and mean one-way faggots! PIGSTOCK! A fricking pig farm! You hate me! They hate me! Everyone hates me! Nobody will cast me! The faculty just wants to fuck me! You want to fuck me! Everyone's a cocksucking pig on fucking clusterfuck pig farm! PIGSTOCK! I can't bear it! I can't bear it anymore! I cant! I CAN'T!!!*"

Damn, I thought, *this shouting might bring the police.*

She was oblivious. She kept heaving her torso at me. With a dramatic flourish she slapped me across the mouth. I took it. It must have turned me on. She was like a Jack in the box that kept springing back up in my face, or maybe one of those slithering creatures with the snapping eggplant head from the *Alien* movies. Her teeth dripped acid. The spray burned holes in my skin.

"Listen," I shouted. "I'm not your rubber room! You can't bounce all your insane shit off me whenever you feel like it!"

Months before, Sally laughed the first time I said this. She repeated it to her mother on the phone. "Robert yelled at me last night. He said, '*I'm not your rubber room!*'"

Her mother found this hilarious and took to repeating it in messages left on Sally's answering machine. "I'm not your rubber room! He really knows you, doesn't he?"

The next time Sally coiled to spit her venom, I reached for her throat. I needed to hold her away, so I could take a look and determine whether this pouncing apparition was indeed my girlfriend and not some jungle succubus out to devour my spirit.

She got quiet. I took my hand away from her throat.

"You tried to choke me," she said in a low voice.

"I didn't even squeeze. Are there bruises on your neck?"

"There better not be."

"Is anything sore?" I touched her neck with my fingertips. "See. You're unmarked. You know I'd never try to hurt you."

"You want to put your hands around my throat every time you see me. You probably want to choke me when we have sex."

"I don't think so."

"You know you can't stand me!"

"I love and adore you. Now come on. Haven't we had enough fun? Let's get some sleep and start over in the morning."

"You'll strangle me in my sleep with my own underwear."

"You're safe with me."

"Safe!" she scoffed. She couldn't have been too worried because she fell asleep before I did.

The next day we both woke up close to noontime.

"You tried to choke me last night," was the first thing she said. "I'll never forget that you did that."

"I'm sorry. You know I'd never really want to hurt you."

She turned her back to me. I hugged her close, caressed her body, nuzzled and kissed her wherever I could. When she responded to this, I rubbed the length of her legs.

"Can I ever make it up to you?" I tugged at her panties.

"Never."

"You're still my lover girl, aren't you?"

She shrugged her shoulders again. "One of these days you'll chop me up into little pieces."

"What would I do with all those little pieces? I don't even own a dog I could feed you to."

"You'd buy one special."

"I'm the only one in the doghouse," I said.

"Yup."

MARS NEEDS MENTORS

I had written a family drama about a family I did not understand: mine. Without the benefit of a psychiatrist or a priest, I attempted to probe the mess of my early home life, the mysteries of a mentally ill dad, younger siblings I barely spoke to, and the faded memories I had of my late mother. The current draft read like second-rate Eugene O'Neill, or maybe "Married with Children" as written by Samuel Beckett, without the laugh track. I wrote sharp scenes and characters, but created precious few scenes with true psychological insight.

I portrayed my dad as a down-to-earth, broken-hearted guy. He was a shot-to-shit god puttering about his own ruined world, or maybe a failed hero without a cause. I probably endowed dad with more dignity than he deserved. The dad I wrote came across as a sort of jobless Prospero walking around his shabby house waving an antique German army rifle instead of a magic staff. In real life, Dad resembled Caliban more than Prospero, except without any real rage or fight in him. My dad was a loser's loser descended from a long line of loser's losers. The Poles had all worked themselves to death in the worst jobs available. And Hell, one of our oldest Scottish ancestors had failed with a brewery business up in Nova Scotia. How the hell do you fail with a brewery? But I still needed to mythologize my dad somehow, perhaps because I felt he was a lot less phony than anyone on the Yale faculty.

Whatever the case, I had completed yet another play that didn't work. Instead of keeping my troubles to myself as I usually did, I decided to make appointments with all of my playwriting professors to see if they could help me.

I walked into adjunct professor Danny Mangold's temporary office hoping for advise. The shared space had no individual decorations. Several visiting artists and scholars used it. Their assigned office hours were posted on the front door.

Danny wore a shawl-collared cardigan with bright black and white designs that looked like a cubist's depiction of a zebra.

"Nice sweater," I said.

"Thank you!"

"A present from your wife?" I asked.

"Yes," he said with a smile. His spectacles were small and round, and made him first appear like a timid bookkeeper, even though he was an artist and a fierce intellectual committed to exploring his Jewish heritage. He enjoyed a successful career as a contemporary playwright and screenwriter. His dramas thrived Off Broadway and on the regional theater circuit. His wife worked as a specialist at the Yale New Haven hospital. Now that Danny had built a fine reputation as a script doctor in Hollywood, I was sure both he and his wife lived very well.

Danny wrote what I would call "I Fucked a *Shiksa* and Liked It" plays. His major characters were always Jewish people who mixed with non-Jews with unwelcome results. At one point in all his plays, a stern rabbinical/father figure would point at the protagonist and say *"What do you know about being a Jew?!"*

It seemed to me that Phillip Roth, Mordecai Richler, and boatloads of other Jewish scribblers had already written hundreds of novels and plays about this sex-obsessed assimilation dilemma. Sally told me it was a cultural thing that I didn't understand. Danny's plays were okay in that solid, well-made sort of way. I just never wanted to see one twice. However, the critics praised Danny's work. Just this year, he'd made it onto the shortlist for the Pulitzer Prize. He had concurrent productions in New York, London's West End, Canada, Australia, and regional theaters all across the United States. He recently declined production offers in Israel because he feared terrorists and bombs. Pussy.

Danny Mangold handed my family drama back to me. "Very good writing," he said. "The scenes are skillfully written. The grandfather character is impressive." After a pause, he added, "I think it's time for you to start writing your next one."

This puzzled me. "You mean I shouldn't keep working on it?"

"Well," he said, adjusting his sweater. "I don't know how you can fix this play."

"You don't?"

"No."

It reminded me of the old New England joke, in which a lost driver stops for directions in upstate Maine. He asks some locals at a gas station, *"What's the best way to get to Augusta?"* After some head-scratching, one of the locals turns to the driver and says: *"Yuh cah-n't get they-uh from he-ah-re!"*

Danny sensed my confusion. "Don't take this play so seriously."

"But it's my family," I said.

"I know," he said. "What I'm saying is that the work it would take to fix this play would be better spent on something new. You've got all the tools: dialogue, strong characters, your own unique voice. Perhaps you should take all of that and invest it in a fresh story. Maybe your next piece is where you'll really break through."

"But this play is scheduled for a production in one month."

"And I'm sure it will be a very fine production and that you will learn a lot from it. Think process, not product."

I lowered my eyes and stared into the crazy patterns of Danny's sweater. It was the only dynamic artwork in the room, certainly more fresh and daring than my family drama. Danny had a gentle but superior smile. His glasses made him look wise and paternal. But now I felt more patronized than parented. I felt like the town drunk getting a lecture from his parish priest: *All right, my son. You'll see what I mean when you sober up.*

"But I don't think this play is finished," I said.

"No play is ever finished. You simply decide to stop working on it. This is a play you needed to write. You wrote it. It's done. Don't be afraid to move on."

"Why should I have to move on? I followed an impulse writing this play. It took me somewhere. Maybe not far enough, but I still think I can get there. I don't know. I was hoping for some advice, a little revision strategy or something."

Danny shook his head. "Only you know the original impulse. It's your life. But I think you have even bigger stories to tell." Danny smiled again, not in a mean or condescending way, but confidently and comfortably. He believed that he knew something I didn't. Maybe he did. But I thought he could have shared more with me. Or maybe he could have at least gifted me with a clue. Don't all magic trolls at bridge crossings give the seeker a secret riddle as he follows his quest? This troll just sat there like a little prince in a loud sweater pulling his precious opinions out of his tight turtle sphincter.

"Thanks," I stood up and left.

I'd become so desperate for advice that I even made an appointment with my nemesis: Playwriting Chair Todd Voorhees. His secretary escorted me into his office, which had all the charm of a police interrogation room. Voorhees sat behind his desk looking as prim and officious as J. Edgar Hoover. He'd recently lost thirty pounds, and now parted his fluffy, feather-cut white hair in the middle. He looked like an intense grade school boy with a rare disease that had prematurely aged him.

"Robert! Sit! At last we meet!"

I'd avoided Voorhees for most of my second year. Now in my third, I allowed him to corner me a few times in the hallways to unload his opinions. He didn't like actual conversation or Q & A. He preferred to rattle off a grocery list of all his most important thoughts while I just sat there and listened.

"Now, Robert. This piece suffers from all the pitfalls of family drama. Here on page one, take look at this. I think you're better than this..." He launched into a fifteen minute, blow-by-blow dissection of every poor choice in my play.

After his critical aria had reached its finale, I paused. "That's all cosmetic," I said, drawing an instant frown from him. "I can cut this or that, change this cliché into something fresher, or switch a dirty word for a clean one, or maybe throw in some extra abstract weirdness for a surprise. That's easy. But the problem, the central problem, you know, whether the play stands up and holds its own ground, or collapses, well...I still feel alone on that one. I mean, Danny Mangold wants me to chuck the play altogether and start my next one."

"He might have point."

"Damn. I thought I'd written a serious play about my family, but no one seems to take it seriously but me."

It angered Voorhees that I would not swallow his wisdom like medicine. "Don't you feel nurtured in this program?"

"Nurtured?"

He explained how he believed playwriting should be taught, even though he was a dramaturge, and had never written. My eyes glazed over. I became sorry that I'd made the appointment.

Well, I couldn't connect with either Voorhees or Mangold. But fortunately I found at least one faculty member who appreciated my plays and championed them in class.

Daniel "Duke" Kinderman wrote theatre reviews for a couple of national magazines. He'd published well-regarded books of theatre criticism. Fellow critics and academics acknowledged him as the preeminent American expert on the plays of Anton Chekhov.

After the first draft of my play about the mayor of Boston was read, Duke stood up and spoke to me.

"Robert, the difference between this play and that terrible Hollywood play you first showed us are enormous. I have some criticisms, but overall, this is fine work. At present the play is overwritten. That's why the class has run overtime. But you can always cut out the crap and put in more good stuff. Please come and see me in my office and let's talk about it some more."

Duke Kinderman was a Brooklyn Jew whose father worked as a labor organizer in the 1930s. Though his parents had good educations, they had little money, and Daniel grew up with lower class boys whose respect he needed to earn with his fists, an agile mind, and a wise-ass mouth. His dad couldn't buy him good clothes, but somehow found money for his tuition at Brooklyn College, where he studied English. There the Duke began to indulge his lifelong obsessions with literature and women.

I saw that his door was open, stuck my head in, and knocked. The Duke's office was decorated with his own books and memorabilia. Bookcases dominated the walls top to bottom. A huge wooden desk took up half the available floor space. He sat in an old-fashion wooden chair with leather padding.

"Have you read all these books," I asked.

"Yes. I've had a little more time to read than you."

I took a seat opposite his desk.

"Was that your girlfriend I saw you with this morning?" asked the Duke as he opened his desk and pulled out a bottle of Jameson whiskey. He winked at me. "My office bottle, like Detective Marlowe." He didn't offer me any.

"Yeah. Her name's Sally Garfinkle. She's an actress."

"Pretty. You lasted a whole year with her, huh?" He held his bottle up to the window to examine its contents. Sunlight glinted off his thick, horn-rimmed glasses, brightening his white beard and thick silver eyebrows. He had a sweeping gray comb-over which started an inch and a half above his left ear.

"Yeah. So far so good."

He squinted as he poured a single into a juice glass, recapped his bottle, and stashed it back into his desk. "I prefer Irish sometimes. Scotch can taste too peaty."

I would have accepted a glass of either, but it was just as well he didn't offer. Better that I listened while the Duke sipped and talked about women and art and women.

In the bookcase beside his desk, I saw the title *Glory Days of Burlesque,* authored by The Duke himself.

"You wrote a book on burlesque?"

"Yes. Good reviews. But it didn't sell."

This worried me. I remember how much he liked my Boston Mayor play. I'd thrown many burlesque elements—broad sexual innuendo, bawdy gestures, male-oriented humor—into that. Did I write dirty old plays for dirty old men?

"I didn't see you with a girlfriend your first year."

"Yeah. My first year was rough. Nothing worked out."

"It never works out. But you can't waste time on disappointments. I've always had a girlfriend. Always! Ever since I was seven years old. If one fails me, I find a new one in two days or less. I don't waste time pining or regretting or wondering what might have been. I never think it's my own fault. I'm the hero of my romantic life! One time I found myself impotent with a woman half my age. She gave me that look. You'll see that look someday. You know what I told her?"

"What did you tell her?"

"'*It must be your fault, sweetheart. This never happened with my last girlfriend, or my wives, or with any of the ladies before. It has to be you,*' I told her with my own frown. She didn't like that one bit. Some women will accuse you of being gay when you can't get it up. I'm non-violent, but I know fellas who'd smack a woman who said that. Anyway, I found a new woman in two days and had no problems with my equipment whatsoever."

Towards the end of our meeting the Duke and I did finally talk about my play a bit. He gave me a short list of cosmetic notes about what could be improved or cut. I left his office feeling almost as empty as I had when I'd left the others.

I went home to my apartment and telephoned my dad.

"Hi, Dad. What's new with you?"

"I'm restoring an old Colt army revolver. A real trench gun from World War I with a lanyard ring! Quite a big hog-leg for close combat in the mud. This one was a real junker. Rusted solid. Some guy found it in a box of tools in his basement and gave it to me for nothing. How are you? How's school?"

"I've written a new play. But it's not finished. I'm not sure how to fix it. Nobody on Yale's esteemed faculty seems to be able to help me."

"Well, good writing can't be easy. If it was, everyone would be doing it. You know, I always wanted to be a writer," Dad said. "I used to read all those paperback westerns, and I thought, *I could do that*. I could...if I knew the land. You've got to know the land. It's part of knowing what you're talking about. The good writers always traveled and learned the land. Joseph Conrad, Mark Twain, Kipling. You know, Louis L'Amour camped out all over the west before he wrote stories about it. It's good to travel some, see the pretty places, do your thinking. I think you've got to enjoy life somehow. No reason why you shouldn't."

I heard the click of a gun's hammer over the line.

"Success!" Dad announced. "I remembered an old trick. Used to do it down at the mill. Cleans gunked up machinery real quick. It'll even unblock toilets. Got to be careful though. What you do is pour acid through the action real fast. Then right after, flush it out with water. The water's important. You forget the water, you'll end up with a piece of scrap."

I heard two more dry-fire trigger clicks over the line.

"Well, it's a gun again," he said. I could hear the smile in his voice. "Shame I can't put some blue on the steel or varnish the grips. But it wouldn't be an antique then, wouldn't be history. A little oil and wax maybe. That's okay. Hell, maybe I'll load it up and fire it someday. Got to go light on the gunpowder. Don't want it to blow up in my hand, you know? You know, I never did shoot anybody. Not once in my whole life. Plenty of people I'd like to shoot. But they never seem to come knocking on my front door. Maybe I'll stop paying my taxes—that's what I ought to do. Someone will come for sure then."

"Yeah. You be careful with that, Dad," I said. "Glad you got your gun fixed. Have a good night."

"Good night, Bob. Take it easy."

As soon as I hung up, my phone rang. It was Sally.

"When the hell are you going to get call waiting?!"

"Why do I need it? The only people I ever talk to are you, or my dad. Can't you wait five minutes?"

"No! So when are you coming over?"

"I'm coming over?"

"Yes, you are. You're coming over right now," she said in a lush bouncy voice that made me see her silky bare behind wagging like happy hound's tail.

"Okay. But give me twenty minutes. I've got to write something first," I said.

"A whole twenty minutes?!"

"Yeah. I need to write it while it's fresh in my head."

After I hung up, I sat down and wrote down what my father had just said about paperback westerns, travel, and gun repair. I underlined my dad's sentence: "*I always wanted to be a writer.*" It sounded like his blessing, as if being a writer was a good thing, and I was living a dream he'd always had, but kept hidden. "*I always wanted to be a writer.*" Yeah. Thanks, Dad. I felt glad that I'd called him. This speech would create a nice little moment near the end of the play between father and son.

I still didn't know how to fix the whole damn script, or whether fixing it would become too big a bridge to cross. In any event, the faculty would cast and stage it in less than one month. I didn't think it would bomb, but doubted it would blow anyone away either, certainly not Todd Voorhees, or Danny Mangold. Oh, well. Bad theater can break your heart, but nobody ever died from it. A playwright is not a brain surgeon, or a race car driver. No one dies if you make a mistake.

I printed out the page, then rushed over to Sally's.

IDENTITY POLITICS, THE WOEFUL TALE OF TEDDY K. LEE PART II

As the final production dates for Teddy Lee's *Rage Train* drew nearer, the Women's Center stepped up their campaign. Every day, young women handed out leaflets in front of the rehearsal hall and carried signs in front of Yale Drama's business offices. Pretty soon Yale's LGBT Center also became involved.

A handful of culturally-sensitive Yale Drama actresses joined in the YWC/YLGBT protest, including our vulnerable Rosalie, female star of the rape play in question. The Women's Center appealed to her to quit the play. Rosalie refused. She compromised by attending group discussions. But trouper that Rosalie was, she always abandoned the Women's Center and LGBT groups in time for her rehearsal calls. The Gs, Bs, and Ts understood. The lesbians were less forgiving. Men, mostly gay, attended these protests too, and also a few straight allies. The signs they toted had slogans like:

> WOMEN <u>CAN'T</u> BE RAPISTS
> WOMEN WHO SUBMIT TO SEX TO PLEASE MEN ARE
> RAPE VICTIMS
> ZERO TOLERANCE
> SILENCE = DEATH
> I LOVE STRONG WOMEN!

Exactly one week before the opening, a protest march assembled in front of the drama school, then marched across campus to a large music hall where the school's various glee clubs and musicians routinely performed.

Radicals from New York City and Boston took the train in to New Haven. Women's Studies professors from Harvard, Brown, and Princeton showed up. Old lesbians with gray ducktail haircuts and faces like Robert Blake, Henry Kissinger, and Harrison Ford arrived. Transvestite and transgendered men also made a show of support. Some were so pretty you wouldn't have to be very drunk to get fooled. Like church matrons decked out in beaded bonnets and glittering dresses, they used the demonstration as an opportunity to flaunt their grandest fashions.

I heard one homeless, toothless old black woman remark: "Damn, a whole lot of trick-or-treat bitches out today."

The Women's Center billed the discussion a "Cross-gendered, Inter-oriented, Culturally-sensitive Call for Peace."

Oletun cancelled rehearsal that day because he wanted to attend the discussion and seize his opportunity to speak.

Teddy reluctantly attended.

Rosalie had a panic attack and could not be located.

I got there early and scouted around for a good seat. The domed ceilings and stained-glass windows impressed me. The acoustics were amazing. As I descended marble stairs into the auditorium, I could hear my footsteps echoing in all corners of the hall. The pipes of an enormous piano organ dominated the back of the stage. A good concert would be a lot more fun than what I expected to witness this afternoon.

On stage, several butch women adjusted microphone stands and speaker systems. A few of Yale's student actresses were in attendance. No Sally. When I'd asked her if she'd like to go, she replied: "Oh it's only a play. Why don't they just stay home and get fucked? Seriously." I wanted to stay home and get fucked too. But I had promised the *Yale Campus News* a story.

The only other Yale Drama face I recognized belonged to Justin Mc-Grommett, a special research scholar from Australia who had earned a lasting reputation for a play he'd written in 1970 that had became the basis for a seminal film which helped launch the Australian film industry. He was red-faced drunk, as usual, and a little too happy to be there.

A tall woman wearing a baggy sweater approached the microphone. Her voice rasped strong, if flat. "We called for this discussion because violence against women is at a crisis level!" She paused for applause, didn't get much, and then launched into a rehash of the statement read aloud at the first protest rally. When she concluded, she opened the floor for questions which weren't really questions. Everyone was grandstanding and preaching to the converted: *Violence is bad. Violence against women is worse. Too many women are victims. Pornography degrades women and makes them targets. Hollywood portrayals of violent acts against women cheapen women's lives.*

There didn't seem to be anything real to argue about. No sane person wants women hurt. I braced myself for an hour of boredom when I saw Justin's hand go up. Great, I thought. An inebriated Aussie sexist should be able to stir things up.

Justin stood up. A young woman handed him a microphone. "You know," he said, "the way you women talk, it's a wonder an American man can get an erection."

A young man in the back of the auditorium stood up. "American men have no problem getting an erection!"

This statement drew applause from almost all the men in attendance, both gay and straight, but especially gay.

"If anyone has any trouble, I can help," trilled one little bald fellow with a cookie-duster moustache.

"This talk of erections is getting me hot," said one guy.

"I'm horny," said another guy.

The bald, mustachioed fellow rose and exited. I wondered whose cookie he'd be dusting. Three more men left together.

The woman speaking raised both arms and tried to calm the house. "Please, people! May I have your attention? We're all here for the same reason. We embrace all forms of consensual sexuality. We support healthy, adult, mutual expressions of love. But the issue here is violence. The issue is rape!"

Teddy Lee raised his hand. A young lady carried a microphone to him. It took Teddy five seconds to utter a syllable. "I...I wrote the play." Teddy fell silent.

Some woman shouted from the back of the room. "Why are there so many violent acts against women in your play?"

"I...wanted to...I wanted to show...something. It wasn't just darkness. Or violence. No. I felt...I tried...I...I...I..." He was all stutters now. Finally he clammed up, tossed the microphone to a seated guest, and rushed to the exit.

"You can hurt a woman onstage, but you can't even talk to one in person?" the same woman said.

"I don't think that man will ever get an erection again," remarked the Aussie.

"Always, *always* talking about erections. I think that man has issues," commented another male attendee.

Then Oletun Osazuwa stood up. He usually dressed in the semi-casual clothes of a British student, button down shirts tucked inside of slacks, and leather lace-up shoes. But today he wore some kind of African man-dress with black and gold designs. He took the microphone and advanced to the stage.

"I am the director of the play. I will speak from the stage." Ollie took center stage. He paused, waiting for silence. When he knew he had everyone's attention, he spoke. "I first read this play one month ago. I read it three times in one night. To me, this became an important play. In my homeland, rape has become a tool of political terror and oppression. It is true all over Africa. For young women in my country, it is very bad. No one intervenes, not the oil companies who drill in our swamps, not the copper companies who strip-mine our mountains, looting all our resources. The United Nations only watches. America and the West pay no attention. Soldiers attack our townships, burn down huts, drag women and girls into the forest to rape them over and over again. Old women too, and young men and boys, when there are not enough females."

The Women's Center became as silent as a funeral home.

"Many of these soldiers know that they have the H.I.V. virus, and deliberately infect their victims, destroying their futures. The infants born of these rapes begin life with a deadly disease for which there is no medicine. Not in Africa, where rape can become a double murder."

I heard a sniffle or two in the crowd.

"It happened to my sister." The crowd gasped. "Yes. She was only eleven years old." Ollie's voice came close to breaking, but didn't. "Women suffer the most. But boys and young men are also attacked. Just as girls are circumcised before they can know what it is to be a woman, so are boys castrated by Witch Doctors, their youth, innocence, and sexuality stolen forever."

Another collective gasp rose from the crowd. A fellow sitting near me flinched and crossed his legs.

Ollie shook his head. "Why do men do such terrible things? I believed that Mr. Lee's play would give us a chance to explore this question. I see the stage as a safe place for humanity to explore the most terrible and inhuman things. As one oppressed citizen, I cannot strike back against the evil men with guns who run over my country and its people. But in the theatre, I try to tell the truth. I try to open minds and touch hearts." Oletun bowed his head. He patted his chest. "That is all I have to say." He flashed a peace sign as he left the stage.

Oletun's statement received loud, if uneven applause. Some clapped hard, the rest cried. A few couples held each other and sobbed. The host reclaimed the podium, but everyone knew that the meeting had ended. Oletun's impromptu sermon rocked the house. No one could follow that. I left before everyone left.

I spent a whole night sifting through my notes, trying to cobble together a fair, yet concise portrayal of what I thought happened with Teddy's play. I praised Ollie's passion for the script, and the protection he offered Rosalie during rehearsals. I commented on Rosalie's courage and artistry. I couldn't think of anything praiseworthy about Teddy, except that he took a risk offering his piece for production. I acknowledged the Women's Center's concerns about artistic portrayals of violence towards women. I praised the civil tone their protest leaders maintained throughout all their rallies.

The very next morning, I walked into the offices of the *Yale Campus News* and handed my finished piece to Skip the Feature Editor. "You are awesome sauce, boss!" he exclaimed.

As I left the *News* office, I noticed that the Women's Center's offices were directly across the hall.

As opening night got closer, Rosalie began to feel the strain of living a double life. In rehearsals, she sprang into her Ms. Randy Rapist mode, dashing across the stage like Robin Hood with a plastic rapier. At the Women's Center encounter groups, she became Polly the Penitent Feminist. This demanding dual role soon proved too much of a stretch for even the very best of Yale Drama's student actresses.

After a long afternoon of rehearsing with Ollie, followed by a scolding session led by some of the Women's Center's finest, Rosalie walked into Dean Bill Michter's office in tears.

Michter was a former chain-smoker and current alcoholic who had lost one lung to cancer. After 25 years at the Drama School, he dictated much of its Orwellian office politics. Big Brother Bill served as the Dean of Academic Affairs, besides being the chief instructor at Yale Drama's legendary acting program. His need of rehab was the dead cat stuffed under the living room rug. No matter how many professors or students tripped over it, or how much it smelled, no one dared mention it. Dean Bill drank medicinal portions of vodka during his morning and afternoon classes. At night, he switched to whiskey.

There were rumors that Bill carried on sexless affairs with the more vulnerable actresses under his tutelage. He was impotent, so these trysts consisted of tender embraces, whispered sweet talk and stifled sobs. Without revealing her sources, Sally told me this. I couldn't help but believe it.

By pure chance, I witnessed Dean Michter's final evisceration of Teddy K. Lee. I needed to copy my own play for a staged reading. The copy center was directly across from Dean Michter's office. As I waited for thirty full-length plays to be copied and bound, I turned and caught a glimpse of Teddy Lee crying in Bill's office. His girlfriend, Joanna Hansen, sat beside him stroking his arm.

"The play isn't ready," shouted Dean Bill. "I should never have consented to a production."

I tiptoed closer. I felt a bit foolish, but after all I'd witnessed, I couldn't help my curiosity.

"What's your angle?" Dean Bill demanded.

"*Angle?*" asked Teddy, utterly confused.

"My actors have to take great emotional risks with your material. But you write this thing, this offhand thing, full of violence and darkness, and what do you expect? Is this therapeutic for you? Are you purging your own demons?"

"I don't know," was all Teddy could say.

"Or maybe all you're doing is brandishing your penis in our faces? Maybe you need therapy. You know, you can see a shrink for free down at the Yale Student Health Center? Half of my actors go there. The waiting room in the mental health unit looks like the Yale Rep Green Room. Think about it. Maybe get a prescription. Sometimes a little pill changes everything."

"I am not mentally ill!" barked Teddy. It excited me to see him display a little fire for a change. He leaned forward in his chair and actually looked straight into Bill Michter's bloodshot eyes. "Maybe it's not my play—maybe it's your acting students who aren't ready for something fresh!"

Dean Michter got up slowly and pushed his door shut. What happened behind that door, I can only guess. What I can presume is that it didn't go well for Teddy.

My feature came out the next day. Editor Skip cut it in half and completely rearranged it. Any praise of the Women's Center's concerns got deleted. Skip moved one provocative quote I used in the opening paragraph to the very end of the article. It came from an old Army guy covered in flags and medals, who was out protesting the protest. I recognized him as one of those old school Vietnam vet types, forever bitter about hippies and radicals of any stripe. Why I stopped to talk to him, I don't know. He gave me an earful:

> "It's censorship! They want to control what authors write, and how they write it. If that's not censorship, what the hell else would you call it?! The ladies at the Women's Center ought to be ashamed of themselves! My best friends died in Vietnam protecting their right to free speech! But would these young women fight for my rights, or for the dramatist's rights?! Heck no! They just want free

speech for everyone who agrees with them and nobody else. And that's the truest thing you'll hear today!"

★ ★ ★

To dump insult upon absurdity, Teddy cancelled his show the morning before the first performance. After all the fuss and muss, and many a tornado in a tea cozy, not a soul would see it. When Teddy heaved himself into Michter's office and demanded that his show be cancelled, Dean Bill wavered, not sure whether he wanted to cancel it after all. He'd pressured Teddy all week to pull his show, but who was he to *demand* that his show be cancelled? Todd Voorhees came in to consult. Todd and Bill soon agreed that since Playwrights Collaborative Projects are "all about the playwright," of course Teddy could pull his own play.

That afternoon a crowd queued up in a sunny courtyard just outside a small Yale Drama theater. The news moved fast down the line of would-be patrons. A dozen folks representing the Women's and LGBT centers arrived. They seemed dismayed. It took a while for them to realize that they should cheer. I wondered if most were secretly disappointed that they'd missed their chance to watch the hated play.

The next time I saw Teddy, he was holding a beer can. His eyes looked red and wet behind his rimless spectacles. From that day forward, I never saw him outside of class without a beer in his hand. Teddy soon turned into an experienced drunk who knew how to start strong, build a solid buzz, and maintain it throughout the day. He would taper off at night by nursing beer after beer. The alcohol entered his system at a measured pace, like steady drops of pain-relieving opiates from an I.V. drip.

Everyone in the Drama School seemed to forget about Teddy's ordeal – everyone, that is, except for Teddy. We playwrights sympathized with him and told him as much in private.

The next time I saw him at a bar, I said, "You got a raw deal, Teddy. You got played by folks with an agenda that had nothing to do with you. Bunch of opportunistic bastards."

Teddy grunted.

"Can I buy you a beer?" I asked.

Another affirmative grunt.

The staff of the Women's and LGBT Centers no longer stalked Teddy. They forgot about him. The only personality still burned into their memory banks was me, Robert Rachaborski, that hack Bobby Rack bastard who wrote the feature article that called them enemies of free speech. Sometimes when I walked across campus I got hissed at by angry women I didn't know. Lesbians with rockabilly pompadours muttered "asshole" as they passed me by. One morning, a woman who looked like Joe Pesci in a studded motorcycle jacket bumped me with her shoulder and growled in my ear, "Fucking shithead!"

It felt good to be despised. Sally loved me madly. Dykes who didn't know me at all hated my stinking guts. Nobody was indifferent. It made my blood rush and skin tingle. Why couldn't Teddy feel the same way? I no longer blamed the feature editor of the *Yale Campus News* for sharpening my news copy into a weapon. I defended art that would never apologize. I was the point of the spear, or at least the strap-on.

But Teddy preferred indifference. He wanted everything to disappear, to pretend that it had all been nothing but a bad dream. He worked on his next piece for two whole years, never showing a single page of it in class. He adapted a classic children's fantasy novel for the stage. It seemed appropriately regressive and safe for a drunken playwright who would probably never write another original play for the rest of his life.

I still think of Teddy as a pussy for crying in Bill Michter's office that day. But for all the tuition he paid, Teddy deserved someone on his side. We all did.

***

A month later, another drama student staged his own adaptation of Georg Buchner's *Woyzeck* in the Yale Cabaret. The original nineteenth century German play portrayed a starved, broken down soldier who is dehumanized, driven mad by his superiors and later stabs his wife in an unhinged fit of jealousy. The vigorous student director embellished the events. His concept included golden showers, thumping synthesizer music, and the graphic slaughter of the wife. He used exploding blood squibs and gushing tubes to simulate arterial blood loss. Bursting sacks of twist pasta stood in for brain matter during one long bludgeoning scene. When the lead actor fell to the ground to embrace and mount the gory corpse, several audience members left the theater. Somehow that production escaped the attention of the Yale Women's Center and their LGBT allies.

Sally and I watched this production of *Woyzeck* together. She had a thing for serial killer stories, so we stayed for the whole bloody spectacle.

"It's a twenty page play and it lasted for-fucking-ever. Sheesh. That sure sucked," I growled when it was over.

"What do you mean? It was brilliant!" insisted Sally.

"Come on." I reached for her hand. She jerked it behind her back. I pretended to leave. She ran after me and punched my arm. We fought all the way back to her place.

Meanwhile, in other parts of Yaleland, Teddy K. Lee nursed a well-built buzz with beer after beer. Rosalie Bryant likely dined with yet another polite medical student who would never marry her. And Dean Bill Michter was stumbling around his apartment in an alcoholic blackout after placing several incoherent phone calls to former female students.

It was an ordinary night at the Drama School.

LONG DAY'S JOURNEY BACK TO BED

When our classes finished, Sally and I met in the street and raced to her place. She was kissing her way down my chest when the phone rang. An answering machine took the call.

"Hi, Honey!" said Sally's mother. "Are you there, sweetie? I want to talk to you about your father's plans for Sunday." Sally's father ran the biggest patent, copyright, and intellectual property law firm on Madison Avenue. Sally let go of me and ran for the phone. There was no such thing as a short conversation with Sally's mother. I bent my business back into my shorts, grabbed one of Sally's fashion magazines, and plopped down on a couch. I watched the minutes tick away while Sally and her mom debated the details of a family outing planned months in advance. The women in Sally's magazine were a bit anorexic for my tastes, but kept me aroused.

"I'll have to take a taxi, Mom," said Sally. "What do you mean 'Dad just saw the credit card bill'? Did he say something? Why are you always starting trouble for me? I have to eat, don't I? I am not getting fat! Mom, you're so horrible to me!"

It took ten more minutes for Mom to convince Sally that she wasn't fat. They did agree that all the other actresses in the Drama School were fat horses who didn't watch their figures.

Sally dropped her pen while Mom listed important instructions for Sunday. She frog-jumped across the floor in her attempt to retrieve it. Her buttocks bounced in her leotards. I put down the magazine and pulled down my shorts.

Sally snatched up the pen and looked at me. "Put that away," she whispered. "Girl scout cookies," she explained to Mom. "Robert opened a box. I don't want to be tempted."

"The best cookies in town," I said.

Sally laughed out loud after one of her mom's comments. She covered the phone. "Mom says that the kind of asses the actresses have around here might get them a black boyfriend, but won't get them a part on a TV show."

I didn't laugh. I liked big asses. I imagined a parade of big bare asses parading just for me. I struggled to stay put and not rape Sally while her mother listened. I let this fantasy overtake me as Sally wiggled about the room with the phone jammed in her ear. "Jesus!" I shouted out loud.

Sally raised her eyebrows. "That was Robert," explained Sally. "He's going stir crazy. We have to go to a play soon." Now that Sally's mom knew we had to leave, the pace of their conversation intensified. Topics changed without logic. "Mom, I don't need a new winter coat. Well maybe little Myron shouldn't go to summer camp again if he's only going to get bullied. Don't bleach your teeth, Mom! You'll look like a vampire. Your smile will glow in the dark. I don't know why she got cast. Yes, she's a cow and she got cast. Maybe I was supposed to moo for the director? We have to go! Love you! Bye!" She hung up.

Sally crossed to the couch and fell down beside me.

"No time for a quickie?" I asked.

"Nope."

Dean Bill Michter demanded that students attend each other's dreary projects. The only way to beat the system was to sign up and not show, but you always ran the risk that some snitch bitch stage manager would rat you out.

Sally and I arrived six minutes late. We Bogarted the last available seats in the back row. The audience was packed with actors who chattered like randy chimpanzees. They saw each other every day, but still found new things to scream about.

"Did you see Jomo's recital?! Like butter! Who knew he had such a yummy voice! I wanted to cry!" said one actress.

"Oh my God! I did cry!" replied another actress.

I turned to Sally. "I was once a substitute teacher, and I'm not sure which is louder: a classroom of junior high kids or a room full of adult actors."

"What show is this?" Sally asked.

I glanced at the program and grimaced. "*Contrapuntal Cantata, Girly Flights of Fancy, and Fugues of Immutability.*"

"Jesus. What is it? A lesbian orgy? Who wrote it?"

"Marla Starrett," I said.

"Is she gay?"

"No. But she looks like a hockey player. Imagine Wayne Gretzky in a summer dress."

"Is that her?" Sally nodded towards a large woman in a black sweat-shirt, high-water pants, and silver granny glasses.

"No. That's the stage manager, Allie Breen. She *is* gay."

Allie held two granola bars in one hand and a bottle of Yoo Hoo in the other. She pushed the granola bars into her face.

Sally whispered. "Poor girl, why does she eat so much?"

I pointed out Marla. "That's the playwright."

Sally waited until Marla turned her head to check the size of the house. "God, she *is* a hockey player!"

"Shhhh. I think her mother up in Canada heard you."

Marla stood up to welcome the crowd and point out fire exits. "In the highly unlikely event of a fire, please follow the signs." She ended by saying, "Thanks for coming to my show."

The house lights dimmed. I slid down in my chair. "This will be a long one," I whispered. Sally rested her head on my shoulder, picked up my hand, and laced her fingers through mine.

A band of light spread across the stage. A man with an enormous tool belt waddled into the scene. He said nothing for what seemed like minutes. At first, the audience was uncomfortable. But soon our unease downshifted into disinterest. A second character sauntered onto the stage whistling *Pop Goes the Weasel*. She wore cut-off overalls, a t-shirt, a backwards baseball cap, striped sweat socks, and double-laced high top sneakers. She asked, "Did you get that door open?"

"Which door?" asked Tool Belt.

"The door," said Whistling Woman.

They went on like this, asking which door, what door, and who would open which door when, and with what. I heard the first yawn from the audience. I checked my watch. I heard sighs and creaking chairs. The audience stopped waiting for anything to happen, and just waited for the play to end. Perhaps some existential ruse was being played on us? Could it be a masochistic, mass hysteria that was holding us in those ass-numbing, metal folding chairs? The play dared the sane to flee.

"God, we could be home having fun," I whispered.

Sally patted my arm. "You're being so good." We made angry faces at each other. I growled under my breath. Sally growled back. We stopped growling when folks shushed us.

The play waddled on. For three hours, two lazy locksmiths rambled about the stage. One of them was a mythical Key Man who carried a giant ring of clanking keys. None of the keys worked in the locks. They knocked on doors and whispered epigrams, aphorisms, and Gertrude Stein-bites through keyholes.

I was snoozing when Key Man dropped his keys. They thudded on the floorboards. I woke up with a snort. Sally squeezed my knee. I saw Marla grab her face. Sally pressed her lips to my ear and whispered, "Will the Key Man ever get to put his big key into one of those glowing keyholes?"

"I don't think we'll be so lucky." I watched the actor gather up the giant keys. They sounded as if they'd been made from pig iron. The play ran three hours, with intermission, but felt as long as an overbooked flight to Australia.

At the two hour and twenty-five minute mark, the Key Man shoved a golden key into the giant upstage door with a ruthless grunt. The audience leaned forward, thinking something would finally happen. Yes, the key turned. Yes, the door opened. Yes, the Key Man got to the other side. The door closed behind him. It felt like something had reached a conclusion. But for twenty more interminable minutes, the woman in cut-off overalls continued a mournful conversation with the glowing keyhole. The lights faded. After an indecisive pause, everyone clapped politely. When the lights went up after curtain calls, I grabbed Sally's hand. "Let's get out of here!"

"Wait," she said. "We have to congratulate the actors. You should congratulate the playwright."

"For *what??!*"

"Just be a good boy."

While Sally comforted her fellow actors, I hovered off to the side. As misfortune would have it, Marla Starrett came my way. Two playwrights were congratulating her. Her father and mother were stroking her shoulders. Her dad wobbled about, plump and pale. In his sagging grey suit he looked like an insurance lawyer. Marla's mom was tall and thick and topped with a pile of dyed red hair. She looked like she could not only fry the bacon, but butcher the hog as well.

As a man whose mother had always been sick and unavailable, and whose father was forever heartbroken, other people's parents fascinated me. Marla's folks seemed so solid and healthy. They looked like direct descendants of pioneering stock, the ablest of over-achievers, and a poster family for the American Dream, even if they hailed from Canada. I stood in awe. I wondered what they thought of their daughter's unbounded dramaturgy.

Marla's cool eyes caught me. She squinted while I moved out of her way. I had no choice but to mutter "Congratulations."

"Thank you," she said with a forced smile.

I decided to join Sally and pretend interest in the actors. But before I could move, Marla spoke to the back of my neck.

"Robert."

I turned. "Yes."

"Were you snickering at my play?"

"Excuse me?"

"I thought I saw you snickering."

I shook my head. "No. I don't think so. If I yawned or something, sorry, nothing to do with you."

Marla looked skeptical. Her father glared at me as if I'd just shot their family dog. Her mother's mouth tightened.

I got away fast, and ducked into the dressing room where Sally was playing the Jewish mother for an insecure actor.

"You did a lovely job. Sensitive," Sally said. "Such an odd, difficult play. Give yourself all the credit."

"Do you think I ruined the momentum when I dropped the keys?" Travis Magee was a thin and pink-skinned actor, with a blonde pompadour, and puffy blow-job lips. He busily hooked loops and studs back into his tongue, nose, lips, eyebrows, and ears. He had enough rings in his face to hang a shower curtain.

"Of course not," Sally said, turning to me. "We thought it was part of the play, didn't we?" She and I nodded together.

"Oh it was just hideous up there when it happened! Hideous!" shrieked Travis. His voice rang stout and manly up on stage, but the girl skipped out of the bag now.

I found Travis amusing. "Good job," I told him.

He beamed at me. It was flattering to have such a pretty young boy flashing his eyes and teeth at me. "You're a playwright, aren't you," asked Travis. "What would you call this kind of piece? A language play?"

"All plays are made out of language."

"What do you mean?"

"Well, you know. They're not made of bricks."

"Hmmm. Maybe this one is made out of keys?" said Travis.

Sally shot me a look, as if to say, *Take it easy, big guy.*

I knew that dressing rooms were not the place for serious talk about art. After the show, be quick and congratulatory. Be loud with your praise and exit fast on an encouraging note. But I was in a mood to preach. "It's all words. You put one word next to a second and it creates a third thing. If it becomes something more, maybe you've got a play." I paused, wrangling with my next pronouncement. "This thing today, I don't know. It could be like Pinter or Beckett. But Pinter has menace, that scary vaudeville. You don't cry, but the laughs and fear creep up your back. And with Beckett, the heart is always there. But this play, it's all brain and no heart."

Sally looked away. Travis regarded me as if I were a psychedelic platypus with a flashing bow tie. Then he broke into song. "*If I only had a heart!*" he belted out like the Tin Man. I got out of there before he started in on "Over the Rainbow". As I was on my way out, he turned to Sally. "Oh my God, can you imagine how heavy those fucking keys were? I felt like a slave in chains up there! Auction my little ass off!"

I went out for a smoke. Ten minutes later, Sally came out.

"Let's go home," I began walking.

"We need to eat. And how about a drink?"

"Okay. We'll grab something on the way."

Sally walked slowly, a sleepy grin on her face. "What's the rush, big guy? I don't know if I should let you take me home," she said. "You might have plans to rape me."

"I just might." It felt good to be her playmate again.

"I never heard of anyone raping the willing. But there's always a first."

By the time we made it to her place I was charged and eager for release. But before we could get any real groove on, I popped like a teenaged virgin.

"What happened," Sally asked. She unpeeled the condom and held it up to the light. "Ha! That's new!"

I retreated to a far corner of the bed. Sally slid over and wrapped her body around mine. "That was hot."

"I guess that long-ass play got me all pent up."

"That poor Key Man and all those heavy keys."

"The *Key Man*," I repeated. "What the fuck?"

Sally laughed. Then I laughed. Everything seemed better. We held each other in the dark and waited for more good times. The night was on our side.

THE FINAL HOEDOWN

I persuaded my father to take the train from Boston to Connecticut for my commencement ceremonies. "You can have my bed," I told him. "I'll sleep at Sally's. She'll keep you company while I'm up there sitting with the graduating class."

"I don't know. I don't think so," he grumbled.

"I'm only going to graduate from the Ivy League once, Dad."

"I heard New Haven, Connecticut is a depressing place."

"You heard it from me. Listen. I've been stuck here three years. You'll only be here two days."

"I guess I can come. Just this once," he said.

**

I was almost surprised when I saw Dad step onto the platform at New Haven's Union Station. He wore scuffed yellow work boots and a green-striped polyester golf shirt covered with runs, tears, and loose threads. His blue jeans hung loose on him, faded and droopy. He'd hemmed the pant legs himself with coarse black thread. A one-armed Parkinson's sufferer could have stitched them with more precision. Nothing fit right. With his raw, open face, my father looked like an overgrown boy in hand-me-down clothes.

"Hi, Dad," I said as I took an army surplus satchel out of his hand. "That shirt of yours has seen some combat."

"It's the dogs. Their claws pull at the fabric."

"Maybe I've got some clothes you can wear."

"I don't need anything special," he snapped.

"I just don't want you scaring my girlfriend away with that raggedy homeless get-up."

"If she can tough it out with a prick like you for this long, she can't be scared of much!"

Dad was in his best scrappy form. I patted him on the shoulder. "Let's take a cab to my place."

"How far is it?" Dad's lips pursed into his regular penny-pinching expression.

"Too far. Don't worry. I'll get the fare."

On the steps outside my building, I saw the large Irish-American family of graduating Yale Drama actor James McAdams. The McAdams men, father, grandfathers, uncles, in-laws and all, wore the finest, form-fitting new suits. The elegant McAdams ladies wore bright happy dresses. They all had perfect white smiles. Jimmy Mac, as James was called, stood on the top of the steps while his family looked up and admired him. James had already been cast in movies and TV, and still received healthy residuals from three national commercials he'd booked and shot before even attending Yale Drama. A furnished apartment in Manhattan already awaited Jimmy Mac. Five top NYC agents asked for his signature on a contract. He signed with the best.

"Hi, Mac," I said as I smuggled my father by.

"Oh hi!" said James with an automatic smile.

No eye contact or introductions were exchanged.

"You'll sleep there," I told Dad as we entered my studio apartment. He looked at my queen-sized mattress, which was on the floor.

  "Pretty low to the ground."

"The brass bed is being polished. The canopy is at the cleaners. Have you ever eaten Indian food?"

"I don't think I have."

"There are lots of Indian restaurants in New Haven because of Yale's Medical School."

"I guess they need plenty of doctors over there."

"Yeah, but most stay here, where the money is."

"Smart."

I pressed two clean towels, a wash cloth and a new bar of oatmeal soap into his hands. "Why don't you take a shower? Then we'll eat." I didn't want to order him to wash up, but Dad didn't smell too fresh, more like rancid onions and unwashed armpits. "Does he wash?" Sally had asked me just days before. "Of course," I half-lied. Dad made me honest by taking a long hot shower with no extra prompting. Meanwhile, I searched around for some clothes which might be loose enough to fit him and laid them out.

I had a size 46 silk sport jacket which fit my shoulders and chest, but floated everywhere else. It was a thrift-shop find with Italian labels. A black nylon golf shirt would look stylish enough underneath it. I checked inside Dad's satchel and found a pair of dark blue work pants that were nearly new.

I also found his Beretta 9mm automatic pistol—for security purposes alone, I'm sure. Well, at least I'd know where to locate it in case any lawless intruders or ninja assassins burst into the apartment. *You're not taking that to my graduation, Dad,* I said to myself. Besides, there was no way he could conceal it under that silk sport jacket.

Footwear was the tricky part. Dad was a 10½-11 while I was a big ol' 13. I located some black navy oxfords in the bottom of my closet. They pinched me, but would probably fit around his swollen ankles—undiagnosed gout, most likely. Dad didn't like doctors. When he came out of the bathroom toweling his ears, I pointed at his new outfit. "Okay. Time for the big TV makeover. Oprah and her studio audience are waiting."

The black shirt fit tightly on him, but stretched. His blue pants were hemmed high. I gave him some dark socks to bridge the gap. The oxfords floated about his toes, but didn't ride his heels when laced up. Dad could walk in them. The real magic happened when he donned the Italian silk jacket. It fit him like a king's plush velvet robe. The Cinderella story was almost complete.

He stood there like a waxwork. "Okay. Now I'm all duded up. What happens next?"

"We go and eat," I said.

He grabbed his filthy baseball cap and twisted it onto his head.

"No. That's not going to cut it. Hold on." I dug in my closet and pulled out a new Yale Drama School cap. "Now folks will know where to point you if you get lost."

Dad looked more than half-human now. To the untrained eye he appeared a whole human. Give him a desk, two secretaries, a wall safe, a couple of law and business degrees on the wall, and you'd think he was the boss of a very important company. *RACHABORSKI ENTERPRISES: We Deal Big.*

Dad stood perfectly still in his new wardrobe. He watched me for his next move. His lips curled into an uncertain scowl. He could only hold eye contact with me for a few seconds at most, then his eyes became unfocused and wet. Though unspoken, it was embarrassing for his son to dress him.

"Okay. One more thing," I said. "The finishing touch. The masterstroke. The mark of the artist!"

"An ostrich feather up my ass," said Dad with an empty expression.

"Better than that." I found a pair of classic Ray Ban Wayfarer sunglasses and slid them onto his face. "Now you're swingin'. The world's last original Beatnik."

Dad smiled for the first time that day. "A real cool cat."

"A gas, man. Give you a pewter hip flask and a Greek fisherman's cap, and you could be Jack Kerouac's long lost brother."

"Gerard," said my father. "Gerard was his older brother, who died of rheumatic fever. Jack was only four. He never got over it. He kept searching for another big brother. Never found one, just a bunch of misfits, hustlers, and too much booze. Jack thought Gerard was his guardian angel. Maybe so...for a while."

Dad could roll deep on a subject when he got going. I knew he'd read most of Jack Kerouac's books before I was born. Before we both got lost down Jack's long, lonesome dead-end road, I changed the tune. "Now we're going to go out and search for some Indian food. Let me call Sally and let her know we're on schedule."

"Hello," answered Sally in a wobbly voice.

"What's the matter?"

"Is he there?" From the tension in her tone, you'd have thought it was a hostage situation.

"Yeah. The eagle has landed. Do you want to meet him here first, or at the restaurant?"

"I'll come over there. Do you think maybe...?" Sally hesitated. "Couldn't Ted or Rey be with him tomorrow, instead of me?"

"Rey is graduating with me. I don't even know if Ted's in town. Come on. We talked about this. Just give him some company. Keep it light. Easy and breezy." I waved at Dad. He looked away.

"I'm nervous. I'm scared about what you told me. What's wrong with him?"

"Nothing you can't handle." I wasn't about to discuss my father's issues in front of him. I kept things upbeat. "He'll be crazy about you. Just be your sweet pretty self. He likes people." I winked at Dad.

It felt odd, negotiating a meeting between two emotional cripples. Meanwhile, my inner world went entirely neglected. What about my anxieties and concerns for the future? The man of the hour was me, a young artist poised to face the big bad world with an MFA degree, no savings, and forty thousand dollars worth of student debt. I was the Yale grad about to reach out and grasp that rare Ivy League parchment that poor little underprivileged boys and girls aren't supposed to even dream about, much less touch.

Sally kept moaning and groaning over the phone. She was all woe, and how come, and why me, which made me mad. "If you don't come over here right now, don't ever come over again. *Finita la commedia.* Okay? Grow up and get moving." I hung up.

Dad looked glum.

I patted him on the arm. "She'll be here."

Sally could have made in ten minutes if she walked fast, but she arrived in twenty. I buzzed her up. She gave my apartment door a spirited rap-a-tap-tap. I opened up.

"HI!" she shouted and walked into my arms. She hugged me hard to let me know she was still scared. I took her by the hand and led her to the round table in the center of my studio.

"Do you want a beer? All I've got here are tall boys."

"Fine," said Sally.

"Coffee, Dad?"

"Okay."

Sally wore a pink belly shirt and skin-tight jeans that rode low. I was used to her dressing sexy, but I hadn't expected it tonight. I could see she'd strapped on one of her special bras, the kind that made her look enormous, and in complete contravention of Newton's laws of gravity. Her bare midriff shined smooth and trim and her nutty brown skin had its usual warm Mediterranean glow.

After two years, Sally's perfect shape had spoiled me. But now I saw her through my father's eyes. My mother had suffered with bad skin and never weighed less than one hundred and eighty pounds since her junior year of high school. She was the only woman my father married or loved.

I loved Mom too, but never really knew her. She delivered me at the age of 23, but got sick with multiple sclerosis the week after I was born. She would have been diagnosed even sooner, but being pregnant with me held her in remission. Afterwards she could barely walk or contemplate a productive life. Her sanity started to slip.

Then Mom got religion, hard. Often, she left me unsupervised in strange rooms with strange children while she gathered and prayed with her holy roller friends. If I told her I was hungry or needed to pee, she became greatly irritated that I would let such trivialities interrupt her direct ecstatic communion with the Lord. Soon all that mattered to Mom was prayer and miracles. Birth control didn't seem to count for much either, because she carried and delivered two more children, even though she could barely walk.

It took Mom twenty-four more years to die, the last twelve spent in long-term care medical facilities. Dad never remarried, or even dated again, as far as I knew.

"So," Sally said. "You must be so proud of Robert! He's told me about how hard things were growing up in Boston. But tomorrow he's graduating from Yale University. He's a survivor. Isn't that so marvelous? He is blessed."

Dad made an effort to avoid his usual cynicism. "Well, at least he's doing what he likes to do. I always wanted to be a writer."

"Robert is so talented."

"Uh-huh," Dad grunted without much commitment.

I assembled an antique coffee dripper in the kitchenette. I brought Sally out a beer. "Sally's the real talent. She's got perfect comic timing."

"Oh yeah. I'm a real laugh riot. I've done plenty of improv and stand-up and sketch comedy. The problem is that I want to be taken seriously as an artist. Does my Bobby take me seriously?"

"Like a heart attack."

Sally raised her eyebrows.

"As serious as double-pneumonia, overdraft fees, and a court date before a judge."

We gave Dad the full Bogie and Bacall routine. If ever there were film noir characters, it was us in that room.

"We're not always at each other's throats, Mr. Rachaborski."

Dad withheld comment. Sally reached over and hugged my waist as I set down coffee for my dad. Then she bit my arm.

"Ouch!"

"Sorry," she said with a saintly smile.

"Just don't bite my dad," I replied.

Dad looked embarrassed. Sally frowned. I went to get my own cup of coffee. I changed my mind and grabbed a beer.

When I returned, Dad and Sally were silent and staring at the floor. I knew my father felt shy and out of place. Sally, however, looked disturbed. She had that fight-or-flight look that often surfaced when we weren't getting along. She didn't want to be there, not at all, not with my gloomy dad, and maybe not even with me. She felt abandoned and angry because I was leaving Yale Drama School tomorrow, without her. She would have a whole extra year to deal with all by her lonesome, without me to talk her down from trees, hold her hand, and whisper endless endearments and reinforcements into her ear. *Bastard*, she was thinking. *How could you go and leave me behind?*

I could read her thoughts in her hunched shoulders, knitted brows and brooding mouth. Her eyes glowered at me as if I were the parent who wouldn't take her out for ice cream anymore. This was my Sally, who I expected to escort and care for my tragic father on my most important day. For her first meeting with him, she'd decided to dress like a party gal leaning over a pool table in a pick-up bar. I didn't think she'd have appreci-ated it had I shown up all muscle-bound and menacing in tight jeans and a wife-beater tank top to meet her parents. Then again maybe she would, just to rub it in her mother's face.

I dropped a reassuring hand on my father's shoulder. "She's just pissed because I'm graduating and moving to New York. She's got another whole year here to contend with all alone, without my love and protection."

"Do you think she'll live," Dad deadpanned.

"Oh...one way or t'other," I said.

"What do you mean?" Sally protested. "You know how happy I am for you! You're going to visit me, right? You won't forget where Grand Central Station is? Ninety minutes to New Haven."

"You know I'll be living on that train," I said.

"If you don't, I'll be dying here without you."

Was this us talking? Or had Raymond Chandler and Billy Wilder writ-ten our script?

I slid my chair over and hugged her. "Don't worry so much. You know I've got to move to New York to become a big famous playwright."

Sally nuzzled my neck and rubbed my thigh. As usual, her kissing and stroking became too sexual for mixed company. She knew we'd spend the night at her place after I stashed my dad.

"Let me clean up, then we'll go eat." I picked up Sally's 16-ounce beer can. It was empty. She pulled at me as I stood. My father looked away. There was no going back to Boston now.

***

The waiter at the Royal Palace restaurant wore a white turban and sported a bushy gray beard so thick you could hide two of my dad's pistols there. From his red eyes, oily skin, and the way his arms jittered as he yanked out chairs, I could tell he was hung over. There wasn't a single customer in the place. All twenty tables sat empty. At first, the waiter tried to seat us at a cramped, four-person table.

I pointed out a more spacious table. "How about that one?"

"No. That table is for a large party."

"But there's no one here." I waved at the empty room. "This place is a barn."

"The dinner rush is coming."

"When? It's almost six now."

Normally, a standoff like this would launch Sally into her pushy, New York broad mode. I braced myself, getting ready to feel sorry for the waiter. I'd never seen Sally lose in a customer service situation. But today she was so pissed at me and mortified by my father that she folded her arms, sulked, and stared out the window into the night.

"Look, why don't you go sneak a big Kingfisher beer in the kitchen and straighten yourself out?"

The waiter blinked and shivered. "You must go. I cannot serve you."

That woke Sally up. She snapped out of her brooding funk. "May I please speak with your manager?"

"He is not here."

"Please give me his phone number."

"I can only call him for emergencies."

"*This* is an emergency. Telephone him. Now. I would like to speak with him. Go ahead. Pick up the phone, dial the numbers. Get us all connected."

"I cannot do that! You must go!"

"Oh, no. No. Oh good God, no. Do NOT raise your voice to me. What time does he come in? My boyfriend lives right across the street. We walk by this place every day. We will find and speak to your manager. I will tell him personally how you drove the only paying customers out of his empty restaurant on a Sunday night. I think he'd like to know that, don't you think so? Do you have other job skills? Do you have family who will take you in? Have you ever applied for government assistance?"

Sally tossed her purse onto the largest table in the restaurant and plopped down in an empty chair. "I'm hungry."

The waiter said nothing. I sat down. Dad sat down.

"Bring us two large King Cobra beers with glasses, plus water for all three of us," I said. This is how I asserted what little was left of my masculinity.

The waiter walked away. Our beers didn't arrive quickly, but they did arrive. I suspect that he drank one himself before facing my queen cobra again.

★★★

If there had ever been anything good, sane or salvageable in our relationship, we'd lost it like a cat out of a car window on a cross-country trip. The cute early core of our love wandered alone now, lost and crying beside a blue highway.

245

I acted cool about graduating and leaving Sally behind for her final year, but inside I worried about not having such a ready, entertaining girlfriend. She was grim about my leaving and wore the mask of a wronged woman. She might as well have worn a veil and a black pillbox hat.

With all of this on our minds the very last evening before the commencement ceremony on the wide Ivy League green, we did the worst thing possible—we went out to a bar, an old bar that reeked of stale beer, sawdust, and soaked floorboards. We isolated ourselves in our own padded booth with the names of a century's worth of students carved with pocket knives into the wood-paneled walls. Then we drank whiskey after whiskey like a couple of rogue villagers in a gothic novel who had to boost their courage to do something awful, bloody, and irrevocable.

I feared the big bad world I was about to graduate into with nothing but an MFA parchment in my hand. But Sally didn't give a flaming unholy fuck about my future. I would not be there for her next year—that's all that mattered.

In all proper well-reasoned reality, our relationship was doomed before it began. In the fantastical land of grad school, between my student loans and her parents supporting our romantic adventures, we could pretend we were carefree lovers in a French New Wave film. But out in the real world, with bills piling up in our mailboxes, we'd last as long as a pair of butterflies in a lava flow. I could never afford Sally out there where street reality applied. She dated successful, Manhattan lawyers before she met me, men much like her father, men who scored more in a single case than I would probably ever make in a whole year. That's who she would return to when things got tight.

Who knows how many rounds we drank or how fast we drank them? It didn't take long to numb our brains. Our capacity for reason devolved to the level of snapping crocodiles.

"You're leaving me!" she shouted. Her well-trained voice shook the walls and stirred the buzzing barflies. They shut up and looked our way. The jukebox, normally inaudible under the din of yapping drinkers, played the dullest sort of classic rock, like Eric Clapton pretending he was Jamaican. A drift of yellow smoke hovered above us.

"I'm just graduating," I said.

"You won't visit me! You won't! I KNOW YOU WON'T!"

The manager moved from behind the bar.

"I'm afraid I will," I slurred.

"Are we okay here?" asked our waitress.

"No," snapped Sally. "You'll find a girl in New York."

"I can't afford a girl in New Haven."

"Oh, I'm sure you'll find a way," said Sally before she paid the waitress for our last round, and then wiggled two fingers for another.

"Can we go home?" I asked. "I have to graduate tomorrow."

After we finished our last drinks, I got up and walked to the door alone. I waited while Sally made up her mind. Then I went outside to enjoy a cigarette in the night air. After I lit up, Sally appeared. We walked home. Few kind words were spoken.

Back at her apartment, I located some beer that I'd left in her fridge two days before. I took out a can and popped the top.

Sally grabbed my wrist and tried to separate the beer from my paw. "No. No more."

I yanked my arm away. We'd been matching each other drink for drink all night. Why put on the Carrie Nation act now?

"Then you have to get out!" she screamed.

"Get out to where? My dad's sleeping in my bed."

Sally grabbed her phone and dialed. "Mom?! Bob's here!"

It was on now. Whenever she called Mom for assistance, it meant the start of a long night, with much sobbing, consoling, shouting, screaming, and endless streams of breathless promises and teary-eyed endearments.

"Why are you calling her?! Things aren't crazy enough?!"

"He's drunk!" shouted Sally. "Yes. Yes! We've been drinking. Yes, Mom. Mom? MOM?!"

I leaned forward, mashing my face into Sally's, and shouted into the receiver. "We're drunk, Mom! Yep! Crazy drunk off our asses! It's been an orgy of whiskey and cigarettes with your wild, wicked daughter! Wish you were here!"

We wrestled with the phone. Sally shoved me away. She listened to more of her mother's scolding and instructions, and then set down the phone without hanging up.

"You have to get out!"

"Get out where? Where am I going to go?"

"Out in the hallway."

"What's there?"

"You'll see."

Sally somehow herded me out into the hallway. Before I knew it, a metal security door that weighed hundreds of pounds slammed shut in the face of the fella graduating Yale tomorrow.

I stood alone in the long, empty hallway with a fresh can of beer in my hand. After I finished the beer, I started knocking. No answer. I stopped rapping with knuckles, and started slapping with open hands. I switched to fists, punching the door like a heavy bag. Despite my keen impersonation of "Raging Bull" Jake LaMotta, there was no response. "Open up! Open it! LET ME IN!" Now I was kicking the door.

What am I doing out here, my drunk brain asked itself. *What happened to our celebration? How come we aren't cuddling up in the cave together? Why am I out here with nothin'? I'm the big guy. I'm the big graduating guy. Where's my baby? Where's my happy honeypot? Where's my baby boo? Moo? Where are you? Where's my honey? Why did you take it all away? I want my honey. Please. I need it. Give it back. Bitch better give me my damned honey! I WANT MY HONEY!*

Had I said all of this out loud? Oh dear. Apparently so.

After a while, I must have remembered my four years of Tae Kwon Do training. I proceeded to throw perfect side-kicks, pivoting off my back foot, and landing with full force on Sally's door. Then leaping kicks that began to dent the metal and remove chips of paint. I left my mark, but couldn't achieve entry. I gave up and took the elevator downstairs.

The fat rockabilly doorman with his dyed pompadour and droopy handlebar moustache didn't even look at me.

Fifteen minutes later, I unlocked the door of my apartment and woke up my father. His hands were under the covers. I imagined one of them held his 9mm pistol, his "peace of mind".

"It's just me, Dad," I said. "Sally won't be accompanying us to my graduation tomorrow. She couldn't bear it. I'll sleep on the floor."

* * *

Four weeks after graduation I still lived in New Haven waiting for my next move. One morning I spotted Dean Wodehouse and Professor Voorhees waiting at a crosswalk. I walked by them without a word, a glance, or a nod. My job at the Natural History Museum brought in a little money. New York City was the goal. That's where an emerging playwright emerged. Boston could only be a backward step. Somehow, by summer's end, empty bank account be damned, I would transplant myself into an apartment in Brooklyn, Queens, or across the Hudson in New Jersey.

Sally and I hadn't spoken since that disastrous night before my graduation. I received phone calls which either stopped after three rings, or answered me with silence when I picked up. I would lift the receiver, say "Hello," wait some seconds, then return the silent phone to its cradle. If I waited longer, I might hear hushed breathing, a sigh, perhaps a sob.

"Robert."

"Sally." After a pause, I asked, "Why don't we meet and go for a walk? I don't feel like sitting down. I don't want to be indoors. I could come over and wait downstairs at your place. Twenty minutes?"

"Okay," she said.

I walked fast to Sally's place. I waited at the end of the canvas awning that extended from the lobby out to the cab stand.

Sally soon appeared. She wore a white sleeveless blouse, a brown miniskirt and espadrilles. When I saw her, old feelings rushed through me. Why was I here? Why wasn't I home where I could just forget and heal?

We did not touch or kiss. I walked. She stayed by my side.

"I missed you," she said.

"I missed you, too," I admitted without breaking stride.

We walked for two blocks before speaking again.

"My Dad was angry about the door. It wasn't cheap."

"You mean I really broke that huge thing?"

"Yes, you did."

"I couldn't help myself. I'm so terribly in love."

Sally scoffed. "Pfff. If only."

Manhattan was Sally's usual summer playground. But her parents hadn't been able to find a free sublet for her this year. Most summers, Sally stayed in her grandmother's ridiculously inexpensive, rent-controlled apartment in Greenwich Village while Granny Garfinkle traveled in Europe. Other times, Sally's parents traded use of their Florida home, and various time shares for an NYC pad to stash their daughter. No such luck this year. Unless Sally wanted to bunk in her parents' Scarsdale house, she was grounded in New Haven. Out of sweet old Jewish guilt, she'd volunteered for a children's theatre project, in which she would help little ghetto girls and boys on summer break to write and produce their own short plays. She was good at it. All the children loved Sally's fun, noisy spirit.

We crossed through downtown and found ourselves on a bridge overlooking the interstate that linked Boston to New York and points south. To our left, a slope of manicured grass fronted a luxury hotel. A bright golden banner hung above the hotel's entrance welcoming a convention of Baptist ministers.

"That grass looks good," I said. "Want to sit on it?"

"Okay," she said.

We circled around to the hotel. The grass grew soft and thick. Gentleman to the end, I took off my shirt and laid it out so that Sally's linen skirt wouldn't get stained. We stared into each other's eyes. We leaned into each together. The sexual tension was electric. But an abyss awaited our first misstep.

Against all good sense, against all the hard-won wisdom of our brutal history, Sally and I wanted each other. Our foreheads touched. We fitted our noses side by side and breathed each other in. Sally's hair smelled like honey on fresh baked pastry. Her lip gloss could only be cherry. After a whole miserable month our first kiss was a punch to the core. I wrapped my hand around the small of her back and pulled her close.

She began to cry. Now I felt like crying, too. But I boxed that old violin and let hunger take the lead. I slid my palm up under her skirt, kept on sliding, and filled my hand with half of her behind. She kissed me harder and faster.

"No."

Over Sally's shoulder, I saw a dozen Baptist ministers in bright five-button suits smoking outside the hotel. I had to hand it to those black reverends. I'd never have the audacity to wear golden sharkskin, velvet teal, or electric mulberry suits with two feet of tails. They observed our groping, made comments and started laughing. Then their wives came out. The women were dressed even more elegantly, in tall feathered bonnets and immaculate pastel dresses. They must have known their men well, because they chased them back into the hotel.

Sally kissed me as if sex was all that she wanted. I wanted to touch her in all the ways I knew that would free her, but it wasn't meant to happen. Not here. Not yet. As we broke from a long kiss to catch our breath, I rolled away and stared up at the open sky. I felt a harmless ant crawling on my arm. I could hear other insects singing between the sounds of speeding cars. The stray clouds above didn't remind me of anything.

"I should take you home," I said.

Sally smoothed her skirt, then sat up.

I stood. She took my hand and I lifted her to her feet.

Damned, but downtown New Haven was depressing, with half its stores closed, homeless folks camped in neglected doorways, and no activity at noon on a weekday. For two years, Sally and I hopped all over the bricks of this town like we owned it. We lived out a romance here, made lots of noise, enjoyed ourselves plenty, and probably made most of our peers gag.

Now that the degrees had been handed out and the leases expired, you saw with new clarity the dead birds, used condoms, and broken glass in the gutters. New Haven and Yale and the School of Drama was just one more playground from our childish pasts. The town had become our theatre, the only place where the real drama took place, because it certainly wasn't on Yale's stuffy stages. Sally and I played for laughs and did most of the laughing ourselves. We believed we owned the town, down to every last cherry tree, ivy clad wall, and fake gas light, plus all of its dark clouds, low moons, and ragged skies. We were sure that we defied gravity on a daily basis. But it was our youthful hormones, not helium or witchcraft, that held us aloft.

Now Newton's Law would apply again, with extreme prejudice, and the asphalt wouldn't remember us any more than last night's rush hour, a dead horseshoe crab flattened by a tire, or the early morning trash truck grumbling out of an angry alleyway.

The old bounce done bounced away.

As Sally and I approached the midpoint between our apartments, I asked her, "Can I take you home?"

"It's too soon." She backed into the doorway of a candy store which had gone out of business and held out her arms.

"Come here."

I didn't move. "Maybe we should meet up again tomorrow?"

"Can't you come hold me?"

She looked vulnerable in that empty doorway, like somebody's lost little girl. I wasn't sure if she was still mine. Stepping in there to embrace her seemed absurd to me, another nutty love game with made-up rules. *No, I couldn't take her home today. But yes, I could kiss her and call her Princess, and snuggle in the secret doorway.* Sally had always enjoyed sneaking into doorways or dodging around corners for a discreet kiss or cuddle.

"Let's talk tomorrow," I said. "Want me to walk you home?"

She stayed put. Her eyes shined wide, wet and bright. I refused to step closer. In the past, I abandoned her when our disagreements reached a standoff. But I wasn't going to do that now. Stay or go, our pain held us in each other's orbits. I couldn't cut and run. I hovered and matched her forlorn gaze with my own.

"What?" I said.

Her eyes stared into mine. She said nothing.

We waited for each other.

It was a warm spring day in our first year. I had good mojo moving inside me, and someone I could hold onto who wasn't going anywhere soon. I felt forgiven and full. The sidewalk answered all my footsteps in the affirmative. And if someone stopped me and asked, *Do you know where I might find Mr. Lucky?* I'd grin and say, *You're looking at him.* Memory may overstate the case, but let's just say that I rolled with an awesome and swell-looking babe, and felt a hell of a lot happier than usual.

It was an impromptu date. We had no classes and nothing to argue about. One of us said, *Let's take a walk.* Then, later, *How about stopping for a drink?* We laughed. We touched. She surprised me by jumping up into my arms. A shuffling gray geezer in a public park caught our gymnastics and shouted, *That's the way! Get it while it's good!*

We spied a few crispy characters in that big sunny barroom we settled into: motorcycle jockeys, men with shady jobs, and red-faced muscle dudes who couldn't decide if they were gym rats or barflies. Some of these hairy Joes and Jeffs crossed the line between looks and leers, but I heard no trash talk. No one invaded our space. It was best they hadn't, because I felt invincible that day. I know I'm just one vessel of clay, with no more natural stardust than any of God's creatures, but I stood mighty on that particular afternoon, and you'd have had an awful knock-down drag-out effort proving otherwise. My woman, my bright angel who lit up a shining path and showed me a shortcut to paradise, adored me. Sally had fast become my only real teacher at Yale. She brought and taught the important lessons. How many times had I called her crazy, dumb, stupid, hateful, pill-popping, and impossible? Too, too many times.

But it's best to remember beyond all that, and to ignore bad professors with bigger egos than hearts and more degrees than doings, parents too busy or troubled to filter the world for fearful and curious children, past the old battles and bad words, the doubts and dread, the tears, a violence that couldn't be helped.

She was my first real love.

After probably our third round of margaritas, she and I quieted down. We stared at each other for minutes, unblinking, each meditating on the magic of the other.

"Am I beautiful?" she asked, breaking the silence.

I nodded. I smiled.

She leaned in, nose to nose. *"Am I?"*

"Yes."

She searched my eyes, mouth, and face for lies.

"Now why would I tell you anything but the truth?"

THE AUTHOR

Robert Curtis grew up in Hyde Park, Massachusetts. He attended UMass, Boston, and earned an MFA degree in Playwriting from the Yale School of Drama. He wrote a number of stage and screenplays, and also a good deal of poetry; he won awards for two of those poems at Los Angeles City College, where he continued to study writing. He loved Jimmy Van Heusen and Sinatra, Bukowski and George V. Higgins, Robert Mitchum and Warren Oates. He enjoyed hiking in Griffith Park, talking movies and politics (The Friends of Eddie Coyle and Bernie Sanders topped his list), and the company of his many, many friends. He performed as a singer later in his life, as singing became a passion of his. He died at age 50 in Los Angeles in 2016.

www.ingramcontent.com/pod-product-compliance
Lightning Source LLC
Chambersburg PA
CBHW021219260626
47172CB00002B/504